The tendrils were snaking into Ascaros's hair and curling along his face. Where they touched him, Isiem saw his friend's skin blanch white and then go corpse-gray, while the smoke grew thicker and more solid. The russet brown of his hair, ordinarily touched with vibrant red, began to go gray too.

It was feeding on him. The shadow was stealing Ascaros's life, hoping to create its own—but it wouldn't succeed. It *couldn't*. The shadowcallers would crush it before it got that far . . . and then his friend would have died for nothing.

And they were willing to let him die. Right here, in front of all the gathered villagers. Isiem saw that plainly. If Ascaros couldn't wrest himself free, they would let the nightglass kill him.

He rushed forward, shoving Ascaros away from the mirror. The female shadowcaller snarled, drawing a hand back to strike him, but the tall one with the circlet of chains shook his head and she froze.

"Let him try," he said. "I want to see what he does."

Isiem scarcely heard the man. The shadows had let go of Ascaros, but only so they could twine around Isiem instead. They were *cold*, colder than the sharpest winter wind, and the same tingling burn followed their touch. He gasped, and with watering eyes stared into the mirror . . .

The Pathfinder Tales Library

Nightglass

Liane Merciel

Cover art by Tyler Walpole.
Cover design by Andrew Vallas.
Map by Robert Lazzaretti.

Paizo Publishing, LLC
7120 185th Ave NE, Ste 120
Redmond, WA 98052
paizo.com

ISBN 978-1-60125-440-5 (mass market paperback)
ISBN 978-1-60125-441-2 (ebook)

Publisher's Cataloging-In-Publication Data
(Prepared by The Donohue Group, Inc.)

Merciel, Liane.
  Nightglass / Liane Merciel.

  p. ; cm. -- (Pathfinder tales)

  Set in the world of the role-playing game, Pathfinder.
  Issued also as an ebook.
  ISBN: 978-1-60125-440-5 (mass market pbk.)

  1. Imaginary places--Fiction. 2. Magicians--Fiction. 3. Good and evil--Fiction. 4. Fantasy fiction. 5. Adventure stories. I. Title. II. Title: Pathfinder adventure path. III. Series: Pathfinder tales library.

PS3613.E727 N54 2012
813.6

First printing June 2012.

Printed in the United States of America.

For Peter, who did all the stat work
so I could just tell the stories.

Book One
Monsters

Prologue

"You should not be here," the woman whispered. Her fingers fluttered over Feisal's face, light and erratic as blind butterflies. Fear made her eyes enormous. "You must not be here. The white ones will find you."

Feisal tried to lift his head. Couldn't. Everything from his neck down was cold and dull, utterly unresponsive to his efforts. The numbness frightened him worse than pain would have. Pain meant he was alive, if hurt. Numbness meant . . . what?

Curly-furred sheepskins covered most of his torso, but they had slipped off one of his shoulders. By tilting his chin down, he could just glimpse the stiff gray flesh, puckered with withered rings as if some enormous many-mouthed leech had sucked not only the blood but the life out of his body.

"Where am I?" Feisal whispered. "What's happened to me?"

"Hush," the woman said. Her back was to the fire, and it was too dark for him to see her face, but he thought he heard kindness in her voice. Kindness, and exhaustion. And fear.

Gently, the woman lifted Feisal's head and held a wooden cup to his lips. Splintery dried leaves floated on the steaming liquid inside. "Drink."

He did. Warmth suffused him. Then a soft, suffocating heaviness.

He slept.

The woman was gone when he woke.

Feisal sat up. He was in a small cottage, its single room partitioned into three smaller spaces by folding wooden screens. Paneled shutters covered the uneven windows. Although seams of daylight showed above and beneath the shutters, it was dark enough in the cottage that Feisal could only make out the general shapes of things.

He got off the pallet, intending to lift the shutters and let some light in, but stopped just before reaching the windows. Something dangled in the middle of each one, on the far side of the shutters: a crude doll-shaped fetish made of wicker bound with human hair. Their faces were blank, wrinkled balls.

What had the woman said? Something about "white ones"? She'd been terrified of them, whatever they were. Not just for herself, but because she feared they might find him.

Perhaps she'd had a reason for leaving the shutters closed. Licking his lips, Feisal stepped back.

He lit a candle instead. Holding its flame over his body, he saw that the wounds that had frightened him so badly the previous night—if it *was* the previous night; he had no idea how long he'd slept—looked much better. The dead grayness was gone. Welts still dappled the right side of his body in an odd looping pattern, but the flesh appeared to be a healthy pink under the layer of greasy ointment the woman had rubbed into his wounds.

What had *done* that to him?

The last clear thing he remembered was talking to his employer, Luswick, as they sat around a campfire waiting for the company's dinner of sourbroth and beans. They'd argued over which road to take as they neared the southern Uskwood. Feisal, mindful of the forest's reputation, had wanted to follow the trade road that skirted its periphery. Luswick, who fancied himself the best Pathfinder in Isger, wouldn't hear of it. To him, an unmapped forest cried out for chronicling, and none of Feisal's arguments could sway him. None of the other mercenaries had even tried to dissuade the eccentric.

"The Uskwood *is* mapped," Feisal had protested before they crossed the border. He'd seen the inked deerskins himself. They weren't especially sophisticated, true. The Nidalese kept all the good maps to themselves and forbade their sale to foreigners, so the only maps available were those drawn by unlettered borderlanders or itinerant peddlers. But they showed the things that mattered. A forest, a few small settlements. Roads. What more was there?

Luswick had snorted hard enough to flap the ends of his bushy white mustache. "Guesses, boy. There are *guesses*. Scrawls and doodles by illiterate amateurs, one step removed from sailors' lies and 'here be dragons.' Not *maps*. No, this place cries for an expert's hand. Besides, there's treasure to be had."

What treasure, he'd never specified. The most Luswick would tell any of his hirelings was that he was on the trail of some Desnan artifact—not enchanted, he claimed, but valuable nonetheless as a historical relic of the faith. Why the Pathfinder believed it was in the

Uskwood, how he intended to find it, or what it even *was,* he stubbornly refused to say.

Feisal remembered little of their journey. The Uskwood had been strangely cold, strangely hushed under its canopy of unmoving leaves. Its shadows had seemed to stretch longer than they should. He'd pointed that out to Luswick and the others—how the shadows reached toward them from the wrong angles, going against the sun—but Luswick had only nodded, recorded it in his journals, and dismissed the phenomenon as a harmless curiosity.

For a while Feisal had let himself hope the chronicler could be right. The forest was an eerie place, and he never came to like it any better, but it didn't seem dangerous. Nothing disturbed their camps; they never saw so much as a pile of bear scat among the trees.

Until the night a storm brought the dark down early, trapping them inside the wood.

Eerie, that storm was. Unnatural. It hadn't touched the trees. Even Luswick, seeing that, had stopped talking and moved closer to their campfire. High overhead, wild winds raked the clouds to shreds and lightning stabbed the tatters . . . but around them, silence reigned. It was as if an enormous glass dome encased the forest. It shut out any breeze, any raindrop that might have splashed into the perfect, deathly stillness.

The air had . . . thickened, too. Feisal put a hand to his throat, remembering. He hadn't been able to breathe. Dizziness had overwhelmed him, and in that choking delirium he had imagined *shapes* moving in the dark. Snakes. Or whips, maybe. Had they moved on their own, or had someone held them? He couldn't recall. But there had been pale figures, pale faces, floating in the gloom . . . and they had passed him by, because he was already dying when they came.

Then oblivion. Until he woke up here.

Putting the candle down, Feisal pulled on a spare set of trousers and a clean shirt. The clothes he'd been wearing that night were nowhere to be seen, but his other belongings—excepting his weapons, he noted sourly—were piled neatly beside his pallet.

So were some of his companions'. Luswick's sketchbook sat among his saddlebags. Feisal picked it up, flipping through the maps and notes written in the Pathfinder's blocky, familiar hand.

He tossed it away. Luswick treasured that book above his own life; he would never have abandoned it while he still drew breath. So he was dead, or as good as.

Was it worth it? For an unfinished map of the Uskwood's shallowest reaches?

Feisal turned the book over with his foot so he wouldn't have to look at its owner's mark. He was standing beside it, wondering if he dared search the cottage for his missing weapons, when the woman bustled back in. She carried firewood under one arm, a bucket of water in her other hand, and a freshly plucked chicken tied to a sash at her waist. Daylight washed over her from the open door, revealing that she was younger and more careworn than Feisal had initially realized. Her hair was soft brown without a streak of gray, but her face was deeply lined.

"I feel much better," he said. "Thank you."

"Rest," she said, not unkindly. Her accent was heavy, but Feisal couldn't quite place it. Was this how villagers spoke in the Uskwood?

She didn't look at him, instead busying herself with hanging the water bucket in the hearth and dumping the firewood on the floor. The door closed, leaving them both in shadow. "I am not surprised you feel better. The white ones' curse fades quickly if it fails to kill. But you are not well, not yet, and you will need all your strength to evade them."

"What happened to my companions?" He gestured to Luswick's book.

"Dead."

"All of them?" He knew the answer to that, or thought he did, but he wanted to hear someone else say the words. Let her be the one to make that horror real.

"Better if you think so." The woman arranged her firewood in the hearth, piled kindling beneath it, and struck a spark to the heap. "In truth, I do not know. We only found you."

"The others could still be alive?"

"No."

"But you said—"

"We found you, so you lived," she said impatiently, straightening and taking the chicken over to a bloodstained board. With swift, practiced strokes, she chopped the bird into stew-sized chunks. "Two of the others were dead: an elf woman and a young man with an old rope scar around his neck. We buried those. If anyone else was in your company, the white ones took them. They may not be dead, but they do not live."

"That doesn't make any—what do you mean?"

"They give their captives to the shadow. Or . . . other things, sometimes, but most often they sacrifice to the shadow. Do not think to rescue your friends from that fate. Even if they still draw breath, they are your friends no longer."

Feisal exhaled, struggling for calm. It wasn't just frustration at her cryptic answers that beset him. It was fear. The men who had vanished were all gifted with magic; he and the dead ones were not. There was only one place in Avistan where albinos hunted wizards and fed them to the living dark. But he needed to hear it. "Where am I?"

The woman rinsed her bloody hands in a bowl of water. She emptied the water into her stewpot along with the chopped chicken. "You know that already."

"Where?"

"Nidal."

Nidal. Cursed land, cursed people. Feisal sank bonelessly onto his pallet, closing his eyes. All his strength had fled. Her answer was not a surprise—of *course* he was still in Nidal. He was likely still in the Uskwood, which guarded the darkest of that nation's secrets. But he had dared to hope, when he woke alive and unmaimed, that somehow a miraculous benefactor had found him and carried him away.

Because he could think of no reason that he would still be alive, and unhurt, in Nidal.

He'd heard the stories all his life. At the end of the Age of Legends, when Earthfall shattered the world and cast its sundered empires into darkness, the people of Nidal had struck a terrible bargain. In the cataclysm's wake, ash blotted out the sun; nothing green could grow. Facing an endless winter and sure starvation, the Nidalese swore allegiance to a dark and twisted power. In exchange for eternal servitude, they were granted the gift of survival. After a fashion.

Life in Nidal was not as it was elsewhere. Feisal didn't know how many of the tales were true and how many were fanciful exaggerations, but if it was one in ten thousand, it was too many for him. He had advised Luswick to give the Uskwood a wide berth for precisely that reason. Pangolais, the darkly glittering heart of Nidal, was said to lie in the depths of that forest, and to be the source from which all its terrors sprang.

Despite his best efforts, those terrors had found him after all.

His hands were shaking. Feisal concentrated on stilling them—on attaining that one small measure of control over his own terror—and failed. Completely. His hands obeyed him no more than his near-dead body had the night before.

"Where?" he asked again, hoarsely. If he was close to the edge of the forest, perhaps he could slip out. Even on foot, he might make it across the border. If he was near the Menadors' passes, or a caravan road, or anywhere else he might find merchants, travelers, *anyone* willing to shelter a stranger in their numbers . . .

The woman paused before answering, probably wondering whether he was half-witted, but eventually she caught his meaning. "A village. I will not tell you its name. When the time comes, I will tell you which way to go, and that is all you need know. Anything more might bring trouble to us."

If you get caught. She didn't say it, but she didn't need to. Feisal understood her implication clearly.

"I suppose that means you won't tell me your name, either."

"No," she said, with a faint smile.

"Can I call you Lyrael?" he asked, naming one of Desna's legendary priestesses. According to the tales, she'd appeared to wayward travelers lost on starless nights, and had guided them gently through the dark to safety. Considering the circumstances, Feisal thought, it was an appropriate name for his benefactor.

The woman's smile vanished. She turned away from him abruptly, lifting her stewpot in rag-mittened hands and setting it over the fire.

"I'm sorry," Feisal said. "I didn't mean to —"

"Yes," she said. "Yes, you can call me that."

Day by day, Feisal's vitality returned. He hobbled around the cottage, doing what small chores he could, but Lyrael refused to let him venture outside. Knowing where he was, Feisal felt no temptation to disobey her. If he escaped Nidal alive, it would be by Desna's good graces and hers.

He occupied himself playing with Lyrael's son, Isiem, a three-year-old boy with long white hair. Not white-blond, as many children had, but stark white. The child himself was not much darker. Head to foot, he was the color of new-fallen snow . . . and of the pale ones who had hunted the Uskwood on the night of the storm.

Feisal didn't ask Lyrael about that. Neither did he ask where the child's father was, or how she eked out a living alone with one young child in her home and, judging by the bump under her apron, another on the way. It wasn't his concern, and prying would have been a poor reward for her generosity—the woman was already angry enough that her son had unwittingly told Feisal his real name. So instead he watched the boy, playing simple games and retelling the handful of stories he remembered from his own childhood. He wasn't much of a talespinner, but *any* story seemed to fill the child with wonder, no matter how clumsily told.

When he wasn't mangling folktales for Isiem, Feisal watched the village's life through the shuttered windows. What little he could see didn't look so fearsome. People drew water from a communal well, gossiped in the grassy square, carried firewood and game from the forests. They dressed like the commoners he'd known in Isger, although their homespun tunics were drab and plain, with none of the brightly colored embroidery or glass beads that even the poorest Isgeri girl prized. In all, the Nidalese seemed ordinary.

But wicker dolls hung in all their windows, and he never saw them outside after dark.

"What are the dolls for?" he asked Lyrael one night. She sat by the fire, humming a wordless lullaby as she darned holes in Isiem's clothes. Behind one of the wooden screens, the child was already sleeping.

"The dolls?" she echoed, looking up.

"The ones in the windows. Everyone has them here. Why?"

Lyrael set the needle down. She folded the half-darned sock in her lap and stared into the flames. A knot of dried sap hissed and popped in the hearth. "To show we are loyal," she said.

"I don't follow."

"It is said that the white ones can see through the eyes and speak through the mouths of those dolls. We put them in the windows so that the white ones know that we are the faithful subjects of Nidal."

"But the dolls don't have eyes," Feisal said. "Or mouths. They all just have blank cornhusk heads."

"And they sit outside the shutters, yes." Lyrael picked her needle up and resumed her work. "If their eyeless heads see anything, it is what we do outside, not in our own homes. Well, we are only ignorant villagers. If we do things clumsily—make our dolls without eyes, or forget to put them in the right places—it is only to be expected. The white ones will hiss and snarl, and we will grovel for forgiveness, and when they go away we will doubtlessly make the same mistakes again, stupid as we are."

"A clever cover for your rebellion."

"Clever or not, it is limited." She gave him a pointed glance. "Small rebellions we can survive. Large ones remain beyond us. We are still the subjects of Nidal, and its rulers are not all as blind as their cornhusk dolls." Dropping the finished sock in the basket by her chair, Lyrael picked up a shirt and began mending the rip in its sleeve. "You have your strength back. It is time for you to go, before the white ones catch your scent. Travel quickly, and go by daylight, and they will not find you. Their hunters are seldom abroad before dusk."

"Which way?"

"South. Your friend's maps are well drawn. In a day or two you will reach the parts he covered. They can guide you from there, if need be, but once you are out of the Uskwood, the danger will be past."

Feisal nodded slowly. He dug Luswick's book out of the pile of his belongings and paged through it until he came to the chronicler's last map: the one that showed the southern Uskwood, and the lands that lay beyond.

He'd memorized the map during his long days of enforced idleness. He had no further need of it, except as a reminder of his dead friend's last journey, and that was a memory Feisal intended to forget as soon as he could.

Lyrael, however, might find a better use for the Pathfinder's final work. She'd shown courage by taking him in and cunning by keeping him hidden. She was strong enough to raise a child alone in a realm whose very name still made Feisal feel a thrill of fear. For the sake of that child, and the second babe who would shortly join him, she might wish to flee someday soon.

If she did, she'd need a map.

He tore the page free. Ripping Luswick's book felt like sacrilege, but Feisal ignored that pang of conscience, creased the map down the center, and offered the folded sheet to Lyrael.

"Maps don't just show the way into places," he said. "They show the way out, too. You might like to have this someday. For the children, if not yourself."

She took the page cautiously, using the tips of her fingers. For an instant she stared at the yellowed paper as if all the secrets of the universe were written inside—those that could bring her dreams to life, and those that would summon her nightmares to slay them. Then she tossed it into the fire.

"A gracious gift," she said, as the paper curled and charred, "but perhaps you did not hear me. We are in Nidal, and its rulers are not blind.

"Leave in the morning. I will not wake to watch you go."

Chapter One
The Festival of Night's Return

The shadowcallers arrived the night before the Festival of Night's Return. They were true shadowcallers from Pangolais, not the white druids who usually came, and Isiem gathered with the other village children to watch them ride into the square.

He had seen shadowcallers before, of course. They visited Crosspine every fifth year, as they did all the little villages, to test children for the gift of magic. But Isiem had been only six the last time they'd come, too young to attract their notice, and he barely remembered anything from that visit. This year he was eleven, old enough to stand their test, and excitement warred with nervousness in his belly.

His mother hadn't wanted him to go, Isiem knew, but she hadn't had the power to say no. The shadowcallers were, somehow, beyond his mother's word. That made them even more fascinating . . . and more frightening, too.

Wide-eyed, he watched as the shadowcallers came down from their horses. There were two men and a woman, all on black geldings draped in dark stones and silver. The horses were strange ones; their manes and tails seemed to flow off into shadow, and their hooves made no splashes on the rain-muddied roads.

Their riders were stranger still. All three were tall and thin, pale as ghosts in the moonlight. They wore deep gray robes, cut tight around the body but wide below the waist, with loose, billowing sleeves from the elbows down. Silver chains circled their throats and silver rings glimmered on their fingers, each one set with a smooth black stone.

The taller of the two men was the most unsettling of the trio. A circlet of spiked chains wrapped around his brow, starred with beads of dried blood like so many small gems. His long black hair was matted with blood; it hung to his shoulders in ropy dreadlocks, crusted with the residue of his self-mortification.

"M-m-may I take your horses?" Belero asked, hurrying from his home. Crosspine was too small to have a proper inn, let alone a hostler to look after guests' horses, but Belero had one of the largest houses in the village and, since his children had been carried off by plague, often rented his spare rooms to travelers. He knew horses as well as anyone in the village did, but these silent animals had him visibly unsettled.

The three shadowcallers exchanged a glance and a smile. Their smiles were unkind, Isiem thought; even from this distance, he could sense their cruel amusement. It made him uneasy. He slipped away from the other children, retreating to the doorway of his own home.

"You may," the woman said. She handed her reins to Belero. The others followed suit, although the shorter man removed something from his panniers first. It was a round object slightly bigger than Isiem's head, and it was swaddled in black velvet that looked unimaginably soft. He cradled it tenderly to his chest as the shadowcallers followed Belero to his home.

The object fascinated Isiem. He felt an ineffable pull toward it, as though whatever lay beneath that swathing velvet was a lodestone that drew upon his soul. He took an uncertain step forward, wondering if he might be able to peek at the thing without causing trouble, and jumped when a hand fell upon his shoulder.

It was his mother's. He hadn't heard her open the door, so enthralled had he been.

"Come inside," she said, pulling him in. The door closed behind him with a thump. "Don't go back out tonight."

Isiem nodded, slightly dazed but obedient. The magnetic pull had vanished. Although he still wanted to see what the shadowcaller kept under that velvet wrapping, his mother's fear, and his memory of their malice, held him back.

Thinking of their smiles made him remember something he'd wondered earlier. "Why did they laugh at Belero?"

She beckoned for him to sit next to her chair by the fire. When he did, she stroked his head, holding him close as if he'd just escaped some great danger. "Because their horses aren't real. They're shadow and magic; they never needed tending. In a few hours they'll vanish, and Belero will have fed and watered empty stalls."

"Does Belero know that?"

"Yes."

"Then why did he do it?"

"Because he knows, as we all do, that their contempt is what keeps this village safe. If we're stupid yokels who can't tell false horses from real ones, then surely we don't know enough to evade their other sorceries. Ignorance is safety." She pinched his chin, turning his head so that his eyes met hers. It hurt, but there was such intensity—such raw *fear*—on his mother's face that Isiem bit back his protest. "Do you understand me? *Ignorance is safety.* And nothing they offer you, nothing they promise, is real. It's all shadows and lies, like their horses."

Isiem nodded, as much as he could. "I understand," he said, although he didn't.

"Good." She held him a moment longer, searching his eyes, and then let go. "They will test you tomorrow. Remember what I told you."

"I will." He paused. "My father had magic, didn't he?"

"He did." She sighed and lifted her darning basket into her lap. "Go to bed, Isiem. Don't wake Theron."

"I won't."

He didn't sleep, though. He lay in the darkness, next to his younger brother's snores, and listened to his mother pray.

She prayed quietly, as she always did, in a soft breathless whisper with her head bowed over her basket. "Starry Lady, Winged Dreamer, hear me and help me tonight. Keep my children safe on the morrow. Keep the darklings' mirror blind. The night is yours, Desna, Starsong . . . don't let the pale prince reach through it tomorrow. Don't let him take my boys. Please. Please . . ."

Her voice quavered and broke. Isiem saw the shape of her shoulders, silhouetted by the fire, hunch under the weight of helpless sobs.

His mother cried as quietly as she'd prayed, but the sound of it followed him into sleep.

Despite the unsettling events of the night before, Isiem woke early on Festival morning. He scrubbed his teeth hastily with charcoal and cold tea, helped his brother dress, and put on his own best clothes for the occasion. Then, without waiting to see whether Theron followed, he darted out to the village square.

Already it was bustling. The true festival wouldn't begin until nightfall—no proper Kuthite ritual was conducted in daylight—but, while Isiem couldn't deny the spectacle of the nighttime celebrations, he had always preferred the lighter moments of the day.

One of the men hoisted his little daughter onto his shoulders so that she could put the finishing touches on the effigy of Shelyn, the goddess of beauty. At sunset, the effigy would be set ablaze to burn through the night. The girl draped her garland of late-blooming flowers carefully over the effigy's brow, earning a pat of approval from her father. Other children were putting cedar splints and bundles of dried herbs at the base of the wooden goddess, ensuring the night fire's smoke would smell sweet.

Isiem thought it was a pity that something so pretty had to be burned, but he had to admit there was something awe-inspiring about the pillar of flame that took the effigy every year. This year's was larger than ever, and more elaborately painted; the shadowcallers would surely be impressed by Crosspine's piety when they saw it.

On the other side of the village square, boys were outlining the penitents' path with a scattering of blood-red maple leaves. At midnight, when the Festival of

Night's Return reached its climax, the young people of the village would walk that path, stripped bare to the waist and flagellating themselves with whips as they prayed for Zon-Kuthon to guide them through the darkness and the winter that was coming. The more fervent worshipers—or, Isiem thought, the ones who most wanted to impress everyone with their toughness and tolerance for pain—would use spiked chains, as the clerics in Pangolais were said to, instead of braided horsehide.

The passing of the penitents marked the end of the ritual. Afterward, the young people disappeared. A few left to tend their injuries, but more went off to couple. Isiem had watched them do it every year of his young life, and while he did not fully understand what drove them, he knew on some wordless level that the intensity of the experience, however brutal, awoke some dark passion in its participants.

That was a long while off, though, and there was a full day of Festival to enjoy before then. Isiem spotted Ascaros, one of his friends, walking alongside a donkey-cart of early apples and sweet yellow squashes that his mother was bringing into the village to sell.

Ascaros was two years younger than Isiem, and lately Isiem had begun feeling that his friend was too occupied with babyish things for them to remain as close as they'd been, but any distance between them was forgotten in the excitement of Festival day.

"Isiem!" Ascaros waved with childish enthusiasm. He was a slight boy, almost girlish, with curly brown hair that his mother let grow until it fell past his shoulders. "Are you planning to stand for the magic test?"

Isiem balked, embarrassed by his friend's ignorance. "It's not a *choice*," he said, joining the younger boy beside the wagon. "You *have* to stand for the test. Everyone does."

Ascaros shrugged, unfazed by his error. "I hope they pick me. I'm going to be a great wizard—a Midnight Guard like my aunt."

Isiem fought the urge to roll his eyes. He'd heard Ascaros brag about his never-seen aunt a thousand times. All the children had.

"If your aunt's a Midnight Guard," he asked, also for the thousandth time, "why are *you* still swilling pig-bone soup in Crosspine?"

Ascaros shrugged again. He opened his mouth, readying some ridiculous excuse, but closed it again at a glance from his mother. "Maybe I just like it here," he said lamely.

Isiem laughed, unable to help himself, and an instant later Ascaros laughed too. Snatching an apple from the cart, Ascaros tossed it at the older boy's head, then ran off. Isiem caught the apple and gave chase half-heartedly. After a few steps he stopped, feigning great interest in eating the fruit rather than making a fool of himself in front of the whole village.

Already the Festival was beginning. Belero and the other village men wore fanciful costumes, disguising themselves as blue-spotted pigs, horned Chelish devils, and buffoons with harlequined hats and long pointed boots. The women wore silver and white, braiding white flowers into their hair and around their waists if they couldn't afford full Festival dresses. They drank and danced and played games of skill or chance, and even Isiem's mother was caught up in their joy.

Too soon the day was done. After a perfunctory prayer to Zon-Kuthon, Belero set a torch to the effigy of Shelyn, and the villagers gathered in a circle to watch it burn. Isiem stood with them, feeling a great solemnity as the red heat washed over his face and the night grew chill at his back. Parents held children, courting couples held each other, and all Crosspine bade summer farewell. The long nights were coming, as they had in ages past. Beauty could not save them; it was weak, and it died with the cold. Only the Midnight Lord could protect his people from the hostile dark.

Into that silence, punctuated by the snap of burning timber, the shadowcallers came.

Isiem hadn't seen them at all during the day. They'd taken no part in the festivities. Like all the other shades of the Uskwood, it seemed, they emerged with the stars.

The tall man with the circlet of chains came first, trailed on either side by his companions. In his hands was the object that had entranced Isiem the previous night, but now its velvet cloak had been pulled back and it lay revealed to the villagers' wondering eyes.

It was a shallow disc of opaque black stone, perhaps obsidian or onyx, polished to a reflective sheen. The shadowcaller held it reverently, even fearfully; he kept his head high, and never glanced down at the object in his hands.

At the end of the penitents' path he stopped. With crimson leaves rustling at the hem of his robes, he turned to address the villagers. "Who will look into the nightglass? Who will come forth to be tested?"

Slowly the village children formed a line. Some needed a push from their parents to step forward. A few were struggling not to cry. Ascaros came confidently, without hesitation . . . and yet, Isiem noticed, the boy measured his paces so that he entered the line after Isiem himself did.

"Worried the glass might eat you?" he whispered.

"Hardly," Ascaros murmured in reply. His large brown eyes stayed fixed on the black mirror. "Just didn't want to show you up by going first. Wouldn't be fair, forcing you to follow a great wizard."

"I'm grateful," Isiem said, and then the line began moving, and they stopped talking.

One by one, the children of Crosspine looked into the shadowcaller's ebon bowl. Some gazed at it with fear, some with respect, some with desire . . . but whatever they hoped to see, or the shadowcallers hoped to see in them, they did not find it. One by one, they were dismissed.

Long before he was ready, it was Isiem's turn. He pressed his sweaty palms together and came forward.

"Look into the nightglass," the tall shadowcaller said. "Tell us what you see."

Isiem nodded, swallowed, and looked.

The nightglass was . . . glass. And yet it was not. Darkness pooled in its center, melding with the smooth black sides so that he couldn't tell empty air from stone. At the edges, the nightglass was thin and translucent, delicate as a gray dragonfly's wing. Along the sides, between center and edge, reflected starlight stretched into shimmering silver arcs, distorted by the mirror's curve.

In the spaces between those blurred lines of starlight, something small and indistinct moved. Isiem caught his breath, wondering if he'd imagined it . . . but when he looked again, his doubt vanished, along with his awareness of who he was and where he stood.

It was as if the nightglass swelled somehow, or he himself shrank, so that instead of being a boy looking at a piece of polished stone no larger than his head, he was a mouse confronted with an enormous black doorway. The starlight was almost gone, muted to glimmerings of gray that danced about the doorway's edges. Darkness stretched beyond it, and that darkness was alive.

No, Isiem realized, not really *alive*. It moved. He saw faces shifting in the dark—ravenous, misshapen faces, with hollow eye sockets that sagged below their noses and wrinkled mouths full of fangs—but there was no life in them. Not truly. It was hunger that animated them. Hunger, and envy, and a desire to consume his life so that they could fuel some brief semblance of their own.

At first there was only one, and he wasn't sure of that one. But soon others joined it, forming a mob at the door. They strained at him, reaching out with fingerless hands and licking at their lipless mouths, but they could not come through. Not unless he opened the way for them. Isiem understood that instinctively, as one understood the logic of fairytales or dreams: the darkness could not come into his world, his home, without an invitation.

That is so, the shadow-creatures whispered in voices that he heard without hearing. *Summon us, and we will serve you. There is so much we can give. Power. Wealth. Eternal life, eternal youth. Magic.*

No, Isiem thought. He wanted to say it aloud—he wanted to shout it, and flee—but his limbs and his jaws remained stubbornly locked. *I don't want anything you can give me.*

You are foolish to refuse, the shadows said. *Foolish, foolish child.*

Isiem didn't answer. He focused entirely on pulling away from them, and from this strange never-world inside the mirror. It was hard, as taxing as forcing his way through waist-deep snow against a brutal headwind . . . but he did it, and came back to himself with a start.

Cold sweat plastered his shirt to his chest. He was heaving for breath, so winded he could scarcely stand upright. The pale moonlight was so bright it seemed blinding.

The female shadowcaller leaned toward him. Her eyes were completely black from lid to lid. They had no whites, no pupils or irises. Isiem had never been close enough to notice before. He wished he wasn't close enough now.

"What did you see?" she asked.

"Nothing." He forced the lie through numb lips. *Ignorance is safety.* "I didn't see anything."

"Nothing?" she echoed, disbelief clear in her voice.

"Nothing." Isiem turned away from the penitent's path, resisting the urge to flee outright. He tried to sound calm, even a little disappointed. "I'm sorry."

She nodded brusquely, already dismissing him. Ascaros stepped up next, and Isiem hesitated, wanting to give his friend some warning or reassurance before he looked into that bowl. He couldn't think of what to say, though, and he was afraid to attract the shadowcallers' notice again. Instead he moved to the side and stopped, curious to see how Ascaros reacted.

It didn't look nearly as dramatic as it felt. Ascaros just stood there, staring into the nightglass. His face was pale, but then he was always pale; his expression was rapt, but Isiem couldn't tell how much of that was real and how much was his friend's desperation to prove himself a wizard.

Then he saw that something was rising from the polished stone. Smoke, it seemed, or shadow . . . but it could not be smoke, for it coiled against the wind, and it could not be shadow, for there was nothing to cast it. Swiftly it spun upward, reaching for Ascaros's face with gray tendrils. The boy remained motionless, his eyes starting from his head and his face drawn taut as he gazed through the unnatural smoke into the mirror.

"Such power," the shorter man breathed. "Such potential. That he can not only *see* the shadows in the nightglass, but call them forth with no training at all . . ."

"But can he control them, or will they consume him?" the woman asked. Her silver necklaces clinked softly as she tilted her head, watching. "Power without control is worth less than nothing."

The tendrils were snaking into Ascaros's hair and curling along his face. Where they touched him, Isiem saw his friend's skin blanch white and then go corpse-gray, while the smoke grew thicker and more solid. The russet brown of his hair, ordinarily touched with vibrant red, began to go gray too.

It was feeding on him. The shadow was stealing Ascaros's life, hoping to create its own—but it wouldn't succeed. It *couldn't*. The shadowcallers would crush it before it got that far . . . and then his friend would have died for nothing.

And they were willing to let him die. Right here, in front of all the gathered villagers. Isiem saw that plainly. If Ascaros couldn't wrest himself free, they would let the nightglass kill him.

He rushed forward, shoving Ascaros away from the mirror. The female shadowcaller snarled, drawing a hand back to strike him, but the tall one with the circlet of chains shook his head and she froze.

"Let him try," he said. "I want to see what he does."

Isiem scarcely heard the man. The shadows had let go of Ascaros, but only so they could twine around Isiem instead. They were *cold*, colder than the sharpest winter wind, and the same tingling burn followed their touch. He gasped, and with watering eyes stared into the mirror.

Once again the starlight blurred before him, and he had the eerie sense of space stretching, or his own reality shrinking, so that the nightglass engulfed him in its vastness and the old world fell away. The shadows had greater definition here: what seeped through the ebon doorway were not shapeless tendrils of smoke, but thin black fingers, impossibly long and triple-jointed. Each one was tipped with a fragment of bloody bone.

Release me, the gaunt face between those fingers hissed. Starlight whirled in its eyes, imitating the whites of human eyes. They were almost real. Almost sighted to the living world. *Release me to feed. The bargain was struck. Release me, and my power will be yours.*

No, Isiem thought back.

Then you will die. You do not have the strength to send me back.

That was true. Isiem had no idea how to close the mirror's gate. He didn't even know if it *could* be closed.

But there were other truths as well. *You'll die too*, he thought, and then amended: *or at least you won't be free. I can't stop you, but the wizards waiting here can, and they will not let you escape into the world. Go back, and return another time.*

I am already here, the shadow-creature insisted, but Isiem felt its hesitation. Its tendrils, or fingers, unclenched their grip. They undulated in the air, darting toward the shadowcallers and retreating just as swiftly before making contact. Then they pulled back from the living world, back through the nightglass, back into the ebon doorway.

Quickly Isiem severed his connection to the magic. The nightglass's distortions receded; the autumn night returned. Sound came back to him. Scent. Trembling, he closed his eyes. He smelled smoke from the burning effigy, heard distant laughter from late revelers and the relieved sobs of Ascaros's mother.

"You will come with us," one of the shadowcallers said. Isiem didn't know which one. But he nodded shakily, surrendering to his fate. Of course they would take him now. He'd given up his pretended ignorance to save Ascaros. And although he was afraid of what that might mean for him, he had no regret about interrupting the shadowcallers' test.

His mother was wrong, Isiem thought. Not everything they promised was shadows and lies. They promised death, too. And that was real.

Chapter Two
The Midnight City

They took two other children from Crosspine: a brother and sister named Loran and Helis. The girl, near Isiem's age, was a coltish thing, starveling thin, with a tangle of black hair that hadn't seen comb or scissors in months. Her brother, only eight, was among the youngest children to stand for the test. He kept close to his sister's skirts, rarely venturing a sound. Both wore rags that were more holes than cloth, and their shoes were only bags of greasy leather held up with drawstrings around their ankles.

Isiem didn't know either of them well. They came from one of the forest farms outside Crosspine, and he'd seldom had occasion to talk to them. He didn't have the chance to renew even that slight acquaintance before they left the village. Something ugly had happened in the night, and the shadowcallers were in a hurry to return to Pangolais.

Their silent black horses had emerged from the stable's shadows in the morning, and with them came two more for the children to ride double. Isiem hoped the mount he shared couldn't sense his dislike. The inky gelding carried him and Ascaros smoothly, even though neither of them had ridden before, but it felt . . . wrong. There was no warmth to its body. Isiem couldn't feel its heart beat, and it didn't seem to breathe. It didn't seem *real*, and at any moment he thought it could dissolve into swirling air, dropping him to the ground.

The shadowcallers didn't seem to notice. They were still preoccupied with whatever had happened in Crosspine. Isiem didn't know what that was, but he had noticed that they'd left under a cloud of silent resentment. The villagers voiced no protests—they couldn't, not against shadowcallers from Pangolais— but they had watched the strangers go with flinty eyes.

"You couldn't restrain yourself a little?" the female shadowcaller snapped at the shorter man as they rode into the Uskwood.

"We are permitted to share in the rites of penitence," he replied haughtily, keeping his focus straight ahead.

"Oh, most assuredly. But the girl was a simple villager, not a petitioner for the Joymaking. What were you *thinking*?"

"Lamion. Chorai. Enough." The shadowcaller with the circlet of chains did not turn in his saddle, but the other two straightened and fell silent immediately. "Lamion is correct: it is permitted to share in the penitents' rites. And Chorai is correct as well: one should practice restraint among the uninitiated. They are not prepared for the full measure. Will the girl live?"

"She should," the shorter man—Lamion—muttered.

"Any permanent damage?"

"Maybe one of the eyes."

"You truly are an idiot," Chorai marveled. "Pray the Triune never hear of this, or you'll spend the rest of your years cleaning the Joyful Things."

"I see no need to trouble the Triune with such a trivial matter," the tall man said. "A village girl may have some scars. Lamion will learn greater care. That ends it."

"As you will, Amrael," the other two chorused, and they rode on in silence. The black-leaved branches of the Uskwood closed overhead, casting their path in dappled shadows that shifted—but never relented— as the sun moved distantly through the sky. A wind whispered through the wood, but no wildlife was to be seen or heard; there were no birdsongs trilling from the trees, nor squirrels leaping among the boughs.

There *were* animals in the Uskwood, Isiem knew. Trappers brought their meat and pelts to sell in the village, and he himself had seen the white webs of the wood-spiders stretched across entire trees. But all the beasts of the forest were under Zon-Kuthon's sway, and the Midnight Lord wanted no interference with his servants' return.

"What did you do?" Ascaros whispered into Isiem's back an hour later. The shadowcallers had ridden a little farther ahead, giving them enough space that the children felt they could whisper to each other without being overheard. "With the nightglass, I mean. When you pushed the shadow away from me."

"It wanted to be free. I told it that even if it killed you, or me, it wouldn't be. The shadowcallers would just banish it. That wasn't what it wanted, so it went back into the glass."

"It talked to you?" Ascaros sounded astonished.

Isiem glanced over his shoulder at the younger boy, surprised in turn. "It didn't talk to you?"

"No. I just . . . I looked into the glass, and I saw a shadow . . . or something like one. I couldn't see it clearly. It reached for me, and it . . . it went *inside* me, somehow. I could feel it moving, and I could feel myself getting weaker, but I couldn't do anything to stop it. Then you pushed me, and its hold broke."

"It wasn't like that for me," Isiem said.

"What was it like?"

He shrugged uncomfortably. "I saw a doorway, and things in the doorway that wanted to go through. They couldn't unless I let them. I didn't want to let them."

Ascaros was quiet for a while. Then he asked: "Why did they have to ask you, and not me?"

"I don't know."

Another silence fell. Leaves spiraled through the air ahead of them, falling in slow circles untouched by any breeze. Their horses trotted on soundlessly, leaving no tracks on the mossy earth.

"I'm not sure I want to be a wizard," Ascaros confessed.

"It doesn't matter," Isiem said. "We're going to Pangolais."

Three days later, they reached the city.

Black-leaved trees towered over Pangolais, shrouding its glassy streets and obsidian buildings in constant shadow. Neither sunlight nor moonlight touched the Midnight City, yet it glittered like a sea of stars. Silver twinkled on banisters and decorative spires; pale moonstones gleamed serenely on the brows of the citizens who walked the wide avenues. Great gray moths flapped among the trees' branches, and their wings were luminous with spectral dust.

Amrael led them through the hushed streets toward a soaring building of smoky glass. Its pointed arches and long narrow windows drew the eye upward, as did the twisted spikes that crowned its towers in silver and steel. Clerestory windows, tinted in a thousand shades of gray, created a ceaseless play of shadows as the ghostly lights of Pangolais fell through them from both sides.

Eerie, fluid sculptures flanked the two great doors in the center facade. As they drew nearer, Isiem saw that the sculptures depicted nude human forms, male and female, that clenched their maimed fists around spiked chains to hold themselves above an onyx sea. The base of each carved figure dissolved into amorphous swirls, melting into the waves.

"This is the Dusk Hall," Amrael said. "You will begin your studies here. Lamion."

"Follow me," the shorter shadowcaller said, dismounting. The other two rode away, leaving the children to climb awkwardly off the horses on their own. Isiem, stiff-muscled from the long ride, barely managed to keep from falling. Loran, less fortunate, landed hard on his backside. After a gasp and a moment's stillness, he pushed himself back to his feet. Tears started in the child's huge brown eyes, but he bit his lip and refused to sob.

Lamion paid him no heed. He pulled open one of the doors and stepped into the shifting gloom. The scent of incense and hot metal drifted from its depths, along with an undercurrent of burned flesh. "This way. The horses will see to themselves."

The children followed in a huddle. On either side, arched windows rose above them, inlaid with steel traceries that evoked sharply pointed, lightless flames. Black and white candles mounted in iron sculptures stood between the windows. The few sculptures Isiem saw, before he stopped looking, were of gaunt, twisted men and flayed women whose mouths had been sliced wide to hold the candles' ends.

They were not the only entrants in the Dusk Hall. Others passed them; students or teachers, Isiem couldn't tell. To a one, they were thin and pale, and they moved with the peculiar, graceful lassitude of Pangolais's natives. Some were dressed in glossy black leather, some in matte white. A few wore the soft gray robes of shadowcallers. All ignored Lamion's charges.

Halfway down the hall, Lamion stopped at an ornate door and withdrew a key from a hidden pocket. Suffering figures, wrought in black iron, covered every inch of that door. Each broken body was set like a gem amid a filigree of spiked chains and studded lashes. The keyhole was a wound gouged into the side of a stylized rendition of Zon-Kuthon, also cast in black iron. The tines of the god's crown clicked into his skull, one by one, as Lamion turned the key in its lock.

"Go," he told them, stepping aside. "The Joyful Things must see you."

With an uneasy glance back at the shadowcaller, Isiem led the children in.

A wide hall stretched before them. Black iron beams and curved braces encased the ceiling in elaborate trusses, as though the hall itself were held in bondage. More black iron sheathed the massive pillars that ran down the center of the hall. Candles flickered in serrated lines on both walls, perfuming the air with musky resins and molten wax.

Under that heavy, masking fragrance, the place smelled thick and foul, like the stink of an invalid's sheets in summer. It was the smell of disease, and of others' indifference to that disease. The hall felt cold and lonely; grand though it was, Isiem was sure that the shadowcallers rarely lingered here.

The ironwork on the pillars held odd, egglike shapes hoisted high above the children's heads. They resembled huge maggots, pallid and featureless in their cocoons of bent metal—but as Isiem walked toward the first one, it blinked open eyes he had not known it had.

"Ah," the thing croaked in a rusty, gurgling voice. Its face was a soft white sack of flesh, its mouth a wet glimmer between pouches of suet. Yellow sand caked the corners of its pinkish eyes. Caged from the neck down in iron, the creature could not wipe the crusts away. "Young blood. Come, children. Let me taste you."

It was a man. Hairless, limbless, locked immobile on a pillar in this seldom-visited section of the Dusk Hall . . . but at one point he had been human, whatever he was now. Isiem watched in astonishment as the man's iron cocoon descended along the pillar with a rattle of heavy chains. The other hanging cripples had opened their eyes as well. They did not speak, but they watched with an unblinking hunger that recalled the nightglass's shades.

When the limbless one was level with the children, the chains groaned to a halt and his iron egg-case stilled. "Come, children," he said again. Dried saliva crusted his shapeless chin. A sour smell emanated from the innards of his cage.

Isiem held back, too frightened to obey. The other boys quailed with him. Helis, casting an angry look over them all, shoved between them to approach the crippled man.

"I'm not afraid of you," she announced, crossing her arms and closing her eyes. "Do it."

"A lie," the limbless one replied, his words thick and wet with yearning, "but I will." His tongue rolled out—long, long, infernally long—and engulfed her head in its slimy, blue-veined coils. Helis issued a muffled protest, but the tongue wrapped around her face suppressed it.

For an agonizing stretch of time, the two remained fixed in their positions. Spittle dripped from the cripple's tongue onto the girl's squirming shoulders. Finally, as Helis swayed on the verge of suffocation, the creature let her go.

"You will do," he said, licking his fleshy lips. "Your spirit is not weak, and your fear is . . . exquisite." He turned a glutton's grin on the rest of them. "Who will come to me next?"

"I will," Isiem said. He took Helis's place, shut his eyes, and tried not to flinch as the wet, warm flesh came slithering out to envelop him.

The stench of the thing's tongue would have choked him even if the tongue itself hadn't. It writhed over him, prying and slobbering. Just as he thought he would scream from the horror of it, the limbless one pulled away.

"Good," he pronounced with a smack of his lips. "You, the little one. You next."

Isiem stepped back. He wiped his face on the bottom of his shirt and watched as Loran and Ascaros were taken by the tongue in turn. When it was finished, and the crippled one had deemed each of them satisfactory, the chains began clanking again and the iron cocoon creaked its way back up the pillar, bearing its grotesque burden.

"Go," the Joyful Thing said. "You are worthy to begin your training. In Zon-Kuthon's name, I declare it so. To the end of the hall with you, young blood. You will find your rooms there. Do not think to come back this way without a proper escort. We have our eyes and our mouths; we will call the alarm. And then things will go badly for you, my tasty little ones. Oh, very badly."

Their rooms were waiting, as the creature had said. They looked like cells, albeit comfortable ones. The steel traceries on these windows thickened into bars. Their doors locked only from the outside, and their narrow beds, lofted over equally narrow desks, were arranged so that there was no place to hide.

The children scarcely had time to choose their rooms—Isiem and Ascaros to one, Helis and Loran to another—and deposit their scant belongings before a new shadowcaller came to them.

This one was a woman, strong-jawed and severe, with black hair pulled into a tight knot at the base of her skull and her left sleeve buttoned over an arm that stopped at the elbow. She looked them over as a farmer might examine a new litter of piglets, deciding which to keep and which to slaughter young.

"You're early," she said. Her voice was as hard as the rest of her. "The rest of this year's cull isn't here yet."

The three older children looked at each other, none sure what to say. Isiem felt as if he were being accused of something, but as far as he knew, they hadn't done anything wrong, and he didn't know how to remedy the trouble if they had.

Adults tended to like eagerness, though, so he tried that. "May we begin early, then?"

The woman laughed, a sharp brittle sound. "What's your name?"

"Isiem. Of Crosspine."

"Forget that last part. Your piddling little village has no more claim on you. If you come from anywhere, it will be the Dusk Hall, or Pangolais. If you prove unworthy of

those names, you will never have cause to use them."
She paused, fingering the buttons on her empty sleeve.
"You are here because the nightglass sensed some
spark of magic in you and the Joyful Things tasted no
impiety. That means you have potential. It does not
mean you will succeed, or survive."

"What will?" Helis asked.

"Strength. Skill."

"I have strength," the girl said, raising her chin.
"Teach me skill."

The woman laughed again, but this time there
was a different note to it. "I suppose you may have
one brief lesson." She held out her hand, showing
them the silver ring she wore. It was the same as the
other shadowcallers': a band of silver brushed with
countless tiny scratches that left the metal a lustreless
gray. A smooth black jewel, the size of Isiem's smallest
fingernail, sat bezeled in its center.

"What do you sense in the ring?" she asked.

Isiem stared at the stone, gritting his teeth in
concentration. At first he felt nothing, and wondered
if she wasn't playing a prank on them . . . but then he
opened himself, as he had when he freed Ascaros from
the nightglass, extending his thoughts and senses in
some way that he could feel instinctively but did not
know how to define. And when he did, and looked upon
the black-gemmed ring with new eyes, he saw a nimbus
spring up around it, like the hazy aura that surrounded
bright flames on the coldest winter nights.

"I see . . . light," Helis said. "A misty halo."

"Yes," the woman breathed. "Now draw it out. Shape
the magic. Follow my movements, my words." She
raised her other hand, curling her fingers through a
slow pattern as if playing some invisible instrument.

At the same time, she intoned three words, or perhaps only one word that comprised three syllables. Isiem didn't recognize the language, but the sounds struck a chord in his soul. He repeated them carefully, and heard Helis echo them at his side.

The aura intensified. It became clearer, stronger; he could discern shadowy faces swirling in its frosty nimbus. They opened their mouths in silent screams, broke whirling apart, re-formed and screamed again. An overwhelming sense of grief and pain came from them, and a ghostly charnel stink.

"Death," Isiem whispered. "The magic is death . . . and pain. So much pain." He blinked, clearing the alien sights from his vision.

"Necromancy. Yes." The woman seemed pleased at his words. "You are a clever boy to sense so much with your first spell." She glanced at Helis. "Perhaps the two of you have some promise, if not the others."

"They're just children," Isiem said, feeling a need to excuse Loran's and Ascaros's inability to do whatever he and Helis had.

"Do you imagine that matters?" the woman asked icily, her flicker of approval vanishing. "Should childhood entitle you to be incompetent?"

Yes, Isiem wanted to say, but he didn't. He could tell from her abrupt coldness that it was the wrong answer, but he had no idea why. Nonplussed, he stared at her until the shadowcaller turned away from them in a swirl of velvet.

"There is no excuse for incompetence in the Dusk Hall," she told them over her shoulder as she departed. "None. You had better learn that very quickly if you have any intention of becoming wizards rather than corpses."

"I'm tired," Ascaros announced as soon as she was gone. Without another word to any of them, he retreated into his room and shut the door.

After a moment Isiem followed him. The younger boy was already bundled in his charcoal blankets, face to the wall. As quietly as he could, Isiem changed into his sleeping shirt, snuffed the room's lone candle, and climbed into his own bunk.

Ascaros wasn't sleeping, though. In the stillness he stirred, turning back toward Isiem.

"Why did you call us children?" he asked.

"Because we are," Isiem whispered back, surprised.

"You didn't say that, though. You said '*they're* just children." Loran and me. Not you."

Under his blankets, Isiem squirmed. He'd only meant to make the shadowcaller forgive them, not to insult his friend . . . but it seemed he had doubly failed. "I didn't mean anything by it. I'm sorry."

Ascaros didn't answer for so long that Isiem wondered if his friend had fallen asleep. When he finally spoke, his voice was muffled and unsteady, as if he were on the brink of tears and had pressed his face into his pillow to hide them. "No, you were right. We're children. Just stupid children dreaming of magic."

"That's not true."

"I didn't sense anything in that ring." Ascaros let out a long, shaky breath. "Nothing. I tried, but . . . it didn't come to me."

"The nightglass answered you," Isiem reminded him. "The Joyful Thing accepted you."

"The Joyful Thing." Ascaros shuddered. "Is that what becomes of failures?"

"I don't know."

"I just wish . . . I wish . . ." He broke off, unable to hold the sobs back any longer.

"Abandon your tears," Isiem told him. It was a phrase that the Kuthite priest in Crosspine had been fond of repeating. He'd died years ago; Isiem barely remembered him. The priest had been a reclusive man, unpleasant and ill-liked, and when he took sick, no one lifted a finger to keep death from his door. But he'd had Zon-Kuthon's blessing—the only person Isiem had ever known, before the shadowcallers, who did—and he had often told them that the Midnight Lord loathed the weak. In this place, surrounded by Zon-Kuthon's devout, those words seemed good guidance.

"Abandon your tears," Ascaros repeated. His laugh was unsteady, but it wasn't a sob. "That's what we'll have to do now, isn't it? Accept the Joyful Things' caresses, master whatever spells they care to teach us, never leave the parts of the Dusk Hall we're permitted. . . and abandon our tears."

"You can do it."

"I know." Ascaros turned over again, directing his words to the wall. "I will."

Chapter Three
Bargains

There were no seasons in Pangolais.

Days melted into weeks, into months, into years, and life in the Dusk Hall never changed. Under the gaze of its unliving statues and half-living Joyful Things, children prayed, practiced spells, and—somewhere along the way—learned to leave childhood behind.

Over a hundred students came to the Dusk Hall that year. Several failed the Joyful Things' test; those remained wrapped in the cripples' tongues until their struggles stopped and they collapsed for lack of air. Then the shadowcallers carried them away, dragging them down to the lightless cells in the Dusk Hall's depths.

Sometimes, in the silences of the nights that followed, Isiem could hear their screams. More often he could not.

The survivors needed no further reminders of failure's price. They kept to the south side of the Dusk Hall, where their classes and living quarters overlooked three small courtyards, each one a jewel-like garden of night-blooming white flowers and exotic plants with dark dappled leaves. The north side, separated by a larger courtyard paved in squares of silver-streaked marble, was reserved for shadowcallers and students of Zon-Kuthon's faith. Other than the library and the cathedral where Kuthite services were held, those rooms were forbidden to the new arrivals—as were the dungeons hidden under the Dusk Hall's solemn grandeur.

Few were tempted to test that prohibition, and none had time. The newcomers threw themselves into their studies, spending hours bent over the long, low tables in the Dusk Hall's perpetually twilit libraries. They spent hours more in circled lecture halls, attending lessons on everything from the history of the horselords who were their honored ancestors to the rites of propitiation for Zon-Kuthon's heralds.

They studied the Shadow Plane, a warped reflection of the real world where all was drawn in shades of gray and nothing was substantial. There, distances stretched long and snapped close unpredictably. Landmarks dissolved like dunes of black sand in the wind, only to rise again in new places. *Things* lived on the Plane of Shadow that did not, could not, exist in the daylight world. It was a strange and surreal realm, largely indifferent to puny human toils. And it was the source of many shadowcallers' spells, so the pupils of the Dusk Hall devoted months to the study of its workings.

Above all, however, their lessons concerned magic.

The spells they learned were more innocuous than Isiem had expected. They called no shadowbeasts to hunt innocents in the night. They didn't even offer sacrifices of their own blood over fire, as evil wizards did in the dimly remembered stories of his childhood. Instead they practiced minor ward spells, imbuing themselves with thin weaves of energy that could be used to deflect other magical attacks. They learned to conjure ghostly lights and imagined sounds, to manipulate small objects at a distance, to create sparks of flame and bursts of wintry cold. The only necromancy their teachers showed them was defensive: a method of unraveling the spells that bound undead to this world, weakening their hold on false life.

Isiem was not, however, reassured by the seemingly benign forms that their lessons took. He understood that these spells were but a prelude: a necessary foundation so that when they *did* attempt the darker and more dangerous forms of magic, they would not immediately be destroyed.

He almost didn't care.

Isiem was *good* at magic. He had a gift for it. Spells came easily to him, and once learned, were not forgotten. Often he could intuit more advanced forms from the simplified shapes of cantrips, enabling him to leap ahead of the other students and impressing the senior wizards.

His skill bought him respect, approval, and a certain measure of safety. The teachers of the Dusk Hall did not tolerate failure. Clumsy students were subject to discipline, and discipline in Zon-Kuthon's house was no light matter. Isiem took pride in his talent and cultivated it for its own sake . . . but he was also acutely aware that same talent sheltered him from the lash.

Not all his fellows were so fortunate. Of the three who had come from Crosspine, only Helis matched him. Ascaros struggled. Some things the younger boy learned almost instantly, faster than Isiem himself did, as though the knowledge was already in him and needed only a reminder. Other things he could not learn at all, no matter how furiously he sweated over his books or how many times he repeated the words.

As the months passed, Ascaros became surly and withdrawn, often sinking into black sulks that forced Isiem to physically drag him out of bed, lest his friend be punished for failing to attend his lessons. Ascaros's nails grew long and hooked; his curly brown hair became a wild tangle that fell over his eyes, isolating him from the world. The lack of discipline shown in his appearance earned the shadowcallers' ire, and so the boy would shear his hair and cut his nails and, for a while, maintain their standards of seemliness. But the weight of his anger and depression always pulled him back down, and within weeks he slipped back into disarray.

Yet even Ascaros fared better than Loran did.

The child wasn't stupid. He was afraid. He was too young, had grown up too isolated. The Dusk Hall overwhelmed him. His sister, struggling with her own studies, had little time to coddle him. Ascaros and Isiem had still less, although they did what they could. The other students, sensing Loran's weakness, avoided him, and month by month, his loneliness exacerbated his fear.

One evening, as the students gathered around a nightglass, Loran's terror came to a head.

The mirror—which Isiem now knew went by many names, of which "nightglass" and "nightmirror" were the most common—was a small one, scarcely larger than Isiem's palm. It was the first time any of them had been allowed to gaze into a nightglass since they had been tested, and Isiem felt a thrill of fear when their instructor—Dirakah, the one-armed woman who had shown them her ring their first night, and who had proved no softer since—lifted the black velvet that veiled it.

He was not the only one to react that way. A disquieted murmur rose from the other students, but it soon died out: they were Nidalese, aspiring wizards of the Dusk Hall, and well accustomed to subduing their fear. If Dirakah thought them ready to face the nightglass, then they would be ready—whether or not they themselves believed it.

One by one, the thirteen students in the chamber came forward. Each took a saucer of cold clotted blood that had been collected from the kitchen chickens slaughtered that morning, then returned to his or her place in the semicircle facing the glass.

"It has been two years since you came to the Dusk Hall," Dirakah told them. "In those two years, you have learned the beginnings of magic. It is time for you to move beyond trivial things and prepare yourselves for true power.

"Each of you has gazed into a nightglass once before, and each of you has felt the vastness that lies beyond. All that can be imagined can be wrought from the Midnight Lord's shadows . . . if you have the strength to bend them to your will, and the gift to bind them." She beckoned Isiem forward. "Come. Try. Call the shadow from the glass, and offer it your sacrifice. The blood it tastes will shape it—not always, not perfectly, but sufficiently for tonight."

Isiem bowed his head to her, rose, and approached the nightglass. The black mirror stared back at him, waiting, from its pedestal of worked iron.

Drawing a measured breath, Isiem focused on it as he had that night in Crosspine, willing himself to look beyond the nightglass and into the pooled darkness at its heart. Starlight swirled across its polished surface, although there were no stars in the sky above Pangolais and no windows in the chamber through which they might shine.

He let the vortex of impossible light carry him into the nightmirror . . . and, as he had before, felt the world fall away.

The gate of shadows greeted him. It was different in this mirror—like standing at the brink of a forest pool and gazing down, rather than standing before an onyx archway. Dark, elusive shapes stirred in the depths, swirling the cold black water without creating so much as a ripple on its surface. Some of them felt peaceful as they slid past his awareness, most uncaring, a few dangerous.

Isiem singled out one of those shapes and concentrated his will upon it, alternately coaxing and compelling. What he did was not like any spell he knew, precisely; it felt less like entangling a living creature in his magic than like spinning sound and light into illusion. There was *something* real in the nightmirror's pool—he felt it twisting and writhing in his grasp, reshaping itself to fit the contours of what he imagined—but it had no substance. It was ephemeral as a ghost, and when it finally drew near, lured up to the surface, he felt nothing from it but hunger and sucking cold.

His physical body felt sluggish and numb, but he still had control. Isiem raised his dish of chicken blood to the nightmirror in offering.

This is a poor cold meal. The shadow-thing's voice was more akin to the touch of a frigid wind than any sound. Yet it stretched to take the blood despite its complaint, sending a tendril of darkness out of the nightmirror into the practice chamber.

A second murmur rose from the assembled students as the shadow-creature manifested before their eyes. Isiem ignored them, keeping his focus entirely on the shade he had summoned. The instant that it touched the blood, a physical shock rolled through him: the ghostly thing he had called suddenly solidified, became *real,* in a way it had not before. He fought to keep it in the shape he had envisioned. It felt like trying to hold up a collapsing roof with bare hands . . . but bit by bit he succeeded, and the shadow poured into the form he chose.

It was a vulpine thing, its face lean and clever and cruel, its teeth white as winter stars. Lidless, slanted eyes shone between a pointed nose and pointed ears. A ruff of melting darkness, somewhere between spikes and fur, wreathed its too-long neck. Its shoulders, and whatever else might exist of its body, remained within the mirror.

"Impressive," Dirakah said. "Now send it back."

Isiem nodded, scarcely feeling the gesture. He withdrew from the nightglass, simultaneously releasing the shadow-creature's imagined form and pulling it apart at the edges. It unraveled like an unfinished garment, dissolving back into formless darkness with a mute howl of frustration.

"Good." With that curt note of approval, Dirakah dismissed him, turning her attention to the next student in the circle. "Perahni."

It took her twice as long, and what she finally coaxed from the mirror was little more than a shapeless mass of coils ending in disjointed spiders' legs, but ultimately Perahni called a shadow-creature to drink her offering too. Other students followed, with greater and lesser success, until it came Loran's turn.

The boy stood hesitantly, edging toward the nightglass with sidelong steps. Fear radiated from him. He held his dish of chicken blood steady, and he did not shrink from gazing into the curved black glass . . . but he held himself closed to the shadows in its depths. Whether because of something that had happened during his test in Crosspine, or because of all the misshapen monsters he'd seen the other students call forth, Loran was unwilling to open his own soul to the mirror. And, being unwilling to use his own mind and spirit as the lure, he could conjure nothing from the glass.

Isiem saw it clearly. If he saw it, Dirakah could hardly fail to do the same—and, indeed, her lips thinned in displeasure and her hand twitched toward the thin black rod she kept tucked in her belt. She did not take it out, however, and Isiem's trepidation grew. If she wasn't going to beat Loran with the rod, it only meant she had something worse in mind.

"Step away," she told the boy.

"Yes, mistress." Loran bowed over his untouched bowl of blood and backed away from the glass. Shivers wracked his skinny shoulders, and he set the bowl down rather than let it fall from his trembling hands. Making a mess would only have worsened whatever was coming.

"You are afraid." Dirakah stood, walking toward her student with icy implacability. Her heels clicked on the floor's polished stone. "Your fear makes you fail."

Loran watched her come, too frightened or emotionally exhausted to do anything but stare at her with the huge frozen eyes of a mouse pinned under a serpent's gaze. "Yes, mistress."

"There are worse things to fear than the nightglass's shadows. Perhaps you require a reminder."

"If—if you deem it so, mistress."

"*If?*" Blinding-fast, her rod sliced through the air, striking Loran's cheek. He crashed to the ground and lay there without protest, not even reaching toward his wounded face. A broad pale swath striped his cheek; as

Isiem watched, the white flesh turned a mottled red, and a line of blood welled in its center. "You do not say 'if' to me, worm. 'Yes.' All you may ever say to me is *'yes.'* Do you understand?"

"Yes, mistress," Loran mumbled. He did not blink as blood trickled from his wound toward his eye. Neither did any of the other students. They watched his punishment with practiced stillness, unmoved as gray-robed statues.

"Dirakah." The door eased open, and a dark-haired man in shadowcaller's robes stepped in. It took a moment for Isiem to recognize him as Lamion, one of the trio that had taken him from Crosspine; the man was not one of the Dusk Hall's instructors, and Isiem had not seen him in the years since. He looked much the same, apart from a few threads of gray in his hair and a new series of scars across his right hand.

"What?" Dirakah snapped without turning around.

"The Chelaxians are here with a new string of slaves. Good ones. They will go quickly. You'd best hurry if you want to secure any for your students."

"These half-wits don't deserve good slaves. I should make them feed the shadows from their own wrists for their idiocy." But she drew back from Loran, breathing hard as she looked over the gathered students. After a moment she pointed to Isiem. "Take that one. Have him choose. He's the least stupid of today's lot, for what little that's worth."

Lamion glanced at Loran prostrate on the floor, curled his lip in a sneer, and nodded. "How many do you want?"

"One, and only if that one can be had for something approaching a reasonable price. I'll not waste the Dusk Hall's gold for the benefit of these fools."

"As you will." Lamion bent a knee briefly and retreated from the doorway. "You. Come."

Immediately Isiem left the circle and followed Lamion into the hall. He fell in quietly behind the shadowcaller, walking one step to the side and three behind, as he had been taught. The older man did not address him, or give him so much as a glance, until they were out of the Dusk Hall and walking along the wide, curved streets of Pangolais.

"Have you been to the markets?" he inquired as they passed beneath a pair of towering iron lampposts that resembled the trees overshadowing the city. Pallid globes of light hung among the trees' thorned black branches, drawing a constant swirl of gray moths.

"No, master," Isiem replied.

"They are a spectacle."

It did not take long for Isiem to see what he meant. The city's market square was a vast expanse of flat gray stone. Gargoyles and contorted statues, wearing crowns and needled gorgets pierced through their stony skin, overlooked the bustle from freestanding plinths and the grand buildings that hemmed the square.

Some of those statues were not carved of marble or limestone. They were living bodies that had been flayed and broken, drained of blood, then pinned into oddly beautiful configurations with lengths of sharpened steel. Those enormous needles were enchanted to keep their prisoners alive and suffering beyond all mortal endurance. High above the teeming crowds they hung, with only their feeble gasps and the occasional twitch of a finger to show that they were anything other than pure ornament.

Few in the crowds seemed to notice their torment. The market's wares held more interest for them—and for

Isiem, too. He saw barrow-carts piled high with long white radishes and dark furled mushrooms dug up from the depths of the Uskwood; he walked past jewelers' stands draped with filigree necklaces, earrings, bracelets—all in silver, all set with glowing gemstones in white or gray or black. Anything he could imagine, ordinary or rare, seemed to be displayed on a table somewhere.

Slender noblewomen picked through trays of cosmetics that promised to accentuate the whiteness of their skin, darken their lips, or lend the shimmer of crushed nightmoths' wings to their eyelids. Scarred Kuthite priests tested razors and studded lashes on themselves or on the tongueless slaves staked by the merchants' tables for that purpose. Shadowcallers in flowing gray brushed past peasants and artisans, ignoring the mumbled obeisances that the latter were always quick to offer.

And then they came to the slave market, and Isiem was truly overwhelmed. Elsewhere he had seen things strange and wondrous . . . but here, for the first time, he saw *people* who were utterly foreign to his understanding of the world.

Some of the slaves on the rope were huge. Some were tiny. Many were inhuman. Their skin was ruddy or golden or a deep rich brown that amazed him; none had the ghost-pale complexion of a Nidalese. Their hair was not only ash or white, but flame or brass or brilliant sun. One small, large-mouthed creature, barely half the height of a human, had extraordinary blue eyes and wild spikes of purple hair. Next to it was a hulking female with bronze-capped tusks and callused gray-green hide that, over the creature's slabs of muscle, gave her the look of a walking statue. Isiem gaped at them openly, too astonished to hide it.

"Congratulations, novice, you'll pay double the price now," Lamion muttered, although he seemed more amused than irritated by Isiem's reaction. "Let me do the bargaining."

"What are we looking for?" Isiem asked. As his initial surprise dissipated, he realized with some puzzlement that many of the slaves appeared to be old, very young, or sickly—not what he would have expected a slaver to choose for the long and arduous journey into Pangolais.

"Emotion," Lamion said, walking down the line. "Emotion and experience."

"Emotion?" Isiem repeated, uncomprehending.

"Others buy slaves for their deft hands or strong backs. *We* seek sacrifices for our art. I saw that Dirakah had you practicing with the nightglass. Surely you must have noticed that its shadows demand to be fed—and that they come into the world stronger and surer once they have eaten."

"Yes," Isiem said, remembering the foxlike creature he'd drawn out of the mirror, and how abruptly the feel of the thing had changed once it tasted his offering of blood.

"Those shadows need us. They need *life*. They have none of their own. Warm blood—the taste of life— is precious to them, but more precious still are the dreams and emotions that living people possess. The memories. It doesn't seem to matter much what the memories *are*, only that they're strong ones. Vivid. Fear, hate, love, it's all the same to them. The intensity is all they care about. It makes things easier for us, and more profitable for our friends from Cheliax."

Isiem felt lost again. "Easier?"

Lamion gestured contemptuously at an old man in the line. Like all the other slaves, he was bound with a loop of enchanted rope around his wrists and ankles. The soft gray strand flexed perfectly around its prisoners, avoiding any abrasion while keeping them confined in bonds stronger than steel. Yet even that seemingly fragile restraint looked absurd on the old man's liver-spotted wrists. He could hardly stand upright; any fight in him had died decades ago.

"Who would buy that one?" Lamion asked. "Look at him. The necromancers of Geb might pay a few coppers for his bones, but he's worthless to anyone else. Except us."

And him, and his family, Isiem thought, but he held his tongue. Lamion clearly thought nothing of that; it did not matter a whit to him that all these slaves could hear every word he said. In the shadowcaller's eyes, these creatures were not people.

"His memories are what matter," Lamion continued. "His pain. If he can suffer, he has worth—to the shadows, and so to us."

"Do we need him?" Isiem asked hesitantly. The shadowcaller gave him a curious look, but he did not seem angry, so Isiem pressed onward. "Can we not feed the shadows ourselves, instead of relying on these poor creatures?"

"You do." An auburn-haired woman stepped out from the canopied tent near the slave line. Turquoise-studded silver pins held her hair in an elaborate crown of braids. She was slim and pale, like a Nidalese, but she was not one of them. Her pallor tended toward gold, not white, and although her dress was black leather like a Kuthite's, it was trimmed and slashed in red. The emblem of Cheliax was worked in crimson on her breast.

Lamion did not seem pleased to see her. "Suryan."

"Lamion." She gave him a radiant smile and raised her hands in mock-affectionate greeting. "Who is this charming child you've brought me?"

The woman's effusion seemed to increase Lamion's annoyance. The shadowcaller stepped back, withdrawing into a shell of unfriendliness. "Isiem. He's new."

"He must be. You haven't crushed all the questions out of him yet." She regarded Isiem with the same too-charming smile. Her eyes sparkled: now blue, now green, now somewhere in between. He wondered if she used some minor magic to change their hue. "New as you are, however, you must have seen that the people of Pangolais are . . . different. A lassitude envelops this city. Its people are wan, thin, silent. You might say they're shadows of themselves. Or, perhaps, that they've *fed* shadows of themselves."

"Suryan," Lamion said again. This time it was a warning.

She ignored him. "You must have seen, too, that most of your fellow students do not come from the city, but from the little villages farther from Nidal's heart. If they've started letting you out of the Dusk Hall, you may have noted that there are few children in Pangolais. I've been visiting this city for a decade, and I doubt I've seen twenty children in all that time here. Why is that, do you suppose?"

"*Suryan*," Lamion snarled.

"Ah, the truth is prickly." She turned to Isiem, encompassing the market around them with a wave of one hand. Her nails were painted blue-green, too. "The Nidalese *do* feed their shadows. Constantly. Every breath you take under the trees of Pangolais is taxed for their sustenance. And even so, all these people giving up their vitality can only sustain the gloom over Pangolais. To call beasts from the darkness, you need more—yet if you fed them with your own blood, drained as you are, it might kill you. Therefore you need our charges to pay the toll."

"Which is why we've come," Lamion said sharply. "If you could cease your fairy stories long enough to sell some."

"I suppose, owing to our long friendship, I might do you the small favor of negotiating for one or two." Suryan's smile twinkled, although her eyes stayed cold. "Which would you like?"

Lamion nodded toward Isiem. "Choose."

Choose. The immensity of the decision rooted Isiem to the ground. How did one choose who was worthy to live? If Lamion's intimations were true, and the intensity of a sacrifice's emotions strengthened the shadowbeast that fed on him, then it was likely—no, it was *certain*—that the sacrifice would be tortured first. No Kuthite would let an opportunity to inflict suffering pass.

Whoever he chose would be tortured and killed. And if he didn't choose anyone, he invited that fate upon himself. Isiem had been in the Dusk Hall long enough to know that.

It was a briefly tempting thought—one way out of his dilemma—but as he faced that thought, and the finality of it, Isiem quailed away. He didn't have it in him to choose death. Not the kind of death Zon-Kuthon's adepts would give.

How, then, could he do the least harm?

"Tell me about that one," he said, pointing to the little creature with the shock of purple hair. A whimsical pattern of colored dots, garishly out of place in Pangolais, had been tattooed up one shoulder and the right side of its neck. Three feet tall and bizarrely bright-eyed, the purple-haired creature looked the least human of the slaves in line. If it was a monster, as he hoped, his choice would be easier.

Suryan went back into the canopied tent and returned with a ledger held open on one hand. She flicked through a few pages, then read: "Quilli Brightburst. A gnome. Lost her tongue and freedom for preaching treason in Westcrown. Magically gifted, although she will need a new tongue before that's of much use. The price is eleven platinum crowns."

Lamion was staring at the gnome with naked hunger, but he shook his head reluctantly at mention of the price. "Too much. Gnomes are expensive."

"Experience and emotion, wasn't that what you wanted?" Suryan glanced up from her book. "Gnomes surpass all others for that. And then there is the matter of the Bleaching. Gnomes crave new experiences. Need them. Die without them. You can make them do *so* much in the name of novelty, and then deprive them of it entirely in the end . . ."

"I'm well aware," Lamion snapped. "Eleven crowns is too much. Choose another."

"What about that one?" Isiem indicated the tusked, heavily muscled woman. Her forehead was ridged with ritual scars, her eyes small and suspicious. She carried herself with a subtle tension, as if she expected danger to leap out from any direction and did not intend to be caught unawares. And yet, Isiem imagined, there seemed to be a certain fatalism to her as well, as if she had already accepted that her end would be bloody and viewed that as no great tragedy.

"Atan," Suryan read aloud. "A half-orc. Formerly the property of House Henderthane. Offered on the open market after rebelling against her rightful masters and allowing a defeated foe to escape instead of bringing him to House Henderthane's diabolists as commanded. Suspected of allowing others to escape on previous occasions. Exceptionally strong, but impulsive and defiant. Ideal for the gladiator's ring."

"Less so for beginning students." Lamion crossed his arms. "That one is likely to be too much trouble for them. Still, with so much violence in her soul . . . what are they asking?"

"Sixty platinum crowns, or two good fighting slaves to House Henderthane in exchange."

The shadowcaller snorted. "Half that would be an outrage."

"Henderthane sets the price. We only ask it," Suryan answered with a shrug. "According to the entry, she is quite accomplished in battle. Good at finishing her foes in a showy mess. Audiences like that."

"The old man," Isiem suggested, feeling a twinge of desperation. Lamion had discarded all his suggestions so far, giving him some reprieve, but the shadowcaller couldn't reject every slave in the line.

"Edovan. Called Leadthumb for his heavy hand on the merchant's scales." Suryan closed the book. "I know the lictor who transferred this one. He said the man was suspected of arson and murder—it was rumored that he'd burned down a competitor's shop, killing the family in their beds as they slept above the blaze—but only fraud and deceit could be proved. Leadthumb chose a term of slavery rather than paying off his fines. Too much of a miser to give up his gold, even at the cost of his freedom."

Or too worried about his family's penury, Isiem thought. He wanted to believe the lictor's tale. His choice would be easier if he could believe this old man had murdered a whole family out of greed . . . but he wondered whether that was why Suryan had told the story. Maybe it was just a subtle way to push the sale by salving his conscience. Maybe there was no murder, no arson, only false accusations of fraud, and Edovan Leadthumb, unable to shake his accusers, had sacrificed himself so that his children wouldn't have to starve.

He'd likely never know the truth. Did it matter?

Why not accept the comforting answer? What harm could it do?

It's cowardice. Isiem looked away, not wanting to meet the slaves' eyes. But they were everywhere, all around him. The only place he could look without seeing them was skyward, and there he found his gaze caught by three suffering bodies pinned together in an ornamental circle by gleaming silver needles. Their shattered arms and legs were arrayed in graceful whorls within the wheel, creating a filigree of flesh.

The nearest victim's eyes were gone, pecked out by carrion birds or gouged as part of his torture, but the ragged black pits held Isiem fixed.

"How much is that one?" he heard himself ask.

"The original price was five crowns, but I'll give him to you for four. We make no promises as to his soundness."

"We'll take him," Isiem said.

He never saw Edovan Leadthumb again.

Lamion did not ask Isiem to choose any other slaves, perhaps because he was impatient with how long the boy had taken to pick the first. He made the rest of the selections himself, haggling viciously with Suryan over their prices and, when he was finally satisfied that the cost was cheap enough, signing a contract for their delivery. Then he led the boy back to the Dusk Hall, leaving the Chelaxians to bring their living wares later. The shadowcaller offered Isiem no hint of what the slaves' fates might be, and Isiem didn't ask, assuming that he would find out in due course, whether he wanted to or not.

But he never did.

He never saw the slaves come to the Dusk Hall's subterranean dungeons, and none from that day's purchase were ever used in his classes. Others came, and others died, but Isiem never learned what befell the old miser he had purchased from the Chelish line. He never had the chance to ask whether the lictor's story was true, or why Leadthumb had chosen slavery instead of paying for his freedom.

And in that unknowing was another hard lesson: that he might never know the ramifications of his own choices, and that he still had to make them as best he could. Isiem might flounder in a sea of half-truths and uncertainties, and he might never learn whether he had chosen correctly, but he still had to act, to choose *something* without hesitation, when the opportunity to do so came.

Because that opportunity would be fleeting, and refusing it meant leaving the choice to shadowcallers— to Lamion, or Dirakah, or worse. And that, after his visit to the slave market, seemed an even greater cowardice than he could bear.

Chapter Four
Gifts

I'm running away," Loran said.

Isiem and Ascaros exchanged a look. Helis, reading on her bed above them, snorted.

"You can't run away," she told her brother. "Where would you go? What would you do? You're *eleven*, and you can't even get out of the Dusk Hall."

"I don't care." Loran turned over onto his belly, hiding his face between his crossed arms. Bruises dotted his skin in a panoply of blues, purples, and dirty yellows, vanishing into his sleeves. The gloom of the students' chambers masked the boy's expression as much as his arms did, but nothing hid the misery in his voice or the scars of the shadowcallers' chastisements. "I'll live on the streets if I have to. I'll eat rats. Drink from puddles. It has to be better than this."

"It gets better," Ascaros said cautiously, closing his own book. Over the past months he had emerged from his own turmoil and found a certain degree of comfort in his studies. The gaunt angles of his cheekbones had softened slightly as he returned to a normal weight. No longer was his hair a greasy shag; now it was washed and brushed and pulled back in a neat tail, like Isiem's own. The reddish tints in his hair were fading, though, becoming murkier day by day, as if the shadows of Pangolais were stealing its color.

Loran shook his head. His words were muffled; he was chewing on his lip again. "It got better for *you*. But you have a talent. Maybe not like Isiem's, but it's something. I don't have that. I never will. My lot's only going to get worse."

That was likely true, Isiem judged. He'd watched with increasing dismay as Loran flailed in the wake of Dirakah's beating. The boy's aptitude for magic was marginal at best, and the disaster with the nightglass had shattered his confidence. Month by month, cowed by his continuing failures, Loran had retreated deeper into timidity.

It was a choice that might kill him. As the spells they learned grew stronger, and the consequences of losing control became greater, their instructors had become more severe. Mistakes didn't earn beatings anymore. The last time a student had botched a spell in one of Isiem's classes, the shadowcaller had made her flay a finger-thin spiral of her own skin from wrist to elbow. The girl had obeyed in perfect silence, knowing that any cry of pain would double her punishment. Afterward the shadowcaller had healed the wound, but only enough to keep infection at bay. A week later, the shape of it still showed raw and pink on her arm.

Loran had fared worse. Isiem seldom saw the boy during their daily lessons; he was older, and more skilled, and had long ago moved to more advanced studies. But he often visited the siblings' room during the quiet hour after dinner, when the students had some time to themselves, and he had seen Loran trying to pull a stoic mask over his suffering.

Never sturdy, the boy had shrunk into a wide-eyed waif. His ears and nose had always seemed too large for the rest of his face, but now they were the only features with any definition at all. Loran kept his eyes downcast and his mouth shut tight, as if he were always holding back cries. His lower lip was covered in scabs; he gnawed at it constantly, using the small pain to distract himself from larger ones.

Isiem sometimes wondered why the shadowcallers had taken the child, or why they didn't send him to some other task. It was clear that Loran would never be a great wizard. He might never master anything beyond a cantrip. Perhaps he was too young, or too frightened, or lacked the sharpness of mind necessary to grasp arcane theory . . . but whatever the cause, the result was the same. Wizardry was beyond him.

"You'll need a plan," Isiem said quietly.

"You can't mean to encourage him." Ascaros said, aghast. "We'll help him do better. Revisit his lessons with him. Practice cantrips after dinner."

"We've been doing that." And as far as Isiem could see, it hadn't improved anything.

"No one leaves the Dusk Hall." Ascaros sounded desperate. "They'll kill him if he tries."

"I'd rather die," Loran muttered. "At least then this would all be over."

Helis slammed her book shut with a thump that made her brother jump. "Don't be stupid. You aren't going to die, and you aren't going to run away. All this talk is idiocy, and I won't have you two"—she glared at Isiem and Ascaros—"indulging it. Out. Now."

"She's right," Ascaros murmured as they walked from the siblings' room to their own. The hall was empty, but the continual dance of shadows through the Dusk Hall's many-tinted gray windows surrounded them with the flickering illusion of motion. "He needs to study, not daydream about running away. And that's all it'll ever be—a daydream."

"Aren't we allowed to daydream here?" Isiem asked mildly. He opened the door and held it for his friend.

Before Ascaros answered, he closed the door and made a series of swift gestures. A mote of white light, no bigger than a firefly, winked into existence and hovered over his palm. If any magic were nearby, the mote would change color. Both boys watched it intently, holding their breath as they waited to see whether it would shift toward the yellowish tint that meant divination.

The spark stayed white. No enchanted eyes were on them. Ascaros let his cantrip expire. Then, at last, he answered: "No. Not about escaping."

"I'm doing it to protect him," Isiem said.

"How?"

"He can't hurt himself daydreaming. As long as Loran spends his time *planning* to run, instead of actually *doing* it, he won't get in trouble. If he tells us his plans, we can point out all the flaws in them. There will be many, I'm sure; we both know he'd never make it past the Joyful Things, let alone out of the Dusk Hall. Then he'll have to think up ways around those problems. He might finally accept that there's no escape. But even if he doesn't, we'll keep him from doing anything stupid, and we'll have that much longer to help him with his magic."

Ascaros exhaled, looking simultaneously deflated and relieved. "All right." He pulled his shirt and trousers off, folded each with neat, efficient motions, and squared them atop the drab gray stack of his other garments. Nothing was out of place by a hair—it never was—but Isiem still glanced over to make sure. Any untidiness would draw the night watchers' ire.

There was none, however, so he just reached over and snuffed the candle burning in the wall ledge by his pillow. A moment later, Ascaros extinguished its twin.

"*Can* we help him?" Ascaros asked into the dark.

"Maybe." Lying on his back, Isiem blew a soundless sigh toward the ceiling. "I don't know. He's too afraid to grasp the magic. Every time he comes close, he flinches back, like he thinks it'll burn him. I'm a poor teacher, anyway. I don't have the patience."

"He isn't smart enough," Ascaros said.

"He's young."

"And not smart enough." After a pause, he added, "I'm not saying that to be cruel. Only because it's true. It makes things harder. This place . . . I don't know if you see it. Everything comes so easily for you. I'm not saying you don't work hard—I've seen the hours you spend at the library, the stacks of books you bring back here—but you don't know what it's like to struggle just to follow what the lecturers are saying. You don't know the *fear*."

"There've been lots of times I haven't understood things in lecture," Isiem objected.

"It's not the same. If you don't understand something, it's a good bet at least half the class doesn't either. You've never had to weigh whether it would be better to ask a lecturer something, and risk getting ridiculed or beaten for your stupidity, or forge blindly into a spell and risk it failing, or turning upon you, or worse.

"I've seen you ask questions in lecture. You don't flinch. You don't understand why *other* people flinch. I don't think you even notice. That's the luxury your intelligence buys—that you can talk theory with the instructors, and they're patient, even pleased, when you ask about variations while the rest of us are just struggling to comprehend the basics. You've never had the terror of wondering whether you're the last to understand."

"Are you jealous?" Isiem asked quietly.

"No." The answer was an exhalation into blackness. "I was, when I first realized what was happening. Now I'm more worried for you than I am for myself. The instructors barely notice me. I'm in the great middling mass, not exceptional one way or the other. It's safest there. *You* they notice. You they know. And that's dangerous, I think. Nothing good comes of the lecturers noticing you." Ascaros's bed creaked as he turned over. The scent of hot candlewax and burnt wick drifted past. "Anyway, my point was just that you don't feel the fear. I do. And I don't think Loran ever escapes it."

"You did."

"Not by suddenly getting smarter." There was an odd note in Ascaros's voice, as if he hesitated on the cusp of a confession he wasn't sure he wanted to make. Isiem sat up, curious, and saw that his friend was also sitting up in his bed. "I found . . . another way."

"What?"

"Do you remember my aunt? The one in the Midnight Guard?"

"How could I forget? It's only been three years since we left Crosspine and you finally stopped bragging about her."

Ascaros laughed weakly. "Right. There was one story about her I never told."

"Impossible."

"Oh, it's very possible." There was a smile in his voice, but it drained out as he went on. "I only met her once that I remember. She was a stern woman. Much like Dirakah, now that I think of it . . . all the way down to her dead arm."

He fell silent for a while, so Isiem prompted: "Dead arm?"

"Her left arm was withered and gray. Like an old gnarled stick. I think she could move the fingers, a little, but that was about the only use she had of it. I always assumed it was an old spellwound, but that was just an explanation I made up for myself. When I asked her about it, all she told me was that if it was my fate to know, I'd find the answer on my own."

"That's not much of an answer."

"I didn't think so either. Not when I was nine. But since we came to the Dusk Hall, and especially over the past year or so, I've begun to understand what she meant."

"What was that?"

Ascaros gestured to the candle by his bed. Its wick flared into flame, gradually steadying into a glassy white blaze. He moved into its light, turning his left arm outward so that the inside of his arm, which had been concealed against his body earlier, was plainly visible.

A patch of skin on his inner elbow, a little larger than Isiem's thumbprint, stood out sharply. It was scabrous and crusty where the rest of his skin was soft, a dark wrinkled gray where the rest was smooth white.

Isiem sucked his breath in. "What —"

"It's the mark of my family's magic. Of our original sin, I suppose." Ascaros pulled away from the light, returning to his bed. The white candle went out, trailing a thread of pale smoke. "I'm not a wizard, Isiem. I never got better at the incantations, the studies, any of it. All I did was learn how to tap the magic in my blood. Some spells . . . some of them just come naturally to me. Like there's an instinct waiting to be awakened, or a memory waiting to resurface. When I watch those lessons . . . I don't understand, not really. I never know what the lecturers are talking about. But I don't need to. I see the patterns in my head. It's like—like hearing a song once, and knowing how to play it because you know the notes. You don't need the music written on a sheet. You already know the *sound*. That's how it is for me."

"Sometimes."

"Sometimes," Ascaros agreed. "If the spells don't come by instinct, they don't come at all. I've been able to hide it so far, but sooner or later the instructors will have to suspect. When they do . . ." His blankets rustled as he shrugged. "It has to be possible to survive the Dusk Hall as a sorcerer. My aunt did it."

"If I can help, I will," Isiem said. He didn't know much about sorcery. The shadowcallers made no secret of their scorn, disdaining such inherited powers as the province of savages and lesser races. Ascaros's secret would likely earn him expulsion, or worse, if it became known.

No wonder Ascaros had worried about his survival in the Dusk Hall. Isiem was acutely aware of just how much his friend had confided in him. And yet, as much as anything, he was curious. What *was* sorcery like? "Does it hurt?"

"No," Ascaros said. "All I ever feel from it is a sort of . . . cold, when I'm drawing on the magic in my blood. It feels like the shadows did when they seized me through the nightglass back in Crosspine." He paused. "It frightens me. The cold reaches deeper every time I call on its magic, and the mark . . . spreads. It's like something's claiming me, and its claim gets stronger whenever I invoke its power."

"Then I'll try to help with that, too."

"Thank you." Ascaros's laugh was short-lived and weary. "Anyway. We were supposed to be talking about Loran, not me. I only wanted to explain why the solution that I stumbled upon likely wouldn't work for him."

"We'll find Loran his own answer," Isiem said. "We just need him to listen . . . and give us time."

Fate, however, did not seem inclined to grant either of those wishes.

The day after Loran blurted out his longing for escape, he vanished from the Dusk Hall.

Isiem was terrified when he heard that Loran was gone. He and his friends always searched for magical spies before speaking freely, even in their own rooms, but something might have slipped past them. They were only students, and their instructors doubtlessly had tricks they couldn't begin to imagine.

It didn't have to be magic, either. A curious ear pressed to their door might have undone them. Regardless, if one of the shadowcallers had learned of Loran's childish plans to run off, and had spirited him away to be questioned, then the boy was doomed, and the rest of them likely were too.

But as the days trickled by in an agony of unknowing, it began to appear that they had not, after all, been undone.

Loran had failed the trial of the nightglass again, one of the students in his class told them. Not only had he been unable to call any creatures from the mirror, but he hadn't even been able to look into it. When Dirakah ordered him to touch the nightglass—perhaps intending to force the child to confront his fear—Loran's hands had trembled so violently that he had knocked it to the ground. Although the enchanted glass hadn't suffered a scratch, Loran's clumsiness and impiety had driven Dirakah into a rage.

She hadn't punished him there. She hadn't punished him *anywhere* the other students could see. Instead she had dragged the sobbing, stumbling child into the black rooms below the Dusk Hall, where those who failed to pass the Joyful Things went. That was where the dungeons lay, all the students knew, but none of them had been allowed to go there yet.

No one had seen him since.

Helis was enraged upon learning what had happened to her brother. Isiem had just closed his eyes. If Loran had wept in front of one of the shadowcallers after three full years of study in the Dusk Hall, his fate was sealed. Such weakness in the face of pain was unforgivable.

But before Helis could do anything stupid to get her brother back—or Isiem could do anything to stop her—the shadowcallers returned Loran of their own accord.

He had suffered. The boy said not a word about it. He had learned his lesson about stoicism; he kept his eyes lowered and his mouth shut. But the marks were plain on his body.

Loran walked like an old, old man. He shuffled from place to place in a daze, seeming hardly aware of where he went or why, and he clutched at a ghostly wound in his side. Neither Isiem nor Hellis could find any indication of what pained him there, but they found countless other injuries that he did not seem to notice. Burns, cuts, abrasions of rope and rasp—all partly healed, none fully so.

Worse than those were the holes that riddled his thighs and the flesh between his ribs. Some were small as a fingerprint, others nearly as large as a crabapple, but apart from their size they were all hideously the same: empty spaces where the skin stretched taut and translucent as a drumhead over its shell. Underneath was nothing—no flesh, no bone, not even blood pooled to fill the wound. Only murky darkness, glimpsed through a window of dead-looking skin.

"What could *do* that?" Ascaros marveled, holding a candle to the wounds as he examined them in the privacy of the siblings' room.

"I'll kill them," Helis swore. Tears trembled in her eyes. "I'll kill them all for what they did."

"You won't," Isiem said sharply, "and you aren't stupid enough to try. Loran needs you. Do you think anyone else has the patience to nurse him through this? Look after your brother, or he's dead."

Helis's jaw worked silently as she ground her teeth against his words, but after a long while she nodded. "All right."

Later that night, when the two of them were alone in their own room, Ascaros said, "He's dead anyway, whatever she does." He said it evenly, as he might have reported the results of an elementary practice divination.

"Maybe," Isiem said.

"There's no maybe about it. He's broken. Whatever they did to him in the hidden halls, it shattered his body and mind. He might survive the former, but he's no use to anyone after the latter. I just hope Helis doesn't throw her own life after his."

"He might recover," Isiem said. "I don't think they would have returned him if he were just going to die. This is meant to be a lesson—and if they thought the lesson were best learned by forcing us to watch them kill him, they'd have done that in the chapel."

Ascaros gave him a dubious look, then blew out his candle and rolled over.

But Loran did get better. Slowly. They kept him out of his classes and took turns bringing his meals to Helis's room, where his older sister fed him, one bite at a time, until he was strong enough to hold the fork himself.

Day by day, the cloudiness faded from his demeanor. His gait lost its dragging heaviness, as if invisible weights had dropped from his feet. His awareness of the world returned.

And when his wits were fully restored, and he remembered where he was and what lay before him, Loran ran.

The boy never warned the others of his plan, if indeed he had one. The first inkling Isiem had that his friend intended to flee came after it had happened.

He was in one of Dirakah's classes, practicing a simple mending spell again and again as their instructor paced along the circle of students, slashing at their clothes with a long razor. If a ripped shirt was not repaired by the time she came back around to that student, Dirakah's next swing was harder, slicing through cloth into flesh and bone. Halfway through the hour, several students' clothes were bloodsoaked tatters.

In the midst of their suffering, a bell tolled. It sounded only a single peal, but its echoes rang strangely in the Dusk Hall: each seemed simultaneously louder and quieter than the last, as if the actual *sound* diminished with each reverberation, but the *presence* of it became stronger and more oppressive. As one, the students stopped their spellcasting and looked up in confusion. Dirakah paused as well, canting her head toward the open doorway like a hawk waiting for an unsuspecting hare to break cover.

The bell's bronze echoes died down. In the quavering silence, a new clangor broke out: a shrieking cacophony of iron. The rattling rain of chains pouring down, the shriek of spinning saw-wheels, the stuttered scrape of hooks sliding across stone—there was too much, too fast, for Isiem to distinguish all he heard.

It all meant one thing, though.

"The Joyful Things," Dirakah hissed. Snapping her razor shut, she strode from the room.

The students shared an uncertain look. Some of them stayed where they were, afraid of reprimand. Others followed Dirakah.

Isiem, impelled by curiosity and a tingling, nameless anxiety, went with the latter group. He rushed through the long halls, carried along by a growing tide of students as other interrupted classes emptied from their rooms. He wasn't afraid, precisely, and he wasn't sure what had happened, but he knew in his bones it was bad, and he wanted to meet the trouble head-on instead of waiting to see if it would come for him.

But it wasn't really about him at all.

The Joyful Things had descended from their pillars. Their bloated pale faces shone with unholy glee above their black cage-cocoons; the spiked chains that bound them had come loose, stretching around their pillars and grasping at the air in a monstrous manifestation of hunger. In their midst, Loran stood cornered, a small white fish caught in a net of thrashing iron chains.

"He tried to flee," a Joyful Thing crooned, and the others took up the cackling chorus. "He tried to run! He is afraid. Unworthy, unworthy."

Other shadowcallers were arriving in the chamber. Some came alone; some came accompanied by knots of fearful students. All looked upon Loran without pity.

Dirakah held up her hand. The Joyful Things fell silent. The clatter of their chains ceased.

"This one has proved undeserving of his gifts," she said. She drew up her hood and stopped before the circle of chains. Something about her pose and position struck Isiem as ceremonial, hearkening back to a rite they had studied but which he could not immediately recall.

Another shadowcaller approached the circle and stopped. He lifted his hood over his head, letting darkness obscure his face. "He has refused the gift of knowledge."

"He fears the gift of magic," said a third shadowcaller. She took up a position opposite from the other two, forming a triangle around the Joyful Things' circle.

Two more hooded shadowcallers came forward, transforming the triangle into a five-pointed star. "He cringes from the gift of pain," said one. The other intoned: "He is blind to the gift of shadow."

"He denies the gifts of Zon-Kuthon," Dirakah said, "and he is not one of us." The ring of chains parted, and she stepped through. One by one the others followed, bringing their star within the circle, and the black iron chains closed around them again.

"We offer him to you, Midnight Lord," they said in unison. "We offer his flesh to cloak your servant. We offer his life to sustain it. Reclaim your gifts from this unworthy one. Welcome him to your court."

Throughout their chant, Loran had not moved. Their final words, however, seemed to strike terror into him, shattering his shell of icy paralysis at last. He ducked, spun, and darted between two of the shadowcallers, trying to flee the circle of chains.

He didn't make it to the perimeter. Three of the chains struck at him like metallic serpents, piercing his wrists and stabbing through one of his ankles. As the boy thrashed and bled, more spiked chains coiled around him, immobilizing his limbs and wrapping tight around his throat. A collar of blood wept dark from his neck.

"Bring me the mirror," Dirakah said.

One of the younger shadowcallers hurried to obey. Isiem caught a glimpse of Helis standing in a corridor on the far side of the room, momentarily visible through the press of instructors and students. Her face was white and frozen, her eyes huge with shock. She didn't seem to see him, and soon the crowd swallowed her up again.

Moments later, the shadowcaller returned, holding a small nightglass. Although nothing but its size distinguished this black mirror from any other, Isiem thought it might be the one from which he had first summoned a shadow—and to which Loran had refused to bare his soul, beginning his fatal spiral of failure in the Dusk Hall.

The shadowcaller brought the nightglass to Dirakah. With measured steps, each one clicking on the floor's smooth gray stones, she brought the mirror to Loran. The Joyful Things' animated chains jerked the boy's bleeding hands up to receive it, then wrapped his fingers in spiked iron coils and forced them around the edges of the glass.

"We give this one to you, Zon-Kuthon," Dirakah said, as Loran stared helplessly into the black glass. The other shadowcallers, within the ring and outside it, echoed her words in an unearthly chorus. "We ask you to make him worthy."

Darkness spilled from the glass. It came in sooty tendrils, wreathing the mirror and reaching toward

Loran, and it undulated in the air as if in response to the shadowcallers' chant.

As shadows flowed out of the mirror and wrapped around Loran's head, a colorless reflection of the boy's face gradually took shape in the glass. Initially it was formless and featureless, little more than crude white smudges with empty gaps to signify its eyes and mouth. It gathered detail swiftly, however, and it seemed to become more vibrant, more *real*, as the living warmth drained out of the boy in the shadows' grasp.

The pale duplicate rose from the nightglass like a swimmer surfacing from a pond. It did not come out fully—perhaps it couldn't—but it thrust its face toward the pinned boy's and trapped him in a kiss, and when its lips met Loran's, its being flowed into his. Isiem caught a glimpse of amorphous shadow, trailing a mass of inky tentacles, as it poured from the nightglass into Loran's mouth . . . and then it was *gone*, all of it, leaving the mirror blank.

Loran reeled, choking, in the chains' grip. The Joyful Things' chains held him mercilessly, wrapped and impaled, and after several painful minutes his struggles stilled. His head drooped low; his feet dragged limp.

Then, slowly, he looked up. His eyes were liquid black.

"Let me go," he said. The voice was still Loran's, but . . . different. The inflections were gone. The boyishness. Isiem took a step back, disconcerted by the strangeness of hearing another presence speaking through his friend's mouth.

The chains retracted, releasing his gouged hands and pierced ankle. Loran opened and closed his hands stiffly, as if unused to the motion. He did not seem to notice the bloody holes punched through his palms.

"This flesh is not strong," he said, "but it will serve. As will I."

"As do we all," Dirakah said. Again the shadowcallers echoed her words. "As do we all."

The phrase seemed to be the signal that whatever had happened was at an end. The Joyful Things withdrew their chains, licking at the blood that clung to their spikes, and creaked back up their pillars. Loran left without sparing a glance for his sister. The shadowcallers dispersed. Many herded their students back to their classes, but Dirakah ignored hers.

As the others filtered away, Isiem walked over to Helis, who stood rooted to the ground in the hallway. She didn't turn until he touched her elbow, trying awkwardly to offer comfort.

"They killed him," she whispered, too shocked for tears. "He tried to run, so they just . . . they just *killed* him."

"He isn't dead," Isiem said, not sure he believed his own words.

Helis shook her head fiercely, knocking his hand off her arm. "My brother is dead. They killed him and put some other *thing* in his body. That isn't Loran. They killed him, and I'm going to kill them for it. Don't even try to talk me out of it, Isiem. I'm going to kill them all."

Chapter Five
Faith

Days passed before Isiem spoke to Helis again.

He saw her in the classes they shared, but they couldn't talk frankly in front of the other students or their instructors, and Helis always disappeared after they were released from their lectures. She seldom visited the dining halls or the library, and she avoided her room.

That room, once their sanctuary in the Dusk Hall, had become a lonely, almost haunted place in the wake of Loran's transformation. All of Loran's belongings were already gone; the boy had moved out immediately after the ritual, leaving a bare bunk opposite his sister's bed.

The empty space weighed on all of them, but it had crushed Helis. Isiem hadn't seen her set foot in the room since her brother was given to the shadow. Wherever she was sleeping, it was not in her own bed.

Each day saw her frailer than the one before. It was as if grief had rasped away the core of her being, leaving a translucent shell of a girl. She seemed almost to float, ghostlike, through the Dusk Hall. Isiem was afraid for her, and a little afraid *of* her.

But for far too long, he never had a chance to say a word.

Finally, late one night, he saw her walk past his window. It was summer, and although that did nothing to lift the gloom of Pangolais, it did make the evenings warmer.

As he gained seniority, Isiem had been able to move to a better room—albeit one still shared with Ascaros—and now his chamber overlooked the grand courtyard at the center of the Dusk Hall. He liked the fragrances that drifted in from the nocturnal gardens, and on warm nights often left his windows open to enjoy them. Isiem was still awake, luxuriating in that small sweetness, when he saw a girl drift by on bare feet. She was shrouded in white, her long black hair flying wild in the wind. Helis.

Isiem left his room to follow her. He walked quietly, not wanting to disturb her fugue, but he did not try to hide. If she sent him away, he'd go.

She never glanced back. Swaying from step to step, as if moved by music only she could hear, Helis crossed the Dusk Hall's central courtyard. Isiem held his breath, afraid that she might try to leave through the great doors—a path that would take her past the Joyful Things, and perhaps to a fate like her brother's—but she did not turn east to the doors. Instead she went west, turned her face to the sky, and with surprising nimbleness began to scale the carved stone walls.

High above his head she stopped, sitting on a narrow ledge between two of the enchanted, luminous spheres that hung over both courtyards like caged moons. Great gray moths swirled around her, brushing across her brow and tangling in the black net of her hair. In that moment she was beautiful as a fairy queen, and as inhuman. And as terrifying.

She looked down. "You can come up if you want," she said.

He did. The climb was harder for him than it had been for her. Twice Isiem slipped and caught himself, heart pounding, moments before his head would have shattered like a bloody gourd on the ashen stones below. Helis offered him no help. She sat there, watching him with abstract curiosity, until he heaved himself, sweating, onto the ledge beside her.

"What are you doing up here?" Isiem asked when he caught his breath.

Helis shrugged. She'd already looked away from him, and was toying with a moth that had crashed into one of the globes. Shimmering dust fell from its wings, coating Helis's fingertips, as the insect struggled hopelessly to return to the air. "It's peaceful above the gardens. Restful. I like it. Sometimes I pray."

"To whom?"

She smiled and took her hand away from the moth's wings. Carefully, deliberately, Helis crushed its head with a fingernail. "There's only one god here."

"Does it give you . . . solace?" Isiem asked, fumbling to understand. The Midnight Lord was powerful, and his clerics were skilled in repairing the damage they caused; perhaps Helis had turned to his faith in hopes of helping her brother. "Hope?"

"No. There's no hope. There's no cure." Helis lifted the moth's body by a bent black leg and dropped it onto a heap of small, winged corpses. They were screened by her knee, and Isiem hadn't noticed them before, but when she shifted he saw that there were hundreds of dead moths in the pile. "I went through everything in the library. The shadowcallers had to know why I was there, but they never tried to stop me. I suppose they knew there was no reason; I was hardly the first to look. So many had come before me that all the books fell open to the same pages."

"That could have been a trick," Isiem said. "The books could have been bent that way. A feint to throw you off."

"Don't you think the same idea occurred to me?" Another moth was fluttering on the ledge, not far from where the first had died. Helis stroked its twitching antennae with an odd gentleness. "I looked beyond those pages. It wasn't a trick. I was hoping it could be broken like a curse—not something I can do now, but someday . . . but no. It's not as simple as that."

"What *is* it?"

Helis caressed the moth's wings, rubbing them translucent. Glimmering silver flakes dusted her skin. She pressed a finger to her small, perfect lips, leaving a shining print. "What happened to Isiem—what happened to *all* the souls seized by the shadow, century after century, ever since Earthfall—is not possession, and not transformation, but a little of both. One of the hungry shadows was invited into his body. Not to possess him, but to *become* him. It has mapped its soul against his, taken his memories for its own, adopted his *being*— his habits, fears, aspirations—to guide its stolen life."

Isiem nodded, finding the news grim but not surprising. What she told him only reinforced the teachings of the Dusk Hall.

Most of the creatures that inhabited the shadow realm were neither benign nor malevolent, but simply oblivious to the mortal realm. They had their own world: a gray and twisted reflection of the one inhabited by men, but not an inherently evil one. The doings of humanity concerned such beings no more than birds concerned the creatures of the deep black sea.

Some, however, watched the mortal world jealously, craving the warmth and vibrant solidity that their own existence lacked. Although the hungry shadows were few in number, they were by far the most likely to be encountered by a mortal wizard, for they flocked to gates between the worlds.

They were also the ones most often called, for they were the most easily controlled. The other creatures of the shadow realm wanted nothing from the mortal world, and being indifferent, they were difficult to command or cajole. But the ones who lusted after life . . . *those* would leap to do a shadowcaller's bidding. All they asked in return was a drop of blood, a captured memory—something that gave them, however fleetingly, a taste of what it was to be alive.

That taste would buy their obedience, for a while, but the hungry ones always wanted more. Every student in the Dusk Hall was warned of that danger, again and again, until the words circled in their skulls as they slept: *drop your guard, and the shadows will take you.*

It had never occurred to him, though, that the shadowcallers might deliberately give one of their own to the dark.

"Can the shadow be driven out?" Isiem asked.

Helis shook her head. "Not by you or me. Not by any magic I know. It's devoured pieces of him, mind and body, and insinuated itself into the gaps. Like one of those fungi that sends its threads all through a living rat, tangling its fibers into blood and brain. You can't pull out the parasite without killing the host. It's too much a part of him, now, and what's left of him is too much part of it."

"What will happen to him?"

"Eventually the shadow will kill him. It's not of this world, Isiem. It doesn't *belong* here. It consumes life just by its proximity. Loran's life energy is sand in its hourglass. It might try to stretch its time by adding more sand—getting the shadowcallers to heal its stolen body—but eventually it will run out. It might be years from now, maybe even decades, but it will run out. Someday."

"And then he dies?"

"If he's lucky." Helis pinched the moth's bald wings and, with sudden savagery, rolled them into wrinkled, translucent twists between her fingers. She broke off its legs one by one and tossed the crippled insect onto the pile of the dead, where it rolled helpless as a Joyful Thing plucked out of its cage.

Isiem stared at the garden below them, trying and failing to grasp the full implications of what he had heard. White-throated flowers and umbral leaves rustled at a passing breeze. Moths spun around the branches of the sour apple trees, their wings reflecting the distant glow of the courtyard's hanging spheres. One drifted past Helis's shoulder and perched in her hair, just above two of the strangled corpses of its kin.

"Go away, Isiem," Helis sighed. "Go to sleep. It's late."

"You'll be well?"

A strange, sad smile touched the girl's lips. She nodded, very slightly. The dying moths trapped in her hair renewed their flailing. "I'll be fine. Go to bed."

He went. And, after only a short struggle with his conscience, he slept.

In their fourth year at the Dusk Hall, two months after Loran's change, the students began their initiation into the mysteries of Zon-Kuthon.

All of them, as children of Nidal, had spent their lives surrounded by the Midnight Lord's worship. They had gathered around his fires at the Festival of Night's Return, sat vigils in remembrance of their ancestors on the Day of Salvation, and submitted to the Joyful Things' tasting and testing of faith before entering the Dusk Hall. They saw the scars willingly suffered by his petitioners, and they sensed the fear that suffocated the faithless. All were familiar with the Prince of Pain . . . and, at the same time, all were strangers to him. Not one of them had communed with the god directly. Not one could channel his magic.

Over the course of the following year, that changed. A true shadowcaller was versed not only in arcane magic but in the divine, and in Nidal that meant one thing: embracing the glory and cruelty of Zon-Kuthon. Each of them walked a different path to reach their god, but all came to the same destination, and none of their roads was easy.

For Isiem, the moment of revelation came in the endurance of pain.

The rites of the Midnight Lord's worship were never gentle, but the initiation rites could kill. For a full day and night, the initiates were locked in the Dusk Hall's cathedral, kneeling in lines and circles and chanting in constant prayer. Exhaustion and terror soon took hold of them: the ache of sore knees and stiff muscles warred with the fear of what would happen if they moved.

Everything about the rite was designed to disorient and overwhelm its participants, bringing them to the brink of the numinous. Dizzying smoke spilled from the censers overhead, lashing the initiates with slow, breaking coils. The cathedral's candles wept blistering wax onto their backs; the chants of their superiors drowned them in a tide of solemn song. The thousand shadowlights of Pangolais spun around them, creating the illusion of motion among the sculptures that writhed in stony suffering on the cathedral's walls. In

Isiem's dazed, drugged vision, those marble men and women seemed to convulse in rapture . . . but, on a second glance, they were only stone again.

His own agony was no illusion. He had not been allowed to move except when the shadowcallers overseeing the rite ordered all the initiates to change positions, and it seemed that every such change was a worse contortion than the last. The shadowcallers paced constantly through their ranks, spiked chains whirling, and struck at any initiate who was improperly bowed. Isiem had taken two such blows, and he thought the shadowcallers' chains were laced with poison, for the wounds burned with a feverish, shivering thrill.

At midnight the great bells tolled, shuddering through the worshipers' bodies and souls. A hooded priest stood before the altar, holding a chain of glowing iron. Although tens of yards long, it was no thicker than the band of a lady's ring. Many-faced hooks blossomed along the chain like flowers on a vine, each one shining bright and hot as the never-seen sun. Isiem squinted his watering eyes, blinded by the chain's shimmering heat.

"Raise your heads and be humbled," the hooded priest said. The intonation was strangely distorted; Isiem couldn't tell if the speaker was male or female, young or old, coaxing or commanding. The priest spoke with the voice of a god: all that came through was power and the promise of pain. "Open your mouths and be still."

Isiem lifted his head toward the priest and opened his mouth. The initiates to either side of him did the same. Sweating and straining, they held their positions until the hooded priest came to grant them communion. The chain spilled between his—her?—fingers, its serrated radiance stitching the ranks of bowed initiates together through the infinity of gloom.

The priest stooped over each of them, seizing their tongues and pulling them taut. In her-or-his other hand the chain came up, its cruel fire-flower of hooks glowing, and, in a sizzle of scorched blood and saliva, was driven into each of their tongues.

When his turn came to take the communion in hot iron, Isiem screamed. And in that instant, near-blind and paralyzed with pain, he felt the unbearable touch of his god.

Endure, it said, as euphoria swelled and crashed through him like a flood-swollen river bursting its dam. *Survive. Master the pain. There is no purer test of will, no greater show of strength. And no greater ecstasy than to stare down suffering and prevail.*

Isiem made no answer. Even if he'd been capable of speech, thought was far beyond him. It was all he could do to stay on his knees instead of collapsing on the cathedral floor.

All around him, students moaned or gasped or wept around their own mouthfuls of searing agony . . . and he could *feel* them, could share in the bewildered bliss that they found on the far side of pain. The spiked chain joined them in suffering and in faith, and the intensity of the experience, amplified over a hundred souls or more, overwhelmed Isiem completely.

He did collapse, then, and he was far from the only one. The cathedral was littered with the writhing bodies of initiates and the shivering clatter of barbed links against flagstones. Isiem lay among them, half-sensible, and watched as the chain slowly stilled and its fiery flowers, quenched in blood, grew cold.

But the euphoria did not leave him. It stayed, filling him with fear and wonder, even as Dirakah stooped beside his helpless body and pried the iron hooks from his tongue.

"Be welcome in our faith," she said, and carried the chain away.

Their lessons changed after the initiation. They spent less time on arcane theory and more on the rites and sacred teachings of Zon-Kuthon. Their classes moved from the south wing of the Dusk Hall to the north side, and they were permitted to pass the Joyless Things freely. While the caged cripples had prevented them from escaping before, they were no longer needed. Once initiated into his faith, the students were bound to the Midnight Lord; wherever they went, there would be no escape. One and all, they were his. And so they were free to spread and strengthen Zon-Kuthon's presence in Pangolais.

The *Umbral Leaves*, the holiest text of their faith, eclipsed their scrolls and spellbooks. The powdered gems and murky tinctures of their wizardly studies vanished from the classrooms; in their stead, the students practiced with razors and vises, learning to cut and crush flesh with all the artistry their god demanded.

It was a shattering experience for Isiem, and not only for the obvious reasons. The students were required to suffer as much anguish as they inflicted—often they inflicted torments on each other, reversing the roles of victim and torturer many times in each lesson—but, harrowing as the pain was, worse was what he saw it *doing* to them.

They were changing. Under the weight of that constant trauma, all of them were changing. Sometimes, amidst the haze of blood and iron-scented smoke, Isiem would catch a glimpse of Loran's face twisted with fear and rapture: rapture for the intensity of sensation that the boy's mortal flesh afforded, fear that he might have damaged it too greatly and would be forced back to the numb emptiness of shadow if his stolen body failed.

It was an expression that his lost friend would never have showed, and the sight of it on that once-familiar face forced Isiem to see how alien Loran had become. What was in him was not human, and its yearning to experience humanity only reinforced how very foreign it was.

Isiem couldn't bear it. Nor could he bear what he saw in Helis, who sometimes seemed to have traded her own soul for something bleaker than her brother's. She gave herself to the pain with an intensity bordering on anger, as if she could obliterate her memories in its inferno. No matter how grievous the harms they were asked to cause or endure, Helis never held back; if anything, she went further than their instructors desired. She truly did not seem to care if she killed or died, and the enormity of her indifference frightened him. They were friends, or had been, but now he felt that he scarcely knew her at all.

For his own part, Isiem just wanted to survive. As their studies continued, drawing them deeper and deeper into Zon-Kuthon's embrace, his sense of right and wrong went spinning away. If morality was a compass, his had lost true north—and, lacking that core certainty, Isiem could find nothing else to orient him.

Was it wrong to torture a helpless slave, if serving as their practice subject was all that kept that slave alive? Was it still wrong if he inflicted the same pains on his closest friends, and suffered them in turn? Not eagerly—not because he was able to take any pleasure in it, as more devout Kuthites seemed to—but because he, too, survived only by the lash?

If it was not wrong, was it *right?*

Isiem didn't know. He was increasingly unsure whether he cared. Questions of that sort seemed relics from another world, as irrelevant to his own life as the intricacies of Tian chrysanthemum ceremonies or the proper protocol for greeting Taldan dignitaries in a foreign court. They were things that existed in books, and they had no place in shadow-swathed Pangolais.

What existed here was pain, over and over, in infinite variations that admitted no possibility of release.

Not even their instructors were immune. The shadowcallers took their turns serving as the students' subjects, although Isiem noticed that some of them tended to avoid certain students. In particular, Dirakah seemed careful not to place herself at Helis's mercy.

"Of course she is," Helis said when he asked her about it. They were perched above the courtyard's garden again, sitting among its caged lamps and spiraling moths. "She's afraid of me."

"Because of Loran?"

"Yes. She's right to be." Helis smiled—that melancholy, faraway smile she'd only showed after her brother's sacrifice. She lifted a stunned moth up to brush a kiss across its wings, coating her lips in silver dust. Extending her hand delicately over the precipice, she blew the moth off her finger, sending it spiraling downward on translucent, useless wings.

Isiem watched the moth fall with troubled fascination. "Why?"

Helis shook her head lightly and patted his knee. Her hand left a ghostly outline of shimmering powder on his leg. "Go to sleep, Isiem. It's none of your concern."

If Dirakah *was* afraid of Helis, however, she showed no fear of anyone else. Nor did she show any fear of death.

If anything, she seemed to court it. More often than anyone else, she served as their subject in practicing the Kuthite arts. To her, their lessons were ancillary. The real dance was between Dirakah and her god, with the students serving merely as the means by which the shadowcaller flirted with destruction. She was addicted to the intensity of life at oblivion's edge, and she chased it at every opportunity.

As their arts advanced, the less pious shadowcallers stopped offering themselves. A flogging was one thing; any Kuthite could take that, and a clumsy hand with the lash was scarcely more dangerous than a deft one.

The great tortures were another matter. A mistimed touch on the Crystal Chimes would kill the subject and, perhaps worse, shatter the instrument's delicate blades. A misspoken incantation into the Veil of Whispers could result in both the invoker and her victim being drained to death by its gray gossamer.

Day by day, the difficulty of their arts rose higher, and the potential for lethal mistakes became greater. One by one, the shadowcallers stopped taking their places on the torturer's table. Most of them put prudence above piety, and did not want to risk dying at the hands of beginners. Soon the students' work shifted entirely to slaves.

Slaves . . . and Dirakah. She, alone among the shadowcallers, never quailed. When it came time for Isiem and his fellows to practice the Needled Choir, it was Dirakah who lay bound on the table before them.

The Needled Choir, like most of the great tortures, was a performance piece. It was not meant to wring information from its victim, nor was its primary purpose to inflict pain. It was, rather, meant as a spectacle to delight and intrigue the audience, and was most often conducted in Zon-Kuthon's cathedrals during the celebration of his high holy days.

For the Needled Choir, bound victims were laid on tables arrayed like the spokes of a wheel, with their heads pointed inward and their feet radiating outward. There might be as few as three or as many as twelve; Chellarael of Nisroch, who was infamous for her excesses, had once conducted a Choir of forty-eight arranged in two concentric rings. Today's exercise had only three: a pair of condemned prisoners requisitioned from the Umbral Court's dungeons, and Dirakah.

Deep, soft pillows, covered in white satin to show blood better, held each victim's head and shoulders bent back to expose their necks more cleanly. The victims' mouths were sealed—only with cloth wrappings, for this exercise, but in a true performance they would be stitched shut, or even maimed with knives and acid, then magically healed into a smooth whole. However it was done, the purpose was to leave the victims silent and unable to breathe through their mouths. Until they sang through the needles, they would make no sound again.

Three of those needles rested on a white satin cushion near Isiem's hand. He glanced at them and swallowed, trying to hide the nervousness that thrilled through him.

Each of the steel-tipped needles swelled into a hollow alabaster reed designed to be pierced into the victim's windpipe, where it would stand upright and vent the victim's trapped breath into fluted notes. A scarlet ribbon hung at the end of each needle; during the performance, it would flutter in the channeled breath, flapping like a geyser of blood.

The insertion, however, was a delicate task. If the needles were thrust in too deeply, or imprecisely, they could pierce the carotid artery. Clumsy placements could also ruin the victim's voice, or allow air to escape and bubble under the skin of the face and neck—a phenomenon that, once it was discovered, gave rise to its own tortures, but was still considered a grievous failure in a performance of the Needled Choir.

If Isiem did botch the needles' insertion, the responsibility for healing lay entirely with him. Earlier in their training, a shadowcaller had always stood ready to remedy their worst mistakes with magic, but now that they had all advanced sufficiently in their prayers to command their own curative spells, the students were expected to keep their own subjects alive.

The slaves they used were not expensive, and the condemned were virtually worthless, but Isiem was queasily aware, however much he tried to heed his training and ignore it, that a human life lay at his mercy. In the eyes of the world, the measure of his failure might be a few pieces of gold, but in his own, it would be far worse.

A roll of drumbeats broke through his introspections. The ceremony was starting. Taking up a scarlet-flagged needle in one hand, Isiem exchanged a tense look with the students on either side. To his right, Helis stood by the other prisoner from the Umbral Dungeons. To his left, a hollow-eyed youth named Serevil leaned over Dirakah. Neither of their faces betrayed any hint of the anxiety Isiem felt. He hoped his own was as impassive.

The drumbeats died. Holding his breath, Isiem watched from the corner of his eye as Helis held her reed high over her victim's throat, then plunged it down with a dramatic swoop. Her aim was unerring, her control complete: the needle pierced the prisoner's windpipe and stayed there, emitting an unearthly shrill. Its crimson flag lashed the air once in a straight line, then subsided into twisting contortions.

The drums picked up again. Now they insinuated themselves around and beneath the mournful haunt of Helis's reed, accentuating its song instead of overwhelming it. Their erratic stutter evoked a failing heartbeat, and when it fell into a long, tense lull, Isiem knew his turn had come.

Sideways between the third and fourth tracheal rings. It had been easier on the corpses they used for practice, with the correct incision point inked on stiff cold flesh . . . but, after a frozen instant, Isiem found that same point on the living man. Offering a quick prayer that his hands would be steady and his aim true, he plunged the needle down.

It caught for an instant—the windpipe was tough, and although the needle was sharp, it took some force to push it through—but he executed the movement flawlessly, and he did not strike too deep. A second eerie note rose from the prisoner's punctured throat, joining the song that Helis had begun.

Moments later, after the drums had risen and dwindled again, the third student raised his reed to complete their song.

Isiem had already taken a half-step back when he noticed that Helis had not moved back with him. Curious, he stole a glance at her, although he knew it would draw a reprimand from his instructors if any of them noticed. *Any* deviation from the appearance of singleminded concentration was a flaw, but looking to other participants for guidance was a serious one.

No one noticed. And what he saw piqued his interest even more: Helis had torn a bit of loose fleece from her sleeve and was rolling it surreptitiously. Her lips moved in a slight, soundless murmur; clearly she'd practiced delivering that incantation subtly. From even a few steps farther away, her gestures would have been invisible, and the reeds' drone drowned out her whispered chant.

But to what end? Isiem recognized the spell she was casting—they had all learned the same simple illusion early in their studies—but he could not discern its purpose. Helis moved back, taking up her proper position for the ceremony's end, and nothing seemed to have changed.

Then Serevil swept his hands down, plunging in the last reed, and Isiem realized in a flash of horror what she had just done.

Blood fountained from Dirakah's throat: a vertical flood of it, painting Serevil's astonished face and the floor behind him and the nearest circle of the audience in hot red gouts. A horrible wet gurgle choked in the reed. Its crimson pennant, soaked through already, rippled with each new spurt like lakeweed caught in the continuing flow of Dirakah's lifeblood.

In moments the shadowcaller would be dead. Not because Serevil had killed her, but because Helis had. A minor illusion to shift the incision point from Dirakah's windpipe to the great artery in her neck was all Helis needed to kill the woman who had led her brother's destruction.

And Dirakah *would* die, unless Isiem stepped in. So would Serevil. No one was permitted to intervene with any of the great tortures except the torturers themselves. The risk of disaster was ever-present; it was no small part of the audience's thrill.

But that did not mean the students could not be punished for their failures. Serevil was already doomed to suffer for injuring a superior; if Dirakah died, so would he. That knowledge seemed to have paralyzed him. The youth stood white and unmoving, too stunned to react. Blood dripped from his cheeks and hung in garnet drops on his eyebrows.

There was no chance that Serevil would recover from his shock in time to save Dirakah. Pushing his own ambivalence aside, Isiem strode forward, steeling himself to call upon Zon-Kuthon's uncertain mercy. As he prepared to utter his prayer, Helis grabbed his wrist with a hand like a manacle of ice.

"No," she hissed, too softly for the audience to hear.

"Let me go," Isiem said, trying to pull away.

She did not release him. "*No.* Dirakah has courted this end for years. Do you think this is anything she didn't expect? Anything she didn't *want?* She *deserves* this."

"Does Serevil?"

Beneath the hood, Helis's eyes grew hard. "Is he any better?" Her hand tightened on his wrist, hurting him. "We're all monsters, Isiem. We *all* deserve this."

To that he had no answer. The prayer faltered on his lips, failed.

And under their hands, Dirakah died.

Chapter Six
Seeing Darkness

"Are you happy?" Isiem asked Helis the next time they sat together above the courtyard garden.

She looked up from picking at the tatters of her sleeve. Already there were so many holes in it that the gray wool looked like Taldan lace. "Happy?"

"Content. Satisfied. *Something*. Now that you've had your revenge."

"No." Helis shrugged, waving her ruined sleeve over one of the black iron claws that caged the lanterns below them. A moth dancing around the globe's ethereal glow blundered into the cloth and was caught. She pressed the trapped insect to her wrist, suffocating it slowly against her pulse. "It was a thing that needed to be done, and now it has been. There is no happiness in that. Only the fulfillment of fate."

"That wasn't fate," Isiem said. The anger in his own words surprised him. He paused, gathering his composure; open emotion was unbecoming of a Nidalese. "You killed her. Not the impartial hand of destiny. You."

"And you," Helis said, lightly and almost playfully, as if they'd been sitting at a game of chance and he had drawn a losing card. She plucked the dying moth from its woolen trap and carefully pushed the insect into her hair, just above one ear, as though it were a flower. "You killed her too, Isiem."

"No."

"Yes. You could have stopped me. You didn't. She died."

"That isn't the same as killing her."

"Of course not," Helis said, turning her little smile down to her soft white hands. One of the moth's antennae was trapped under the nail of her forefinger: a bent black fissure across her fingertip. She picked it out and let it fall, spinning, into the garden below. "Yes, I see that now. It is entirely different."

But it *was*. Isiem held fast to that thought in the days that followed. The memory of his passivity overwhelmed him with guilt, although he saw nothing he could have done differently. His only other choice would have been to betray Helis—to cause her death, instead of standing silent at Dirakah's—and that was no choice at all. Their friendship had become a frayed and feeble thing, but Isiem wasn't ready to discard it entirely. Not when it was one of the last links he had to his life before the Dusk Hall.

So he had held his tongue and stayed his hand as Helis committed murder with the hands of another, and now guilt dogged his every step.

Little of that guilt was for Dirakah. The shadowcaller had been a vicious and coldhearted woman, and she had courted the Midnight Lord's last embrace for years. If there were any tragedy in her finally receiving what she'd wanted so long, it was in the desire, not the consummation. Isiem felt no pity for her.

Serevil, though . . . that was a heavier weight to carry. Serevil had only been a student, no better and no worse than any of them. That death haunted him.

And the worst of it was that he didn't even know if Serevil *was* dead. No one knew. After the disaster of the Needled Choir, he'd simply vanished, swept away along with Dirakah's body and the injured prisoners. None of the other students had seen him since. In the silence that followed Serevil's disappearance, every terror in their collective imagination flourished—for what, they all wondered, could the shadowcallers possibly do to him that would be worse than the horrors they'd already witnessed?

Isiem had no answer for that. He only knew that he bore the blame.

To escape it, he threw himself ever deeper into his work. It was easier now that their focus had shifted back to true magic. Having mastered the great tortures, the students were allowed to return to their wizardly studies. A few found themselves called to Zon-Kuthon's side, and chose to concentrate on the rites and invocations of the priesthood. But most, Isiem included, were privately relieved to let that part of their schooling pass. They were all born Nidalese, and they could withstand the terrors of the Midnight Lord's gifts without flinching; but even they, whose forebears had lived under his rule for millennia, seldom *welcomed* those gifts.

True magic, unstained by Zon-Kuthon's touch, was easier to embrace.

And it was well that Isiem thought so, because their instructors pushed them to new heights every day. It was as if they were determined to make up for all the time lost to the students' religious studies, and did not care how they did it.

Day after day, the students were pounded with a relentless torrent of lectures, experiments, practice sessions. Day after day, they struggled not to drown in the flood. They learned to enhance the magical resonances in precious materials suitable for crafting into enchanted items, and how to blend rare resins into inks that would hold the ephemeral echoes of magic. They mastered the tedious labor of gem-setting and woodcarving to make worthy receptacles for their spells. They copied cryptic diagrams and repeated incantations in long-dead languages until their hands cramped and their tongues ached, and then they pressed on for one more spell. Always, always one more.

Those who failed went to the shadow.

The same fate, they learned that autumn, had befallen Serevil. After months of silence, he reappeared in their classes without a word of explanation, as if he'd never missed a day. But he was not as he had been: vertical slashes striped his face with white scars, both his ears had been burned to curled husks of leather, and his eyes were no longer human. Only the void stared out from those eyes, and few in the Dusk Hall could meet them.

Isiem couldn't. He spent the first few days after Serevil's return working himself into a frenzy of exhaustion, and when that failed to push the guilt away, he sought out Helis.

She had forsaken her usual haunts. As the evenings grew cooler, she visited the gardens less often, not because of the chill, but because she had taken to spending her nights in the perpetual twilight of the Dusk Hall's library. Most of the students, including Isiem, found those creaking, crooked shelves and gloomy piles of books unsettling, and spent as little time there as they could. Helis, however, seemed to take solace from its musty loneliness.

It was there that he finally found her, drifting among the leatherbound stacks. She was skeleton-thin under her cloak of black hair, every bone in her face drawn sharply in starved beauty. A shroud of silvery moths fluttered luminous in the dark around her—an intricate illusion, woven for no evident purpose save to amuse her. Upon brushing Helis's skin or clothes, the moths shriveled into decrepitude and tumbled, age-broken, to the ground, only to re-form from the dust within moments and rejoin the whirling dance.

"Helis."

She looked up, startled. An illusory moth drifted toward him. It passed through his candle's flame, burst into fire, and dissolved into glowing ashes. "Isiem."

"Serevil is back. Shadow-seized."

"I know." She crooked a finger at the falling sparks of the candle-burned moth. They spun back together, whirling into a fiery spectre—the shape of an insect sketched by shifting, burning motes. The sight seemed to enchant her. One by one the other moths in her illusion exploded into flame. They continued their dance as burning ghosts, the unreal light of their wings spinning off the gilt on the books all around her.

"That's all you have to say about it? You *know*?" Isiem started forward, reaching out to seize Helis or strike her, but caught himself at the last moment and stopped just short of touching her. If showing anger was anathema to Nidalese, making physical contact without invitation was unimaginably worse—a breach of etiquette that could easily lead to the loss of the offending hand. Slaves and prisoners had no right to their own bodies, but that was a mark of their low status. They were non-persons. Free Nidalese were inviolate.

But it was tempting. It was supremely tempting.

Isiem raked a shaking hand through his long white hair. "All of this was for revenge, wasn't it? Retribution for what they did to Loran. And now you've inflicted the same fate on another student—another *boy* no more deserving than your brother. Is that what you wanted? Is that what you hoped for? To give another innocent soul to the shadow?"

"They aren't innocent," Helis said softly. "None of us are innocent."

"I don't care," Isiem snapped. "Stop. You've had your revenge. Dirakah is dead. It ends."

"It never ends." She laughed: a short, breathy sound of hurt. "It's eating him, Isiem. The shadow in Loran. It doesn't *understand*. How to live—how to keep *him* alive. It doesn't understand flesh. It forgets to sleep, it doesn't eat . . . it mortifies his body constantly for the thrill of feeling pain."

"And now Serevil will suffer the same." Isiem scowled, cupping his candle to protect the flame as he turned back toward the door. "If you want to find a way to free Loran—if such a thing can be done—I will help you. However I can, I'll help. But this foolish, futile quest for revenge . . . it has to end. Promise me that, Helis. Please."

She shook her head, retreating past a shelf of time-dulled tomes. Her burning moths snuffed out one by one, returning the library to its dusky gloom. Isiem hadn't realized how much light they shed; with Helis's illusion gone, his candle's flame was a puny thing. He couldn't see anything but the black-bound books and dusty shelves crowding at his elbows. Helis was invisible in the dark, although he could hear the whisper of her footsteps receding.

"Please, Helis," Isiem whispered, unsure whether he meant it for her or himself.

She did not say a word. But he heard the rustle of her sleeve, and he saw the wick of his candle bend suddenly, crushed into its wax by an invisible hand. The flame died. Midnight engulfed him: the absolute lightlessness of Zon-Kuthon's rule.

Heavy-hearted, Isiem dropped the useless stub and blindly he felt his way out of the black.

Winter came subtly to the unchanging city of Pangolais. The eternal trees did not turn their broad black leaves, nor did those leaves fall. Under their canopy, the shadowed days and nights melded into one, and no change in their length could be told. No crops ripened among the white paths and onyx obelisks of Pangolais; no beasts fatted themselves for a long sleep until spring. Only the moths danced under the caged lights of the Nidalese.

But the evenings' humidity lightened, and the early morning chill grew sharper, and an air of anticipation began to suffuse the libraries and study chambers of the Dusk Hall. With the advent of winter, six years after their arrival, the students' work was finally approaching its end. Next autumn, one way or another, all of Isiem's class would leave the Dusk Hall.

Only one task remained before they finished their novitiates and apprenticed to individual masters: the crafting of a scrysphere.

On one level, a scrysphere served as a benchmark of the student's ability. A wizard capable of enchanting one was powerful enough to be useful to the Umbral Court and knowledgeable enough to avoid dishonoring his teachers; his creation was proof of his skill.

But the test of the scrysphere went beyond that. Other spells, equally demanding, made for more impressive demonstrations of wizardly skill—hurling fireballs, taking on the shapes of wolf or mountain cat, riding the wind on invisible wings—but none of them held the scrysphere's place in Kuthite theology. Not even the spells that commanded darkness or pain shared the same prestige, for their magics were fleeting, while the scrysphere endured.

And so, too, did its sacrifice.

The crafting of a scrysphere demanded a tithe of flesh from its creator. Most wizards contented themselves with giving up an ear, the joint of a finger, a small toe—the smallest acceptable losses, and the most easily concealed. Those who wished to flaunt their devotion plucked out an eye, mirroring their god's mutilation; Cuvandos the Shadow-Sighted, a legendary archmage, had earned his sobriquet by sacrificing both of his. In their stead he had worn his scrysphere on a black silk band tied over his scarred, empty sockets, signifying that he had forsworn mortal sight in favor of the arcane.

For that was the purpose of a scrysphere: it enabled its creator to see from a ball of polished onyx, as if he himself stood in its place. And that purpose was exceedingly valuable to the Umbral Court.

A scrysphere was small, easily concealed, and invisible to most methods of magical detection. It could be easily slipped into the decorations of a visiting Chelish dignitary's room, hidden among the sooty rafters of a tavern where would-be rebels conspired, or even worn as jewelry to a private soiree. And because a scrysphere was difficult to detect, the constant threat of observation kept the treasonous cowed even when they were not being watched.

Isiem, alone in his room, wondered whether anyone was watching *him*.

Unlikely. And even if they were, they'd see nothing damning. His work today would be seen as commendable eagerness to leave his student days behind and take up a shadowcaller's mantle.

The treason would come later.

Exhaling slowly, Isiem closed his eyes and sought serenity. He needed to remember everything about this experience, so that he could transcribe it faithfully onto a scroll that would enable others to command the same magic he was about to attempt.

There was a thriving clandestine market in scrolls at the Dusk Hall. Not every student could master every spell; the sheer volume of their studies meant that, inevitably, some minor magic would go neglected amid the rest. Isiem himself had let some of the cantrips and elementary spells fall by the wayside—a necessary sacrifice so that he could devote his time to more demanding forms.

For the most part, their instructors overlooked such minor failures. But when a spell was required, as the scrysphere was, and was difficult enough that many students failed to learn it properly, then a great demand arose for scrolls that trapped the magic for them.

In order to graduate from the Dusk Hall, students needed to create a scrysphere at some point during their final year. They did *not* need to understand the arcane theory behind its workings or the metaphysics of their sacrifice of flesh. They only needed to produce the finished ball of onyx and demonstrate its magic. For their purposes, then, a scroll was *better* than a book-scribed spell.

And that meant there was a great deal of money to be made by whoever could provide those scrolls.

Isiem fixed on that thought, trying to ignore what his hands were doing, as he reached for the bulbed needle to begin.

The needle was not metal or glass, but the entire preserved head of a mosquito-like parasite—a winged, pigeon-sized thing with a hollow proboscis that it used to drain the blood from its victims. Trappers in the Uskwood caught them and sent the corpses whole to Pangolais, where they could be more delicately flayed. The parasites' heads were dipped into rubber sap, adding strength and flexibility to their paper-thin skin, and sold as syringes.

Squeezing the hollow head to expel the air trapped inside, Isiem opened a vial of black liquid with his other hand. Tears of the night, that liquid was called. It was not of this world. Supposedly the tears were wept by mortal men and women trapped on the Plane of Shadow, just before they succumbed to its endless night. The shadowcallers gathered it, and Isiem did not like to wonder too long about how.

He let the inky fluid fill the syringe. It rose through the proboscis, past wax-stoppered nostrils, into the resin-coated head. Although Isiem had drawn only a small amount of the liquid into his needle, it seemed to expand to fill all available space; the head swelled between his fingers, and darkness roiled behind the empty rubber shells of its eyes.

Uneasy, Isiem pulled the needle away and stoppered the tiny black vial. He drew a breath, steeling himself, and then slid the dead white needle under his skin.

He had chosen to give up a toe. Working as quickly as he could without compromising his precision, Isiem used the needle to trace the prescribed arcane sigils in his flesh, outlining its shape in droplets of ink.

As soon as he squeezed out the first drop, however, the magic flared into a life of its own. The tears of the night swelled under Isiem's skin, spreading wisps of watery darkness through his flesh. A shivering chill wracked him, sudden and disorienting.

It was only a *toe*. It shouldn't hurt so much. And yet the magic working through his body was dizzying, a vortex of unreality that sucked at his bones, devoured his muscles, swallowed and silenced the weak drum of his pulse. The injected shadows consumed him, leeching his life away to feed something . . . something *else* . . . and the crimson thread he'd tied as a tourniquet at the base of his toe seemed a flimsy barrier indeed.

Trembling, sweating, Isiem finished the last rune—and as soon as it was drawn, even before the final drop of ink had spilled out, he hurled the deflated syringe-head away and reached for the cleaver resting by his knee. Swiftly he brought the blade down, severing the shadow-poisoned toe and cutting off his ordeal—this part of it, at least—behind a wall of searing, blissfully cathartic pain.

Who could do that to an eye? Isiem wondered, as with shaking hands he lifted the severed digit to the dish under the scrysphere. He was vaguely surprised to see a dribble of red blood from the stump of his toe; it had seemed so far removed from human flesh, so drastically transformed already, that he had not thought it would bleed.

But it did. And as he placed the shadow-swollen bit of meat and bone into the sacrificial dish, that blood dissolved into something like smoke, rising upward to wreath the unfinished scrysphere in a haze of crimson and gray.

The rest of the toe crumbled in on itself, as if reduced to ash by some invisible flame. Then the powdered bone and soot turned to smoke and spiraled up with the rest, leaving the dish perfectly clean.

The scrysphere drank it all in. Soot and smoke and scarlet threads of evaporated blood spun around its glossy sides and funneled into the sigils that Isiem had etched into the stone the night before. Those sigils shone steadily brighter as the magic gathered within them, like smoldering embers stirred by the wind. And then, as they devoured the last of Isiem's gift, they vanished altogether from his sight.

Isiem blinked. The smoke was gone, the sigils were gone. The scrysphere was a smooth polished blank. And he saw himself through it—distorted, murky, as though he looked upon the chamber through a pane of dark and bubbled glass. But even so, he *saw*. Through his own eyes and the scrysphere at once.

It was impossibly disorienting. Isiem closed his eyes, putting a hand to his swimming head . . . and yet he could still see. Struggling with the unfamiliar perspective of eyes not his own, he fumbled his way across the room to retrieve a spare shirt from his closet, then back to the scrysphere's stand. Carefully Isiem dropped the shirt over the sphere, and sighed with muted relief when that ended the doubled sight.

He'd have to practice. He would have to practice, and accustom himself to viewing the world through the scrysphere's eerie lens. But he had, at last, a way of seeing whether Helis meant to honor his plea.

A week later, he hid the scrysphere in the library.

Chapter Seven
Exorcism

"Helis has stolen a nightglass."

It was the beginning of summer. Isiem and Ascaros were alone in their room, in a rare respite between classes.

"She's using it to commune with a demon," Isiem continued.

Ascaros shrugged. He plucked one of the scrolls from the case Isiem had brought and held it up between two fingers. "This is a scrysphere?"

"After you mutilate yourself and feed your flesh to the shadow, yes." Isiem grimaced, remembering.

"I'll survive. It's magic I'm bad at, not cutting. How much?"

"Nothing," Isiem said, surprised that his friend would even ask. "I don't need your money. I need your help. Helis is *summoning a demon*. Not just to speak with it. All winter she called lesser spirits to learn this demon's name, and all spring she researched charms and controls before finally calling it forth. She's been planning this half a year or more."

"Planning what?"

"I don't know." Isiem shook his head in frustration. "Something for the Festival of Night's Return. Something terrible."

"And what of it?" Ascaros rolled the scroll into a neat cylinder and slid it into the sling that held his left arm. He told the rest of the students that the arm had been broken as part of an exercise in Kuthite piety and that he was allowing it to heal naturally to prolong the pain, but Isiem knew the truth. The sorcery was spreading in his friend's blood.

As if sensing his scrutiny, Ascaros folded his good arm over the useless one and gave Isiem an even look. "What would you have me do? Ask her to stop? You tried that, and it was useless. Tell the instructors? They'll kill her or give her to the shadow. Sabotage her by stealing the mirror? Then *I've* got a nightglass, and damned if I want that kind of trouble. There are no good answers, Isiem. The best we can do is keep our heads low and our mouths closed."

"That's the best we can do," Isiem echoed flatly. "Really."

"Yes," Ascaros snapped. "Really." He stepped past Isiem, heading toward the door, but as his hand closed on the handle he turned back. The anger receded from his voice, leaving weary resignation and, perhaps, a touch of sorrow.

"I'm sorry. I would help you if I could, but I have my own troubles." Ascaros untied the sling binding his left arm. He pushed up his sleeve, revealing a band of gray, wrinkled flesh that encircled that arm from elbow to shoulder. Fingers of withered gray stretched toward his chest and crept down his inner wrist. A faint, spicy odor clung to the discolored skin, redolent of the Osirian fragrances they used to mask the stink of decay in the Dusk Hall's corpse rooms. It was not an unpleasant smell, but in this context it was unsettling.

"I knew it was bad, but . . ." Isiem trailed off, unable to put his shock into words.

Ascaros gave him a pained smile and shook his sleeve back down. "Every time I cast a spell it worsens, and we've been working quite a lot of magic these last few months. It's dead—all that gray flesh. Completely dead. I've burned it and felt nothing. I've cut into it and seen no blood."

"And the smell?" Isiem asked quietly.

"A precaution. It doesn't reek of death yet. At least I don't think it does. But I wonder when it will start, and who might notice when it does." Ascaros pushed his useless arm back into position, tied the sling into place once more, and collected a tall black staff leaning in the corner by the door. It was a new affectation, although it already seemed familiar in his hand. Pierced silverwork adorned sections of the staff, and through those censer openings, more Osirian fragrance spilled.

"Let it go," Ascaros advised him, opening the door. "I'm not asking you to close your eyes to what Helis is doing. You should watch her, and be wary, and keep yourself safe. But let it end there. Her fate is not yours to decide, or mine. We have our own paths, our own problems. Do you truly need to take on the troubles of another?"

"If you will not help me," Isiem said, "the scroll will be three hundred gold sails."

Ascaros hesitated, but reached for his coin pouch. "Costly."

"Survival is."

Two nights later, when Isiem knew that Helis was away practicing the great tortures and the scrysphere showed that the library was empty, he went down to meet her demon.

It seemed darker than he remembered. Colder. The shelves seemed to loom over him like hostile sentinels; the gaps between books seemed alive with whispering shadows. Dull bronze and faded parchment accented the gloom without relieving it.

Helis kept her stolen nightglass tucked high up on a seldom visited shelf, behind a musty treatise on the geneaology of the great houses of Westcrown before Aroden's fall. Isiem eased the book out of the way, taking care to avoid cracking its spine. Age had dulled its once grand gilt and dried the leather to a fragile shell; no doubt Helis had chosen that book in part because anyone who disturbed it too roughly would damage the bindings and betray his hand. But Isiem was careful, and the mirror slid out smoothly.

It was a small one, no larger than the palm-sized glass the shadowcallers had used to test them as children at Crosspine. Isiem unwrapped it cautiously, conscious of a tight dryness in his throat.

The mirror was wholly unreflective. A pit of darkness in his hand. He swallowed past the dryness, weaving the first threads of magic that would awaken the nightglass's gate between worlds. It wasn't a true spell—it hadn't enough force or shape to be a cantrip, even—but it might give him more control over what answered the nightmirror's call.

He'd barely begun when something—some*one*— yanked the nascent magic from his grasp. It spun out into a shape of unimaginable complexity: a chrysanthemum whose every petal was a dragonfly wing, and whose every vein in those wings was the edge of a continent. Isiem caught only a glimpse before it swelled into a nova and contracted to a single point, and darkness filled the world where it had been.

In that darkness rose a voice, slow and black and burbling, as if every word were contained in a bubble that belched from the depths of a tarry swamp. It was the voice of a demon—not a creature of the shadow realm, but a true *demon*, the essence of malevolence made flesh—and its foulness was indescribable.

What is Helis thinking? Students in the Dusk Hall were expressly forbidden from consorting with demons. Even full shadowcallers seldom dealt with them. Demons were infinitely treacherous, inconceivably malign, ever hungry for the corruption of human souls. Again and again their instructors had told them: nothing a demon can offer is worth the risk of contact. There were countless other paths to power—slower, perhaps, but safer and surer. Only fools conjured demons.

Yet here Isiem was, speaking to one through a stolen nightglass.

You are the watcher, it said to him, in words that were not words. There was a pause for the gathering of thoughts, or for the gathering of energy to force the demon's thoughts into a semblance of human ones. *I have felt your eyes on us as we talked.*

"Yes," Isiem admitted, donning a mask of impassivity. The fiend's thoughts seemed to crawl across his soul like slugs, leaving trails of sticky slime he could not wipe away.

Yet you come to me, not her. A chuckle, wet and stinking. *What treachery do you plan?*

"What does she want from you?"

Destruction. A swirl of distorted images filled Isiem's mind: people crowding the grand square of Pangolais, heatless white torches burning on sleek pillars around the throng. Elaborate effigies in white and gray wood, carved but unpainted. The Festival of Night's Return. The vision was stretched and murky about the periphery, as if he were watching it through a crooked and dirty glass—but he recognized the city and its people, and the high holy day of Zon-Kuthon.

In the image, three shadowcallers raised a nightmirror to the heavens, calling the children of Pangolais to come forth and be tested. There were not many children in the city—there never were—but the ritual went on all the same. Four boys and girls stood in a wavering line, uncertain as Isiem himself had been at his own test those few forever years ago. And as the first of them gazed into the glass, chaos erupted.

Shadows spilled from the mirror. Ugly, muddy, long-clawed shadows leaped from the nightglass, springing onto children, parents, any festival-goer they could reach. The wizards of the Dusk Hall threw up translucent shields, and the clerics of Zon-Kuthon called on their god to save them, but the ordinary Nidalese had no defense. The shadows leaped upon them, prying open people's jaws and squeezing themselves into screaming mouths. And when they were within, the screams stopped, and their victims blinked, and their eyes were black and empty over wide, wide grins.

It wasn't a true vision, Isiem knew. Prophecy was unreliable since the death of the god Aroden. What the demon had showed him was only a stage-play of illusions on a scaffolding of shrewd guesses. But it was more than enough to disturb him.

"That is her plan?" Isiem asked. "To give innocents to the shadow?"

To give them to my servants. They are seldom fed. Your shadowcallers do not like us. This will be a wondrous feast for my loyal ones.

"A feast for them. But not for you?"

I am bound. My joy must come in the watching. It is enough.

"How are you bound?"

By virtue. Another gurgling chuckle, fouler than bog gas. *A virtuous man died to bind me. Only another virtuous man's flesh may house me. Otherwise I will wait here a hundred hundred years, blind and bodiless in this realm. Twenty-seven such years have passed.*

"What if I could find you that virtuous man?"

Who would give his flesh for me to wear? Yearning warred with disbelief in the demon's thoughts. *If you could find me such a man—if you will give me freedom—then, little watcher, I will give you treachery. Any treachery you want.*

Isiem nodded. He pulled his awareness from the nightglass, gratefully severing his connection to the demon's world, and slid the heavy book of genealogies back into place on the shelf. Coins jangled in his pocket as he stepped away: Ascaros's payment for the scroll.

Not enough for a virtuous man. But, if he sold a few more, it might be.

The next weeks passed in a haze of sleeplessness and overwork. Every spare moment that Isiem could snatch from his studies was spent locked in his chamber, feverishly scribing scrolls. Mostly he penned scryspheres, reliving his own torment and sacrifice again and again as he set down the magic for others to use, but he was willing to write any scroll for which a fellow student might pay him. His fingers were ink-stained, his concentration ruined, his soul weighted down by the memories of pain . . . but scroll by scroll, coin by coin, Isiem gathered the gold he needed.

It wasn't only the slave he had to buy. The slave would have to be kept somewhere away from the Dusk Hall, and his keepers bribed into silence, so that Helis would not learn of his plans. Isiem would have to pay off the guards in the market, a few clerks, two or three senior shadowcallers, perhaps a cleric if the slave took sick or was injured . . . and then there were other things he had to buy, and other preparations to be made, that dwarfed the cost of all the rest. The apothecaries of Pangolais could procure any potion or poison known to humanity, but their services did not come cheap.

Two weeks before the Festival of Night's Return, he finally had enough.

Drawing on a hooded cloak, Isiem left the Dusk Hall in as much secrecy as he could muster. The Joyful Things would know he'd gone, of course, but they wouldn't know where, or why. No one else needed to know even that much.

A gray drizzle was falling through the black-leaved trees of Pangolais as Isiem made his way to the slave markets. Rain slowed the market's bustle, but there were still buyers seeking bargains and sellers ready to put on a show. Isiem hurried along the outskirts of the square, keeping his head low until he reached the black tent flanked by Chelish pennons.

In Nidal, Isiem thought dourly, a virtuous man was as exotic as any purple-haired gnome or ring-nosed minotaur. He'd have better luck looking among foreigners.

The Chelaxians had two long strings of slaves tethered under the tent. Isiem stopped just outside, where the rainwater dripping from the canopy might provide a little more cover, and waited until the guards' eyes were turned away. When no one seemed to be looking, he muttered a surreptitious plea to Zon-Kuthon, clutching the silvered symbol tucked into his sleeve.

Casting spells at slaves was only a minor breach of etiquette, provided they weren't damaged, but if the Chelaxians got wind of Isiem's particular needs, they'd doubtlessly raise their prices. He wasn't sure he had enough as it was; he could ill afford to excite a dealer's greed. But, to Isiem's enormous relief, no one seemed to notice his prayer.

Of all the unfortunates bound in the slave line, only two were pure-hearted enough to radiate an inner light to his spell. The others might have been honest folk, even generous and kind at times, but they were well within the ordinary run of humanity, and Isiem doubted they'd suffice to entice a demon.

The other two might. One of them he dismissed immediately. She was a silver-haired woman, lithe and comely, with a supernal grace that spoke of divine blood. The price for such a beauty, let alone one of celestial heritage, would be far beyond Isiem's means.

That left one: a youngish man dressed in dirty orange robes. He stood slump-shouldered in his bonds, apparently oblivious to the other slaves or the market's din or the rainwater that trickled through a hole directly over his head, splattering his wispy blond hair. A step to either side would have avoided it, but the dejected man simply stood there, absorbing the rain.

"Who's the broken one?" Isiem asked the merchant overseeing the tent.

The man shrugged indifferently. He was a thin man with a triangular face and slightly protruding eyes that, under pinched tufts of dark hair, gave him a weaselly look. "Some cleric."

"One of Desna's?" Secret worshipers of that goddess, especially in the outlying villages farthest from the Umbral Court's watchful eyes, were a constant thorn in the Kuthites' side. Isiem's own mother had been one of them, and he sometimes wondered if that fact would condemn him too, should it ever become known.

"Come now, kind master." The merchant laughed, although his eyes stayed sharp and cold. "A Desnan, here? In the heart of Zon-Kuthon's most devout realm? You make a great joke to me, yes . . . but a dangerous one. No, he is no Desnan. Would that he were. A true Desnan, in this place, would be worth twice—no, thrice—any of these others. And I include the lovely Zenobai in that," he added, with a gesture at the silver-haired woman.

"Whose cleric is he?"

"Ah. The Dawnflower's, I believe. But it would be incorrect to say he *is* a cleric of Sarenrae's. *Was* would be more accurate. Does that disappoint?"

"Yes," Isiem said curtly. He was quite sure he could not afford to purchase Zenobai, and he was almost equally sure that he would not be able to sell enough scrolls to make up the difference before the Festival. Keeping a woman such as that safe from the casual abuses of slave-tenders would be prohibitively difficult, and he could hardly watch over her himself. But a failed cleric made a poor gamble.

"A pity," the merchant said, although his expression never changed. "Did you need a priest for some particular purpose?"

"A merchant would do as well. If he were the right merchant." Isiem touched the Kuthite emblem on his chest as if in absent-minded consideration.

The Chelaxian paled. "Perhaps you wish to speak to the man? This former priest? He might still be of use for—for whatever purpose you seek."

"I will do that," Isiem agreed. He dropped a small handful of gold on the merchant's table as surety against the loss of his slave. One of the guards was already unbinding the priest. A moment later, the man came to join him at the eaves of the tent, rubbing his skinny wrists.

"What do you want from me?" the priest muttered, keeping his eyes on the mud.

"A name might be a start," Isiem said. He strode away from the tent, turning his back on the slave merchant and his remaining chattel. The drizzle had turned into a real rain, but that was good; it would reduce the number of eavesdroppers in the market. "Walk with me."

"You're not worried I'll flee?"

"You are in Pangolais. No." Isiem slowed as he passed through a screen of marble pillars. The cleric slowed with him, wary but curious. "A name?"

"Bedic," the priest said, after a hesitation. "Why?"

"So that I might call you something other than 'slave.' You cannot have been a slave long if you still have the temerity to ask questions."

"No." Bedic's mouth twisted as if the admission itself was bitter. "It's hardly been a week."

"What happened?"

The priest's shoulders hunched. He puffed a little breath through his lips, obviously reluctant to answer and yet afraid of what silence might cost him. At last, never looking at Isiem, he spoke. "We were in the Uskwood. Two companions—two *friends*—and myself, chasing after rumors and rumblings and old pleas for help from people who were likely dead before we started.

"The druids found us on the first night. I was standing watch, and I should have warned the others, should have woken them, *something* . . . but I didn't. I just fled. The terror that came over me . . ." Bedic put a trembling hand to his face, covering his eyes, then dropped it. "I saw a campfire through the trees. I ran toward it. Whether I hoped to find help for my friends or safety for myself, I couldn't even tell you. But whichever I wanted, it wasn't there.

"The fire belonged to that slaver. I wonder, now, if the druids weren't there to deal with him . . . but it hardly matters. He asked me to sit at his fire, offered wine, pretended concern at my condition—and when he was satisfied that I was alone, and that I might have some value, he signaled his guards to take me."

"And your friends?" Isiem asked.

Bedic shrugged. "I never saw them again. Perhaps they died. Or, if they were less lucky, perhaps they're on the other side of this market."

"The slaver said you were a priest, but that you are no longer. Is this true?"

The priest's blue eyes strayed past Isiem's shoulder and fixed on an indeterminate point in the distance. The tip of his tongue flicked out, brushing his lower lip. "Yes."

"You're lying. Why?"

Bedic smiled tightly. There was no warmth in it, only self-loathing and a kind of grim relief at being caught. "Just before we came to Pangolais, when there was no longer any doubt about where we were going or what we faced, one of the other captives freed his children. Not by cutting their bonds. That would have done no good; we were too deep in Nidal for that kind of escape. He killed them. A loving father with two young children, and he had no better choice for them than death.

"When his children were dead, the father tried to strangle himself. He botched it. The slaver found him slumped and blue with a cord knotted around his throat . . . but there was still a spark of life in the man. So he demanded that I heal his slave."

"And you refused," Isiem said. "You told him you couldn't do it."

"Was there any better choice? Anyway, if it was a lie then, it won't be for long. Sarenrae has no use for cowards, and I've been nothing else since I came to Nidal." Bedic took a shaky breath. "I'm sorry if you needed a cleric."

"I don't need a cleric," Isiem said. "I need a virtuous man."

"Why?"

In sparse words, Isiem told him: what Helis had done, what she planned, how she had bargained with a fiend. The demon's price to betray that bargain.

Bedic shook his head in refusal even before Isiem finished. "You want me to give myself to a demon to save shadowcallers and Kuthite priests?"

"No. The shadowcallers can defend themselves. They are in no danger. It is the common people of Pangolais, not the Kuthite adepts, who will suffer if you refuse. I want you to save innocents. People trapped by their circumstances, as you are."

"At the cost of giving a bound demon a body."

"Yes." Isiem pulled a small vial from his sleeve and held it out for Bedic's examination. Liquid sloshed inside the dimpled glass, its crystalline blue muted to a silvery hue by the twinkling lights of Pangolais. A dragon's hoard in gold, distilled to a bottle no larger than his thumb. "A dying body."

Chapter Eight
The Demons' Festival

The Festival of Night's Return was not the same in Pangolais.

Crosspine was small and at the periphery of Nidal; its villagers were largely left to do as they pleased. Their Festival observed the proper pieties—they weren't *entirely* outside the Umbral Court's eye—but it had laughter, too. Games. Dancing. Merriment.

There was no such joy in Pangolais.

There would be feasting, later, after the rite reached catharsis and the people watched the powerless foreign gods burn, but even that was different in the Midnight City. In Crosspine they'd have roast pig and salted acorn jellies and early summer wine, all served on tables of felled logs. In Pangolais they feasted on the same dishes—and many rarer delicacies—but their tables were not rough pine. Here they ate on enormous, intricate puzzleworks of bone, cut from the bodies of Kuthite sacrifices and bleached by alchemical acids.

The bone tables were meant to signify the hardships, and survival, of their ancestors. In the black days after Earthfall, when great clouds of dust hid the sun and all the world was cast in shadow, the ancient Nidalese had ventured from their god-shielded grasslands to find that other men and beasts, lacking Zon-Kuthon's protection, had died in masses. The Nidalese had stripped the bones from the corpses of their ancient enemies, using them to build temples to the glory of the god who kept them safe.

And in each of those temples they had built a feast table from the same bones, so that they might remember, at each holy meal during those lean cold years, that but for Zon-Kuthon's grace they, too, would have starved or frozen on those withered sunless plains outside the Uskwood.

Today they would feast on similar tables. Not the same ones; thousands of years of use had worn those down to dust. All that remained of the original bones had been collected into a single ceremonial table in the Umbral Court's own cathedral. But the prisons and torture chambers of Pangolais gave up more than enough bones to rebuild the tables for every fall's Festival. At the end of the night's ceremonies, the alchemically treated bones would be burned in an incandescent bonfire, signifying the sacrifice of all those victims to their god's mirth.

Beautiful, and terrible, and ultimately unimportant. Those victims were already dead. Helis's were not. Isiem wrested his thoughts back to the moment. If he allowed her plan to go forward, more than bones would burn in the square tonight.

The Dusk Hall's shadowcallers and their students stood in a loose formation at the periphery of the crowd. More were scattered within the throng in gray-clad groups of two and three, each surrounded by an arm's span of empty space. Close-packed as the crowd was, no commoner wanted to stand too near Zon-Kuthon's true faithful.

At the head of the crowd, atop a three-stepped plinth of bone and black steel, the Black Triune led the masses in prayer. As the familiar words rolled past, Isiem glanced at the priest tethered to the chain on his wrist.

Bedic's pupils were dilated, and perspiration made his forehead shimmer under the Midnight City's witchlights. He'd drunk the bluekiss tincture earlier that day; it would have been too suspicious if he had drunk it in the market square. Isiem had used a prayer-scroll to delay the poison's effects and prevent the cleric from dying immediately after swallowing the draught, but the magic was beginning to fade. In a few minutes it would fail altogether.

He hoped he'd calculated the timing correctly. He needed the priest upright until the demon took him, and then he needed the man to die very quickly indeed. If his spell expired at the wrong moment, the cleric might succumb before the demon could take his mortal shell—or, worse, might survive long enough for the demon to purge the toxin from his blood.

Before Isiem could worry about that, however, he needed Bedic to hide the poison's effects a little longer. In a few moments, the Black Triune would finish their prayer and signal the shadowcallers to bring down the dark, and no one would notice if the priest collapsed in his chains. But until then, he needed to avoid drawing suspicion.

Bedic seemed to realize it too. The priest's white lips moved in his own stuttered prayers. His solitary voice was lost in the measured thunder of the Nidalese chant, and there was no magic in his call; he did not dare invoke Sarenrae's power in this place. But the priest seemed to draw strength from the familiar words, and he managed to keep walking.

At last the Black Triune finished their chant. In unison they threw their arms to the sky, and in unison they collapsed on their plinths, prostrating themselves to Zon-Kuthon tonight as their ancestors had millennia before. In that same moment, Isiem released the spell he'd held prepared, and every shadowcaster in the square did the same.

Darkness, absolute and impenetrable, blanketed the crowd. And in that darkness, screams arose.

Some were pure figments of the wizards' fancies; some were stolen from the throats of Kuthite victims. All sounded of sheer agony. Supernatural cold and wind buffeted the crowd along with the illusory screams, recreating a fraction of the terror that had beset their ancestors in the dark days after Earthfall. There was no need to recreate their despair.

Gradually the screams dwindled and died. The winds howled louder, stronger, colder, whipping Isiem's hair into his face and flapping his sleeves like the wings of some great crippled bird. And then they, too, died, and in the silence the Black Triune spoke again.

"Desolation fell upon us, and the Midnight Lord gave us succor. Death came to hunt us, and the Midnight Lord gave us its leash. Pain tried to break us, and Zon-Kuthon taught us that it held nothing to fear. By his grace we are Nidalese. By his gifts we master the night."

"By his grace we are Nidalese," the assembly echoed, and Isiem relaxed the weave of his spell. Its enchanted darkness loosened, lessened; glimmers of twilight began to seep through, as water might trickle through a basket's rushes. Here and there, shafts of silvery starlight filtered through the gloom.

"By his gifts we master the night," the shadowcallers chanted. As their spells faded, the neverlight of Pangolais returned, but it felt different now. Tense. Breathless. *Hungry,* as if the night itself were a living thing, and one that had not eaten for far too long.

The children came forward to face it. There were six of them, not four as the demon's vision had showed: two boys and four girls, pale but stoic, impossibly young. Their parents ushered them forward with silent pats and too-brief hugs, then receded into the crowd.

In the spaces between the three plinths, two enormous nightmirrors hung suspended within silver rings, each one a moon in eclipse. And in that darkness, that infinite night, cold and envious things waited.

One by one the children approached to face it. Each time, Isiem tensed and waited for Helis to make her move . . . and each time, nothing happened. The children awoke no answer from the nightglass. They went back to their parents in relieved disappointment, and Helis stayed hooded in the audience.

Had she given up? Or had she just had some qualm about pitting her demon against innocent children? Isiem watched, uncertain, as the last of the children walked away and the shadowcallers began to come forward.

Every year their procession was the same. The shadowcallers came to the mirrors in a double file, summoned an unliving beast from the gloom, and led it through the awe-hushed crowd to show their mastery over the terrors of the night. Some offered their own flesh or that of others as sacrifice to show their piety, but whether they fed the dark or not, each of them called it and held it. *Death came to hunt us, and the Midnight Lord gave us its leash.*

What none said, and all knew, was that only their obedience kept those leashes intact. The procession of the shadowbeasts was an exhibit of Zon-Kuthon's power, but it cowed the people as much as it exhilarated them. They were proud, yes, but under that pride was fear. At the first whiff of apostasy, the masters would become prey.

Was that what Helis intended?

She had moved too far ahead for Isiem to intercept her. At least twenty shadowcallers stood between them, and the crowd hemmed them into a narrow line. There was no more room to manuever.

Tugging Bedic's chain as if the cleric were a balky dog, Isiem continued his slow march forward. Bedic kept pace beside him, sweating and stumbling. The poison had nearly overwhelmed the man; anyone who troubled to look at him would see that there was something worse than fear at work on him.

But no one did. The shadowcallers were lost in anticipation, and the common people of Pangolais were distracted by the monsters who had come to walk among them.

Two by two the shadowbeasts took form. Some were horned, some heavy-jowled; some were tusked in flame. Their eyes were black diamond and smoky topaz and pearl. One had no eyes at all, only weeping rifts in its skull.

Every one of the shadowbeasts, whether sleek or shaggy or armored in cracking chitin, seemed strangely indistinct in the night. The force of their presence was undeniable. No one could have claimed they were not *real*. Yet their bodies wavered at the corner of one's eye, like dream-creatures who, infinitely mutable, begin to dissipate the instant the dreamer changes focus. The shadowbeasts, too, were defined only as long as a human will made them so.

That lack of permanence was the shadowcallers' primary source of control. These shadowbeasts existed in this world only by the will of Zon-Kuthon, and so a rebellious beast could be unraveled. The threat kept them tractable, as much as any such creatures could be. Demons offered no such assurance.

Isiem could see Helis now. She had reached the end of the line, and walked separately through the empty space before the suspended mirrors. Although she wore a shadowcaller's robes, as they were all required to do, hers were ancient and ragged, their charcoal dye faded to an ashen gray that looked almost white in the gloom. The withered corpses of moths hung pale in the black net of her hair, like flower petals strewn across a bride's coiffure.

She's going to a funeral, not a wedding.

Isiem's grip tightened on the priest's chain. "A little longer," he whispered hoarsely. The cleric nodded weakly, his eyes closed as he fought to stave off death's grip for another few minutes. Isiem turned back to watch his old friend—willing, uselessly, that she turn back from the brink of destruction. Bedic was doomed, whatever happened, but Helis need not be.

"Iskarioth," Helis whispered. Her voice cut clearly through the hush. The nearest shadowbeasts, and some of their masters, lifted their heads toward her plea. They recognized that it was no shade's name she called. *"Iskarioth."*

Who calls? The voice was as Isiem remembered—and yet nothing like it. What he remembered was a frail shadow of the demon's full, crushing presence, just as the memory of a nightmare lacked the paralyzing force of the night terrors themselves. His feet were stone, his spine weak as a wilted stem. He stood trembling and unable to move, and all around him the people of Pangolais stood locked in equal fright.

"Helis of the Dusk Hall," he heard his former friend say.

What would you have of me? There were eyes in the mirror now. Three of them. Five. A dozen. A hundred, swirling around one another like rotting leaves caught in an inky whirlpool. All of them shone with the same malignant brilliance.

"Chaos," Helis said.

What do you offer me?

"Chaos," she repeated, the word thick with yearning.

Terror spiked through Isiem, breaking him free of the numbness. "No," he croaked.

The eyes in the mirror turned to him. One by one they blinked in a spiral of milky amusement. *No? Who calls?*

His throat was dry. Painful. But he scraped the answer out. "Isiem of the Dusk Hall."

What would you have of me?

"Betrayal."

What do you offer me?

"Freedom." Isiem choked on the word. He did not look at Bedic. After all the cruelty he'd dealt in his training, and all the blood on his hands, he still could not face the man he was about to sacrifice. "I offer you a good man. Young. Strong. Pure of heart. I have done nothing to damage his body. Take it, and leave ours. Refuse this girl her wish."

I will. The swimming eyes winked out of the mirror. Isiem closed his own. He heard Helis scream, and he heard the wet percussion of bones breaking inside flesh, and he closed his eyes still tighter.

Beside him, Bedic's chains jangled abruptly as the priest convulsed in his bonds, arching his back so violently that his spine cracked in a rapid trill. Possession was seldom a gentle process, and the sheer force of it, coupled with the poison the cleric had drunk, assured the man's death. Precisely as Isiem had hoped.

Hadn't he?

The chains' frantic song clanged to an end. The cleric let out a hoarse shout, part cry and part croak. The sound was despairing, filled with rage—and overwhelmed by grateful glory. Two voices together, one dying, one furious and fading as the demon was drawn back into its prison, denied the freedom of flesh.

And then they were quiet.

Slowly Isiem became aware of breathing around him, and whispers. The crowd. The proud and faithful Nidalese, alive because a foreign slave had traded his life for theirs.

Because I traded his life for theirs.

A hand closed on his arm above his elbow, pulling him to the side. He looked up, opening his eyes at last. It was a woman: sharp-nosed, stern-jawed, her shoulders held rigidly back and her dark hair bound in a severe knot. *Dirakah?* Isiem wondered, dazed. It did not seem impossible, after everything else he'd seen tonight, that the dead might walk again.

But no—this woman had two arms, and her eyes were the lustrous, empty black of the shadow-seized.

"Come," she said.

"You knew what she would do."

"I guessed," Isiem admitted, turning toward where he thought the speaker stood. He could not see them—any of them. A veil of gray blindness sheeted his vision.

The Black Triune, legendary rulers of Nidal, often employed such spells as part of their interrogations. Blindness made their subjects feel more vulnerable, and their naked expressions were easier for their questioners to read. It also, Isiem knew, served to maintain the shroud of intimidating secrecy around the Triune. Stripped of his most familiar sense, he was powerless. He could not meet their eyes to impress them with his honesty, or try to guess their thoughts from the flickers on their faces.

The effect was calculated to frighten him, and it did. But at the same time, in a way, it was a relief. Isiem had never expected to stand face to face with the Black Triune, any more than he would have expected to stand before the devil-lords in Asmodeus's infernal court. He certainly would never have been able to withstand their stares without quailing. The Black Triune were ancient, unfathomably powerful; they had governed Nidal since it first swore allegiance to Zon-Kuthon, and if they had been human in the beginning, they had not been for centuries since.

What they were today, no one knew. Even wondering seemed dangerous. Sweat crept down his back. "I guessed," he repeated.

"You *knew*." A different voice. Female. "Or are we to imagine that you happened to have a cleric of Sarenrae—a good soul, a *rare* soul, and precisely the key to Iskarioth's freedom—simply by accident? That the cleric was coincidentally drugged to the brink of death just when you offered him to the demon? Are we to accept that all of this was *happenstance*?"

"No." Isiem swallowed. His throat was so dry it ached. "Not happenstance. I knew what Helis planned. I heard her bargain with the demon through a nightglass, and

I prepared myself to break that bargain. But I did not know what she would *do*. Until the very last moment, there was always a chance that she might come to her senses and stop."

"Generous," the first voice said. Was that a hint of approval? Or condemnation? Isiem strained to tell.

"Foolish," said the woman. "What if your cleric died before you could offer him? What if the demon betrayed you instead of Helis? Your plan was fraught with unnecessary risk, and why? Because you believed a madwoman might turn back from her revenge?"

"I had to give her the chance," Isiem said.

"Even after she murdered Dirakah?" The female voice laughed softly at his expression. "Yes, we know about that."

"You knew, but you still punished Serevil?"

"Even if Helis deceived his eye, it was Serevil's hand that drove in the spike. He had the opportunity to heal his victim once he realized his mistake. He did not. That was weakness, and it was failure. It proved him unworthy of his gifts."

"But you did not punish Helis."

"No," the woman agreed calmly. "Because we, like you, wanted to see what she would do. Would she be content with a single act of revenge? Or would she want more? Dirakah was no great loss. We judged it better to wait and watch rather than destroy a promising student whose only sin, to that point, was excessive loyalty."

"We were blind to her scheme with the demon," the first voice admitted. "Had we known, we might have eliminated her immediately . . . but we might have done as you did, and given her the chance to seal her doom. We cannot say your choice was wrong. Or disloyal."

"Loyalty is to be commended." This was a third voice, one that had not spoken before. It was neither male nor female, as far as Isiem could discern, but simply *old*. So old that trivialities such as gender had lost their meaning.

A shiver danced along Isiem's spine. "You will not punish me?" he ventured.

The woman laughed again. "You might perceive it as a punishment, but that is not our intent. You have proven yourself cunning and cautious. Loyal to your friends, but ruthless when they endanger Nidal. We need servants of such quality. So, our loyal servant, you are not being punished . . . but you *are* being sent away. It is time for you to leave the Dusk Hall."

"But I have not earned my ring," Isiem said.

"That is so," the first speaker said, "and that is good. It will cause them to underestimate you." A smile seemed to come into his voice. It did not sound like a kind one. "Gather your spellbooks and bid farewell to your friends. You are going to our allies. The Chelaxians."

Chapter Nine
Escape

He did not go to Cheliax.

He didn't even leave Pangolais, although they did at least allow him out of the Dusk Hall. When the Black Triune promised to send him to the Chelaxians, Isiem soon realized, they did not mean he would be sent out of Nidal. Rather, he was sent to apprentice with a dignitary visiting the Umbral Court: a small, elegant woman whose dark hair and pale skin bespoke the blood of old Azlant. Her name was Velenne, and she was a diabolist.

"It is a distinctly Chelish discipline," one of the Triune had said before they released him. "It would be useful for us to learn all we can of it."

"You want me to spy?"

"We want you to study. Both what she intends for you to learn, and what she does not."

Of course, Isiem thought.

Four hundred years ago, Nidal had been conquered by the empire of Cheliax, one of the great powers of Golarion, and the humiliation of their defeat had rankled for centuries thereafter. Cheliax was itself an ancient and storied nation, with nearly two thousand years of tradition to its name . . . and yet, compared to Nidal, it was but a raw green upstart. For the chosen people of Zon-Kuthon to lose their sovereignty to *any* terrestrial ruler, let alone a relative novice to the world stage, was a bitter blow.

But not, they had come to understand, an accidental one.

In the year 4606, at the dawn of the Age of Lost Omens, the god Aroden died and cast the world into turmoil. The Empire of Cheliax, which had claimed Aroden's particular favor, lost its divine mandate and collapsed into thirty years of civil war.

From that war, the diabolists rose victorious. Sweeping the old faith of Aroden aside, they brought the empire under the rule of the Thrice-Damned House of Thrune—and through House Thrune to Asmodeus, Prince of Darkness, the silver-tongued lord of devils, whom the diabolists worshiped and served.

And the Nidalese came to see why Zon-Kuthon had allowed them to fall under Cheliax's reign. Aroden's Cheliax had distrusted and subjugated their shadow-sworn nation, but Asmodeus's Cheliax welcomed them as allies.

Diabolists came to Pangolais to study the Kuthite arts. Nidalese shadowcallers served in the Midnight Guard of Westcrown and other hotspots of rebellion against House Thrune, using their arcane powers to subdue the very people who had once subdued them. There was a delightful irony in the conquest of their conquerors, and many in Pangolais believed the opportunity was ripe for the Umbral Court to extend its influence even further. Isiem's apprenticeship with Velenne was one small way of doing so.

But, in the beginning, it did not seem that she intended for him to learn anything. While Ascaros and the rest of his old classmates from the Dusk Hall apprenticed under Nidalese masters, learning to weave magic into darkness and pain, Isiem—once the best among them—sat idle. The Chelaxian paid him no mind, except occasionally to order him to make tea or fetch a finished necklace from the jeweler. The latter was more common than the former; the woman loved her jewelry.

Isiem did too. In the long, lonely hours that he spent in his assigned quarters, waiting for the diabolist to remember he was there, he often tumbled her rings and pendants over his fingers. The colors dazzled him: glowing pink spinels, emeralds like mist-hazed gardens, diamonds that split moonlight into rainbows. Nothing in Nidal was ever so vibrant, so full of life, as Velenne's jewels in their scented ivory boxes.

Even the names of the places they'd been found were fascinating. Katheer. Oppara. Nantambu. Each of the stones had an entry in a ledger that recorded its type, price, and point of origin.

The first two things meant nothing to Isiem, but the names of the cities and lands that had birthed such marvels entranced him. He read through them again and again, trying to imagine these exotic places where the earth was not dull muted gray, but brilliant enough to shame the sun. He envisioned gilded cities, fragrant with spice, where birds sang and musicians strummed: places where he would hear joyous sounds, instead of Helis's screams echoing endlessly in his mind. Somehow, Isiem imagined—knowing it was foolish, but unwilling to shake the fancy—there were no shadows there.

One afternoon he did not put the jewels away quickly enough when he heard Velenne's steps approaching.

The gems were tangled across his fingers in webs of gold when the diabolist opened the door.

"Is it so tempting to deck yourself like a Taldan dowager?" she inquired.

"No, mistress." Isiem fumbled with a pair of sapphire earrings, trying to separate their interlocked wires so he could hang them back in their boxes. "I only —"

"Only what?" She stepped into the room and let the ebony door fall shut behind her. It made no sound, but Isiem flinched anyway. "You were not stealing from me, I hope."

"No, mistress." The earrings were hopelessly tangled. He dropped them into the box, closed the lid, and drew a breath before meeting her eyes. "But you give me nothing else to do. I came to study at your side, but it seems you have no wish to teach me."

"Ah. And so you grow impatient, and imagine how else you might profit by my neglect." Velenne smiled, but her eyes remained dark and unrevealing; he could not tell if she was joking. "Well, it is true I have been a poor teacher. What do you wish to learn?"

"Magic. Diabolism. Whatever you wish to teach me."

"Those are three different things," she murmured, nearing. She plucked a green garnet necklace from his nerveless fingers and dropped it into a velvet-lined box. "But one of them, I suppose, you might learn."

Velenne was as good as her word. Over the next several months, she taught Isiem numerous spells. Some were known to him already, but others were disfavored by Nidalese wizards or shunned as anathema. If Velenne were any example, the Chelaxians preferred to rely on conjurations and compulsions to force others to do their bidding. She had little interest in the undead and no reverence for darkness, which she viewed as useful for confounding enemies on the battlefield and nothing else. Spells that inflicted pain amused her, but she did not treat them with the holy reverence that the Kuthites did.

To her, Isiem thought, arcana was just another tool to manipulate. A powerful one, to be sure, and a useful one, but a servant all the same. The diabolist was no fool—she treated magic with respect, and her spellcraft was as precise as any shadowcaller's—but she had none of the bone-deep dread that he, himself, had never been able to escape.

"Why aren't you afraid?" he asked her late one night, after finishing the last of the scrolls she had ordered him to transcribe.

Velenne looked up from her book. "Afraid of what?"

"The magic. You don't fear it."

She gave him a quizzical look, then closed her book, smiling faintly. "You Nidalese. You see traps everywhere. No surprise, really, given what you are."

"And what is that?" Isiem asked, feeling as if he should be nettled but not quite knowing why.

"Slaves. Slaves so thoroughly cowed, so utterly broken, that you're afraid even to look at your chains. As if merely acknowledging your enslavement might tempt punishment from your master—which, to be fair, it might. Zon-Kuthon is not noted for his temperance."

Her blasphemy was astounding. Even after months of studying under the Chelaxian, the things she said amazed him. Isiem bit his tongue. He couldn't rebuke his teacher, but if the Umbral Court knew that he'd sat in silence while she uttered such profanities . . .

What would they do? What *could* they do? The question brought him up short. It was the Black Triune that had instructed him to spy on their visitor, so perhaps they *wanted* him to uncover Velenne's disrespect. If that was so, he served them best by remaining quiet.

And, he admitted in his most private heart, it was oddly thrilling to hear such illicit ideas spoken aloud. The Nidalese *were* slaves. Zon-Kuthon's rule *was* cruel. And Isiem had often, so often, been afraid to admit even to himself how badly his god's yoke chafed. Or that he wore it at all.

"But you're a diabolist," he said. "You don't fear the devils?"

Velenne waved two fingers dismissively and opened her book again. "Not as you fear your master. I serve, yes. But I also command. I have a contract: my duties and obligations are set forth clearly, as are the risks I take and the rewards I might win. There is no uncertainty, so there is less fear. I know what I face, and I accepted it freely. But you . . . you didn't even strike your own bargain, did you? You stumble in the fetters your ancestors forged, bound by terms you never negotiated and barely know. At any misstep, you risk punishment, but you've only the vaguest idea where the true path lies. And so you live in terror. Even now, you're afraid that someone is watching, aren't you? Looking for transgressions you don't know."

That cut too close to the bone. "Why are you here, then?" Isiem blurted. "If all you see in us is such horror, why come to Nidal?"

"To witness the warning," Velenne replied coolly, turning a page. "Imperial Cheliax, in her wisdom and glory, has chosen to walk a path not far from yours. It serves us well to remember what might happen if we bargain poorly."

"That's what we are to you? A cautionary tale?"

"Everyone is a cautionary tale. You needn't be insulted on Nidal's behalf." She glanced up, brushing a lock of hair behind one ear. "Really, you should be pleased. Your masters will be delighted you've uncovered such sedition. Few spies are so successful."

He shrugged her mockery away. "Are those the only choices? Slavery or servitude?"

"Those are the only choices for us. And they aren't really choices, are they?"

He had no answer for that. Velenne read it on his face, smiled again, and set her book aside. "Ah, you're afraid of me now. Or angry. Which is it?"

"Neither."

"You shouldn't lie to your betters," Velenne said. Unhurriedly she stood, loosed the ties of her soft gray robe, and walked past his cramped desk on the way to her bedroom. Two steps away, just as the first whisper of her perfume reached him, she beckoned for her student to follow.

Isiem felt the blood drain from his face. Something fluttered deep in his stomach. It was not a surprise, precisely, that she might invite him to her bed—master shadowcallers frequently took such liberties with their students—but after months of inaction he had assumed that Chelish customs were different, or that she simply had no interest in him. Learning otherwise, *now*, after such a perplexing conversation, was . . . disconcerting. And, he realized with a flicker of uneasy surprise, he was afraid of disappointing her.

"I can't," he said, swallowing.

Her smile did not waver. "It wasn't a request."

She had that right, if she wanted it. Isiem stood. Then he hesitated, uncertain again. "You never told me why you aren't afraid of the magic."

"Because I control it," Velenne replied, as if stating a most obvious fact. "And you fear it because you control nothing." She rested a hand lightly on his arm, then closed her grip. He could feel her nails dig in through the cloth of his sleeve.

"Nothing," she repeated, amused. "Come."

She taught him more about that, too, as the days rolled into months. Yet no matter how diligently Isiem applied himself to those lessons, he sensed that it was never quite what she wanted.

Velenne liked pain. She liked inflicting it and enduring it, and Isiem came to believe that her predilections played some role in why she had come to Nidal. Certainly she seemed to delight in their refinements of the torturer's art. His training should have made him adept enough to please her, and yet it seemed he seldom did.

"What am I doing wrong?" he asked her once, in the dim hours between the end of night and the beginning of morning. Velenne was a blur of warmth and fragrance in the darkness beside him, but he knew that she had her back turned to him. "I love you. I want it to be right."

The sheets rustled as she rolled over. Her hair brushed his shoulder and swung away. "Love?" she repeated, inflecting the word with a wealth of irony. Neither of them had uttered it before.

"Yes."

"Ah." There was a pause, as if Velenne were considering what to say next. Then she shrugged and, in a determinedly light tone, said, "Did I ever tell you about the first boy I loved?"

Isiem had no wish to hear the story, but he could think of no polite way to decline. "No."

"I call him a boy, although I suppose he was a man—albeit boyish in many ways. His name was Ederras. Ederras Celverian. Scion of a storied noble house, paladin of Iomedae, dedicated fighter for the freedom of Westcrown." She laughed quietly, tracing her fingertips along the inside of Isiem's elbow. He shivered, but did not draw away. "He was brave and beautiful and bold, and oh so innocently stupid.

"My duty was to spy on him. I was new to diabolism then, and less well known in Cheliax than I am now, so my superiors believed I should be able to infiltrate the Wiscrani rebellion easily. I arrived in the city with a false name and a background full of lies, and immediately I set about seducing Ederras Celverian. No magic; he might have sensed that and grown suspicious. Only charm. So it took a very long time, but in the end he succumbed.

"He wore armor the first night he came to me, as if that would protect him. It didn't, of course, but I broke a nail on his plate. He never did it again. And for a while we were . . . happy. Truly happy, I believe. Both of us. I didn't file the reports I'd taken on him or his compatriots. I even helped him, in small ways, and counseled him away from mistakes. Because I had come to love him—really *love* him, forthright and foolish as he was—and I wanted to shield him from the disasters he was inviting.

"Oh, I knew it was doomed. Or maybe I didn't. Stranger things have been known to happen in Cheliax; it is a country made for strange allegiances. Perhaps I wanted so badly to believe that I even convinced myself we could be one of them. But we weren't.

"I don't know why he decided to break into my private belongings. I suspect his father was behind it; he wanted Ederras to get rid of me and start getting babies on some mousy little noble-born wife. But it might have been his own idea. Anyway, he had one of his friends in the rebellion force the locks on my closets.

"They found everything." She paused, and took a breath; Isiem could almost see the self-mocking smile curl upon her lips. "My books, my tools, my recorded observations of all his friends' treasons. I had never reported any of it—I loved him too much for that—but he didn't ask. Didn't care, I imagine. The revelation of my nature was damning enough.

"That night he came to me in armor again, but this time he did not take it off. He told me that he knew what I was, what I had done, and that justice demanded my death.

"I said nothing. I *did* nothing. I was too devastated to defend myself. And I think because of that, he could not bring himself to finish it. Oh, he tried. But Ederras was a truly righteous man, and it wasn't in him to kill an unarmed woman, even if that woman was me. So he held back from delivering the last blow." Velenne made her odd little laugh again. She ducked her head, nestling her cheek against Isiem's side, as if even in the darkness she wanted to hide whatever was on her face. But she did not stop.

"He left me there, bleeding on the brink of death. I never saw him again. I suppose he married the faithful little wife his father wanted, or went off to throw himself against demons in Mendev. Perhaps both. For my part, I did my duty and turned in my observations. The Hellknights took his friends, and my work was done in Westcrown. That was the end of it."

"Why are you telling me this?" Isiem asked. It was an effort to force the question past the constriction in his chest.

"You're supposed to be spying." She brushed a kiss against his neck, plainly aware of his torment and just as plainly amused by it. "Don't forget it. Love only gets in the way."

He never reported her sedition.

He never reported anything, although there was much about their visitor that would have interested the Umbral Court. Velenne's candor was breathtaking, and although Isiem wondered how much of it was genuine unconcern and how much was meant to bait him, the answer almost didn't matter. It was enthralling. No one dared *think* such things in Nidal, let alone say them.

Velenne said anything she wanted. And although Isiem never did, bit by bit he found himself silently sharing her thoughts. About fear, and enslavement, and the crushing terror of being held to someone else's bargain. About freedom.

"I want to go to Cheliax," he told her one night as they lay entangled in sheets and sweat. He hadn't intended to say it; the words had slipped out on their own. The idea of running away had been more and more in his mind lately, although Isiem tried to tell himself it was only an idle fancy. There was no real future for him with Velenne, and no chance of escaping Nidal.

But he couldn't quite crush that last ember of hope, and when he heard what he'd said, he froze, wondering how the diabolist would react.

"What?" She propped herself up on an elbow, looking down on him with a mixture of concern and merriment. Her hair fell across her shoulders in loose tangles.

He took a breath and plunged ahead, committing himself to the plea. "You won't stay in Nidal forever. Take me with you when you go."

Her eyes widened. Then she laughed, breathily and almost soundlessly, for a very long time. Sitting up, Velenne gestured to a black-thorned candelabra resting on her vanity. A spark ignited the nearest of the candles, then jumped up to the next and the one after, drawing an arc of fire in its wake. The flickering flames seemed to echo the diabolist's laughter. "You want me to help you run away."

"Yes."

"Do you have any idea what happens to runaway slaves?"

"If they're caught," Isiem said with more bravado than he felt. "I won't be."

"In Egorian? You would be. There are some who can melt into cities and vanish. You are not among them. Besides, it's too predictable that you would run away with me. I would be questioned, and I would give you up. Immediately. The only way to avoid it would be for me to run as well, and I have no interest in that. I am quite attached to my position."

The air seemed to have fled from the room. Isiem cast his eyes downward, feeling unutterably foolish. "I see."

"No, you don't. You want to be free?"

"Yes."

"You should." Velenne leaned in, tracing her nails across his shoulders. "I've been pushing you toward it from the beginning. But to realize that desire, you must have a plan. A *real* plan, not a child's belief that some benevolent fairy will sweep you away by magic. And it will have to be of your own doing, or with the aid of expendables, because anyone you enlist to help you is likely to be destroyed—either by your pursuers, or by yourself, to cover your tracks."

"On my own, then."

She gave him a brief, tight smile and pulled away. Disapproving, Isiem thought, that he was not more ruthless. "On your own. As you will. You should stay away from cities: you have none of the skills needed to hide in crowds or survive among strangers. The wilderness will serve you better. Few there will recognize you for what you are, and fewer will care."

"The Uskwood is full of eyes. I can't hide there."

"I said the *wilderness*. Not Zon-Kuthon's garden of nightmares. Western Cheliax is filled with godsforsaken wastelands where traitors and dissidents hide."

Isiem was dubious. "And how do I get there?"

"Oh, that part's very simple. You persuade the Black Triune to send you."

Book Two
People

Prologue

Parsellon Alterras, Provisional Governor of Devil's Perch by the grace of Her Infernal Majestrix Queen Abrogail II, poured himself another glass of brandy, swirled the amber liquid while staring at it with every appearance of thoughtfulness, and wondered for the ten-thousandth time why his uncle couldn't have purchased a better office for him. This arid spit of striped red rock lacked any semblance of prestige. Its people were a fractious and independent lot, as stubborn as the rocks they called home—and as poor. Governing Devil's Perch had yet to line his pockets with anything but dust; all this place had ever given him was an overabundance of headaches.

One of those headaches was babbling at him right now.

Parsellon pinched the bridge of his nose and eyed the man over the brim of his brandy glass. He'd already forgotten the fellow's name. Horvus? Sorlos? Some unshaven miner who drank too much and bathed too little and spent his days trying to scratch crumbs of gold from the unforgiving spires of Devil's Perch.

When he'd first come to this godsforsaken place, Parsellon had believed that the gold mines might make his ten-year term as governor worthwhile. True, the posting was remote, and the newly established town of Blackridge—what was intended to eventually pass for the provincial capital—hopelessly dull. But if there *had* been gold here, he would have done his duty to Imperial Cheliax faithfully and without complaint, and then retired to Egorian to enjoy his well-earned spoils.

There was no gold. If there had *ever* been gold in Devil's Perch, which Parsellon heartily doubted, it had all been mined out long before he arrived. All that remained were rumors and stories and desperate idiots chasing them through the canyons.

Well, the sooner he got rid of this idiot, the sooner he could enjoy his brandy without having it spoiled by the man's odor. "Remind me again what you wanted?"

"A claim deed for a parcel around Crackspike," the man said. He fumbled a greasy piece of leather from his back pocket and held it out to the governor.

Parsellon glanced at it long enough to ascertain that it held a crudely rendered map and waved the ill-smelling thing away. "A claim deed, you say?" That could be worthwhile. In order for Imperial Cheliax to recognize a miner's claim on a previously unstaked piece of land, the miner had to formally file a request for it and be granted a deed. The filing fees on such deeds were not formalized. In theory, this was because the value and size of parcels varied, so a uniform fee would have been unfair. In practice, it was an open invitation to bribery. The Provisional Governor could set his fees as high or as low as he pleased—which would have been very useful, if anyone ever bothered paying them.

In fact, as Parsellon had learned soon after coming to Blackridge, hardly anyone did. The pitiful excuse for a town he governed had only the barest semblance of a militia, so there was no real enforcement for such deeds. Even more damaging, there was no reason for anyone to want or need a legal claim, because all the land in Devil's Perch was worthless. No one could farm it, livestock starved and died on it, and there was nothing but sorrow to be mined.

But if this idiot wanted a claim deed, who was he to refuse? Provided the man could pay the filing fees. "These things can be expensive, you realize," Parsellon said, stroking the scarlet velvet stole of his office. He'd had it trimmed with a band of gold brocade: a bit of an overstep, since only paracounts and higher were accorded gold in the courts of Cheliax, but one he judged unlikely to hurt him. These louts didn't know any better, and no Egorian aristocrat would be setting foot in Devil's Perch anytime soon.

He hadn't offered his guest any brandy. The miner— Sorvus, *that* was his name—stared at the governor's drink with open longing before shaking himself and returning to the matter at hand. "I can pay."

"That's a large parcel you're requesting." Parsellon glanced at the charcoal-sketched map. "It will have to be surveyed, checked for prior claims, registered before Her Infernal Majestrix's clerks in Egorian . . ."

"How much?" the miner interrupted.

The Provisional Governor decided to overlook the man's impertinence. If he felt entitled to be so rude, he was clearly an eager mark. "Fifty golden sails," he decided aloud. An impossible sum, unless the miner really had struck something worthwhile in those rocks.

"Here." Sorvus dug a callused hand into a dirty pocket and came up with a handful of dingy gray rocks, which he spilled over the top of the governor's desk. He untied a filthy sack from his belt and tossed that alongside them. The sack's mouth sagged open, revealing grains of blue-black dirt. "Weigh it."

"You can't pay the fee in *rocks*," Parsellon said, annoyed.

The miner squinted at him. He unhooked the horn-handled knife at his hip and scratched it along a particularly wriggly-looking rock, one shaped like a spoonful of batter dropped into hot oil. A shining line of white followed the dull blade's score.

Silver.

That was why none of the hedge charms to find gold in Devil's Perch had ever worked. There *was* no gold in those rocks. The fortune of the lawless west was silver.

Parsellon's fingers twitched. He knotted them tightly in his ample lap. "Where did you find that?"

"You'll take my claim deed?"

"Consider it signed."

Sorvus nodded and spat on the floor. The governor didn't correct him. "Two miles north-northwest of Crackspike," the miner said. "Found these nuggets washed up after a canyon flood. The rest at the bottom of a water pit I dug. It's in my parcel, mind. I've claimed it."

"It is yours," Parsellon assured him. He didn't take his eyes off the silver. If all of that was pure, he had . . . what, a hundred gold sails' worth sitting on his desk? Two hundred? How much was the man carrying? How much had he *found?* "That's strix territory, though, isn't it?"

"They call it theirs, aye. The black buzzards are thick up there. Probably why nobody found the strike before—or lived to tell about it if they did. Which brings me to the second favor I came to ask you."

"Ask."

"Send word to Citadel Enferac. We'll need Hellknights to keep the swoops at bay if we're to get the silver out of Crackspike. It'll be hard enough mining ore out of those rocks without worrying about the strix. Scare them off, or I'll never get the men I need to make my find good. A company or three of Hellknights will go a long way toward convincing outsiders it's safe enough to come and work here."

"You'll need that many workers?" Parsellon asked.

"Oh, aye, no question of it. The find's good."

"Well, I'd be remiss in my duties as governor if I didn't do all I could to help Devil's Perch flourish." Parsellon gestured to his bodyguard, Thantos, a hulking and taciturn man who had not budged an inch from his post by the door for the entirety of their conversation. The provisional governor sometimes wondered whether the man blinked. "Quill and paper, if you please."

Wordlessly Thantos set them before him. Parsellon dipped the quill and, glancing occasionally at the miner's map, sketched out the area to come under Sorvus's claim. Then, with a flourish, he signed his name at the base and pressed his official seal to the paper.

"There," the governor said. "Sorvus's Strike is yours. I shall have my clerk draw up a copy to send you before the day's end. The original, of course, must go to Egorian to be properly recorded. Rest assured that I will dispatch it as soon as the appropriate security measures are arranged. It's quite a claim you've made here. We wouldn't want it to get lost. But the strike, my good man, is yours." He motioned to his brandy carafe. "May I offer you a toast to fine fortune?"

"I wouldn't say no," Sorvus replied. The apple of his throat bobbed.

"Thantos! Another glass." Parsellon poured a liberal measure and offered it to his guest. And another. And, when the man continued to swill good Chelish brandy like Isgeri barrel-wash, a third.

Five glasses in, Sorvus was blind drunk. Parsellon, who had nursed his original glass throughout while toasting his guest's every sentence, gave the inebriated miner a confiding smile.

"So tell me," he said, "just how much silver *is* there in your strike?"

"Don't know." Sorvus set his glass aside unsteadily and tried to lay a finger alongside his broken nose. He missed, although he didn't seem to notice. "A lot. I went upstream when I found that bit I gave you. Found . . . a lot. Under the rocks it's soft. You can . . . you can shovel it right out." The miner mimed throwing a shovelful of dirt over his shoulder, nearly upsetting his glass. He didn't seem to notice that, either. "Looks like sludgy black dirt, but you cook it down with salt and mercury and you can see, it's silver. It's all silver. Barrels of it. *Wagons*."

"We'll need soldiers to protect that," the governor mused. "Or Hellknights."

"Aye." Sorvus tipped the last of the brandy down his gullet. "The swoops didn't trouble me none, but I'm just one man and I know the canyon ways. We'll need a lot of workers to mine out the strike, and they won't know the first thing about surviving out here. Maybe if I could hire men from Pezzack, but . . ."

"There will be no traitors tolerated in Devil's Perch while I'm governor," Parsellon said firmly. Softening his tone, he added: "Besides, how would that look to the throne? Or the Hellknights?"

"Not good." Sorvus grimaced. "No Pezzacki. That means outlanders. Lots of 'em. And that means trouble with the strix."

"Let me worry about that. You just enjoy your good luck. There'll be plenty of time for work soon enough." Parsellon stood and nodded toward Thantos.

The towering bodyguard took the miner's shoulders, helping him gently but inexorably toward the door.

When the miner was gone, Parsellon yawned and cracked his neck. His eyes fell on the greasy leather map, which Sorvus had neglected to pick up before he left.

Wagons of silver . . .

Thoughtfully, he rubbed the soft, dirty leather between his thumb and forefinger. That much wealth would make Devil's Perch a magnet for prospectors, and everything that went with them: cooks, barkeeps, whores, dealers in horses and mining equipment . . . rough trades, to be sure, but profitable. Very profitable. And they'd all be under his jurisdiction.

His gaze strayed back to the center of the map. Crackspike. An ugly little landmark, that was. The first team of prospectors to run afoul of the strix, nearly twenty years ago, had been tortured to death. While bloody but still alive, they'd been staked out for the venomous yellow hill ants to devour, and they had been left there until nothing remained but bare bones.

Then the black-winged bastards had gathered up their victims' bones and cracked them apart with their own mining tools and made the whole thing, broken spikes and broken bones and all, into a morbid sculpture in the shadow of one of their holy stones.

That was Crackspike: the strix's way of saying that the barren red rocks were *their* land. Human interlopers were unwelcome.

Hellknights didn't die as easily as prospectors, though, and with Citadel Enferac's support, the governor was quite confident that the strix could be pacified.

Securing that support, however, could prove costly. The various Hellknight orders were always interested in raising their power and prestige relative to rival orders, and in extending the rule of law over an uncivilized land . . . but convincing them to protect a single man's silver claim, however rich, could be a difficult proposition.

Considerably easier if that claim belonged to the throne. Considerably more profitable, too.

The door opened. Parsellon looked up as Thantos stepped in, wiping a spatter of mud from his breeches. "What do you think of all this?"

"Lot of changes coming," the big man replied. "Probably a lot of blood. You want me to start hiring swords?"

"A sensible precaution, if you can find good ones. We'll still need the Hellknights, though. Find a fast rider who can take a message to Citadel Enferac. For Vicarius Torchia's eyes only." The Provisional Governor tapped his fingers against his desk, looking at the map again. "That miner . . . Sorvus. Does he have a wife? Any kin?"

Thantos grunted. "He had a woman for a while. A Pezzacki. I forget her name. Pox-scarred, but not bad to look on. She left two years ago. Went back to Pezzack. It's a hard life for a woman out here."

"It's a hard life for anyone. Any issue?"

"You mean children?" Thantos shook his heavy head. "No. A sickling son who died. Think that's why his woman left. No other kin."

Parsellon nodded thoughtfully. "That's a shame." After a final glance, he rolled up the map and slid it into one of his desk drawers. "When you send the rider to Citadel Enferac, tell him to mention to Vicarius Torchia that the man who found the silver strike was, regrettably, killed only a day after making his claim. A robber, most likely. He was flashing his money around too much in a bar. These things happen in a lawless town."

"They do," Thantos agreed neutrally.

"This tragedy only underscores the importance of having Hellknights here to keep order."

"It does." The big man tapped the hilt of the knife at his belt, then reached for the doorknob. "I'd best dispatch that rider soon. Wouldn't want his tidings to prove stale. Make the other arrangements, too. Anything else?"

"Is there a tailor in town at the moment?"

"Widow Lascia takes in washing. Believe she does a little mending, too."

"Good." The governor plucked the stole from his neck and held it out to his bodyguard. He hated to give it up, but if he was going to draw the eye of Egorian to his long-ignored corner of the empire . . . "Tell her to take off the brocade."

Chapter Eleven
Devil's Perch

W e are grateful for your government's assistance in these trying times. Imperial Cheliax is blessed to have such steadfast allies."

"We are honored to serve," Isiem replied. At twenty-five, he was the senior of the two shadowcallers seated before the desk, and so he spoke for both of them.

Vicarius Torchia nodded, accepting the statement as no more than his due. An iron mask forged to resemble a Hellknight's helm concealed his face. Gray eyes, gray hair, a gray wolfskin cloak that seemed better suited to a barbarian warlord than the Chelish wizard he was: that was all the lord of Citadel Enferac showed to the world. Around his neck he wore the mummified claw of a bone devil, studded with ruby-headed pins between its knuckles, in lieu of a formal symbol of office. The devil's claw made the same point, and more graphically: Citadel Enferac was a place where the denizens of Hell served men, willingly or otherwise.

Throughout Cheliax and beyond, the Hellknights commanded respect—and no small measure of fear. Implacable, pitiless, and iron-willed, they modeled themselves after the armies of Hell and enforced the law at any cost. They owed allegiance to no king or country— not even to Her Infernal Majestrix, to the Chelish throne's eternal irritation—but they could, for the right price, be persuaded to assist in stamping out rebellion.

Even by the standards of the Hellknights, the Order of the Gate, based in Citadel Enferac, was unusual. Most Hellknights relied on sword and shield, but the crimson-cloaked signifers of the Order of the Gate wielded magic as their primary weapon. It was said that no secret escaped them—meaning both that the Order of the Gate could ferret out any secret they wished to know, however well concealed, and that they revealed none of their own.

So it was said. Whether the saying was true remained to be seen. The Hellknights were allies of Nidal, just as Cheliax was. But every wizard seated in this room had his secrets, and each of them wanted the others'.

"Honored to serve," Torchia repeated. He smiled, showing a flash of his own teeth through the mask's visor. They were long and yellow, almost devilish. "You've done well with that so far. The two of you distinguished yourselves in Westcrown. I have, accordingly, a new proposition to put before you."

"What might that be?" Isiem asked. He was careful not to look at his companion, a younger shadowcaller named Oreseis, whose hair was already pure silver although he was only twenty years old. The two of them had served together in the Midnight Guard of Westcrown, but their patrols had seldom overlapped and Isiem had never gotten to know the man well. He had no idea what the Vicarius meant when he referred to Oreseis's distinguished duties, and so he kept a neutral face.

"Crackspike."

"I am not familiar with that name," Isiem admitted.

"Her Infernal Majestrix Queen Abrogail II has recently come into possession of a substantial silver claim in the region of Devil's Perch. Its original owner met some fatal misfortune and left no kin, so his claim reverted to the throne. The miners' settlement is called Crackspike. After some local landmark, I believe." Vicarius Torchia steepled his fingers and rested his chin atop them. The near-black rubies on his chained rings glimmered. "The mine's wealth is vital to Imperial Cheliax, but its extraction is proving difficult. The region is rife with hostile creatures. They must be pacified so that the mines can be brought to their full potential. This is, you may appreciate, a matter of some importance to the throne. Your aid would be a boon."

"You called them 'creatures,' not people," Isiem said carefully. "They are not human?"

Torchia shook his head. "I speak of the strix." He unlaced his fingers and lifted the devil's claw on its chain, regarding the wizened gray flesh as if he might read Crackspike's future in its palm. "Black-winged creatures with burning eyes. They eat the flesh of men raw from dripping bones. They know no mercy, and they deserve none."

"They must be formidable foes if you're seeking our aid against them."

The Vicarius shrugged. "They know the land, and they have no compunction about using terror as a weapon. The strix have always been restive subjects of the throne, and now that men are moving into Crackspike in larger numbers, they have become even more savage. Their atrocities demand answer."

"Do we have a free hand to pacify them," Oreseis asked, "or would you prefer more . . . restraint? They *are* the throne's subjects."

"They might have been, had they chosen otherwise," Vicarius Torchia said. "Instead, they are rebels. Do as you will with them."

"What do you suppose the odds are that this assignment is really a reward for distinguished service in Westcrown?" Oreseis asked as he walked with Isiem back to their rooms in a far wing of the citadel.

"It isn't," Isiem said. "This is just a ploy to keep us from spying on the internal workings of their order. We might stumble on something worthwhile if we stayed in Citadel Enferac, so we're being sent to some remote reach of Cheliax where there's no risk of our seeing anything more important than snakes and scorpions and dust. For supposed friends of Nidal, the Chelaxians have never trusted us far."

The Nidalese were staying in a single drafty room high in Citadel Enferac's eastern tower. Their rank would have afforded them individual quarters in a less remote reach of the citadel, had they wanted that, but they preferred to stay together in an isolated hall. One room was easier to ward against scrying, and fewer ordinary interlopers were likely to wander up this way.

Isiem unlocked their door—black iron and weathered wood, almost gloomy enough to belong in the Dusk Hall—and locked it again, using a different key, once they were both inside. His own key offered far more protection. As long as they remained in this room, their voices would be silenced against eavesdroppers, and their doings would be shielded from magical eyes.

"I wouldn't trust us either." Oreseis pulled open a drawer and took out his spiked prayer chain. He took out a small black sack as well, offering it to Isiem. "But perhaps we can turn this to our advantage. Western

Cheliax is a wasteland, but that only means there will be no one to watch us. No vicarius, no lictors, no suspicious Chelish nobles. We'd be poor Nidalese indeed if we couldn't find *some* advantage in this."

Isiem opened the sack. It held a dozen candles. Each was a squat, fat taper, yellowish and soft, with a wick of braided human hair. Consecrated to Zon-Kuthon, the candles had been made of fat carved from the living bodies of sacrificial victims; their wicks were woven of those same victims' hair. When lit, they enhanced Kuthite meditations with visions of remembered pain.

He snuffed out all but two of the candles already burning in their room. Beeswax, being expensive, was reserved for high-ranking Hellknights and magical rituals; the Nidalese were given tallow to light their evenings. The smell was unpleasant, but at least it would mask the equally foul odor of their vision candle.

"Anyway," Oreseis said, "Torchia can send us away, but we won't be completely blind to his order's intrigues. I'm leaving a scrysphere with one of his charming little disciples."

"What does she think it is?" Isiem asked, amused. He took a candle from the bag, lit it, and thrust the stub end into a holder. "A sweetheart's necklace to remember you by?"

"Something like that." Sitting on the bare stone floor, Oreseis began winding the barbed prayer chain around his calves in preparation for his nightly communion. "It *is* a well-made piece. And I gave it some small enchantment to make it useful, so she'll keep wearing it even when she finds a handsome new Hellknight to take my place in her bed."

"Clever."

"If you'd done something like it for your diabolist, we might not have to be here now."

"If I had tried something like that on her, I certainly wouldn't be here now. Velenne was not a forgiving woman." Isiem moved across the room and sat crosslegged on his bed. The blankets were coarse wool, scratchy under his thighs. Leaning back, he willed himself to relax, waiting for the candle's visions to begin. "But she is not in Citadel Enferac."

"Does that disappoint you?"

"It relieves me. Shouldn't you be praying?"

"Of course." Oreseis relaxed into his bonds for a moment, then shifted into a kneeling position, driving the chains into his legs as the barbs were caught between his flesh and the floor. Blood began to seep into his petitioner's robe, already crusted with the residue of past prayers. "Shouldn't you?"

"I prefer magic to piety."

"They are one and the same. You know this."

They are not, Isiem thought. The candle's smoke reached for him, redolent of burning hair and bubbling fat, and under that a whisper of dark, sweet incense.

He closed his eyes and inhaled.

They left Citadel Enferac the next day.

Twenty Hellknights and armigers traveled with them. Vicarius Torchia claimed their escort was an honor guard, in addition to serving as much-needed reinforcements for Devil's Perch and its outlying settlements, but Isiem knew that the Hellknights' true purpose was to keep an eye on their Nidalese allies—and, perhaps, to delay them as well. Had they been traveling alone, the shadowcallers might have used magic to speed their journey, but they could not leave the Hellknights behind, and they did not have spells enough for their entire company.

So they rode. They made a motley company: the signifers in crimson cloaks, the Nidalese on black steeds woven of spells and shadow, and scattered between them, like copper beads between gems, the curly-coated, potbellied goats that bore their food and supplies.

Isiem thought the goats looked faintly absurd with their bulging panniers and strapped-on water barrels, but they could survive on poorer fodder—and less of it—than horses or mules, and they were sure-footed on the rocky mountain trails. The Hellknights lost their first destrier to a broken leg on the second day, but the goats never stumbled.

There was much for them to stumble on. The western Menador Mountains were not as high or cold as some of Avistan's other ranges, but they were deadly nonetheless. Citadel Enferac sat above a valley that fed its horses and supplied its soldiers. To reach the lowlands of Devil's Perch, they had to go up before they could go down. It was not an easy journey.

They began their journey amid pale granite, gnawed by ancient glaciers and sliced by rivers. Canyons furrowed the peaks; treacherous scree slopes skirted their bases. Icy mists billowed down from the blue-white glaciers above them, sweeping over the riders and their mounts in ghostly crystalline veils.

"It must be difficult to reach the citadel in winter," Isiem said to the Hellknights' leader, a scarred and stocky signifer named Erevullo, as they rode through a pass that was little more than a crooked crack in the mountains. Walls of sheer stone hemmed them in on either side, close enough to bump the heavily laden goats' burdens. A single heavy snowfall would block it, Isiem judged; a hard spring rain would flood it. Splintered bruises in the walls showed where rain-washed boulders had tumbled through in past years.

"Impossible," Erevullo confirmed. "On horseback, that is. Many of our visitors come by other means. The rest must wait until spring."

"Doesn't that hinder your work in the field?"

"Not as much as you might imagine. Most of our work is done by single agents. As we seldom rely on brute force, it hardly matters that we cannot easily send armies in winter." The signifer shifted his weight in the saddle, trying to find a more comfortable position. "It is true, however, that the strix complicate matters. Not only do they harry lone riders, but they hunt our imps and birds out of the sky. It's a nuisance. If we are to maintain any worthwhile presence in Crackspike, we will need alternative methods of communicating with the citadel. I may ask you to assist with that when the time comes."

"I would be honored," Isiem said. Erevullo grunted in acknowledgment, and rode on.

A week after they left the citadel, the barren snow and stone gave way to thick forests of stern green pines and silver firs. Occasional broad-leafed trees dotted the slopes with red and gold, already fading toward crinkly brown as autumn slipped into winter. One morning brought a heavy fall of wet snow. It melted by sunset, but it made Isiem grateful that they were out of the passes. Up there, the snow might have delayed them for days.

Bold black squirrels with tufted ears and red-tipped tails scolded them from the branches, mocking the armigers' threats to shoot them. Now and again Isiem glimpsed distant lakes shining like tourmalines set in silver, or heard the laughter of unseen streams chasing each other down the mountain. But for the most part it seemed to him that water was growing scarcer as they descended.

Once they stumbled across a mountain clearing where a titanic battle had been fought only days before. Mature pines were smashed like kindling around the periphery; enormous claws had gouged ten-inch tracks into their trunks. Blood and coarse brown fur littered one patch of churned earth, and the smell of rank animal musk lingered heavy there.

Amid it all, a single chipped, white scale lay, soft rainbows shimmering in its depths like mother-of-pearl. One of the Hellknights picked it up and flipped the palm-sized scale to Erevullo.

"What do you make of that?" the Hellknight asked.

Erevullo frowned, turning the scale over in a gloved hand. "Dragon. Or drake." He gestured to the two other signifers in their party who had winged familiars. "Eyes to the sky. Most likely it's flown off after feeding, but we'll take no risks. If your pets see anything—*anything*—call the alert. I've no wish to end my service in a dragon's belly."

But none of their birds or imps saw anything. The dragon was long gone, if dragon it was, and whatever it had killed in that clearing seemed to have sated its hunger.

Isiem, awed to have crossed paths with such a powerful creature and relieved to have come no closer, kept the scale. This was an old land, he felt, and beholden to its own wild powers. Drakes and dragons were unimpressed by human thrones and gods; Cheliax might claim these lands on a map, but those who lived among these rocks had no use for its laws.

Gradually the trees dwindled to sparser, scrubbier remnants, then vanished altogether as the party continued its descent. The mountains' gray stone gave way to red and dun and white, dotted with blue-green needled bushes whose names Isiem did not know. Tall grasses swayed like golden seas between the steep wind-carved stones, while narrow-winged birds skimmed lazy circles overhead.

Isiem watched those birds for a long while. Hunters or scavengers, he didn't know; these hills were home to both vultures and hawks. But they made him think of the strix, and wonder which those would prove to be. Killers, or just eaters of the dead?

The birds dipped behind a lonely ridge to the west. Isiem watched a little longer, waiting, but they did not return. Sighing, he flicked the reins and turned away, rejoining the group that had ridden on without him.

Chapter Twelve
Crackspike

Crackspike was chaos.

Isiem had never seen anything like it. Everywhere he looked, men swarmed like ants: hammering, shouting, digging, driving. *Building*. They were willing a town out of nothing, forcing some semblance of civilization on a land of inhospitable rock and sun, and the sheer vitality of their enterprise amazed him.

The town was a bare sketch—an idea, really—amid clouds of dust. Two-thirds of its buildings were nothing but foundations and wooden frames. Enormous copper vessels and iron pans sat in stacks between piles of lumber and barrels of salt and mercury, all waiting to be used in the as-yet-unbuilt mines that were to make this place's fortune.

Most of Crackspike's people had no real homes yet; they lived in tents or covered wagons or one of the boarding houses built of mountain pinewood so green it spat sap every time a nail went in. Pigs and scrawny chickens wandered freely through the confusion, poking along the roadside in hopes of forgotten food.

A few of the buildings were finished. Alehouses, gambling parlors, a brothel whose walls were shaggy with dust-coated beads of sap. A sash of painted linen hanging from the brothel's balcony proclaimed it the Desert Rose.

Isiem had stopped under that banner, marveling at the miners' appetite for vice, when an unshaven man with a cracked silver nugget in place of a front tooth sidled up to his horse.

"It's a fine place," he said, nodding toward the banner with a smile likely meant to be encouraging. "Posie's girls can do anything you want. Be any*one* you want."

"What do you mean by that?" Oreseis inquired, nudging his shadow-steed toward them.

"Posie's only got five whores, but she taught 'em all a bit of magic. Illusion. So they can be whoever or whatever you want. You like redheads, for a few extra bits of silver you can have one for an hour, sweet as strawberries and cream. You're a dwarf who's feeling lonely and missing the ladies of your kind, well, might be one of Posie's girls could help you forget that for a while. If you don't ask her too closely about growing up in Janderhoff, anyhow." The man sucked his silver tooth, causing it to whistle through the crack. "Might find something in there that appeals even to suchlike as yourself."

"Thank you for the information," Isiem said. "We'll keep that in mind."

The man grinned, touched the brim of his hat, and walked off. Oreseis watched him, shaking his head slightly. "What was that about?"

"Entertainment. He probably knows one of the girls and is hoping we'll give her a good story to tell. Or perhaps he's just deeply concerned about our wellbeing after that long, depriving journey in the wilderness."

Oreseis's mouth twisted wryly. "No doubt. Do you really think the girls use illusions?"

"It's a simple spell for a good deal of profit. Why not?"

"It's a disgusting use of magic." Oreseis said it without heat, but Isiem knew his companion was fully capable of leveling the Desert Rose and murdering every person inside for the perceived infraction. As if the unthinking forces of the arcane needed a Nidalese shadowcaller to defend their honor.

He held his tongue and turned away. "We should go to our rooms."

They were staying in the largest and soundest of the boarding houses. Erevullo had commandeered it, and no one in Crackspike dared defy a Hellknight's order. The Chelaxians took the lower rooms, with the Nidalese assigned to quarters above them. That way, Isiem knew, it was easier for the Hellknights to watch the shadowcallers' comings and goings.

The townspeople seemed equally suspicious. Isiem caught them staring at him from the corners of their eyes and making superstitious gestures when they thought his back was turned. There were no children in Crackspike, as far as he could see, but he had no doubt that their mothers would have scooped them away from the Nidalese if there had been.

"What's wrong with them?" Oreseis muttered, annoyed, as the two shadowcallers ascended the stairs to their rooms. The steps were the only part of the boarding house that didn't have irregular beads of sap oozing along the seams, and only because so much dust was trodden into the boards that they looked like baked clay. "You'd think we were worse than the strix."

"To them, we might be," Isiem said. "They know the strix. Some might have seen them, fought them, even killed them. The black-winged ones might be dangerous, but they're familiar. We are not."

"We're human."

By our lights. But theirs? Isiem pushed open their door. Two coffins sat on the floor. There were no beds. Only the coffins, hammered together from uneven pine, each one filled halfway with coarse gravel and dirt.

"Is that a threat?" Oreseis asked blankly from the doorway. He stepped inside, eyeing the coffins. "Are we meant to infer that these people mean to bury us?"

Isiem shook his head. Realization dawned on him, and with it a wave of sudden hilarity. He sat on the floor, eyes watering with the effort it took not to laugh aloud.

"No," he managed, waving off Oreseis's suspicious look. "It's not a threat. It's a courtesy." He sifted a handful of reddish gravel through his fingers. The rocks made little knocks as they bounced off the coffin's fresh-sawn boards. "This is meant to welcome us. They think we're vampires."

"Vampires," Oreseis repeated. *"Vampires."* He sank down alongside Isiem, tapping his pale fingertips against the side of his own coffin. Then he laughed, helplessly, and Isiem joined him in shoulder-shaking, nearly silent mirth.

"They did see us walking in the sun, didn't they?" the younger shadowcaller asked between gasps for breath.

"Maybe they thought we had protection. Or were some different kind of vampire. Ancient. Shadowy. Blessed by Zon-Kuthon." Isiem shrugged. "Ask them what they thought, if it matters so much to you. But it's a common mistake. Even in Westcrown, many people thought all Nidalese were vampires."

"I only hope their information about the strix is more accurate than their vampire lore." Oreseis regarded the coffins a moment longer with amused disgust, then splashed the road dust from his face with the water set out for them and wiped his muddy hands dry.

When his companion was finished, Isiem did the same. The dust remained thick in his hair, dulling its ivory hues to beige, but a real bath would have to wait. "We'll soon find out."

They left as soon as the armigers delivered their belongings to the room. Isiem had disguised himself as an orc-blooded porter, bull-necked and thick-armed, with enough scars on his mottled gray skin to suggest that he had his reasons for seeking refuge in western Cheliax—and that asking after those reasons would be distinctly unwise.

Oreseis wore a woman's face, and made his illusionary identity as unobtrusive as Isiem's was memorable. He took the role of a wife turned widow on a hard road: sandy hair the same color as the dry desert grass, a once-pretty squarish face scored by wind and sun and weariness, gray-blue eyes that had seen love and lost it and looked on the world without hope of seeing it again.

"It's a masterpiece," Isiem said, awed by the depth of feeling in his companion's illusion.

"It's a memory," Oreseis replied. "I took her from the shadowgarms in Westcrown. She was grateful to have been rescued . . . for the first day. Then she realized that she wasn't going home." He plucked at a lock of illusory hair. "I like to remember her, now and again."

"Of course," Isiem said neutrally. He removed a tiny effigy of a pulley from one of his bags, cupping it in his palm for the moment and concentrating to add another simple spell to his illusion. When he felt the overloaded pack on his shoulders lighten to a feather's weight, he dropped the pulley back into his luggage and headed for the door. "Good luck."

Outside the sunlight was blinding and the bustle undiminished. No one raised an eyebrow at Isiem's disguise; to him it felt outlandish, but there were much stranger refugees in western Cheliax. When anyone paid him any notice, it was to sweep him with a calculating eye and call out an offer of work.

One of those offers seemed promising: unloading lumber from a logger's cart and reloading it onto the wagons of the mine overseer who had purchased the timbers. Most of the other laborers were the miners themselves, and their talk was full of rumors and dire predictions about the strix.

Isiem accepted the job immediately, although the pay—a scant handful of copper for an afternoon's hard labor—was insultingly low. He kept his head down, his mouth shut, and his ears open, hoping that the locals shared the usual prejudice against half-orcs' intelligence. Whether they thought he was a savage or a dullard, they surely *wouldn't* think he was a spy.

And they didn't. The miners spoke as freely as if he'd been just another log. They talked about Posie's girls, sweethearts back home, the wide-ranging deficiencies of their camp cook . . . but no matter where their conversation ranged, it always circled back to the strix.

"It needs answering, what they did to Chastain and her girl," one of the men muttered, hoisting another timber down from the stack. His name was Orwyn, and while he held no supervisory rank as far as Isiem could tell, the others listened when he spoke. "One thing to kill a man who can defend himself. Even the way those bastards do it—always slow, never a clean death. But what they did to those helpless women and children . . ."

"You can't kill children," the stolid, slow-moving man next to him agreed.

"It needs answering," Orwyn repeated.

"Who's Chastain?" Isiem asked. "I'm new."

"Not that new," Orwyn said, "or you didn't come from the east. Otherwise you'd know what we meant already."

"West," Isiem said. Improvising, and taking a gamble on his audience's sympathies, he added: "Pezzack."

That turned their puzzled looks to slow nods and tightened mouths. Pezzack was a hotbed of dissent and sedition in tightly controlled Imperial Cheliax. Rebels and malcontents gravitated to that chaotic outpost in the west—but, owing to the years-long blockade of its port and the military checkpoints on its roads, few reached it. Fewer left.

Openly expressing solidarity with a Pezzacki was stupid to the point of suicide, particularly with a company of Hellknights in town, but judging from the way the men around him relaxed, Isiem believed he had guessed their sympathies correctly. Crackspike attracted a certain type: men who were unafraid of danger and hard work, but on whom the yoke of civilization sat uneasy. Especially diabolists' civilization. They might not say it, but most of these men felt they shared some common ground with the people of Pezzack.

"Chastain's from Whisper Creek," Orwyn said, punctuating his story with grunts as he heaved timbers down from the wagon. "Halfway between here and Blackridge. Not much of a town, but gentler than this. Posie sent for her to work at the Desert Rose. She brought her daughter—just four years old, sweet as a peach, most darling thing you ever saw. Posie told her that Crackspike was no place for the girl, but no mother likes to be parted from her child, and Chastain insisted.

"They traveled with a party of miners and dealers in dry goods. Flour, beans, dried meat. Always a need for food in this camp. I don't believe any of them were trained knights or the like, but they were good strong men and there were near thirty of them, not counting Chastain or her girl, so we didn't think the swoops would trouble them. They're cowardly, those vultures. They strike by night and kill the unwary. They don't risk attacking anyone who might fight back."

"They didn't this time, either," the stolid man muttered.

"No, they didn't." Orwyn spat off the side of the wagon. "Treachery and cowardice, that's all they know. Treachery and cowardice and cruelty."

"What did they do?" Isiem asked.

"First they poisoned the oxen. They'd sown crimson devilgrass all along the trails from Whisper Creek to Crackspike. There's rarely room to carry enough fodder on the wagons, so the animals have to graze as best they can. The strix knew that. The oxen ate their devilgrass and died. In agony, kicking over their traces and goring anyone foolish enough to come near. Two men died with them—one crushed under his wagon, the other struck with a horn wound that festered."

"They had no healer?" Isiem asked.

Orwyn gave him a sour look. "They didn't want an Asmodean, and there was no other to be had. You might not have heard, but Her Infernal Majestrix has taken a personal interest in our silver mines. The devil-priests don't take kindly to competition, so oftentimes it's a choice between their prayers or no one's. Chastain's party decided they'd take the gamble. So there was no one to heal their oxen, and no one to heal them.

"Next the strix shot their guide. It was an assassination. They murdered him when he wandered off the road to take a piss. No one saw them do it; there wasn't any chance to take revenge. And without their guide to read the rocks and riverbeds, the rest of the party was lost. Soon they were stranded. They didn't have enough oxen to move all the wagons, and they didn't have any way of knowing where to go. They wandered around in circles. Backed down canyons, chased after dead ends. The sun beat on them, and the heat. Shade's hard to find, for all the high rocks out there.

"Their food and water held out for a while, but in the end the desert won. And in their last extremity, when they were dying of sunstroke and thirst, the strix showed them no mercy. They swept down and butchered men too weak to fight back—and Chastain, and her child. They defiled the bodies and threw them back on the trail for the next group of travelers to find."

"It needs answering," the slow man said into the silence that followed.

"It does," Orwyn said.

"How would you answer it?" Isiem asked.

"The same way they dealt it," Orwyn replied. "Without mercy."

Chapter Thirteen
Reprisals

The whooping woke him.

It had been the better part of a week since Isiem had talked to Orwyn and the others around the timber wagons. Both he and Oreseis had spent the intervening days asking questions under a succession of guises. Mostly Isiem chose illusionary identities whose mysterious disappearances, like the Pezzacki half-orc's, could easily be laid at the Hellknights' door; when such people vanished, it burnished their knights' reputation for ruthlessness and raised few questions about where they had gone. Sometimes, so that people would not wonder why the Nidalese never showed their faces, he went undisguised.

But whatever face he chose, and whomever he approached, Isiem learned little about the strix. Wild rumors and speculation abounded, but accurate observations seemed scarcer than waterfalls in the desert.

Some said the strix were winged devils in more than name—that the diabolists of House Thrune had deliberately summoned them from Hell and set them loose on the people of western Cheliax so that they could offer protection from the threat they themselves had created. Some said the mine overseers had struck a secret bargain with the strix, allowing them to feast on lazy and unruly workers in exchange for leaving the others unmolested. A few claimed—never when they knew Isiem was listening—that the strix were not living creatures at all, but rather Nidalese thralls who had escaped from the shadowcallers' control and hid in the deep recesses of Devil's Perch because no light could reach them there.

The only sure thing anyone knew was that the strix had murdered Chastain, her daughter, and everyone accompanying them—and that the outrage demanded retribution.

That thought leaped to the fore of Isiem's mind when he heard the whoops that morning. Pushing off his blankets, he went to the window and pulled the curtain to the side.

The street below was crowded with cheering men gathered around four sweat-stained riders on lathered horses. A dark-winged figure staggered on foot between the riders, and two more broken, winged forms dragged in the dust behind them. The ropes that bound the corpses were not tied around their ankles, but threaded through gashes in their calves.

Fastening his shadowcaller's robe as he went, Isiem hurried down the stairs.

Every citizen in Crackspike seemed to have mobbed the street. He glimpsed the Hellknights pushing forward through the fray, Posie's girls leaning bare-shouldered on their balcony, and miners and laborers who had come fresh from their work, wearing clothes sweated through and caked with dust so many times that the men seemed made of mud.

The creature who had attracted all their notice seemed oblivious to the crowd. The strix hobbled between the riders with his head lowered between his enormous, bedraggled black wings, unresponsive to the curses hurled his way or the occasional gob spat on him by a spectator. The riders and their horses, spattered with similar missiles, were less restrained; they answered with imprecations fiery enough to burn a Hellknight's ears, or—if the spitter was foolish enough to be identifiable, and in reach—vicious blows from their quirts.

Isiem ignored them, along with the occasional shrieks from the bystanders they struck. It was the strix that interested him.

This one was a juvenile, he guessed, and male. Head to toe, it was the color of coal. Its eyes were enormous and eerily luminous, reflecting a green-violet iridescence in the bright hot sun. There were no whites or pupils that Isiem could see, although it was difficult to be sure with the creature's head bowed. Its ears were thin and sharp, lying flat against its skull. It went barefoot, its toes and fingers alike tipped with short translucent talons, and its clumsy pigeon-like gait suggested that it did not often find reason to walk upon the ground.

Above all, however, it was the strix's wings that commanded attention. Bent and broken, they still towered over the men on horseback. The feathers were a glossy, oily black, touched with a peacock shimmer like the plumage on a loon's throat. There was an undeniable grandeur to those wings, even as the creature who bore them tottered crippled and diminished on the earth.

"How did you catch him?" one of the whores called down.

"Hunting," the lead rider shouted back. "This one"— he jerked the strix's rope as if the creature were a balky dog on a leash"—thought he'd catch a few of our mules for dinner. That was his mistake. The other two came to free him. That was theirs. They didn't care to be taken alive, so I thought it only right to oblige them."

"Are there any others?" Paralictor Erevullo asked.

The rider hesitated, winding and unwinding the reins around his hand several times before answering. "I can't be sure," he admitted, "but I don't think so. These two rushed in blind, they were so upset we'd caught their friend. Any others would've done the same, if they were out there. Anyway, we didn't see no more."

Erevullo nodded curtly. He gestured with a gauntleted hand to the battered strix. "We will take that one. In the name of Her Imperial Majestrix Abrogail II."

The rider opened his mouth to protest, then closed it, returning the Hellknight's nod even more brusquely. "What about the others?"

"Sell them to your tavern to stuff as a showpiece. Cut them apart and sell the pieces as keepsakes. Or just throw them by the roadside and let dogs feast on the corpses." Erevullo shrugged. "They are of no use to us. Do as you will." The paralictor turned his flinty eyes on Isiem. "It is said that the Kuthites of Nidal are unrivaled in extracting information from their charges. I trust this reputation is well founded."

"It is," Isiem answered.

"They don't speak no civilized tongue," the rider interjected. "Just screeches and devil squawks. We couldn't get nothing sensible out of none of them."

"Language is no obstacle," Isiem said. He turned to Erevullo. "Is there somewhere we might work without interruption?"

The paralictor waited for the rider to untie the strix's rope from his saddle horn. Upon receiving it, Erevullo tossed the mudstained hemp to Isiem. "One of the alehouses has a cellar. They were using it as a dungeon of sorts. It's yours." He motioned to one of the other Hellknights, a signifer whose clean-shaved scalp was tattooed with spiked swirls of red and black. "Odarro. Show the shadowcallers where they will work."

"This way." The bald signifer turned on his heel, leaving the riders and the crowd to look on in confusion that soon turned to abuse of the two remaining strix. Whether their victims were alive or not, the people of Crackspike seemed all too happy to beat them and spit on their feathered remains.

Tugging his captive along behind him, Isiem left them to their sport.

The cellar Erevullo had spoken of was beneath the Long-Bottomed Lady, the largest of Crackspike's three ramshackle taverns. It was a cramped and dingy space, illumined by wobbly shafts of light that spilled through the tavern's floorboards. Barrels of beer and jars of white whisky crowded every available inch. A coating of sandy grit clouded the vessels, although the tavern always drank through its stock within days.

It was only on account of the liquor that the owners of the place had undertaken the trouble of digging a cellar and laying in a wooden floor. Spirits were unconscionably expensive in Crackspike, which had to import all its necessities across miles of hard road. The owners of the Long-Bottomed Lady wanted to protect their investment, and the easiest way to keep thirsty miners from stealing their beer was to sit on it.

Isiem wondered whether his work would dent their appetites. He doubted it. If anything, strix blood seemed to whet thirsts in Crackspike. And there would likely be a great deal of blood before he was done.

He wanted to begin gently, though. Confidences won through trust were worth more than secrets extracted through torture; the latter were often fragmentary and peppered with lies. Many Kuthites chose to rely on torture anyway, but Isiem valued effectiveness above piety.

The cellar had no chairs. He rolled two of the smaller barrels from their nooks, arranging them so that they faced one another across a short space. Touching the small clay talisman of a ziggurat in his pocket, Isiem murmured the words that would grant him the gift of tongues. He'd prepared the spell with the intention of questioning some of the miners whose Taldane was shaky, but it would serve as well with the strix.

"Speak to me," he said. The words had an odd, doubled echo as they left his lips. Isiem heard his own voice clearly, but just as clear were the stretched, shrill vowels and harsh plosives of the strix's tongue. He was never sure what the listener heard—but it hardly mattered, as long as he was understood. "What is your name?"

The strix gave him a hostile, unblinking stare. It did not sit on the barrel as Isiem did, but perched on top, its clawed toes grasping the wooden edge. In this light its eyes showed no iridescence; they were yellow as a hawk's. Faint striations of darker gold, converging in the center of each eye, expanded and contracted as it breathed.

"You should answer me." Isiem drew the holy symbol of Zon-Kuthon out from under his shirt and let it rest pointedly upon his chest. "Sooner or later, you must. And 'later' will come at a cost."

"I am not afraid. Pain is nothing." The strix's voice had the same odd echo as his own: familiar human words twinned to piercing shrills and whistles only barely recognizable as speech. Its true voice seemed extraordinarily hoarse; judging from the chapped skin around the strix's lipless mouth and the sunken, bruised-looking circles around its eyes, that was a symptom of its recent hard use rather than the creature's natural tone.

It made the creature's bravado even more wearying. The strix would break. Under the ministrations of a Pangolais-trained torturer, all men broke. And all dwarves, and all orcs. A strix would be no different, however alien its appearance.

Isiem had had his fill of breaking brave rebels in Westcrown. It was tedious, the progression from braggadocio to stoicism to abject begging. Such men clung to loyalty and principle as though it were a raft that could save them. It never did, but the Nidalese wizard had long lost his taste for snapping their fingers to make them let go.

"I could show you otherwise very quickly," Isiem said, "but I will give you the chance to help yourself first. Again: what is your name?"

"*Kirraak,*" the strix cried. Whether it was a name or a curse, the spell didn't translate it.

Isiem decided to accept it as a name. "Kirraak," he repeated, altering the sound to fit on a human tongue. "How were you captured?"

For a long time the strix did not answer. Its chest heaved with silent, desperate breaths. Then it cocked its head downward and veiled its eyes with semitransparent membranes that slid across them from the side, instead of lowering vertically like its true eyelids. "Stupidity. They left a hurt mule behind. I wanted it. Some of their dogs wanted it too. I was butchering the dead mule when the dogs came upon me from behind. They kept me from flying." The strix motioned toward one of the black wings hanging broken from its back. Up close, it smelled of dust and wild oily feathers and a rank undercurrent of infection. "I could not escape when the men came back to see what their dogs were quarreling over."

"And your companions?"

"Untie me." The strix lifted its head and held its arms out, showing him its rope-chafed wrists. The coarse hemp was spotted with blood, red as Isiem's own. "Untie me, and I will say."

Kirraak tensed as Isiem drew a small knife to cut its bonds. The muscles at the bases of its wings flexed, and it crouched slightly, gathering its strength. Isiem noted its tension but continued sawing at the rope.

He wasn't surprised when the strix attacked. He *was* surprised at how fast it was. Isiem was already ducking away when Kirraak snapped the last few strands between its wrists, but he barely had time to put a barrel between them before the strix seized a nearby bottle of brandy and hurled it at his head. The bottle shattered on the wall inches away, raining liquor and glass shards. One splinter nicked Isiem's chin, another his cheek.

"*Krevaar!*" the strix screamed. "I tell you *nothing!*"

Isiem didn't waste his breath on a reply. He shielded his eyes and dodged behind a second barrel. Another bottle hurtled past, clipping the side of his head, but the strix itself did not come. Glancing back, Isiem realized that the strix's wings gave him the advantage in this confined space; Kirraak flinched every time the wounded appendages struck anything, and the creature could hardly move without smacking its massive wings into a wall or keg.

It had fashioned a crude sort of knife from the remains of a broken bottle, though, and Isiem guessed that might prove more lethal than its ineptly thrown missiles. If the strix got close enough to use it.

He kicked a wine rack toward his adversary, sending bottles tumbling everywhere. Two of them slammed into Kirraak's infected wounds, eliciting an ear-splitting shriek and causing the strix to drop its improvised blade.

Isiem seized the chance. Thrusting a hand in the strix's direction, he chanted quickly, nearly tripping over the familiar words in his haste. Magic gathered in him like lightning and lanced out, surrounding the strix in a crackling black halo. Needles of dark energy stabbed into Kirraak.

The strix collapsed, keening in agony. Its makeshift knife cracked under its body, cutting into the creature's arm and chest, but it hardly seemed to notice this insult compared to the wracking pain of Isiem's spell. As the strix's shrieks gave way to whimpers, and then into insensible sobs, Isiem straightened and brushed the glass flinders from his hair.

"You should have answered my questions," he told the strix without rancor. He had not, of course, really expected that Kirraak would. The rebels in Westcrown seldom did; why would a strix be any different? This was just another step in their dance, predictable and inevitable.

Kirraak made no answer. Isiem hadn't expected one. He picked through the shattered glass and liquor pooled around the semiconscious strix, selecting several of the longest, smoothest fragments and laying them atop a nearby barrel. He was careful to arrange them where the shafts of wintry sunlight made them glint in the cellar's gloom.

When he had all the shards he needed, Isiem retied the crippled strix's arms and tossed the rope over a rafter, hoisting Kirraak up onto its clawed toes. Standing in that partly suspended position wouldn't hurt immediately, but in a few minutes it would start to ache, and in an hour or so it would become unbearable.

As an afterthought, and as a courtesy to the Long-Bottomed Lady's guests, Isiem gagged the strix with the wine-sodden remnants of a burlap sack. Then he started another, simpler incantation, and passed a pale hand over the stained rips in his robe. The torn threads knitted back together; the stains faded from the cloth. In moments there was no evidence of his prisoner's defiance.

The illusion of infallibility was crucial to the fear a skillful torturer inspired. Nothing his victims did could be seen to hurt him, or even interrupt his plans. Everything that happened in his domain had to serve his purpose. The strix's struggles, the shattered bottles, the wasted brandy—all of it, as far as the world would ever know, was part of Isiem's designs.

Isiem picked up a sliver of glass and drove it through the joint of the strix's infected wing. Pus and dark blood spurted out. Kirraak screamed again, weakly; its head jerked up once and fell back down, limp.

Coldly Isiem took a second sliver of glass from the barrel and held it poised, waiting for the strix's eyes to flutter open again.

Everything had its purpose.

"Why did you let it fight back?" Oreseis asked.

Isiem shrugged, spooning pork-flecked oat mush from the pot the Hellknights had brought up for them. To preserve their air of inhumanity, the Nidalese did not eat where anyone might see them; instead they requisitioned food from the Hellknights and sent their waste back the same way. The subterfuge worked well enough, but he could wish the Hellknights indulged in better fare. The Chelaxians subsisted on iron rations boiled in conjured water: oat mush, barley porridge, wheat gruel dotted with shreds of dried apples or rock-hard sausage. Practical, and perhaps good for discipline, but even by the standards of a Nidalese ascetic, a Hellknight's trail dinner was a sorry meal.

Still, he'd choked down worse. Isiem thrust his spoon into the gruel and sat on the side of his bed. "I always give them the chance to fight."

Oreseis had already finished his own meal. He sat with his spellbook propped up on bent knees, making a half-hearted pretense of studying the next day's magic. "But why?"

"So I can be justified in what comes after." Seeing that the other shadowcaller did not understand, Isiem sighed and set his spoon down. "By giving my captives a choice, I give them responsibility for what follows. If they choose to answer readily, they escape pain. If they choose defiance, they suffer for it . . . but they know that it was their choice."

"How virtuous," Oreseis said, smirking.

"Maybe." Isiem swallowed a mouthful of gruel, trying not to taste it. The pork, somehow soggy and tough at the same time, actually made it worse. "But it is useful. Men who feel culpable for their own suffering are conflicted. Guilty, angry, distracted. Easier to break." He took another bite, wondering if Oreseis would believe the lie.

It *was* easier to break a man who felt he'd brought his own woes upon himself. But not precisely for the reasons he'd given.

The true reason Isiem gave them the chance to fight was because putting the choice on the victim—putting the *fault* on the victim—removed it from his own conscience. Framing the torture as the consequence of the victim's decision, rather than his own, absolved the torturer of guilt. And after Westcrown, Isiem could not work without that absolution.

Oreseis closed his book and stretched his legs. "Erevullo wants one of us to help his signifers enchant their devilstongue relay." Seeing Isiem's puzzlement, he added: "It's how they intend to communicate with Citadel Enferac while the passes are snowed in. Evidently their usual methods tend to get intercepted by strix spears."

"So I've been told. What's this relay?"

The younger shadowcaller shrugged. "I didn't see the thing clearly when they were unloading it, and of course its magic is unfinished, but it appears to be a brazier of gold and iron, set with rubies and black stones. Obsidian, maybe. I couldn't see clearly. Erevullo told me that they burn the tongues of devils in its flames, and thus carry their messages through Hell back to Citadel Enferac, where other braziers exist to receive the infernal words."

"Can anyone use it, or just diabolists? Does every relay communicate with every other? How much of a delay is there between sending a message and receiving one?"

Oreseis gave him an incredulous look. "How would I know? I've never used it. I haven't even *seen* it in any meaningful way. But obviously we should learn more."

"Yes." Isiem considered it for a moment. "Offer to assist the Hellknights with their relay. Learn what you can. The Umbral Court will be grateful for your report."

Oreseis tilted his head slightly, studying him. "You're the better wizard."

"Making you the less obvious spy."

"And the less adept one." The younger wizard's mouth twisted into an expression that was not quite grimace and not quite smile. "Don't mistake me. I'm honored that you offer me the opportunity. But should I miss some detail that you would have caught, the Umbral Court will be displeased with us both. I cannot imagine the relay is that simple, or Erevullo would not have asked us to help with it—nor would he be so cavalier about giving us the chance to study it."

"Or he wants us to take note of Citadel Enferac's efficiency," Isiem said pointedly, "so that we understand how valuable they are as allies and how dangerous as enemies. We could second-guess his motives for hours and it wouldn't matter. What *matters* is that we have the opportunity to learn more about this device, and you have the skill to study it without arousing suspicion." He softened his tone slightly. "You do have the skill, you know. The Umbral Court would not have tasked you with this assignment if you were lacking."

"Why won't you do it?"

Because I don't want to go back to Nidal. Knowing a secret valuable to either the Hellknights or the Umbral Court would give them a reason to hunt him down, and Isiem intended to offer them none. But what he said was: "Because I have a strix to break."

"Ah." Oreseis nodded. "That need not delay you long. There is a quicker way. Quicker, and holier."

"Oh?"

The younger shadowcaller stood, put his spellbook away, and retrieved something else from his pack: a round object, about the size of his hand, muffled in black velvet.

He held the nightglass up, still veiled. "Send one to the shadow, and he will give us all his kin. Another nation under Zon-Kuthon."

Chapter Fourteen
Flames

That night he dreamed of Pangolais.

Once more Isiem walked among its black-leaved shadows. Birds perched in the trees: crows and ravens of enormous size, strangely motionless. Bone tables filled the great square, as they did during the Festival of Night's Return, but instead of white-spiced dumplings and radishes cut into translucent flowers, the tables held living people. Each one was partially flayed and held in place by spiked chains.

His mother was among them, and his little brother Theron, who hadn't aged a day since Isiem left Crosspine. Next to them were Ascaros, Helis, Dirakah—the living and the dead, faithful and apostate, bound together in silent suffering.

Among them walked men and women in faceless gray cowls. Isiem, too, wore a hooded robe, and he carried a flensing knife in one hand and a chain in the other. He knew, somehow, that it was his duty to finish flaying the victims and bind them more tightly to their altars—and they *were* altars, not mere tables; all of this was a feast laid out for Zon-Kuthon—but he cringed from doing it.

He wasn't the only one to have such qualms. Other hooded figures let their knives slip in purposeful accidents, angling their blades to cut the captives' chains from their flesh . . . and the moment they did, the chains struck up at them like steely serpents, sinking barbed fangs into the would-be benefactors' arms and legs.

Screaming and kicking, the torturers were dragged off their feet. They were not pulled down to the altars, but simply held immobile, as if in offering to someone else. Their hoods fell back to show their faces, and Isiem saw that all their eyes were raw red pits. *Crows' food.*

The birds in the trees took flight, and the rush of their ebon wings filled the air like thunder. Isiem heard the hungry birds shrieking as they circled overhead, waiting to dive. Lifting a hand to shield his own eyes with his sleeve, he tried to take cover behind one of the altars.

A chain stopped him. It lashed around his elbow and climbed to his wrist, crossing his palm with sharpened steel. Blood trickled from the punctures, and suddenly the living chain wrapped around Isiem's arm wasn't a chain at all, but the fleshy tongue of a Joyful Thing, lapping greedily at the blood it drew. It held him down and *away*, preventing him from taking shelter behind the altar.

Isiem screamed. The crows echoed his cry, mocking his pain in a hundred avian croaks and shrieks, and then they poured down in a whirlwind of black feathers. The chains struck at them, too, spearing the birds midflight and binding them alongside the Nidalese to serve as new dishes in the same savage feast. Ebon feathers filled Isiem's vision, and pain—crows' beaks or chains' barbs, he didn't know, couldn't see—stabbed his every limb.

He sat up. Sweat dappled his brow and dampened his sheets. The crows' hunger still echoed in his ears.

Isiem wiped the perspiration from his face and stood, his chest heaving. He could still hear the crows—and as the nightmare's grogginess faded, he realized that the screeches were not an echo of his dream. They were coming from outside. The hollow boom of an explosion sounded an instant later, and then the faraway thud of a body, or bodies, falling to the earth.

He went to the window, pulling the dusty drape aside. Firelight twinkled from Crackspike's solitary street—more light than could be accounted for by taverns' lanterns and miners' torches.

The town was burning.

Curtains of flame swung across the Desert Rose's windows. The Long-Bottomed Lady was an inferno. The sap-filled wood burned like firecrackers, spitting and popping loudly. Smoke flooded the street and rose from the buildings in a great black shroud, suffocating the stars.

Amid it all, people scrambled and panicked and wept, watching their friends and livelihoods devoured by the blaze. One of the Long-Bottomed Lady's owners stood alone outside his tavern, throwing buckets of sand uselessly into the fire's maw. On the other side of the street, a drunk man fought to saddle a white-eyed horse, and got his head kicked in for his trouble. He fell into the smoke, twitching, and the horse bolted into the night.

Black-winged figures wheeled through the pillars of rising smoke. Isiem could barely see them from his window, but he knew that they were strix. He counted twenty or thirty, perhaps more, from the limited vantage of his window. Mostly they kept well out of bowshot, but now and again one of them would swoop down to pick off a vulnerable straggler. In the confusion of the fire, no one fought back.

Where are the Hellknights? They should have been out there protecting Crackspike's people, but Isiem saw no sign of Erevullo or his men. Oreseis, too, had vanished.

Cursing, Isiem pulled on his clothes and grabbed his spellbook, shoving it under his shirt to save it from the flames. He tied a damp handkerchief around his mouth and nose to screen some of the smoke. Then, bracing himself for the onslaught, he hurried downstairs.

The doorways were haloed in wavering scarlet. Smoke rushed up the staircase's slanted ceiling like a ghostly river running in reverse. Pools of oil made burning lakes on the floor—too many pools, and too few of them ringed with smoke-dulled glass.

Those weren't broken lamps. Someone had poured that oil there.

But how could a strix have sneaked into Crackspike to set up an arson? And how would it have known that the Hellknights were unprepared to stop it?

Someone's conspiring with them.

But he had no time to wonder who or why. Not yet. Gasping through the smoke, Isiem plunged through the last door into the street. Behind him, the boarding house burned.

He hadn't expected a fight—while traveling with the Hellknights, he hadn't expected anyone to *offer* a fight—and was poorly prepared for one. Few of his spells were likely to be useful, and fewer would be able to reach the strix in the sky.

There was even less he could do to help the townspeople; Isiem had never been a gifted healer, and his god was not, in any event, especially inclined to mercy. He'd serve them best by driving off their enemies.

With that thought in mind, Isiem looked for the best place to begin.

Crackspike held no good fighting ground. Its buildings offered the only cover in easy reach, and they were all afire—another sign of a conspirator, for he doubted the strix could have set so many buildings alight, and so thoroughly, in the space of a few minutes. But there was a clear space where a damaged tent had collapsed, smothering its own small fire under the weight of its heavy canvas. Isiem went there, ignoring the cries of the wounded.

His plain gray robes gave him some cover in the night. Enough, he hoped, to trick the eyes of aerial foes scanning for targets through smoke and chaos. Isiem pulled his hood over his white hair and waited.

He didn't have to wait long. Two strix dove through the night, so close that the tips of their wings nearly touched, and swept directly overhead as they pursued a man who had just stumbled from the Long-Bottomed Lady's outhouse. The man had one leg in his pants and the other bare. The empty pant leg flapped between his feet, tripping him with every step. Drunk, unarmed, and hobbled by his own clothing, he had no chance of escape.

But he made good bait.

Isiem waited until they were past. The strix never slowed; they seemed completely unaware of him. Perhaps his shadow-gray cloak fooled them, or the scattered fires played tricks with their night vision. Perhaps they were just so intent on their prey, and so certain of their enemies' disarray, that it never occurred to them that a real threat might be lurking in the dark.

He raised his hands, and a flare of dazzling golden motes erupted around the strix like a plume of dragon's breath in the night. Shimmering dust coated their wings, their hands, their eyes—and, abruptly blind, they careened out of the sky.

If the strix had been higher, they might have escaped disaster; even blind, they might have stayed airborne long enough for Isiem's spell to wear off. But they were already brushing the rooftops, and diving lower still, when he struck. They hit the ground hard, one after the other, and out of nowhere a girl was on them, bashing their heads with a burning brand. She wept as she swung the club, but it did nothing to weaken her blows. In seconds both strix were dead, the bloody pulp of their brains seeping through the soft glitter of Isiem's spell.

"Shadowcaller!" It was Erevullo's voice, although amplified far beyond any level human lungs could sustain. "We are here! West of the stable! Join us!"

Isiem looked that way, but through the screen of burning buildings he could see nothing. The half-dressed man that the strix had been hunting was already gone. Above, more black-winged figures wheeled, dipping occasionally as they picked off fleeing Crackspikers.

He took a step westward, then paused and glanced at the girl who had killed the fallen strix. Her brown hair had come loose of its pins, tumbling over wide dark eyes and a snub nose. Traces of paint clung to her lips, almost as bright as the blood on her hands. She was one of Posie's girls, although he could not recall her name.

"Get out," he told her.

She shook her head, frustration and fear plain on her face even in the murky firelight. "They're shooting everyone who runs."

"Use your spells. You have them, don't you?" She nodded, confirming his guess. Isiem went on. "Disguise yourself as one of them. Crippled, so you have to walk. The strix don't kill their own—if there's any question in their minds, anything at all, they won't risk it."

"I can't do the wings." The girl dropped her club. She stared at the bloody wood blankly, as if unsure where it had come from. When her gaze fell across the bodies of the strix she'd killed, she shuddered and wiped her hand on her thigh, leaving a stuttered smear. "The spells Posie taught us aren't that strong."

"Shadowcaller!" Erevullo called again.

Isiem bit his lip. He plucked a small blue bottle from an inner pocket of his robes and, wondering why even as he did it, flipped the vial at the girl.

She caught it reflexively, then stared at the tiny bottle in confusion. "What's this?"

"Your way out. Drink it and run." He didn't wait to see if she listened. Weaving the same spell that he'd imbued into the potion—a stronger version of the minor glamer that, he guessed, the girl had used to hide from the diving strix for a few seconds—Isiem wrapped himself in a shroud of invisibility and walked away.

He went westward, but he went cautiously, and he took a wide swing south instead of heading in a straight line. Any strix who understood Taldane would have heard Erevullo's call and would know to expect Isiem's coming, and he might make easy prey for such a hunter.

Best, then, to be wary.

Past the stables, he saw the Hellknights. A small brazier of gold and black iron sat in the middle of their circle, its gems twinkling ruddily with reflected flames. It seemed the signifers had just begun their work when they were attacked; jars and vials of spell components were scattered at their feet, and a sack of withered, fleshy masses slumped open by the brazier.

Oreseis and Erevullo were with them, but only a third of the Hellknights' number were there, and they were on the verge of being overwhelmed. *Where are the rest of them?*

The Hellknights had overturned several supply wagons to form a semicircular breastworks. The fortification offered them scant protection from aerial attackers, though, and while the signifers' magic kept the strix at bay, they were quickly running out of spells. Their horses were gone, scattered by terror or shot down by the strix.

Charred and lightning-blasted strix corpses littered the rocks around them. The survivors stayed out of spellshot, but they kept the Hellknights surrounded, waiting for an opportunity to strike. In the meantime, they continued to pick off fleeing Crackspikers. Isiem saw the corpse of the man from the Long-Bottomed Lady's outhouse sprawled in a ditch nearby, three flint-tipped throwing spears in his back. He never had gotten his pants on.

Off to the side of the signifers' huddle, a lone strix sat motionless under folded black wings. Silver and glass glinted amid its ruined feathers, studding the joints of its wings: Isiem's needles and the shards of broken bottles from the Long-Bottomed Lady's cellar. The Hellknights hadn't taken them out.

Why is he here? Isiem wondered, before he realized the obvious answer. Oreseis needed to stage a plausible escape for his captive so that the other strix would take their wounded kinsman home. Presumably the strix, once given to the shadow, was supposed to sneak away while the signifers pretended to be distracted by their work on the devilstongue relay. Then he—or the shadow that lived in his flesh—could betray his rescuers from within.

The attack had thrown that plan into confusion. The Hellknights appeared to have actually forgotten Kirraak while fighting for their own lives, but the captive strix seemed unable or unwilling to break for freedom.

And Kirraak's presence also explained why the strix continued to harry the Hellknights, even though they had already lost several of their number to the signifers' spells. They could see what the humans had done, and they would not abandon one of their kin to that torture.

Isiem wondered whether their courage would kill them. If Oreseis had already completed his ritual and given Kirraak to the shadow, saving him could be fatal to the strix. If they took their comrade from the Hellknights and returned him to their tribe, the shadow that lived in his body would betray the location of their lair. The Hellknights would have every advantage in their attack . . . and the Kuthites of Nidal, with their nightglass, would be able to condemn all the strix to the Midnight Lord's thrall. Every last one of them, given to the shadow. Chained to the same altars that already claimed Nidal.

It would save dozens of human lives. Hundreds, perhaps. Even the strix would survive, after a fashion.

That was a worthy goal. Wasn't it? Victory with fewer deaths?

Crouched invisibly by the stables' covered well, Isiem tried to decide what to do.

There was a chance that he could help the Hellknights escape from their pinned position. One of the spells he had prepared the previous night struck fear in the hearts of those it touched. He had intended to use it to terrify his prisoner with visions of possession, but it would work just as well to distract the strix from their attack on the Hellknights. It might even send them fleeing.

But something held him back from casting. The desperation with which Kirraak had fought him in the cellar, the dream of crows and hungry altars . . . or maybe just his old wish, that half-buried childish longing in the

Dusk Hall, to finally be *free* of Nidal and its curse and his servitude to a god he had never loved, but only feared.

Wasn't this what he had wanted? Wasn't this why he had sought the assignment in Westcrown, and then leaped at the chance to work still farther afield? Everything that Isiem had done and planned since his apprenticeship had been calculated so that he might have this very chance. And now that it lay within his grasp, he hesitated.

He felt no great loyalty to Erevullo and his Hellknights, nor even to Oreseis. They were servants of a conqueror who had come to eradicate an entire people—the Chelaxians for silver to fuel their imperial ambitions, the Nidalese for worse.

The strix might be monsters, but even monsters did not deserve that fate. And yet Isiem did not raise a finger to help them, either. It was not in him to turn against his former comrades.

Almost as if he could sense that no answer would be forthcoming from the missing shadowcaller, Erevullo turned back to his own men. "Barseno."

"My lord." The Hellknight's gruff answer carried clearly through the night, despite the crackle of burning buildings and the fearsome devil-visaged helm that masked his face.

"Prepare to lead us out. Mirenna: the stone." There must have been some hesitation, for after a pause Erevullo spoke again, with a sharper edge. *"Now.* We have no choice."

Isiem couldn't hear the subordinate signifer's answer, if there was one. The Hellknights began gathering their weapons and preparing to move out. A hulking man dressed in full plate armor—Barseno, he presumed—readied his shield, raising it high to ward himself and Erevullo against aerial attacks.

As two others covered her with thin bone wands, a female signifer raised a black-veined amethyst to the sky and slashed the palm of her other hand. She gripped the jewel tightly in her bloody fist, holding it for the span of three heartbeats. Then the amethyst shattered with a crack like a frost-burst tree. The signifer was thrown back against the wagons; she cried out in pain, but no one looked her way. All eyes were riveted on the winged devil-woman who stood where the stone had broken. Starlight seemed to surround her in a silvery halo, illumining every detail of her savage grace. But at the same time, the shadows in her movements seemed impossibly deep.

Isiem had never seen such a creature before, although he knew of them from his years in the Dusk Hall. Some said they were fallen angels; others claimed they merely mocked angels by imitating their forms. Whatever the truth, the fiendish warrior *looked* as lovely as any angel, but there the resemblance ended. Her weapons were barbed and brutal, and cruelty radiated from her like heat from a fire. He was awed, and more than a little frightened, that the diabolists of Cheliax had bound the fiend for Erevullo to command, and that they thought Crackspike worthy of her intercession. *How much silver is in these hills?*

The woman was tall, nearly six feet, and her raven wings towered almost as high again over her head. An ebon bow crossed her back, and a rope of burning hair sat coiled at her hip. She was sheathed in mail of glossy black scales that looked harder than steel, but clung to her movements as fluidly as silk. Bruises and cuts,

livid on her porcelain skin, accented her otherworldly
beauty rather than detracting from it.

"Cover us," Erevullo ordered, already turning away.
The devil nodded curtly and, with two dust-swirling
sweeps of her wings, launched herself into the air. Most
of the Hellknights followed Erevullo, but a few kept
their eyes on the strix, bows and wands at the ready.

What followed was a whirling, chaotic combat that
Isiem could scarcely track. Strix and devil fought in
circles through the thin cold moonlight, ascending
higher than his eye could follow and plummeting with
impossible speed. The fiend hurled her burning rope at
her victims, snaring and dragging them out of the sky
one by one. Blood and feathers fell like rain.

The woman who had slashed her hand began another
spell. Ghostly steeds materialized out of the darkness,
and the Hellknights climbed into their saddles. While
their devilish ally kept the strix from following, they
began to ride off. Kirraak remained where he was,
squatting senselessly in the dust, and the airborne strix
redoubled their attacks upon seeing their kinsman so
close to freedom. Fireballs burst in the sky, searing
Isiem's eyes with their brilliance, as the signifers
exhausted their wands to drive the strix off. Stray arrows
plummeted into the dirt. They were abandoning him.

As quietly as he could, Isiem slid away from the well's
limited cover. He had no clear idea of where he wanted
to go, or how he would get there, but the simple fact
that he could *consider* such things made him almost
giddy. He could scarcely believe that the moment was
real—that Erevullo and the Hellknights had just ridden
away, leaving him for dead.

And then the scale-clad devil swept down before
him, filling the air with the scent of blood and roses.

"Who are you, little mouse?" A mocking little smile curved her lips. Isiem had not released his spell, but invisibility was no barrier to the fiend's sight. Her catlike eyes fixed on him easily. This close, the heat radiating from her body was overwhelming. Blood wetted her lashes and ringed her eyes like red kohl. "You have the look of a deserter."

She drew an arrow and set it to her long black bow, but Isiem didn't move. He couldn't. He was fascinated: a mouse in the serpent's gaze, helplessly enraptured by the jewel-bright vision of death. She was so *beautiful* . . . and freedom was so frightening. Perhaps this was easier. The grave would hide him from Zon-Kuthon too, wouldn't it?

"The penalty for desertion is death," the fiendish archer said. And as she spoke, the strange hypnosis snapped, and Isiem remembered that he did not want to die so easily after all. He wanted to *live*.

He was almost too late. Isiem scrabbled for a simple spell—something that might actually trick a creature immune to illusions, and that he might throw out quickly enough to save himself—but he had no delusions about his chances. If the devil wanted to kill him, she would. She had her arrow nocked and ready, and there was no outrunning that.

But she wanted to toy with him, and that gave Isiem just enough time to complete his spell. White mist rose around him, thick and clammy as rain-soaked wool. It blinded them both, but only the devil had reason to care. She screeched in frustration and loosed her arrow even as Isiem threw himself backward, desperately trying to evade her.

He almost dodged. The arrow sank into his shoulder and angled upward through his arm, knocking him sideways in a blaze of pain, but it wasn't the killing shot it might have been. Isiem lay where he fell, breathing shallowly through his mouth and hoping against hope that the fiend would believe he was dead.

There was nowhere to hide. The mists only covered a small space, and he had no magical escape prepared. Fleeing on foot would be suicide. If the devil wasn't fooled, he'd have to fight—and his odds were not much better there. But it was the only option left to him, so Isiem gritted his teeth and eased his fingers silently toward the hilt of the crystalline wand tucked into his boot. He waited, listening for the slightest indication that might tell him where his adversary was, and where he could best aim the deadly cold stored in that wand.

But the bluff worked. He heard her wings flap and felt a buffeting wind as the archer returned to the air. His wound throbbed terribly, sending a new jolt of agony through his side every time he moved. Blood soaked his clothes and the dirt beneath him. The arrow might have been poisoned, or enchanted by some devilcraft. Or perhaps it had just been a lucky shot. Whatever it was, Isiem could feel his strength waning with every breath he took, and knew that if he did not heal himself soon, he would die in his shroud of mist.

Surreptitiously, he reached for another wand, this one silver rather than stone. It resembled a small version of the needles that pinned the human sculptures over the great square of Pangolais, and that was no accident. Zon-Kuthon's healing came with a high price in pain; to craft the wand, Isiem had inflicted careful wounds on a hundred weeping sacrifices, offering their misery to the Midnight Lord so that he might alleviate his own someday.

That day was now. Isiem channeled a thread of magic into the wand and was rewarded with a trickle of healing—not enough to knit his wound or even force the arrow from his flesh, but enough to keep him from the brink of death. He let his hand fall back to the rocky ground.

A clap of thunder sounded close overhead; Isiem could just make out the bluish flicker of lightning bolts through his cloud of mist. The bolts came one after another, too regular to be natural. The scent of ozone and burned flesh drifted toward him. It sounded like the fight was moving away from him, still high above . . . but blind as he was in the fog, it was impossible to be sure.

Then another arrow fell from the sky—a lucky shot or an accident of fate, Isiem would never know. It plunged into his side. Pain blazed through him, and darkness followed.

Chapter Fifteen
The Lonely Stones

Isiem awoke in ashes.

Clotted blood soaked his clothes and the covers of the spellbook tucked under his shirt. Rocks jabbed into his back like dull spears. The ground had leached all the warmth from his body, leaving him stiff and cold as a corpse.

He was mildly surprised to feel the aches and pains of life, once he was conscious enough to register them. Isiem had assumed that if the devil did not kill him, whoever found him—strix, Hellknight, or looter—would.

But he was alive, if barely so. He sat up weakly and began the grisly work of forcing the arrows out of his body. One was a wicked thing of devilish make, barbed and seemingly crafted of brittle glass. The other was not an arrow after all, but a slender spear with a shaft of hollow bone and a head of knapped gray flint.

Neither was stuck deep enough to need forcing through. Grimly Isiem pried them out, pausing twice to wipe his own blood from his hands when his palms grew too slippery to hold a firm grip. When they were out, he bandaged his wounds and drained two of the potions remaining in his satchel, healing some of the lacerations.

Pushing himself up from the ground, the Nidalese wizard plucked at the chill wet weight of his robes with a grimace. He needed new clothes. Dry ones. He'd need food, too. Water. And whatever else he could salvage of his own belongings or the signifers'.

Isiem had no intention of going back, either to Nidal or to the devilsworn heartlands of Cheliax. This was his chance to break those old bonds.

Pezzack seemed like his best chance. Erevullo had called it a viper's nest of rebellion; if a Nidalese deserter was likely to find refuge anywhere in Cheliax, it would be there.

Reaching it, however, meant a hard journey through the mountains in winter, then persuading mercenaries and malcontents to help him disappear.

Isiem was more concerned about the former than the latter. His spells gave him enough of an edge to make survival possible, but he had no illusions about his skill in woodcraft. He could conjure water to drink and sparks to ignite his campfires, but he would still have to hunt, forage, and collect firewood like any dirt-grubbing peasant. And, unlike the peasant, Isiem had little idea how to do any of those things. It had been a long time since his childhood in the Uskwood.

He needed supplies, and he needed money. The discomfort of his blood-drenched robes forgotten, Isiem hurried toward whatever remained of the Hellknights' boarding house.

His heart sank when he reached it.

The boarding house was a blackened skeleton standing in a field of wind-tossed ash. The huge copper vessels used to heat silver ore sat in the desolation like funeral urns, their gleaming sides dulled by soot. Gray flakes swirled over the bodies of men and mules in the street, blowing through the broken spokes of wagon wheels and clinging to empty windowsills like smoky snow. Nothing else moved in Crackspike, as far as Isiem could see; only the ash and the wind played among its cooling corpses.

The monochrome stillness, perfumed with the scents of smoke and fresh death, made him think of Nidal. Not a comforting thought.

Some of the dead had been crudely butchered. What had been done to them did not look like defilement for its own sake; large chunks of flesh had been cut from their thighs and torsos, as if they'd been taken for meat. There were no strix among the dead. It seemed the survivors had removed their fallen kin to pay whatever respects were customary among their kind, and had had enough time afterward to butcher their fallen foes. Whether or not any of Erevullo's Hellknights survived, clearly they had lost control of this corner of western Cheliax.

Isiem had no wish to join the dead. He needed to take what he could find quickly, and then he needed to leave.

Picking up a partly charred tent pole, he began digging through the remnants of the boarding house. Part of its roof and a few fragments of the exterior walls remained intact, but the rest of the upper floor had collapsed. He avoided the teetering roof; its fire-gnawed supports looked anything but steady, and anyway his room had been on the other side of the house.

While poking through the wreckage, Isiem heard a feeble moan rise from the rubble to his left. It didn't sound human. The shadowcaller approached cautiously, a spell on his lips, and held the pole poised equally to crush a skull or pry up a fallen beam.

Pushing a few fallen shingles away, Isiem uncovered a fan of ebony feathers and a bruised, coal-colored hand. *Strix*. The rest of the creature was buried under more rubble, but the little of its body that was visible was enough to show that it was still alive. Its fingers twitched weakly, as if grasping for the light.

Isiem stepped back uncertainly. He was not altogether surprised to discover that it was a strix trapped in the ruins; its voice had given that away. Perhaps the fiendish archer had shot it from the sky and then assumed, along with the other strix, that her victim had plummeted to its death. Perhaps one of the signifers had felled it with a spell. He couldn't see enough to discern the nature of its injuries, and it hardly mattered in any case. What *did* matter was what he intended to do about it.

The safest thing would be to ignore it and walk away. Leave the creature to its own fate. He didn't have to intervene, and there was no benefit to be gained by doing so.

Failing that, Isiem knew, he should kill the strix. They'd done their best to kill him, and the butchered bodies in Crackspike stood testament to their savagery. If this one somehow survived, it might well try to finish what its kinsfolk had begun. Even if it didn't, it had just become the only witness to his survival—the only living being, other than Isiem himself, who knew for a fact that he had abandoned his companions and survived.

And yet he began nudging the shingles and rafters aside anyway, working cautiously to avoid collapsing the wreckage. It was soon apparent that a single beam kept the creature pinned; everything else was just debris.

The strix watched him as he worked. Ash and dust covered its face in a gray mask and crusted its feathered wings, giving it the look of a gargoyle come to life. It never blinked, except when dirt fell into its odd yellow eyes, and it never spoke a word. It barely seemed to breathe. Isiem wondered whether its stillness was meant to unnerve him, or was merely meant as a safeguard against revealing any weakness to a presumed foe.

Either way, he paid it no mind. He had prepared a strength-increasing spell the previous day, having thought that he might need to disguise himself as a rough laborer or would-be soldier again, and although events had obviously bypassed that plan, it seemed the spell might still be useful. Isiem pinched a few bull's hairs from his pocket and chanted its words quietly, sifting the loose brown hairs over his own head.

When he felt the magic take hold, he grasped the end of the beam and hoisted it up, staggering a few steps sideways to free the strix before letting the wood down again. He checked its wounds visually and could see nothing obviously life-threatening. One of the devil's glassy arrows had broken off in its wing, but the injury did not appear to be crippling, and he was reluctant to come close enough to examine it more carefully, given the strix's uncertain disposition.

Still the creature stared at him, unmoving. It made no attempt to rise even after Isiem retreated another few paces to give it more space.

"Fine, then," he muttered, turning his back on the strix and picking up his discarded tent pole. Ignoring the feathered creature, he resumed poking through scorched shingles and collapsed joists.

It took the entire morning, and he was blistered and filthy when he finished, but finally Isiem dug a few worthwhile finds out of the ruins. Oreseis had left his traveling chest in the room, and although his mundane notebooks and spell components were roasted beyond recognition, the shadowcaller's spellbook—warded, as any sensible wizard's was, with all the protective spells he could muster—had survived intact.

So had some of Oreseis's potions, shielded from the worst of the heat by the warded spellbook. Isiem drank one, relieving the remainder of his arrow wounds. Then he took another and held it in his palm, bouncing the leaf-green bottle lightly. On the third bounce, almost before he realized that he'd made up his mind, Isiem tossed the vial toward the injured strix. The creature's eyes widened in surprise, but it snapped its gaunt hand up in time to catch the bottle.

"It will heal you," Isiem said. He mimed uncapping an invisible bottle and imbibing its contents. "Healing," he repeated, slower and louder, although he had no idea if the strix understood Taldane. Nothing in its expression changed. It clutched the bottle but made no move to drink, and after a moment Isiem shrugged impatiently and pocketed the remainder of the chest's contents.

He'd given the strix a chance to save itself. If it was too stupid or stubborn to use that chance, that was on its head.

Already Isiem rued the extravagance of tossing his potion to the creature—they were hardly allies, and he needed every bit of magic he possessed for himself—but something about the strix's mute patience tugged at him. Maybe it was the eyes: that shining yellow-green, so vividly reminiscent of springtime leaves, in a sea of lifeless black and gray. Maybe it was respect for the strix's stoicism, which would have done any Nidalese proud.

Or maybe it was just maudlin foolishness brought on by too many wounds. Whatever the real answer, it was past regretting. His potion was gone, whether the strix drank it or not; he would simply have to conserve the handful he had left.

Using the pole as a walking stick, Isiem hobbled away from the ruins. He spent the rest of the day scavenging through Crackspike, shooing away wrinkly-headed vultures as he relieved the dead of anything that might be useful to him. Knives, clothing, food—if it was in salvageable condition, Isiem took it.

He found a hutch with three wild-eyed rabbits still inside, a henhouse that held a handful of good eggs, and a small kitchen garden with a few straggly carrots and wilted cabbages. He took them all. What he really wanted was a mule, or one of the small shaggy mountain horses, but none of Crackspike's pack animals seemed to have survived, or to have stayed around if they had. Isiem would have to carry his burdens himself.

The only other animal he saw in Crackspike was a gray-muzzled brown dog that resembled a small coyote. Ghostly black stripes ran up and down the dog's mahogany fur, giving it a tigerish look, but despite its wild appearance Isiem had no doubt that the animal had been someone's pet. It circled around him constantly, keeping its distance but watching him with furtive hope. Obviously the dog felt even lonelier in the abandoned town than he did.

Isiem tossed it a raw pullet that he'd found in the Long-Bottomed Lady's kitchen. He had no great affinity for dogs—the few he'd known in Nidal had been wizards' familiars or huge slavering mastiffs used to hunt men—but a dog would be useful in the mountains. It might be able to carry a pack or help him hunt. At the very least, it could guard his campfire while he slept.

But this dog seemed more interested in the chicken than in him. After snapping his offering out of the air, it trotted away with a wave of its bushy brown tail.

Shrugging wryly at the ingratitude of every living creature he'd found in Crackspike, Isiem left the town to set up a tent for the night. Twilight was rapidly approaching, and he needed to start a fire while he could see well enough to build it.

At least there was no shortage of wood to burn in the empty town. Isiem gathered planks and boards until he could carry no more, and then he built himself a bonfire to stay warm through the night. He put another pullet in a covered clay pot and poked that into the side of the fire. The meat was tough and tasteless when Isiem fished the pot back out again, but it was cooked, and it was food.

He ate as much as he could stomach and flung the rest into the night, hoping it would lure the brown dog back to his side. Then he pulled a smoky-smelling bearskin over himself, curled up, and went to sleep on his bed of pilfered canvas.

"Up slow. No fast moving."

Isiem opened his eyes groggily. The blurs that ringed him, stark against a pink desert dawn, gradually resolved into five grim-faced strix. Four of them held flint-tipped bone spears pointed at him. Painted masks of wood and bone rested atop their heads, ready to be shoved back into place with a single quick movement. The fifth, and the only female among them, was a wizened, hunched creature. She wore a fibrous rope knotted with bone and feather talismans around her reedy neck, and her moth-eaten black wings were heavily dusted with pollen. Curlicued scars disfigured her face; he couldn't tell if they were ritual markings or the traces of old wounds. She was the only one who had no mask, although he had no idea what that meant.

It was the female who had addressed him. In a low, inhuman croak, she spoke again. Her Taldane was clumsy and so heavily accented that Isiem could barely understand her. "Up. Slow. Now." The others prodded the shadowcaller with their spears—not hard enough to draw blood, but not far from it.

Reluctantly, Isiem got to his feet. He was stiff and sore again after sleeping on the ground, although better off than he had been the previous morning. The day was sunny but brutally cold; he wrapped the bearskin around his shoulders as he stood. "What do you want?"

"You come. Now. With us." The female hobbled away. One of the warriors came forward and searched him, removing the rest of Isiem's potions and both of his wands. Surrounded and outnumbered as he was, Isiem made no protest. The searcher stepped back, and with jabs of their spears, the others ushered the shadowcaller along.

The strix herded him northwest of Crackspike, into a dry ravine so cunningly hidden by the surrounding rocks that Isiem had almost no inkling it was there until he'd stepped into it. Another two strix waited at the bottom. One appeared to be a hunter or scout of some kind; the upper surfaces of its wings were painted a mottled gray-brown, blending in with the surrounding rocks, while the lower halves were a paler color, presumably to make itself less obvious when glimpsed from below.

The other was Kirraak.

Isiem's heart sank when he saw his former captive. The glass shards in Kirraak's wings were still there, twinkling like false diamonds. The joints around them were badly infected; they were an angry, bloated red, and foul-looking pus seeped from the wounds into the lustreless black feathers. The stink of disease filled the ravine.

Kirraak never blinked. The Hellknights' bonds were still on the strix's wrists, but they did not seem to register. The injured strix sat completely motionless in the rocks and dead dry weeds, his unseeing eyes sheeted with the black of Zon-Kuthon's eternal shadow.

"Your doing," the old female strix said. She pointed to Kirraak's eyes, then her own, and made a quick gesture across her chest. Some sign to ward off evil, Isiem guessed. "His soul is . . . hurt. This you did. You will heal it."

"I can't." Isiem saw that the old one did not understand, and sensed impatience and hostility from the rest. He reached slowly for the pouch of components tied at his hip. "May I cast a spell? It will let us speak more clearly."

The elderly strix nodded. She spoke a few sharp words to her companions in their own clicking, cawing language. Their faces darkened, and some lowered their masks, but they spoke no word against her. Hoping that meant he could act without offending them, Isiem began his spell. He pressed the talisman of the clay ziggurat into his palm, focusing on the universality of speech. Beyond history, beyond race, beyond time . . .

. . . and he could speak as they spoke, and understand as they did. Strix and human shared pure meaning, overlooking the words that served as a superficial cloak for thought.

"I cannot help your friend," Isiem said. "What was done to him has destroyed him. What lives in his skin is no longer your kinsman."

"That is not so," one of the spear-wielders said angrily. "*Itaraak* Quiet Wings is himself. He remembers our hunts together. He remembers the ways and stones of our people. He remembers what you did to him."

"And yet there are things that are different about him as well, aren't there?" Isiem asked. There was no heat in his voice, only weariness. "Gaps in his memories. Things he remembers differently from how they happened, or not at all. Moments where he does not seem to hear you, and other times when he seems to marvel at his own ordinary body. Staring at his fingers, pulling at his hair, poking at his wounds as if delighting in the pain. Is that familiar too?"

The spear-wielder did not answer. But the crone did. "Yes," she said sadly, gazing at Kirraak. The black-eyed strix gave no indication that he had heard her, or that he was aware of any of their conversation. "That is so."

"The most merciful thing you can do for him— and the safest—is to give him a gentle death," Isiem said. "The parasite that possesses him will kill him, eventually, but before it does that it will try to catch as many of your kind as it can. It will try to give them to the same shadow that now inhabits Kirraak." Some of the spear-wielders blinked at Isiem's use of the name, but he couldn't tell what had startled them, so he ignored it and pressed on. "Your kinsman cannot be saved. Kill the ones who did this, if you like. Kill me, too. It won't change anything."

"They are already dead," the spear-wielder who had spoken previously said. Anger twisted his features. "You should die too. You did this to him, and you refuse to undo it."

"It is not so," Kirraak said suddenly, shifting his head to regard them all. "I am as I was. I am myself. I remember our homelands, summer and winter. Take me home."

The other strix exchanged wordless, uneasy looks. The old one never looked at Kirraak at all, though, and by that Isiem knew that she believed him.

"He will lead your enemies to your home if you let him go back with you," Isiem said. He lifted his empty hands in a gesture of surrender. "I am one of those enemies. I know this to be so. It's why Oreseis did it—to give you a poisoned foundling to take home. He will betray you, given the chance."

"He will have no chance," the old one said. "*Itaraak* Fierce Spear. Make his ending quick." The named strix was swift to comply. He flipped his wooden mask over his face, raised his flint-tipped spear, and drove it into Kirraak's neck. The crone watched without expression, although the other warriors muttered and shifted their weight.

When the dying strix's throes subsided, the ancient one turned back to Isiem. "I will think on your fate. Most want you dead. Perhaps the cold and the stones will kill you before I have to decide. That would make the deciding easier. But if you survive, it will not be easy. For any of us."

"I plan to leave," Isiem told her.

"You will not leave until permitted. Flee this *kotarra* place of wood-roosts and you die. But it will be a quick end, if you find you cannot stand the emptiness. Many *kotarra* cannot. We will give you that mercy if you wish it. All you need do is try to leave."

"And if I don't?"

"I make a difficult decision." The crone waved him off. "Go. But not too far."

Isiem did not wait to be told twice. He left them with Kirraak's corpse in the ravine, walking back to his folded-tent bed and the scraps of a life he'd salvaged from Crackspike.

He had no intention of staying put longer than he had to. Just long enough to finish picking the dead town's bones, and then he would be gone. His magic would hide him well enough to evade the scouts' eyes, he was sure. But until then, it could not hurt to let them believe he took their threats seriously.

It was only when he'd returned to the town, and the strix were long out of sight, that Isiem realized the spear-wielder who had confronted him—the most hostile of them all—had been the very same strix he'd saved from the collapse of the boarding house.

Gratitude, he thought, and laughed.

Chapter Sixteen
The Gift of Trust

Western Cheliax was a beautiful land, and a hard one. Isiem learned the truth of both those things in the weeks after Crackspike's fall. The striated ridges of red stone and sere winter plains were lovely to the eye, but they offered little shelter and less nourishment.

Nevertheless he managed to make a kind of life for himself in the ruins. Every morning, as the first touch of sunlight gilded the spires of Devil's Perch, Isiem emerged from his tent and cast two minor spells to conjure tiny downpours: the first over himself, to wash away the night's grime, and the second over an array of scavenged bowls and pans, to provide drinking water for the day.

It would have been easier to pray to Zon-Kuthon for water, but Isiem preferred his cantrips and his motley dish collection. There was something peaceful and pure in the sound of raindrops striking clay—something unsullied by the Midnight Lord's touch. It was as if every morning he washed a little more of Nidal's clinging shadow from his body, and stepped a little further into the cold, lonely, *clean* world of his exile.

That was how he slipped into apostasy: not with any single grand gesture, but quietly, over a procession of days, simply by letting the rituals of faith fade away.

With no one to enforce his obedience, Isiem neglected his prayers. He left his spiked chain buried among the ashes, and eventually forgot where it lay. He accepted the desert nights' bitter cold as his due, and bundled himself in bearskins instead of beseeching his god to shield him from the elements.

And day by day he felt his soul grow lighter, his sight grow clearer, as if he were emerging from a darkness that had blanketed him so long that he had come to accept it, wrongly, as the natural way of the world. It filled him with wonder and fear as profound as that which he had felt while taking the communion of the burning chain—but although this fear was greater, for he faced it alone in an unknown land, he had no wish to give it up. Hungry and weary as it was, Isiem felt a vast peacefulness in the ascetic's life.

The brown dog became his constant companion. It might have been his gifts of food and water that finally won the animal over, or it might just have been that she—for the dog was female—was as lonely as he was. Neither of them had anyone else in this barren place.

He called her Honey, after a vaguely remembered Keleshite tale about a desert monk who subsisted for a hundred years on Sarenrae's gifts of honey and locusts. Isiem had no god and no divinely granted sustenance, but in Honey, he had one friend in his exile, and that was one more than he'd ever had before.

The dog was pure in her motives. She never lied to him, and she never hid anything. Honey wanted food, shelter, a safe place to sleep—and affection. Love. That was what Isiem believed he saw in the dog's liquid eyes:

devotion. As if he, with all his sins and cruelties, could be worthy of such faith.

It was as much a revelation to him as the sunshine. More so: the sun did not care if he lived or died, and it gave him no reason to struggle through the hardships of another day. Honey did. The dog *needed* him, and trusted that he would meet those needs. And so she pulled him through his moments of despair, and gave him the strength to push onward.

But she couldn't stop winter from coming.

The sun rose later each morning, and dusk crept up on him earlier. What Isiem had initially taken for winter in western Cheliax had only been the fading days of fall. A month after Crackspike had burned, the true cold was coming, and he wondered if he and the dog would survive.

Isiem preserved and kept as much food as he could, storing grain in stolen pots and drying what little meat he managed to hunt or trap on racks built from the boards of fallen houses. Often, while dreaming of dumplings and eating thin gruel, he found himself wishing that the Dusk Hall had taught its students to conjure *food*. Spells that summoned shadowy monsters and blasted their victims with supernatural pain might be better for maintaining Zon-Kuthon's reign, but during those gut-gnawing nights in Crackspike, Isiem would have traded them all for one grilled spinefish in a crust of spice.

He was painfully aware that his scavengings were unlikely to see him through the cold months, and while he still hoped to reach Pezzack, he doubted that it would be possible to make the journey before spring. Enduring the winter in Crackspike would be trial enough.

Although the season was already upon him, Isiem did what he could to prepare. Each morning, after conjuring water to wash and drink, he went scavenging through the remains of Crackspike, or wandering far afield from the town in search of survivors—human, strix, or animal.

He never found any. The strix had reclaimed their own injured, finished off any human stragglers they could reach, and butchered the livestock for meat. By the time Isiem found the bones and bloodstains on foot, the winged ones had already made off with the rest. They'd even eaten the dogs.

On one such expedition he found the remains of Erevullo and the other Hellknights, shot down by the strix over half a mile of barren ground. There was little left of them. Some scraps of armor, a tattered black cloak pinned to the earth by a spear, Oreseis's holy symbol on its tarnished silver chain. The rest had been taken or destroyed by the strix.

No one else, it seemed, had disturbed them. Citadel Enferac, locked behind walls of snow and unable to rely on its usual network of winged spies, might still be ignorant of their fate. Erevullo never had gotten the chance to complete his magical device.

Isiem buried the few bones he found, but said no prayers as he did, and left no marker on their grave.

That night, like every night, he returned to his makeshift dwelling, a shell of a house that he had patched with canvas to keep away the wind. He ate a sparse meal and slept with Honey curled beside him for warmth, and he did not dream of the dead.

A week later, on a frosty morning when the ground crackled silver with every step and the air seemed nearly as brittle, Isiem ranged far from the town to forage. In the distance, across a far blue ridge, he glimpsed three hooded riders on tall black steeds.

Slowly he sank to the ground. It did not appear that they had seen him, but Isiem still felt a thrill of fear run up his spine. He did not know who those riders were, but he recognized their steeds: unliving creations of spellbound shadow, siblings to the black-eyed horses he himself had conjured so many times in Nidal.

The horsemen might be Hellknights hunting strix, or they might be shadowcallers hunting him . . . but that they were wizards, and hunting *someone*, Isiem had no doubt.

He watched them a while longer, waiting to see where they turned—west, as it happened, away from Crackspike and toward the place where Erevullo and his signifers had fallen—and then he crept quietly back to his own lair.

For days he had been working on a compact bundle of food, clothing, tinder and tools to use on the journey to Pezzack. Isiem took it now, along with a walking stick and a few dishes, and whistled for Honey to join him as he started north. He wanted to be well away from Crackspike when the riders arrived.

He doubted they'd stay long. Three arcanists, on magical mounts with no baggage train, were not an occupying army. They would find their prey quickly or not at all, and then they would depart.

But until they left, it would be unwise to linger where he might be found.

There was a small cabin in the hills where one overly optimistic miner had tried to work his own stake. The miner was long gone, his dreams defeated, but his cabin remained. It was a full day's walk from Crackspike, mostly along snake-infested dry gullies lined with sharp rocks, so Isiem had considered it of little use while he was still scouring the abandoned town. But as a refuge from troublesome visitors, it was nearly ideal.

He reached it at dusk. Winter had driven the snakes to ground, making the gullies safer but the cabin more dangerous. Any shelter—whether an old boot or a rickety shack—made a tempting place for serpents to hibernate.

Isiem pried open the rope-hinged door cautiously and peered into the chilly gloom. He picked up a pebble, crushed the tiny body of a dried firefly against it as he breathed a word of magic, and threw the softly glowing stone into the center of the cabin. Its light bounced unevenly against the warped plank walls and fell, illuminating a heap of small gray snakes that lay tangled in a corner.

Rock vipers. Not aggressive, as a rule, but easily startled and exceedingly venomous. Isiem sighed inwardly. He would almost rather have found a knot of rattlesnakes in the cabin; at least then he could have taken consolation in the fact that if he died of snakebite, it would have been because something *wanted* to kill him, not just out of frightened reflex. There was something insulting about dying like that.

But rock vipers were what he had to deal with, so Isiem went back outside and unshouldered his pack. He could only hope that the shadow-mounted horsemen he'd spotted earlier were not in a position to see his light peeping through the cabin's many cracks.

Signaling for Honey to stay back, he pulled the largest of the water-collecting buckets from the dog's pack. The miner had left a balding broom lying in the dirt outside his doorway, which made the chore of snake removal much easier. With the broom and bucket held outstretched like sword and shield, Isiem ventured back into the cabin.

The vipers had barely stirred. Quickly, before they revived from their torpor enough to react, Isiem swept the entire scaly ball into his bucket and threw it outside. The snakes might return, unless they froze to death first, but he hoped to be gone by then.

Shoring up all the cracks in the cabin's weatherbeaten planks was beyond his means at the moment, so Isiem drew upon a minor spell instead. He broke a fine silver wire into eight pieces and scattered them around the shack's walls, then stood in the center of the marked area and rang a tiny sterling bell. Instead of ringing audibly, the bell sent out a thrum of silent magic that tingled the hairs along Isiem's forearms and made Honey cock her head to one side.

If anything crept into the cabin overnight, a similar alarm would wake him—hopefully in time to avoid being bitten. In the morning the spell would end and the silver wire would bind itself back together, ready to be used again, but until then the magic would keep him safe. With luck. Isiem unpacked his blankets and bearskins, snuffed his pebble's magical light, and sank into uneasy sleep.

No snakes troubled him that night. In the morning he rose, stretched, and went outside to relieve himself.

While squinting into the frosty sunrise, Isiem glimpsed a tantalizing tuft of green tucked between the hills to the north. *Water.* Where there was enough water to sustain greenery, there would be animals—hares, copperheaded quail, perhaps even larger game. Hunters had sold the meat of scrub deer and antelope in Crackspike, and the animals had to have come from *somewhere.*

It was worth looking. He didn't want to go back to Crackspike yet anyway.

Isiem had only gone a quarter-mile from the cabin, however, when Honey spun and raced back toward the shack, barking furiously. He tried to call her back, but the dog was deaf to his cries. Annoyed and alarmed, Isiem chased after her.

When he was a few hundred yards from the cabin, he saw something explode from a nearby gully in a burst of black-feathered motion. Honey went berserk, charging at the creature with a ferocious display of growls and barks. Isiem stopped short, baffled.

It was a strix. The creature perched on his roof, staring at him. For some reason it had a handful of short ropes dangling from one fist. He couldn't see if there was anything in its other hand. It did not appear to be armed, though, and it did not seem alarmed at the possibility that he might be. It just squatted there, apparently waiting for him to approach.

Uncertainly, Isiem did. Honey bounded to his side, pausing every few steps to growl a warning at the strix on the roof. A stiff line of fur bristled on the dog's back from her neck to her tail.

As Isiem got closer, he saw that the strix was a juvenile female, and that it was indeed unarmed. The "ropes" in its hand were dead rock vipers, probably the same ones he had scooped up and thrown out the night before. Their heads had been smashed flat.

The strix held up its other hand in a closed fist as he approached. It squinched its eyes shut and squeezed its fingers tight . . . and nothing happened. The strix opened its hand and stared at the tiny clay ziggurat in its palm, obviously disappointed. The feathers at the ends of its wings fanned out and dipped downward.

Isiem laughed, unable to help himself. He had never expected to see a strix so literally crestfallen.

"It isn't enchanted," he said, although he suspected the strix had stolen his ziggurat precisely because it couldn't understand a word of Taldane. "It only focuses the spell."

True to his guess, the strix gave him a blank stare. Isiem opened and closed his empty hand in front of him, hoping it would take the hint to throw the ziggurat down. After a moment, the strix made a trilling whistle and, instead of tossing the object gently, whipped the miniature ziggurat at him with a sidearm throw.

Its speed and accuracy were impressive. The ziggurat hit Isiem's shoulder like a slingstone, causing his entire arm to go numb before the pain kicked in. He sucked in a breath and clutched his arm, trying to assess the extent of the injury.

Nothing felt broken, but he'd have a bruise that went down to the bone. A flicker of relief broke through the throbbing pain. A broken arm could have been a fatal injury to a man trying to survive off the land; it might well have driven him back to Zon-Kuthon in hopes of healing. But this lesser wound wouldn't kill him, or even threaten his quiet apostasy, and for that Isiem was grateful. It could so easily have been much worse.

The strix was watching him with open surprise. Not amusement at his pain, as far as he could tell, and not sympathy, either. Only puzzlement. Isiem exhaled and picked his small clay ziggurat from the dirt, finishing the spell at last.

"Why did you do that?" he asked.

The strix went very still. Its nictating membranes slid sideways across its eyes, perhaps in the equivalent of a human's startled blink. "I did not realize you were unwell," it said. Initially the strix's words were hesitant, but when it realized that the spell was translating for both of them, its mouth opened slightly in surprise and then made a small, toothy smile.

"Unwell?"

"You are slow because you are sick, yes?" The strix canted its head at him. Again the semitransparent membranes sheeted across its eyes in a wrongsided blink. "No? You are not unwell?"

"I'm fine, apart from this bruise on my arm."

"Oh." The strix chirruped, hopping a short step sideways on the roof, and raised the dead vipers. "Then why did you not take these foods? They are good meat. But you threw them away. Why?"

Isiem blinked. "You were watching me last night?"

"Yes."

"I didn't see anyone."

"Nor does the mouse see the hawk, unless the hawk shows its shadow. Your eyes are small, and my shadow well hidden." The strix tucked all but one of the snakes into its belt, then began casually gnawing on the remaining serpent's head. Bones and scales crunched between its teeth. "But you are a hungry one who throws away good meat, and this is a puzzlement."

"It didn't occur to me to eat snakes," Isiem answered truthfully. He'd only worried about *them* biting *him*.

"That is stupid."

"Evidently so."

"I will share." The strix flung three dead snakes down from the roof, one after another, although this time it took care to land its serpentine missiles at Isiem's feet. "This is a hard land for *kotaar*. You are starving. Why do you not go to the black riders in the dead place?"

It meant the trio of horsemen he'd seen near Crackspike, Isiem guessed. He scrutinized the strix's face, but saw nothing to suggest it was trying to bait him. That flat inhuman face and those wolflike yellow eyes gave little away, but to the extent he could read anything from it, he thought the strix was genuinely curious. Hoping he was right, Isiem decided to gamble on honesty.

"I am their enemy," he said.

His candor earned another sideways hop and blink. "But you are one of them."

"I was. Then I turned against them and fled. The Hellknights do not suffer deserters. Neither does the Umbral Court. If they find me now, they'll kill me. And I would kill them to keep from going back." He hadn't consciously realized it before, but as soon as the words passed his lips, Isiem knew they were true. He *would* kill his former comrades before he returned to that life.

Again the strix was motionless for several long seconds. Only its feathers moved, fanning gently at the outer edges of its wings. He could almost see the creature thinking.

At length its yellow eyes focused back on him. "You are a traitor to your kin? That is a great sin."

"The Chelaxians are no kin of mine. They are slavers and tyrants. They consort with devils and cause the deaths of honest men." All true, although Isiem had been—and done—far worse. But that grim fact did nothing to diminish the accuracy of his accusations. "And they will not leave you be, not until the last of your kind is dead or defeated."

"Why?"

"They want the silver in your hills." Isiem swept his arm out, encompassing the gray rocks before them and the red-veined spikes behind. "They will not leave until

245

they have it. And they cannot take it safely while your people remain here."

"And you are their enemy."

"Yes."

"You will help us fight them?"

Isiem shook his head. "I don't believe you can. Cheliax is an empire. A great one. They have soldiers, wizards, enslaved devils by the score . . . the cleverest spellcaster I ever knew was a Chelish diabolist. I don't doubt that your people are brave and determined. But you cannot stand against them without being destroyed."

The strix trilled in apparent dismay. It stuffed the half-eaten snake back into its belt; evidently his gloomy prediction had spoiled its appetite. "That is an ugly truth."

"I'm sorry." Isiem attempted a rueful smile. He doubted it touched his eyes. "It seems I'm made to tell ugly truths to strix."

"Yes. This . . . this new tale will need thinking." The strix flapped its wings a few times, preparing to depart. "I will inform the *rokoa*. I think the elders will listen. It is good to have an enemy's enemy as guide, and you do not tell us lies. It was a hard truth about Quiet Wings, but you did not shy."

"I'm sorry about that," Isiem said. "Kirraak. What happened to him."

The strix cocked its head in the other direction, ruffling its feathers twice in quick succession. Its yellow eyes seemed to deepen toward a golden color.

"*Kirraak* is not a name," it said, lifting into the sky. The wind of its wings beat Isiem's hair back in white streams. "It is a cry to be avenged."

Chapter Seventeen
Snakes

After that first encounter, the young strix came to Isiem's cabin more often. Soon she was visiting almost every morning, and their conversations became the centerpiece of Isiem's days. She sat on the roof, and he sat on the doorstep, and they talked until his spell ran out. He had not realized how much he missed the simple pleasures of discourse. Honey was a devoted companion, but it was difficult to carry a conversation with a dog.

Not that the strix's conversations were much like a human's. The more they talked, the more Isiem became conscious of that fact. And yet, for all the strix's strangeness, something like friendship began to develop between them.

Her name was Kirii, and Windspire was her tribe. She was the daughter of the *rokoa*, the old crone that Isiem had met in the ashes of Crackspike, and it seemed that her birth marked her as a child of destiny. *Rokoa* seldom bore fertile eggs; most were too old for breeding, and centuries-old custom prohibited them from taking mates. But every winter the *rokoa* coupled with every male in the clan in a ritual meant to bring them a bountiful spring, and sometimes children were hatched from such rites. Children born in this fashion were considered the daughters of the entire tribe, for it was impossible to know who had fathered them. And they were never sons; as far as Kirii knew, no male had ever been born of a *rokoa*.

Most of these daughters grew up to become legendary *rokoa* themselves, but Kirii seemed cheerfully unconcerned about any weight of expectation that might lie on her slight shoulders. Her nonchalance was a far cry from the dread that Isiem himself had felt grappling with much lesser expectations at the Dusk Hall, but then Kirii hardly seemed to know the meaning of dread. She was not what he had expected from the daughter of a dying people.

"What should I be?" she scoffed when he mentioned his surprise. "The chief of the Black Crags is greatly stoic. He and his tribe have accepted their doom. Our young *itaraak* let their anger eat their pride and power. They have accepted theirs. Many have abandoned their masks, saying that killing *kotarra* is not a sin, so they have no cause to hide their faces. They flee to Ciricskree, the greatest aerie of our people, and kill all who approach, even the birds and the beasts, fearing they might be spies for *kotarra*. It is a life of bitterness and fear.

"If I am not like them, not what you expect, it is because I accept no idea of doom. That idea is not useful. Fixing one's eyes on it makes one blind to all other possibilities, and a *rokoa* must never be so blind. It is like eating snakes."

"Eating snakes?" Isiem echoed, nonplussed.

"You find snakes in your sleeping place. Immediately you fix on the most obvious thought: they will bite you, and you will die. So you think only of being rid of them.

But there are other thoughts you could have as well: they are good meat. Good skins. By thinking in this way you are still being rid of the danger, but also you will have a full belly. And pretty things for your head," she added, touching the band of braided viperskins that she had taken to wearing around her brow.

Kirii paused, then held her long, slim hands up in a fan toward the sun. The little spikes of her claws were translucent against the light. "Then, too, you think always of what you *must* do, and despair eats you if you fail. If you think instead of what you *can* do, then if you fail—what does it matter? This was but one choice among many. You have others. And my people have many choices, whether they see them or not."

"What choices are those?" Isiem asked. "You can't fight all Cheliax, and the Chelaxians will not give up. Don't be lulled into complacency because they haven't marched yet. Only the snow in the passes—and their contempt for your warriors—delays them. They'll come in their own time, but they will come."

Kirii gave him that small, sharp-toothed smile again. She lowered her hands. "I do not know all our choices yet. That is why I talk to you: to find them. But it is not useful to accept this idea of the inevitable, this thing that cannot be changed. Many of my people would see you as our enemy, and think this inevitable. They would kill you. But you are not our enemy, and in killing you they would lose the chance to learn much about the *kotarra* who come to the ground-roosts. This would be foolish. One must always be curious."

"Some would say that curiosity is itself foolish," Isiem said.

The strix made a derisive trill. "Not foolish. Undignified. This is not the same. To be curious is to admit that you do not know a thing, and some find that frightening. But I am young and there are many things I do not know. I find no shame in admitting it."

"But what if I were a threat?" Isiem pressed. "What if I had attacked instead of talking when you tried to steal my focus?" At his side, Honey perked her ears, lifted her head, and stared at the strix for a moment. Then the dog sighed and settled back onto her blanket, pushing her head against Isiem's leg and curling her tail out into the sun.

"You were no threat." Kiriii blinked sideways several times in rapid succession, the nictating membranes blurring across her yellow eyes. The soft feathers at the base of her wings flared and settled in a gesture that Isiem had learned to interpret as laughter. "I watched you before I approached. You stopped praying to the god of chains and you kept a beast that cannot hunt." She pointed to the sleeping dog, and Isiem felt a flash of guilty amusement at the strix's assessment.

It was true that Honey made a poor hunting dog. She was older than Isiem had originally guessed, and her idea of a glorious afternoon was lying on her blanket in the sun while he prepared their dinner. While she could be roused to ferocious barking if she heard something untoward at night, and she insisted on accompanying him every time he left the cabin, Honey was not and would never be much use for catching game.

But he kept her, because the dog was a friend, and Isiem needed friends.

"Fair enough," he conceded. "I suppose it's obvious I'm not much of a danger. But what if I had been?"

"Then we would have killed you or driven you away, as we did the black riders who came after you."

"Ah." Isiem hesitated, not sure he wanted to know, but asked: "What became of them?"

"*Itaraak* Fierce Spear and his warriors attacked them. The black riders did not stand to fight. They fled by some magic, vanishing into the air, and their horses turned into smoke behind them. The warriors killed none and lost none."

"They'll lose some soon enough," Isiem said grimly. He had warned Kirii that the strix should stay away from the trio of signifers—and he was sure now that they were signifers rather than shadowcallers, as the Chelaxians would be in no hurry to admit their failure to the Nidalese. Watching from a distance would have been prudent, but engaging them would only show the Chelaxians that the strix were still a threat to their interests. He had guessed that the signifers were scouts, not raiders, and had been equipped with some means of retreating swiftly in the face of danger. It seemed his guess had been correct, but it gave him no satisfaction to be right. "I told you not to let your kin attack."

"My mother is *rokoa*, not I," the strix replied testily. "I have no right of command. I told them what you said, and they chose not to listen. All passed as you foretold. Perhaps next time they will heed what you say."

"It won't matter," Isiem said. "Next time the Chelaxians will send a war party."

"We killed the last one. When you came."

"That wasn't a war party, and you had the advantage of a collaborator in Crackspike." He noted a slight stiffening of Kirii's neck, betraying her surprise, and smiled inwardly. Strix had their tells, just as humans did. "What happened to that collaborator, anyway?"

"Pezzack." Kirii garbled the word, turning it into a rooster's crow. "She wished to go to a place of freedom. It was worth the burning of all her kin for her to go." The strix trilled again in disapproval, digging her clawed toes into the cabin's roof deeply enough to leave gouges in the weather-beaten shingles. "Very human. But we honored our bargain and showed her the way."

"In exchange for what, exactly?"

The strix released her grip, took a hop to the side, and sank her claws into the wood again, harder this time. "*Cricscaara* poison, flint, and steel. This woman, she was a slave. It was her duty to cook. It was for her a simple thing to slip the poison into their food, and simpler still to pour oil under their beds as they slept their *cricscaara* sleep. Some were elsewhere and did not eat, but they were few. The *itaraak* slaughtered them."

Isiem said nothing. An unexpected weight of guilt had settled on him during the strix's explanation. He'd had no part in the collaborator's betrayal, but nevertheless he felt that he was, somehow, at fault in some way for it.

Pezzack had been his own dream, and while he hadn't been willing to burn the whole world for it, he *had* been willing to abandon Oreseis, Erevullo, and all those Hellknights to their deaths. *They were soldiers. They invited their risks.* And standing aside in a fight between capable opponents was a far cry from burning helpless civilians alive as they slept.

But the temptation was the same, and perhaps even the betrayal itself was only a difference of degree, not kind.

Even if he let himself believe that his own choice was different, and his own betrayal somehow less, it did not change the fact that he was free only because of the monstrous thing that the collaborator in Crackspike had done. Isiem's liberty had been bought in blood. And in his heart of hearts he knew, uneasily, that even if it were somehow possible to trade the innocent Crackspikers' lives back for his bondage, he would refuse that bargain.

Kirii canted her head to one side. "This troubles you?"

"No," Isiem lied. He wasn't the only one learning to read cross-species tells. Stupid to have forgotten that, even if he felt they were friends. And wasn't that another betrayal, in its way? He had befriended the very same creatures who had massacred the civilians of Crackspike. Not soldiers. Miners, traders, whores—ordinary people trying to scratch better lives for themselves out of the hardship of Devil's Perch.

They aren't just creatures, *and this is their homeland. It is natural that they should want to defend it.* But that only made the bloodshed more wearying. In Nidal he had believed that he was trapped by his nation's curse, and that if he could only escape from the spiritual chains of Zon-Kuthon, he'd find the world a brighter place. Instead he had discovered that good men were just as capable of engineering disasters as bad ones, and that the little people suffered and died just the same, either way.

"Why did you butcher the dead?" Isiem asked. He'd never mentioned it before; he had been afraid of offending Kirii, or of hearing an answer he didn't want to know. But now, suddenly, it seemed important to know the full cost Crackspike had paid for his freedom. "*Were* they dead when you cut them?"

"Yes." Kirii's head tilted slightly. There seemed to be more curiosity than offense in her answer, but Isiem was not sure. "All dead. The *itaraak* cut them to show their shame."

"I don't understand."

"It is forbidden to eat the flesh of the dead who were true-people. But *kotarra* are not our people. In Ciricskree it is taught that you are the worst of our enemies, for you have driven many tribes away from their homelands and forced them to seek refuge upon the Screeching Spire. You are cruel and treacherous and more savage than beasts. To them you are not true-people but half-people, like goblins and ogres." She held up her slim, clawed hands, showing empty palms. "I say this not to insult but to explain. These are the beliefs of the *itarii*.

"There is much dispute over whether the killing of *kotarra* is a sin. If it is a sin, the *itaraak* must wear masks to kill, lest their faces be seen and known for breakers of taboo. If it is not, they may go bare-faced. The *rokoa* of Windspire says it is a sin, as you are true-people. The *rokoa* of Ciricskree says it is not, as you are half-people. The tribes differ on this.

"Also they differ on the taboo of *kotarra* flesh. When an *itarii* dies, his body is taken to a place of honor and given to the worms. The worms clean the bones so that they may be returned to the tribe and made into useful things. In times of great hardship, the worms themselves may be eaten, for they have purified the flesh of the dead with their own flesh. In this way, as bones and fodder, we help our kin after death. But the vilest sinners, the outcasts from the tribes—they are not afforded this honor. Their bodies are left to rot after they die, for as they were exiled in life, so they remain exiles in death. We do not take their bones.

"If *kotarra* are not true-people, it is no taboo to eat their flesh. This is what the tribe of Ciricskree teaches. For them it is acceptable to eat your dead. Half-people are not appetizing, but they make acceptable meat. But if you are true-people, as the *rokoa* of Windspire says, then the worst insult is for your bones and flesh to be left on the ground to rot. The *itaraak* cut them and leave them to show contempt. You may be true-people, they are saying, but you are so worthless, so defiled by sin, that the worms reject your flesh and the *itarii* discard your bones."

"That's what they believe?" Isiem said, incredulous.

"It is."

A long silence fell, broken only by the whistling of a dry winter breeze through the ridges and spires of Devil's Perch. Ripples of yellow and white shone on the wind-carved red rocks, each outcropping as vivid as a sunset made stone. Isiem gazed at their desolate beauty, trying to remember whether this was what he had imagined all those years ago in Nidal: a land where the earth held brilliant colors, and yet was no kinder than Pangolais.

Kirii interrupted his musings. "What are you thinking?"

"Snakes." Isiem forced levity into his answer, hoping to convince himself as much as the strix. "I'm trying to find some to eat, but all I see are big fangs hissing at me."

Once more Kirii's feathers fanned up and settled in peculiar mirth. She warbled low in her throat, a sound she had started making to approximate laughter. "It is often so in the beginning, before you learn to hunt."

"I'd rather not make too many mistakes while learning. Those fangs are *very* big."

"A common wish," Kirii agreed, "but one the world seldom grants. You face what comes into your life."

"Thank you, wise one." Isiem made a face. The strix's feathers fluttered in amusement, and she bobbed her head in a birdlike gesture that seemed more human each time she did it.

Learning to mirror human gestures. She wants to build rapport. Isiem knew from his own interrogator's training that such mirrored gestures were highly effective in establishing a sense of empathy between questioner and subject, and that most often people did not even realize that it was being done.

Far from making him suspicious of Kirii, however, Isiem's awareness of her techniques made him trust her more. If she was trying to master that kind of mimicry, it meant that she intended to use diplomacy instead of spears—and, further, that she meant her efforts to be as persuasive as possible. He couldn't say whether she would succeed, but the attempt was worthy of respect.

"I brought you more dungpatty," Kirii said, when it became evident that awkwardness had suffocated their conversation. She hopped down from the roof and unshouldered her pack, pulling out strings of dried meat, cakes of rendered fat and dehydrated berries, and the round blocks of fuel that the strix called "dungpatty"—the dried ordure of ruminants, mainly deer, rock sheep, and the small fork-horned antelope that thrived impossibly on bristles and brambles and coarse brown grass. The strix gathered it, mixed it with unguents of their own devising, and pressed it into sun-baked rounds. In a land where wood was too scarce to be relied on as fuel, dungpatty served in its stead.

It burned at a slow smolder, giving off little light—an advantage to hunters and raiders who could ill afford to have campfires shining like signal lights from the high pillars of Devil's Perch or across the low bald hills. And it sufficed to keep Isiem warm and fed, although the one time he'd made the mistake of trying to grill meat over a dungpatty fire, he had quickly learned why the strix preferred to cook their food in tightly covered pots.

Without Kirii's gifts of dungpatty, he would surely have frozen or starved. He wasn't a horse; he couldn't eat raw grain. The cabin was too far from Crackspike to raid the abandoned houses for wood, and there was nothing else to burn in this desolate corner of the world. The supplies she brought him saved his life—and he had repaid her with nothing but words. Isiem felt a twinge of shame at the thought, as he always did.

Kirii didn't seem to notice. When her pack was empty, she slung it back onto her shoulders and belted it around her waist. The strix's pack was made of dusty leather in an exterior frame of long, lightweight bones. Strix bones.

Truly, they were a frugal people. Kirii's explanation of why the *itaraak* had butchered the unfortunates of Crackspike had surprised him only in the extent of the strix's hatred for humans, not in the detail of how they treated their own dead. She had already told him earlier that their ancestors bequeathed their bones to their kin.

The strix made everything from spear hafts to tent poles from their dead. Few materials in their world were as strong as bone, and none were as light as strix bone. In past ages, conquering tribes had taken the bones of their enemies, but as their numbers dwindled, and the clans turned their spears away from each other, the only bones to be had were those of their own kin.

"The world changes, and our customs change to fit," Kirii had said. "Old taboos fail, new honors arise. We waste nothing. Not even our own deaths."

Clearly she saw no taboo in wearing her grandmother's bones. When her pack was secured, the strix blinked her bright yellow eyes at Isiem. "You need anything else?"

"No," Isiem said. "Thank you. I wish I could repay your generosity."

"You tell us of the black riders and the men in iron horns. This is repayment enough." Kirii shrugged, looking to the sky, and Isiem shielded his eyes in anticipation of the dust that would be thrown up by her wings. "I go now."

Alone again, Isiem carried her gifts into the cabin. He stored the food inside a leaky old rainbarrel the previous inhabitant had abandoned. It was no use for holding water, but it would keep scavengers from getting at his supplies. The dungpatty went in a stack outside, with a square of canvas to protect it from wind and the distant possibility of rain.

Enough daylight remained for Isiem to bring his spellbook out and study by the setting sun. He had not realized what a luxury the simple act of reading could become; in Nidal it had seemed just a wearisome chore. But here, as winter tightened its grip and the sunlight grew shorter day by day, Isiem seldom had time to pore over his spells. The work of survival occupied him from dawn to dusk, and burning dungpatty gave too little light to read.

He owed this, too, to the strix. Without Kirii's gifts of food, clothing, and fuel, Isiem would have had to gather his own, and that would have left him no time for study.

He regretted, now, that he had thought of the captured strix—of all their kind, really—as monsters. Creatures to be referred to as "it," rather than the individuals they were. Isiem had never been particularly sensitive to such nuances, but in his conversations with Kirii he had become more conscious of words, phrases, the cadences and rhythms of language—and the ideas that it clothed. Those ideas took their shapes from words, and his had been sorely lacking. He had considered the strix worse than beasts, when they saved his life every day.

Even the little he could tell them about Nidalese customs and Chelish magic—information that might help them find some weakness in their enemies—seemed pitifully small against that. He owed them more.

Preoccupied by such thoughts, Isiem found himself unable to concentrate. He stared sightlessly at the spellbook's open pages until twilight descended and hid the words. Even then he remained outside, sitting motionless, as the night's chill crystallized around him.

It was Honey who finally brought him in. The dog nipped at his ankles, tugging at his clothes mercilessly until the shadowcaller stood up and opened the door for them both. Without a backward glance, the dog rushed in and flopped beside the tiny hearth, waiting impatiently for Isiem to light the night's fire. As soon as he did, Honey exhaled an enormous, satisfied sigh, and fell asleep within minutes.

Sleep was slower to come for Isiem. He lay awake puzzling over the strix's dilemma long after the night began to wane toward dawn. However he turned the questions in his mind, he could not find the many choices Kirii had spoken of. He could find only one.

The strix could give up their land, or they could give up their lives. That was all. And that, he believed, was a snake too vicious for any of them to swallow.

Chapter Eighteen
Secrets in Silver

A week later, Isiem went back to Crackspike. A brief warm spell in the weather made the idea of travel tolerable, and he believed that the Hellknights would not yet have returned after the strix's attempt to drive them off. It seemed safe, or as safe as it was likely to be until spring came, and by then the elements would likely have destroyed the things he sought.

He hoped to find something in the ruins that would reveal more than he already knew about the Chelaxians' numbers, resources, and level of determination. Maps, diaries, scraps of unfinished spell research—anything that might offer a glimpse into their plans or the tools they might employ against the strix. Enemies they knew, they could defeat.

Isiem was no longer troubled that his allegiances had shifted so completely. He owed Abrogail II no reverence. Seven years in Westcrown had taught him that the soul of Cheliax was in conflict with itself, and that House Thrune was but one side in the war. It was not a war he hoped to see them win.

And so, bundled in the hides of deer and hares, Isiem walked to Crackspike.

Even from a distance, he could see the town had changed. Great furrows rent the ground, as if a swarm of tremendous ants had begun burrowing a nest under the settlement and then abandoned it half-built. The blackened bones of a boarding house tilted drunkenly into the gaps, its foundations destroyed—and in some places, Isiem saw as he came nearer, eaten.

Heavy claws had splintered beams and boards; massive teeth had gouged holes in cast-iron cauldrons. In one of the shallow, crumbling tunnels he saw a clump of pebbly scat that contained bent spoons, a pick head, and three mangled, acid-eaten horseshoes. Honey sniffed the tunnel's side once and backed away, whining, her eyes wide and tail tucked.

Landshark.

Said to be stomachs on legs—bottomless, sharp-toothed stomachs on prodigiously armored legs— landsharks were notorious for their appetites. They tunneled through the earth in constant search of things to eat, and they defined such things liberally. Any whiff of food or flesh on an object would entice them to swallow it. For breakfast, one might eat a cast-iron pot that had held stew a month earlier; for dinner, a bedframe where someone had slept six weeks ago. Landsharks could digest almost anything, and they were always willing to try.

Fresh meat, however, was a favorite. And while landsharks were voracious scavengers, they were even fiercer on the hunt.

The sight of the scat gave Isiem pause. He couldn't tell how old it was, nor did he have the skill to read the creature's tracks. The landshark might be long gone, or it might yet be lurking among the toppled buildings. There might even be more than one.

But he'd walked a full day to search the ruins, and it seemed foolish to let fear turn him away so easily. He had, after all, seen no proof that the creature was still here.

"Go," he told Honey. The dog flattened her ears and continued to back away. She barked once, when she realized that Isiem was not coming with her, but— although plainly baffled by her human's foolishness— she did not follow him in.

Wary, and alert to the slightest tremor that might warn him of the landshark's tunneling approach, Isiem made his way into the town.

Almost nothing was left of it. What the fires hadn't destroyed, the landshark had. It had eaten the canvas and cowhides of the miners' tents and demolished the few standing buildings. What it hadn't devoured or torn apart had fallen into the tunnels it had bored through Crackspike, so that it seemed the land itself was absorbing the feeble scratchings of civilization on its skin.

Wind whistled over the tunnels' mouths. Isiem's feet sank into loosened soil; the smell of fresh-turned earth, already going to dust, surrounded him. In each of the open tunnels he could see piles of dung marking the landshark's progress in a dotted line. As continuously as the creature ate, so it excreted.

It didn't look promising, but Isiem climbed into the nearest furrow anyway. The partly collapsed tunnel came to his chest, but it was not difficult to traverse. Even as he poked around the landshark's leavings, the shadowcaller wondered what, exactly, he hoped to find. The damnable creature had eaten *everything*.

But not everything it had eaten had been destroyed.

In one of the piles Isiem glimpsed a pair of silver cylinders no bigger than his thumbs, their surfaces worn smooth by acid and corroded solid black. A hair-thin line around the center of each one showed where they could be unscrewed.

Most likely the cylinders had been meant for some winged carrier, but only the clasps of the birds' cages had survived the landshark's stomach. Isiem hoped the cylinders had done a better job of protecting their contents. Pocketing them to be examined later, he moved on.

Among the flinders of a jewelry box was a round bronze medallion stamped in the blocky, ornate fashion of Korvosa; a few steps past that, he found the muddied remains of a traveling spellbook. The trampled pages didn't look legible, but Isiem took it anyway. He was sifting through the next pile, hoping to find something better, when the ground suddenly shivered underfoot.

Fifty yards to his left, the boarding house's beams shook like grass stalks in the wind. A long, low rumble sent pebbles jouncing along the bottom of the landshark's troughs. Moment by moment it grew louder, until it sounded like thunder trapped under the earth. Rills of dirt spilled down the sides of Isiem's tunnel; small stones pattered across his feet.

Isiem cursed silently. He didn't have the magic to escape into the air. The best he could do was try to outpace the beast on land.

Shoving his left hand into a pocket, he fished out a curled shaving of licorice root and closed it in a fist. Magic gathered in him, following the shape of his words. Isiem's muscles thrilled with unaccustomed speed; his body felt impossibly light. The world around him seemed to blur and slow, as if everything but himself was trapped in invisible treacle. He felt quick enough to dodge through raindrops—and as long as his spell lasted, he almost was.

But landsharks were deadlier than raindrops. And faster, too.

Thirty feet away, a gray-green plate spiked through the earth, scattering stones and soil. The thunder in the ground was deafening now; the tunnel he stood in felt like an open grave. Frantically, Isiem grabbed at the trough's lip and tried to pull himself out, but his grip crumbled into sand.

The dorsal fin vanished. The rumbling stopped. Isiem hauled himself out of the hole and, kicking away the encumbrance of his deerskin cloak, broke into a flat-out run.

Behind him, the earth exploded. Broken shingles and spidery-clumped grass roots fountained upward along with an enormous, improbably bulky shape: the landshark, leaping impossibly into the sky.

Fifteen feet long from snout to tail, it was a massive beast, heavy yet streamlined, armored in thick gray plates. Its carapace was worn smooth where it rubbed against the landshark's tunnels, caked with packed dirt elsewhere. Long claws capped each of its feet. Pressed together, those claws made curved shovels ideal for swimming through the earth. Separated, they were killing weapons.

The landshark's bulk blotted out the sun. And then, as quickly as it had flung itself into the air, the beast came down. Isiem saw its shadow fall over him and threw himself desperately to the side.

He almost dodged it. The landshark landed with a bone-jarring thud, its blunt claws splayed to crush whatever it could.

Two of its hind toes caught Isiem on the left arm, tearing deep gashes in the flesh and cracking the bone. The blow knocked him hard to the ground, and a flare of pain dizzied him; he choked on a scream. But he kept his senses, barely.

The landshark's huge heavy-browed head swung toward him. Its breath was hot, musty, redolent of steaming earth and acid. Its tiny eyes were garishly orange and utterly wild; its dull yellow teeth, worn down by years of eating rock and metal, were still more than capable of crushing puny human bone. It lifted its foot and began to turn around, chuffing hungrily.

Swallowing his agony, Isiem scrambled away as soon as its foot came up to release him. He thrust a hand at the landshark's open mouth and uttered a short phrase. A ray of pale blue energy streaked from his fingertips, leaving an ephemeral twinkle of frost hanging in its wake. It struck the landshark squarely on the tongue, spreading a starburst of ice across the flat pebbly flesh.

The flare of cold did no significant damage, but it made the landshark recoil. Its saliva froze into a stringy web; it grunted at the unaccustomed shrilling of cold upon its teeth. The creature pawed at its snout, briefly distracted, and Isiem sprang away, yanking open the satchel that held his food.

He swung it in a wide arc as he ran, scattering dried meat and cakes of boiled millet across the ruptured ground. The motion of the flying food caught the landshark's eye, and it lumbered off to investigate, abandoning its unpleasantly frigid prey. Soon it was savaging Isiem's deerskin cloak, flapping the hide from side to side like a rat in a terrier's jaws.

Isiem didn't wait for it to finish. Clutching his injured arm to his chest, he fled. Every step sent a jolt of pain shuddering through his left side, but terror gave him wings. He raced past the spot where Honey waited, pulling her along in his wake, and the bones of Crackspike were far in the distance by the time his spell-granted swiftness faded.

It was a long walk back to the miner's cabin. Without his deerskin cloak to blunt the wind's bite, the cold was merciless. There was no road, and walking across the uneven ground jostled his arm unbearably. From shoulder to wrist, it felt like one constant red-hot throb. In his hurry to get his satchel free, he'd torn his thumbnail, too, and the dull pain in his right hand made an irksome counterpoint to the drumbeat of agony on the left. The landshark didn't follow him, but Isiem found himself bitterly wishing it would, just to put an end to his pain.

Finally he reached the weather-beaten shack. Utterly exhausted, Isiem gazed longingly at the heap of furs on his cot. He wanted nothing more than to collapse into dreamless sleep . . . but his wounds needed tending first. He lit a small dungpatty fire and set a pan of water over it to warm, then gingerly unwrapped his arm.

Blood caked his sleeve. Isiem had to cut it away and wash his arm, gritting his teeth all the while, before he could examine his injuries.

They didn't look good. The landshark's dull claws had pulped the flesh instead of cutting it cleanly. A deep ring of bruises, freckled with dirt, surrounded each of the lacerations.

Worse, the bone was broken in at least two places. Isiem grimaced as he probed it with his fingers. After years at the Dusk Hall and more in Westcrown, he knew the feel of a fractured limb. And he knew, after weeks of living on his own, just how much a crippled arm would hurt him in the wilds.

If he'd stayed loyal to the Midnight Lord, the injury would have been but a minor inconvenience. A few prayers, an evening's obeisance wrapped in his needled chain, and Isiem would have been a whole man again.

But the shadowcaller had abandoned his god, and his god had abandoned him. Zon-Kuthon would not help him now.

And, Isiem thought as he sponged the wounds with a steaming decoction of comfrey leaves and isschis root, he was at peace with that. In a way, it was even reassuring to know the strength of his convictions—and he was well accustomed to paying his price in pain.

In the morning, however, bravery was harder to come by. The pain had kept Isiem from sleeping, and his wounds were ugly even in the soft light of dawn. The rush of energy from his near-death escape was gone; nothing softened his suffering.

He wept, then, alone in the cabin. He wept out of pain and loneliness and despair, and out of self-pity for the life of exile he had chosen. He wept because he had forsaken the god of his country and childhood, and he had not faced a true test of faith until now.

What becomes of the souls of apostates? Isiem didn't know. He knew what his teachers at the Dusk Hall would have said—that such directionless souls were left to wander the empty plains of the shadow realm forevermore, lost and unclaimed, unable to feel or affect the world around them—but he didn't know whether he believed that any longer. Nor did he adopt Velenne's belief that those who reneged on their faith were consigned to Belial's forges, where their souls were melted into raw material and recast to serve the needs of Hell.

Where *did* they go? Isiem feared he might soon find out.

His choices were stark and limited: beg Zon-Kuthon's forgiveness and return to the fold, hoping that the Midnight Lord would accept his contrition and heal his broken arm; turn to the strix for help; or linger on as a cripple and, most likely, die.

The first was unacceptable. The last was unpalatable. That left one option.

Isiem washed and rebandaged his throbbing arm, then wrapped a coyote pelt around his shoulders and went out to study the scraps he'd picked from Crackspike.

He started with the silver cylinders. They came apart easily when twisted, revealing tiny scrolls of a crisp greenish paper so thin it was translucent. Miniscule black glyphs covered each sheet; one of them held a simplified map that depicted the region surrounding Crackspike. Isiem recognized the script as the tongue of devils, but their arrangement made no sense.

Plainly the missives were written in code. Who was Erevullo addressing in such cryptic fashion? *Why?* There were spells that did such things much more easily . . . but perhaps the signifer hadn't known them, just as Isiem had never bothered to learn how to fly.

Or perhaps he'd had some other reason. Until he puzzled out what the scrolls said, Isiem had no hope of unraveling the rest of the mystery.

He spent the remainder of the day working on the cylinders' code and drinking willowbark tea to soothe the pain from his arm. It didn't help much, but it gave him the comfort of doing *something* to mitigate his suffering. Honey, bored by her human's inactivity, amused herself by flinging sticks into the air, chasing them down, and destroying them.

By nightfall Isiem believed he had broken the code, and by the time Kirii came to visit him the next day at noon, he had nearly finished deciphering Erevullo's message.

"You do not look well," the strix observed as she settled on his roof.

"I had an unfortunate meeting with a landshark."

"The hungry digger? We know of him. He is very old. For days he is eating the bones of your *kotarra* wood-roosts."

"Yes, that's where I met him."

Kirii blinked, then covered her small mouth with her hands. Her fine claws gleamed white in the sun as she rocked her weight from one foot to the other. It was not a gesture Isiem had seen before, and he did not know how to read it. "What were you doing there?" she asked.

"I was hoping to learn more about Cheliax's interest in Crackspike—and how far the Chelaxians might be willing to go to take it." Isiem rubbed his eyes with his good hand. He hadn't slept much since returning. "I have some answers, if not all of them."

"Yes?" Kirii hopped to the edge of the roof, peering intently at him. "What did you learn?"

"Where they found silver." Isiem had made a larger and more detailed copy of the map in Erevullo's scrolls, and he offered it up to her now. "This shows the known boundaries of the strike—where they believe the silver is most concentrated. These are the lands they will fight hardest to seize."

Kirii accepted the page he held up to her, but she did not glance at its drawing. "They will fight hardest for this. But they will not stop after taking it?"

"I doubt they'll stop before," Isiem said. "They might stop after. If you can bleed them badly enough, and if the silver runs out in the hills."

"If not?"

He wouldn't lie. "It may be the end of your people. In this part of the world, at least. You could move somewhere else in Devil's Perch, maybe to Ciricskree. Others have, haven't they?"

"Yes. They gave up their names and traditions. They joined the Screeching Spire as pitiable refugees, adopted the teachings of Ciricskree's *rokoa* as their own, and took the lowest of its nests. It is . . . a way to survive, but it is not a thing any *itarii* of Windspire would desire. We are our own clan. One of the last."

Kirii looked away. North, off to the red-black claws of stone that rose sharply over the lesser ridges around Crackspike. Her wings lifted slightly, the feathers raised to catch the breeze. She did not look back. "Your arm. Do you need healing?"

Isiem shifted his arm in its makeshift sling, hoping to ease the ache but only earning another stab of pain for his trouble. "I would be grateful for any medicines you could spare."

"I will ask." She opened her wings to the wind and was gone.

It was not Kirii who returned the next day, however, but four *itaraak*: tribal warriors in breastplates of bone and tortoiseshell, their faces hidden behind the masks that all the *itaraak* of Windspire wore. Fierce slashes of charcoal, chalk, and red clay adorned their masks, signifying affiliations and lineages Isiem couldn't fathom. Two leveled their spears at the Nidalese wizard as soon as they touched the ground, while a third circled in the air to watch for other foes. The fourth, whose mask was crowned with double crests of bone, approached the shadowcaller warily.

"*Kotarra*. You come with us," the strix said in heavily accented Taldane. "Eyes cover. Hands tied. Beast of war stays here or dies."

"Beast of war?" Isiem repeated blankly, then followed the strix's motion to Honey and blinked. "She's not a beast of war. She can barely kill a rabbit." Seeing that the *itaraak* was lost in the thicket of unfamiliar words, Isiem reached cautiously for his clay ziggurat and cast his spell of translation. He did *not* want to be misunderstood.

When the magic had taken hold, he repeated: "Honey's just a dog. A pet. She isn't a war beast. She doesn't even help me hunt, really."

The strix on the ground exchanged glances. Openly incredulous, their bone-masked leader made a feint with his spear at the dog. Honey jumped back in surprise, her tail bushed out, but did not snarl or lunge; instead she looked at Isiem, confused.

"Why do you keep this beast?" the strix's leader asked, as confused as the dog was.

"She's a friend," Isiem replied. "Why are you here? I only asked for potions."

"We have not come to heal you." The strix gestured to the *itaraak* on his left, who shouldered his spear and came forward with a wide band of deerskin in his hands. "We have come to take you to the stone-roosts. Do not resist."

Isiem didn't. He stood motionless as the *itaraak* blindfolded him and tied his wrists crossed in front of him, then bound them again to his waist. The bonds sent agony shooting through his injured arm, but he hid the pain with well-trained stoicism. "Why?" he asked, proud that no hint of agony came through his voice.

"The black riders have returned," the strix said, "and this time they have come in strength."

Chapter Nineteen
Windspire

The journey to the strix's roost was less torturous than Isiem had feared, although it did not begin that way.

For the first stretch—less than an hour, he guessed, although it felt ten times as long—they kept him stumbling blindly along the rocks and gullies. The blindfold smelled of old blood and, after a while, suffocatingly of his own sweat. Isiem stubbed his toes so many times that he was mildly surprised they didn't break off. Twice he fell hard enough to skin his good elbow and his knees.

He heard the *itaraak* exchanging comments around him. His translation spell had worn off long ago and the inflections of the strix's tongue were far different from those of Taldane; still, Isiem could tell that they were increasingly impatient with his clumsiness.

But what was he to do? He couldn't see, the ground was littered with loose rock, and they offered him no help. Grim-faced, he pressed on.

After leading him up a particularly steep rise, the strix stopped for a while. Isiem felt a chill gather around him as they waited, and understood that he was standing in shadow, not sun. *Is there anything tall enough to cast such a shadow in the hills?*

He heard the rattle of bones knocking against one another and the rasp of coarse rope unrolling. Then the strix were ushering him across a bridge that swayed and creaked at every step, and he was listening to the wind howl underfoot. Only a thin guide rope told him where to go—and Honey didn't even have that. The dog had her eyes, though, and somehow she followed Isiem across.

On the other side, mercifully, the walk came to an end.

"Sit," the leader of the *itaraak* told him in strained Taldane. The other strix parceled food out among themselves—Isiem could hear them cracking open sealed gourds and unwrapping brittle dried leaves, could smell smoked meat and herbed yams—but they offered him nothing. Hands bound, broken arm ablaze with pain, he could do nothing but swallow his hunger and wait.

After a seeming eternity the strix began to move again. One of them uttered a word of magic; Isiem's ears pricked at the familiar syllables, although the accent was different and the strix spoke quietly, so that he could not identify exactly what was said. But he was not surprised when, a moment later, he felt a new, larger presence loom upon the rocks nearby. Stone groaned in the grip of powerful claws; the wind rilled over stiff flight feathers. Isiem heard no breathing, though, and he felt no warmth radiating from what was surely a massive body perched above.

One of the strix untied the shadowcaller's hands. "Ride."

The enormous thing they had summoned came down from its rocky perch. Its movements creaked audibly, like the rope bridge had. A sun-baked, dusty smell surrounded it, along with the scents of crushed pollen and dried meat.

The strix took Isiem's hands and guided him, still blindfolded, onto the creature's back. Under its feathers he felt hard bone, with no muscle or fat to pad it. His foot slid as he climbed on, and his toes caught in an empty space between two of its naked ribs. There was no sign that the creature felt any pain at his slip, or that it even noticed. He clung to it weakly with his good hand, unable to maintain a grip with the other.

"What is this thing?" Isiem asked. Whether it was an enchanted construct or undead, he knew for a certainty that it was not alive.

"Gift of our ancestors," the masked *itaraak* answered. "Hold on strong."

"What about my dog?"

"*Tokoaa* will carry it in claws. No hurting."

"I don't think —" Isiem began, but then the unliving thing under him lurched off the ground and the wind stripped his words away. The speed of their ascent ripped at his blindfold, allowing him to glimpse just how quickly the earth was receding—and how sharp it was. The red-veined spikes of stone that gave Devil's Perch its name looked like an army of readied spears beneath them. The shadowcaller squeezed his eyes shut, lowered his body against the bony steed's, and held on for his life.

Hurtling blind through the sky on a mount he could not control and could barely grasp was one of the most terrifying experiences Isiem had ever endured. The wind was frigid, the height unknowable, the strix unfriendly . . . but most frightening of all was his complete lack of power. Nothing was under his control in this journey, and for Isiem there was no greater horror.

He collapsed in relief when they finally landed. It was a lurching, jaw-jarring stop that smashed his tongue between his teeth, but Isiem hardly noticed the sudden taste of blood. All the strength seemed to have been drained out of him by the flight. Honey bounded up and licked his face, pausing occasionally to worry at the leather band covering his eyes. The dog seemed unfazed by her own sojourn through the sky.

The *itaraak* removed his blindfold. Already the thing that had borne him to their home—the *tokoaa*, he supposed—was gone, presumably returned to the place from whence it had been summoned.

But the strix remained, and their city was of such strangeness that it soon drove the mystery of the *tokoaa* from his mind.

It wasn't really a city, Isiem realized after a moment. The crimson spires and crooked black claws of Devil's Perch gave Windspire the appearance of a city crowded with towers, but most of those stony perches were empty. If they had ever been settled, they were desolate now.

The ones still occupied held tangles of rope, netting, and vines, all woven into nests suspended beneath their arches and between their crags. Long, pale bones served as supports here and there, as did leg-thick poles of braided grass stiffened with reddish unguents. The nests were carefully concealed from aerial view; any foes flying overhead would see only the surrounding rock. Isiem saw a few ladders and bridges linking some of the smaller nests in the heart of the settlement, but most were unconnected. He presumed that the very young and very old lived there. The other strix, able to fly from home to home, had no need of ropes to help them.

Despite the chaos of materials used in the settlement's construction, there was a peculiarly unified beauty to the whole. Just as a robin's nest spun order out of jumbled twigs and straws, so the strix had built something verging on elegance from their scavenged scraps.

"*Kotarra*," the masked strix said. "This way." He hopped down a crooked ledge, gripping the uneven stone with clawed toes and spreading his wings for balance as he walked toward a tented nest. The sides of the tent were made of stitched deerhides, lavishly adorned with geometric designs in bone beads and clay paints. A trickle of bluish smoke escaped from a hole near its top.

Isiem picked his way slowly along the ledge, wishing too late that he'd told Honey to stay back until called. The dog trotting cheerfully at his heels was likely to knock him down to his death—and, indeed, once her nose jostled the back of his knee, causing a black flash of panic. It was a *long* fall to the bottom of Devil's Perch.

But he kept his balance, and he soon came to the covered nest's entry flap.

"In," the masked *itaraak* said, standing to the side.

"You're not coming?"

"The *rokoa* asked for you alone."

"Very well." Isiem was acutely conscious of how disreputable he looked. Between his lonely stay in the miner's cabin and the dishevelment of the ride to Windspire, he looked like a sorry vagrant indeed. No good house in Westcrown would have admitted him; in Pangolais he would have been swept quietly off to the Umbral Dungeons to await sacrifice. He had to hope that appearances mattered less to the strix, at least where *kotarra* were concerned.

"Honey, stay," he told the dog, having no idea whether she'd listen. Quickly, before his furry companion could follow and offend the strix, Isiem pushed the tent flap aside and stepped in. The flap fell shut behind him, closing him in smoky darkness punctuated by the filigreed glow of small, scattered bone braziers.

A winged form shifted in the gloom. As his eyes adjusted, Isiem recognized the *rokoa* sitting on a raised cushion fashioned from a tumbleweed padded with felted hair and feathers. She gestured for him to take a similar cushion facing her.

Isiem obeyed. The *rokoa* held a faded, yellowed page in one hand. It had been folded into a frayed blossom. He couldn't make out any of the page's lettering, but when she motioned for him to give her his hand, he understood that it was some sort of spell talisman. Again he did as he was bidden. The *rokoa* touched his palm with a single wrinkled fingertip, and he felt a spark of magic pass between them.

"Welcome," she said. There was no twinning of voices with this spell; he understood her perfectly, but he only heard the clicks and whistles of strix. "We are grateful you came."

"I had little choice in the matter," Isiem replied.

"Not true. You could have gone with the black riders when they first came to visit the ashes. Instead you chose to run, and so my daughter found you. That was a choice. That choice brought you here." The *rokoa* blinked sideways, nictating membranes sliding across her eyes, but only the movement told Isiem that she had blinked. The aged strix's eyes were so rheumy that they appeared perpetually lidded. "Always there is a choice."

Isiem shrugged. "Whether that is so or not, I am here now. Why did you summon me?"

"My daughter says you are a traitor to the *kotarra*. Is that true?"

"The Hellknights would tell you so."

"I did not ask that. I asked if it were true."

"I've learned to be cautious of absolutes," Isiem said. "What is 'true' depends on perspective. Fly above

Windspire, or walk on the ravine floors below, and it might be 'true' that no nests exist—but from the perspective of your people, perched among its ledges, the city is easy to find. When it comes to questions of loyalty, truth is equally a matter of perspective."

"Cleverly said," the *rokoa* acknowledged, "but that is not an answer." She reached for a triangular clay pot and deftly poured two small cups of a steaming, musky-smelling brew. "Do you wish for tea?"

"Thank you." Isiem accepted a cup but did not drink. He cupped it in the palm of his good hand, letting its warmth spread across his skin. "I'm sorry if it seems that I'm evading your question. I have no better answer to give. I believe that I have become a traitor in the eyes of Cheliax and Nidal. In my own eyes . . . I don't know that I was ever loyal. I've wanted to escape for as long as I can remember. I just never believed I could."

"Have you escaped now?" She extended a wizened hand, indicating that he should give his own to her. Reluctantly he put his cup on the floor—the *rokoa's* nest had no tables—and complied. The *rokoa* wove another spell, tapping the jangling mass of necklaces knotted around her wrinkled neck, and a soothing coolness flowed from her hand into his. Bone scraped against bone as Isiem's broken arm knitted; the fever that had begun to take hold in his flesh vanished.

He bowed his head in gratitude. But he still answered bluntly, and truthfully. "I don't know. Maybe not. The Chelaxians seem determined to bring Devil's Perch under their control."

"But that would not be in your interest," the *rokoa* said softly. She picked up the cup she had set aside and drank her tea in a single long swallow.

"My interests are not yours. *You* want to drive the Chelaxians out of the west. *I* have no particular reason to care. I only need to avoid them. I don't need to hold land against them. Leaving would suit my ends just as well—and much more safely."

"Yet you stayed. You told my daughter what you could about their secrets. Why, if it is not in your interest to see them driven from our roosts?"

"Well, for one, I hear you help people get to Pezzack," Isiem replied with a wry smile. The *rokoa*'s expression did not change, and after an awkward pause he abandoned his weak attempt at levity.

"I don't much like Nidal," he confessed. "Faced with death, my people chose to cling to their land at any price . . . and with Zon-Kuthon's blessing, they did. They kept their land, and they lost their souls. I feel they chose poorly.

"The Chelaxians made a similar bargain. The death of their god threatened their empire, and so their greatest house sold itself and all its kin to devils. They held their lands and their power at the expense of whoever they were before.

"To be sure, Cheliax has not fallen as far as Nidal, or as completely. It is an empire at war with itself, riven with rebellion and conflicted down to the last strands of its soul. But the greater part, the stronger part, made an infernal bargain just as my people did, and paid a similar price. Whether they wish to believe it or not, we Nidalese know better. It is no accident that the Umbral Court sends so many advisors to Cheliax."

"All very interesting, these troubles of *kotarra*," the *rokoa* interrupted, "but what has this to do with us?"

"I saw the slaves that the Chelaxians sold in Pangolais," Isiem answered, letting as much of the old anguish show as he dared, "and I saw what became of the rebels in Westcrown. I know what happens to those who defy Imperial Cheliax and lose. I dealt some of those punishments with my own hand. I cannot stand silent in my cowardice and watch it happen again."

"Do you hope for atonement?" the old strix asked. Her face remained a mask of wrinkles, her eyes opaque and unrevealing as opal cabochons. Nothing in any word or gesture betrayed the slightest hint of her thoughts.

Somehow, that very opacity freed Isiem to speak more frankly than he would have imagined possible. He felt that she would not condemn him, whatever he said. "I don't know," he admitted. "I don't know what atonement would be. But I see how badly your people are outmatched, and I do not want you to suffer as you will if you fight and fail. And I see, too, that you are faced with the same choice that Nidal was, and that Cheliax was. Both of them, I believe, decided wrongly."

"Ah," she said. "Yes. The choice between land and soul." The *rokoa* reached into her hollow tumbleweed cushion and brought out the copied map that Isiem had made for Kirii. "My daughter showed me this. Your drawing. The places that the black riders claim." She ran a wizened finger over the paper, sketching out a smaller, jagged shape within the larger one Isiem had drawn to mark the silver strike. "Our summer roost."

Isiem inclined his head in acknowledgment, saying nothing.

"You suggest we should cede these grounds to them? Risk losing Windspire and retreating to Ciricskree in dishonor? Consign our children to the lowest nests, give up the teachings of our ancestors for those of the Screeching Spire? My daughter told you true: our kin would take us in. The *itarii* do not abandon their blood.

But we would live among them as beggars. Is that the fate you would have for us?"

"Yes," Isiem said. The word tasted bitter on his tongue; he could not imagine how much more so it was to hear. No doubt the *rokoa* regretted her kindness in healing him. But the answer, he believed, was clear. "If you fight them, your warriors will die—on the battlefield, if they're lucky; on the altars of Pangolais, if they're not. I don't believe the Chelaxians have any interest in the remainder of Devil's Perch. This land is impossible to farm, too dangerous to hunt. Windspire itself holds nothing of interest to them. All they want is the silver. Were I you, I would let them have it, and protect the lives of my people."

"This land holds our bones," the *rokoa* said calmly. "We hunt here, we raise our young here, we die here. The bones of a thousand generations of *itarii*, all the way back to the first dread storm that carried us from the world of gods. You suggest we abandon all our traditions."

"I suggest you abandon dirt and rocks. The dead are dead. What do they care? Anyway, you will not lose them all. Your people carry the bones of your dead; I've seen them, and Kirii has explained the custom to me. But even if you *were* to abandon them, every last one, I ask you: Which matters more? Protecting your ancestors, or your descendants?"

The *rokoa* trilled a sharp little hiss through her teeth. "That is our choice? Dishonor or death? Over a shiny metal that *kotarra* women hang from their ears?"

"Over silver, yes," Isiem said. "Over silver and Cheliax's dreams of glory. I'm sorry."

Chapter Twenty
Narrowed Choices

They put him in one of the empty nest-tents at the heart of Windspire. The *itaraak* removed the bridges and ladders linking Isiem's nest to the others, leaving him confined to that single small perch, but he could still watch the life of the strix around him.

There were not many young strix, Isiem soon realized, and even fewer old ones. If it were not for the wounded, the clan would have had little need for its linked tents at all. But for every fledgling and elder strix he saw, there were at least three who bore fresh wounds or old scars. Some looked to him like hunting mishaps, but many—perhaps most—of their injuries had been dealt by human hands. And as swiftly as the *rokoa* made them whole, they seemed to return with new hurts.

Not that they had much choice. Everything the strix ate, wore, and used to build their homes came from outside Windspire. A steady stream of scouts and hunters flew in and out of the hidden city throughout the day. They brought in dry dung and tough grass from the lowlands, oblong blue-black berries and flattened red ones plucked from mountain slopes, and whatever meat they could catch or find. Dust-brown snakes, small plains deer, an innumerable variety of birds— they even ate fat white termite grubs, cracking open their mounds and collecting them in basketfuls like squirming grains of rice. Isiem couldn't stomach the things himself, but he developed a profound respect for the strix's adaptability. They were a people who did not let pride slow their survival.

He hoped that would be as true of their politics as it was of their food. The tension in Windspire was impossible to miss, even for an outsider who saw little and understood less. The *itaraak* and the *rokoa* were sharply at odds, often pretending not to see one another and, when they were forced into direct conversation, holding themselves with stiff formality.

The leader of the *itaraak*, a short yet imposing warrior named Red Chest, was especially prickly, and he made no secret of the fact that his hostility extended to the human among them. Isiem stayed inside his tent when Red Chest was about. Kirii said the *itaraak* had gotten his name when, as a youth, his mask was knocked loose during an attack on human settlers. Rather than turn back from the battle, he had spread the blood from a chest wound across his face in a makeshift design and kept fighting. His tenacity was as legendary as his temper, and Isiem had no wish to provoke either.

The other warriors, however, were not much calmer.

Once a young *itaraak* flew to Isiem's nest-tent after an especially heated argument with the *rokoa*. The warrior's feathers bristled with agitation and he held his flint-tipped spear as if he meant to use it, but Isiem was not immediately frightened, only wary. No *itaraak* of Windspire would dream of taking a life—not even a human life—without that mask to shield his soul.

This *itaraak* was bare-faced, so unless he was a visitor from the Screeching Spire, Isiem did not believe his life was in imminent danger. But the warrior's yellow eyes were hot with rage, and the story of Red Chest's name indicated that an *itaraak* could improvise a mask in times of need, so the Nidalese also knew to tread carefully.

"I could kill you," the *itaraak* said.

Isiem had just finished his day's conversation with Kirii, and his spell of translation was still with him. He understood the strix's words clearly, and wondered whether the sight of the *rokoa*'s daughter leaving his nest might have been part of what prompted the spear-wielder's anger.

"You could," he agreed cautiously.

His acquiescence only seemed to incite the strix. The *itaraak* groped reflexively at his brow, reaching for a killer's mask that was thankfully not there. "I could kill a score of you. A hundred."

"Perhaps."

"You have infected the *rokoa* with your cowardice. Because of you we will run from these mewling *kotarra*. Because of you we will abandon our hunting lands to groundlings and black riders. *Our* lands. Lands our ancestors fought and died to keep!"

The *itaraak*'s fury had drawn curious eyes to their conversation. Isiem, conscious of the others watching, kept his own voice low and his manner subdued. "I cannot change the world," the shadowcaller said quietly, "and this is its way."

"We would not lose!"

"You don't know what you face."

"*You* do not know what we would lose," the itaraak spat back, and threw himself from the ledge. For an instant Isiem was afraid that the young warrior had hurled himself onto the rocks, but when he looked down he saw the strix's broad black wings skimming the abyss.

The others were still watching. Tired, and feeling oddly defeated, Isiem went back into his borrowed nest. Alone inside its felted walls, he tried to imagine a tragedy in being forced to abandon Nidal.

He couldn't. His homeland was too dark a place, too cruel. All his memories were of trying to escape Pangolais, or at least lessen its shadows.

It was possible that he might have struggled to stay in Crosspine. But try as he might, Isiem could recall nothing solid of his childhood in that village. The life he'd led there was too long ago, and too short. He couldn't remember his brother's face, or his own mother's. All that came to his mind's eye was a pale shape and a cloud of brown hair, and a vague sense of gentleness.

Was that enough to fight over? Not for him. Perhaps that made him a coward, but Isiem could not see how. Having come to manhood in a poisoned land, he had never set down deep roots, and he could not imagine how another, born to more spiritually fertile ground, might become so bound to it that severing those roots would kill him.

He sat there the whole day, searching through his memories for something that might help him understand the *itaraak*'s anger, but at sundown he still had nothing.

Kirii came to see him again that evening, bearing a covered bowl of savory black seeds steamed with shredded meat and mountain herbs. The food was good, but Isiem had no appetite. He ate without tasting, while beside him Kirii squatted on the precipice and stared into the infinite shadows under their rocky perch.

"I worry that I've advised you wrongly," he said.

Kirii shrugged—another human affectation she had learned to mimic. Her eyes had an eerie shimmer in the dark, like the alien glow of cat's eyes. "You only answer what we ask. We do as we wish with the knowledge."

Isiem swallowed the last of the seeds. "But if I've given you misleading answers . . ."

"We have eyes to see for ourselves, and minds to judge." The strix's eyes flashed, inhumanly bright with reflected firelight. "It is not for you to choose what becomes of our people."

"I just worry —"

"Wrongly," Kirii interrupted, more sharply than he had heard her speak before. "You told us to flee. My mother advised the tribe to flee. The *itaraak* refused. All this time, they have been arguing in circles, talking and talking for hours into days about the best way to go, but never opening their wings. While they talked, the black riders came. Now it is too late. And still they talk."

"What do you mean, 'too late'? The Hellknights haven't found Windspire." Nor did Isiem think it likely that they had found the summer roosts. In the warm months, the strix were a nomadic people, settling in light tents just long enough to hunt and forage, cure the fruits of their work, and return the preserved fruit, grain, and meat to Windspire for storage. They left little to mark their passing, and even if the Chelaxians found those traces, they would be all but meaningless.

"No," Kirii confirmed. "They have taken Tokarai Springs."

"I don't know what that is."

"It is the surest source of water for Windspire. Not the closest, but the only one that never dries. Animals

287

go there to drink. *Okash* trees grow by the water. Tokarai Springs is key to our survival. Without it, Windspire starves, and four other clans suffer hardship." The strix voiced a low, disconsolate trill. "If they realize that, they will poison it, and that is the end for us. We will go to Ciricskree as beggars. If they do not poison it, they will still take it. No one is fool enough to give up good water in the stonelands. That is nearly as bad. It robs us of our spring. So, the *itaraak* say, we have no choice but to fight—and they are correct."

"Let me help," Isiem said. He made the offer impulsively, and was surprised to hear himself say the words, but did not try to retract them. It felt right to help the strix. True, he was in hiding from Cheliax and Nidal, and joining the *itaraak* of Windspire on an open field could expose the secret of his survival . . . but what was the point of that survival if he did nothing to help his friends?

And they were his friends. Or at least Kirii was.

The strix's glowing eyes widened and then dimmed as she blinked twice in quick succession, the opaque membranes sliding rapidly across her enormous irises. "The *itaraak* will not trust you with weapons behind them."

"That seems ill advised. You can scarcely afford to refuse allies now."

"I agree. But the *itaraak* have their pride. And their fears. You offend both."

"Would it offend them as much if I merely offered to play scout?"

Kirii cocked her head to one side. "What could you hope to see from the ground that they would not from the sky?"

Isiem smiled slightly. He turned a hand outward, sweeping it to encompass the nests and ropes and bridges around them, all so cunningly hidden from the air. "Different truths."

Two days later he came upon the Chelish encampment. The strix had blindfolded him again and left him to the east of the Chelaxians, so that his approach would not give away the direction of Windspire if they saw him. Isiem lost most of the first day regaining his bearings, but the smoke of the army's fires led him to their camp by the following afternoon.

And it *was* an army, he realized as he approached. Judging from the number of tents and horses dotted around the tiny patch of green that surrounded Tokarai Springs, at least a hundred soldiers, perhaps a hundred and fifty, were marching on the strix. Cooks and squires scurried among the wagons and lines of horses, but they were greatly outnumbered by armed knights, most of whom appeared to be carrying out their own chores. For a Chelaxian to give up the privileges of rank was no small thing. This was a force pared down to its essentials.

The infernal eye and swirling vortex of Citadel Enferac flapped over a few tents, but the majority of the camp flew the crossed circle of Cheliax. Only a few crimson-cloaked signifers were visible; most of the men appeared to be soldiers in the Chelish army. It seemed Vicarius Torchia had chosen to let the throne deal with the strix rather than send more of his own Hellknights on a task that did not, after all, directly concern his order.

That realization chilled Isiem, for it meant that the strix faced not a single order of Hellknights, but the full enmity of the throne. A dozen had failed, so Abrogail II had sent a hundred soldiers. And if those failed, she'd send a thousand.

He doubted the thousand would be needed. What he saw spread around the spring was more than enough to overwhelm Windspire.

Two of the tents struck him as unusual. Neither was the commander's tent—one was close beside it, while the other was far on the eastern periphery, almost detached from the camp—but they were nearly as large, and both were far more ornate.

The eastern tent was made of a stiff gold brocade covered in metallic green sigils. From such a distance it was impossible to make out the details of its design, but the tent's arcane nature was unmistakable. It shimmered in the sunlight like a chartreuse sphene, all fractured rainbows over a bed of blinding yellow-green. The garishness made Isiem's eyes ache.

Nor did the strangeness end there. The tent's entry flap was enormous; a warhorse could have trotted through without ducking its head or brushing its sides. An entire supply wagon, piled high with sacks of flour and jarred honeycomb and squawking black chickens in cages, seemed devoted to that single tent. Murky, slime-streaked glass tanks squatted near the wagon's front. Isiem couldn't see what was in them, but the contents were clearly alive. The water in the tanks rippled constantly in slow, lazy waves.

Two bald brown slaves, each tattooed with the same sinuous green designs as those on the tent itself, worked outside it. Long scars on their cheeks indicated in the crude, universal parlance of slavers that they'd had their tongues removed. Their eyes were a brilliant, glowing yellow-green, and there was something bestial about their features—flattened foreheads, chins and noses thrust outward like muzzles, a slight sharpness to their ears—that suggested they were not quite human. Devil-blooded, perhaps.

Bronze collars, engraved with yet more runes, encircled their necks and waists. The skin underneath those metal cuffs was roped with layers of old scars, inflicted by too-small collars being struck off carelessly and new ones soldered on. The marks of such cruelty identified them as chattel even more clearly than the cuffs did.

He wondered where they were from, and what enchantment held them. Slaves were hardly rare in Cheliax, but Isiem had never seen any kept in that fashion. These wore collars but no chains, and their minds did not seem to be their own.

Of the tent's inhabitant, he saw nothing.

The other tent, next to the commander's at the center of the camp, was comparatively plain. It was all in black and red, the standard Chelish colors. A jewel-eyed imp perched on its spiked central pole. Isiem didn't recognize the imp, and none of the tent's trappings were unusual for devil-dominated Cheliax, but something about it still tugged at him, tantalizing his memory like a whisper of an old lover's perfume.

Velenne.

As if the lenses of a sailor's spyglass had clicked into place, the tent seemed to come into focus for the first time. He recognized, now, the line of burgundy stitching where an assassin had cut his way into the tent ten years ago. She'd told him that story one night, laughing about the man's fate when she caught him. The ornaments and talismans that dangled from the tent's roof were the same ones that had hung over the windows of her rooms at the Umbral Court, maintaining her privacy against magical spies.

The realization hit him like a punch. Isiem sat down, feeling suddenly suffocated. A tangle of confused emotions rose in his chest. He shook his head, trying to clear it, but no clarity came.

It couldn't be a coincidence that his former mistress was here. True, after the massacre of Erevullo and his Hellknights, the throne would want more accomplished agents to deal with the strix, and Velenne was certainly that. But she hated traveling, and despised being made to leave the comforts of civilization. She had more than enough influence in Egorian to avoid being sent to the hinterlands for any ordinary matter.

Either she had her own interests in Devil's Perch, or she was here because of him. Either possibility filled Isiem with dread . . . and a small, anxious thrill of excitement. He longed to see her again, even as he feared what her presence might mean for the strix and his own chances of freedom. And he hoped, perversely, that she *had* come for him, even if that meant his ruse of being dead had failed. He wanted to believe she cared that much.

The truth, he knew, was not likely to be so sweet. Just as that paladin in Westcrown had been duty-bound to kill Velenne for her betrayal, so Isiem's mistress would be bound to finish *him*. Her position might be reversed, but the answer was the same.

And yet the key to his survival might lie in that old heartbreak.

Hadn't she said that the course of her life might have changed if only her lover had *listened*? She had been willing to turn for him, she'd claimed, and although Isiem doubted that Velenne was still so malleable today, he thought there was a fair chance that she might be willing to hear him out. To bend her sense of duty that far, at least.

"But what will you tell her?" Kirii asked that night when she came to visit Isiem at the small, hidden camp he set up a quarter-mile from Tokarai Springs. Neither he nor the strix wanted him to return to Windspire until his scouting was complete.

"I'm not sure," Isiem admitted. The night was cold and vast around him. He felt very small under the desert stars. Pulling his sheepskin cloak closer around his shoulders, he huddled over his tiny fire, trying to will the smoldering dungpatty to produce more warmth than it did. "The truth, or some part of it. I doubt I could lie to her." It was Velenne who had taught him to read the lies on men's faces, and he was not fool enough to think he could deceive her.

Kirii seemed unaffected by the cold. She squatted outside the firelight, alien and black-winged. "What part?"

"The part she wants to hear," Isiem replied. "The secret to how she can win."

Chapter Twenty-One
Entreaty

That night Isiem could not sleep.

Long after the moon had crested and begun to descend, he lay awake on the rocky ground, wrestling with the words he wanted to send.

What could he say that would persuade Velenne to come, and to come alone? She had always been cautious, preferring to wait until her prey was unwary and strike from surprise, rather than meeting challengers on an open field. Above all, she avoided engaging on enemy ground—yet that was exactly what Isiem would ask her to do.

And she would see him as an enemy now, standing alongside the strix.

Could he make her believe otherwise in the space of a few whispered words? Was it worth trying?

The moon fell into the claws of Devil's Perch, leaving the sky ghostly and lonesome as it waited for dawn. Isiem closed his eyes and prayed for enlightenment, but he had no god to pray to, and no insight came.

In the end, the message he sent on the morning wind was a simple one: *Come to the ravine of skulls outside Crackspike at noon, and I will give you the key to victory.*

Then he slept, relieved of the weight of uncertainty, while the early sun cast light without warmth over his bed.

An hour before noon he woke and went to the appointed place. The ravine of skulls, although not formally named, was easily found. It was a shallow channel cut into the earth by flash floods, which had also washed the bones of foxes and desert hares into the gully. The people of Crackspike had sealed its name by using the ravine to dispose of their waste, including the bones of the animals they slaughtered or lost to hardship. The skulls of oxen and the small fine bones of chickens and geese littered the rough gray rocks, attracting scavengers as large as coyotes and as small as soft-furred mice.

Some of those mice darted for cover as Isiem approached, but he saw no other living things. Somehow he hoped that Velenne would be waiting, even though he had come early to avoid exactly that, but she was not there.

She had been, though. As soon as Isiem glimpsed a small gray mouse darting away with a bit of crumpled honeycomb in its mouth, he knew that. And he was not surprised—or not terribly so—when a smudge of white jade dust on the brow of a nearby horse's skull suddenly expanded into a small, fanged mouth. Isiem was inured to the strangenesses of magic, but it was nevertheless surreal to see a miniature devil's maw open in the fissures of that sun-baked bone.

"No," the magic mouth said in Velenne's voice, a sound so familiar and yet so long unheard that it made Isiem's heart stop for an instant. "We can talk, but not here. Come to my tent at dusk."

Its message delivered, the mouth faded away, leaving the shadowcaller alone in a valley of bones. He stood there a while longer, lost in a welter of thoughts, then shook off his confusion and walked back to his camp.

Isiem spent the rest of the day in study, trying to guess which spells would be most useful to him. Invisibility would get him in, but if the conversation went poorly, no spell he possessed would get him out.

There was a kind of freedom in that knowledge. It lifted away his worry. He would steer across the seas of chance as best he could, but ultimately all his skill and prudence were insignificant against the whims of fate.

Not that he had any intention of surrendering. Isiem chose his spells and prepared each one with care, counting out the components he'd need and tucking them into concealed pockets. Over his frayed shadowcaller's robes, he wore the warmer furs and hides the strix had provided. He tied a small knife to his belt; it was the only weapon he had. Then he packed up his tiny camp and walked a mile away.

Behind a rocky outcropping, the Nidalese wizard sat with his back against a dead tree and listened to the wind until it was time to go. He heard no messages in the arid breeze, as the *itaraak* claimed to receive before their own battles. But then, he did not have the desert in his blood.

What he found instead was a glimmer of serenity. This land was ancient, far older than he, and whatever happened in the Chelish camp tonight, it would outlast him. Men were not its masters; they might have claimed it, and in the ages of Azlant and Thassilon even believed it, but those empires were long gone to dust, while the spires of Devil's Perch endured.

The months of his exile had given him a glimpse of freedom. He'd slipped out from under the shadows, and that was more than he'd expected to have in this life. If he failed, it wouldn't be the end of the world, or even of the strix. Only of himself, and that was a fate Isiem had accepted since he was a child passing the doors of the Dusk Hall.

Sunset came.

Under a cloak of invisibility, Isiem approached the Chelish encampment. He went cautiously, trying to avoid brushing against vegetation or crunching on loose gravel. In the bustle of a crowded camp, such small disturbances might go unnoticed, but Isiem wanted to take no chances.

Walls of striated red stone screened Tokarai Springs, shielding it from the worst of the desert wind but causing the remainder to eddy unpredictably around the gaps and crevices in the formations. Small trees swayed in the rock walls' shelter, a few yellowed leaves still clinging to their winter-stripped branches. Somewhere out of sight, water gurgled quietly. The smells of woodsmoke and roasting meat mingled with a whiff of stink from the latrine pits.

Soldiers, and occasionally a signifer in an iron-brooched red cloak, walked regular patrols around the camp. Isiem's spell hid him from their sight, but one of the Chelish knights had a pack of four huge, brindled mastiffs chained by his tent, and the spell did nothing to conceal his scent.

The mastiffs had been staked at the periphery of the camp, as far from the army's horses as possible. Moving carefully, aware that the wind might shift at any moment, Isiem waited for the next patrol to pass, then slipped through their lines midway between the animals. He was not worried—yet—about triggering protective spells, but as he inched forward he sent cantrips ahead, searching for any hint of wards.

Velenne's tent had no guard. Its entry flap was pinned open, allowing a hint of smoky incense to escape. Red candles burned in the depths like embers dropped by the dying sun. Nothing seemed to move, save a loose thread stirred by the breeze.

Feeling like a mouse braving a lion's den, Isiem crept inside.

Three steps in, she paralyzed him.

Still stooped and facing the carpet, he felt the magic seize his limbs. Isiem struggled to resist, but it was useless. He'd gotten stronger in the years since their last meeting, but it appeared Velenne had as well. Her spell overwhelmed him, and he froze, locked in ensorcelled immobility.

"I'm glad you came," Velenne said. "I didn't really expect you would." Her voice drifted from somewhere beyond his view. Small, clawed hands patted Isiem down, rifling through his clothes and belongings with inhuman deftness. Within seconds the searcher had found all his spell components, removed his flint-bladed knife, and dropped everything on the carpeted floor in a symphony of soft thuds. Then the unseen searcher guided him to a chair, pushed his unresisting body into the seat, and was gone, sweeping up all his dropped belongings in its wake.

"Pardon my precautions." The diabolist dropped into a nearby chair, almost but not quite opposite. The years hardly seemed to have touched her. Perhaps her clothing was a little more sumptuous, the jewels in her ears a shade larger, a few strands of silver in her dark hair . . . but she herself was unchanged. Isiem would have caught his breath, had her spell not already caught it for him. The sight of her was like a gut punch to his memory.

She crooked a finger, and the magic holding Isiem evaporated. "You must understand, I wasn't even sure you were *you*. Our source was not tremendously reliable."

"Someone told you I was here?" he asked, unsurprised but manuevering for time to regain his composure.

"Of course." The corners of Velenne's eyes crinkled in a suppressed smile. She had shaded them with kohl and silvery dust; the metallic powder shimmered in the dim candlelight. "The girl you saved. You gave her a potion to help her evade the strix. She survived, and returned to civilization. Where we found her."

"And questioned her."

Velenne shrugged. "We wanted to know what happened in Crackspike. That was the only survivor we found. Torchia's man never had time to complete his relay, much less send any messages through it, and your newfound friends make it difficult to rely on imps. She was our only source . . . but now we have our answers, and we are here. As are you." She ran a fingernail along the hilt of his flint knife, studying its carvings. "I was not surprised that you feigned your own death and ran. I *am* surprised you allied yourself with the strix. How does that aid your ends?"

"I wouldn't have survived without them."

"I can see that." She clicked her nail against the hilt's carved antler and raised her eyebrows at the motley collection of hides and furs he wore. "And I suppose it should not startle me that you are grateful enough to them that you've come to broker some agreement on their behalf. You always were an optimist about the value of talk."

"I think the value is obvious enough," Isiem said. "It's stupid to fight. The strix won't engage in a pitched battle. They'll raid and run. They'll sabotage equipment, poison livestock, chase off game—all the things they've been doing during your journey here. It's a long road to Devil's Perch, and a hard one. Surely you must know that, having traveled it yourself. And that was with, what, a dozen signifers and a hundred soldiers? Imagine how difficult it would be for a handful of miners. To keep them at bay, you'll have to station soldiers at the mines and send escorts with every wagon. Her Infernal Majestrix can do that, I know. But it's expensive. Doing it cuts deep into profits, and profit is all the throne wants out of these hills."

Velenne watched him intently, her expression one that Isiem knew well: she was trying to decide whether to take the bait.

"You can prevent them from raiding?" she asked, after a measured pause.

Isiem bit his tongue to keep from betraying his elation. "Yes."

"In exchange for what?"

"Certain concessions. Nothing too onerous."

"Specifics, please," she said acidly, and he knew the hook was set. But a hooked fish was not yet a landed one.

Isiem smoothed out his embellished copy of the map Erevullo had drawn. "Here is where the silver lies in Devil's Perch," he said, pointing out the crosshatched areas on the paper. "The strix are willing to let you mine it, provided that you build no permanent structures on the land. The miners will have to live in tents and wagons. No more than two hundred Chelaxians may enter their lands at any time, and no more than twenty of those may be soldiers, spellcasters, or Hellknights."

"Preposterous," Velenne scoffed. "A mine needs more hands—and proper security needs more swords."

"That is their offer. I expect you will find it difficult to sustain greater numbers in Devil's Perch anyway. This land is not a welcoming one." Isiem went on, pointing to a new line he had sketched around Erevullo's finds. The line excluded Tokarai Springs by a considerable margin. "This marks the boundary of the strix's forbearance. Within it, the Chelaxians will be allowed to work. Outside it, they will be deemed invaders and treated accordingly."

"Killed, you mean."

"More likely tortured, then killed." Isiem shrugged. "The strix are a savage race."

"Savages whose promises we should trust?"

"Within the conditions they set, yes. Many would call the Chelaxians savages, and the Nidalese worse, for what we do in the name of law and faith. Yet none would doubt that *our* contracts bind. Would they?" He held her gaze until she gave an incremental nod. "If their terms are met, and their wishes respected, the strix will keep to their treaty."

"If not, we go back to war."

"A war that cannot win you what you want," Isiem cautioned. "Devil's Perch is cruel enough without adding to your foes."

"Why should they concede anything, then?" Velenne asked. "Why give up their fight?"

"Because I advised it," Isiem answered honestly, hoping she would read the truth on his face. "The strix value every one of their people's lives. Every one. That gave me some leverage in arguing that they should accept a treaty.

"They can fight you, and they can win—what happened in Crackspike proves that—but they will lose lives in doing so. If Cheliax will respect the terms of their peace, then their warriors need not die, and so they are willing to offer this chance. But if they believe they've been tricked, every grain of silver you take from these hills will be bought by thrice its weight in blood."

"Colorfully phrased," Velenne observed. She studied his map in silence for a moment, then smiled slightly and adjusted a ring. It was one he hadn't seen before, a brilliant red ruby. "I might be inclined to accept your terms on behalf of the Queen. Paralictor Cerallius, I fear, will not. He will insist upon a thunderous victory in battle, and the total eradication of his foe, to vindicate the pride of his order. The Hellknights' earlier defeats are not to be suffered, you see."

Her tone made the invitation clear. Isiem inclined his head to show his understanding. "But if the paralictor were, regrettably, to fall in the course of that battle . . ."

"I am sure his successor would be more amenable to your proposal," Velenne agreed smoothly. "Maralictor Adarai is a *much* more reasonable man, and he values my counsel highly. I am certain I could persuade him to see the merit in your terms. Of course, to make any treaty palatable to the throne, it would have to be presented as something forced upon the strix after their defeat."

Something in the way she described the maralictor made Isiem wonder if their relationship was more than professional. It was hardly a surprise; Velenne had always taken bedmates in part to establish useful loyalties. Wasn't that what she had done with him, and that Wiscrani paladin so long ago, and gods-knew-how-many in the years since? Why not a Hellknight maralictor, then, especially if the paralictor proved resistant to her charms?

What *did* surprise him was the lack of rancor that he felt in response. True, it had been seven years since their last acquaintance. Long years for both of them, and he too had taken other lovers in that time. But she had been the first, and if what passed between them was not precisely *love*—Pangolais was inhospitable to such tender emotions, and Isiem recognized now that much of what he'd felt had been the turmoil of youth— it had been the closest thing to it in that dark period of his life.

But that was over. Whether his guess about her involvement with Maralictor Adarai was accurate or not, it was clear that Velenne had no desire to rekindle whatever had existed between them.

And Isiem felt some regret at that, but in the main, what he felt was relief. Velenne had been his last bond and the last temptation to return to his old life, and she had relinquished that hold. He was free. Truly free, at last.

She was waiting for his answer. Isiem hoped she had not read the reasons for his pause.

"The strix won't put on a sham battle for the sake of salving Chelish pride," he said. "Especially if it means sacrificing the lives of their warriors. Saving those lives is, I will remind you, the only reason they're offering peace terms."

"Oh, it won't be a sham." Velenne tossed the flint-bladed knife back at him. Isiem caught it clumsily. "Not at all. The battle and its stakes are very real. Either the paralictor dies and the conflict is hard-fought enough to convince the survivors to accept the maralictor's concessions, or we have no agreement. If Paralictor Cerallius wins, your strix are doomed. If the strix win, there will be no terms. Imperial Cheliax will not suffer another humiliation at the hands of inhuman barbarians. The next army it sends will not be inclined to negotiate. Nor, I suspect, will either of us be in any position to influence the outcome. No, this is not a sham, Isiem. It is your one chance to steer both sides toward the peace you want."

"By assassinating your paralictor under the cover of an arranged battle," he said flatly.

"And Uskonos," Velenne said.

"Who?"

She waved a slender hand in the direction of the ornamented, mute-tended tent Isiem had seen earlier. "The arcanist sent by the throne, to help keep tabs on the Hellknights. His grotesqueness offends me."

Isiem raised his eyebrows. He'd known she had a petty streak, but. . . "You want me to kill him because he's *ugly*?"

"Because he's ugly, and ill-mannered, and thinks he can touch me, yes." Her smile was sharper than his knife. "He's also the senior spellcaster here, with somewhat greater authority in the eyes of House Thrune. I have had to reject him thrice since we left Egorian. Once might have been flattering. Twice I might have forgiven. Three times and he needs to die.

"Besides," she added, apparently as an afterthought, "I want his rings. Kill him too, and you'll have your treaty."

She suggested poisoning the man's toads. Uskonos dai Virrtolgo—or Uskonos Greentongue, as the sorcerer was more commonly known—kept a clutch of dwarf thistletoads in the murky aquariums that Isiem had spotted earlier. Velenne said the man had been introduced to the narcotic effect of the toads' secretions while traveling through Varisia, and had brought a breeding pair back with him when he returned to Egorian. Years of addiction to their toxins had stained his tongue green and left him dependent on a daily scraping of the toads' secretions. Deprived of his amphibian drugs, Velenne claimed, Uskonos would go through a painful, crippling withdrawal. It would not kill him, but it would weaken his control of the arcane.

Isiem had no proper poison, but he did have a jug of aquavit—clear, high-proof alcohol—that Velenne had carried all the way from Egorian. The woman had a gift for grudges.

Trivial as her stated reasons for wanting Uskonos dead were, however, Isiem was glad to do her the favor. If there *were* to be a pitched battle, crippling the sorcerer would give the strix a considerable advantage—one they badly needed. For all his bravado in the diabolist's tent, Isiem knew the strix were badly outmatched. Flint-tipped spears and the *rokoa*'s spells were a poor counter to Hellknight signifers and Chelish steel.

But if one of the enemy's best battlemages was a traitor to their cause, and the other was delirious from withdrawal . . .

It was a chance he had to take. Isiem had prepared several invisibility spells before venturing into the Chelish camp. He used another now, cloaking himself from view as he left Velenne's tent and crept toward Uskonos's. Soldiers and signifers strode past him, alert for threats at the perimeter, but never watching for foes already among them.

Outside Uskonos's tent, the two mute slaves were tending a bubbling cauldron of duck meat and chopped onions. One of them held a wire tray of fat dumplings, which he lowered carefully into the broth. The other stretched handfuls of sticky dough into flatbread while keeping an eye on the soup pot. It looked like enough food to feed a dozen men, but the slaves never tasted a single bite. Everything they cooked was reserved for Uskonos Greentongue.

A minute later, the man himself waddled out to supervise the cooking. He was enormously fat. Glittering sigils in green and gold covered every inch of his body, face, and clean-shaven scalp. Brightly polished brass rings clanked in his swollen earlobes; another sagged from his septum, resting on his thick upper lip. A straggly fringe of reddish beard framed his chin. Despite the briskness of the desert winter, creases of sweat darkened his yellow silk robes under his arms and flabby breasts.

Yet for all his bulk, Uskonos Greentongue moved with a ponderous grace. He floated around the pot, sniffing the steam and sprinkling in pinches of fragrant spices while talking to himself in an oddly high-pitched lilt. His pupils were constricted to tiny pinpoints and his speech was noticeably slurred, causing Isiem to wonder whether the sorcerer had already dosed himself with toad venom for the day. Whether or not that was so, Uskonos seemed completely absorbed in his work, and so Isiem crept past invisibly, walking wide around the mutes as he approached the supply wagon.

The toads sat dark and patient in their murky brine. Screens of woven bamboo shielded their jars from the sun, and fronds of soft black waterweeds made it difficult to see inside, but Isiem could just make out the motionless lumps of the amphibians clinging like fleshy bubbles to the glass sides of their habitats.

Their soft, passive bodies turned his stomach. Isiem hurried forward, trying not to slosh the jug. He set it on the wagonbed and climbed up after it, contorting his body to stay in contact with the container so that it would remain invisible. Once on the wagon, Isiem pried the bamboo screens from the aquariums and, working as quickly as he dared, poured half the aquavit into each one.

Although he took pains to avoid telltale splashes or gurgles, it was impossible to keep the liquid from swirling violently as the clear spirit mingled with the cloudy water. The toads dropped off the walls, disappearing behind the waterweeds. A few tried to jump out, but their squat legs were clumsy, and Isiem pushed them back with the bamboo screens. A glance in his direction would catch the tampering, but Uskonos was enraptured by his cooking, and the mutes were attentive to their drug-addled master, and no one looked his way.

In moments the jug was drained, the lethal aquavit dissolved into the toads' bath. The amphibians' kicks and struggles stopped. Isiem climbed down and tucked the empty jug under the wagon, trusting to the shadows to hide it long enough for him to escape.

He was past the camp lines when the first scream sounded. Uskonos had discovered his pets' fate, and from the sound of it, his fury was fearsome. Velenne had spent the hour dining with the paralictor and Chelish officers in the commander's tent, ensuring her alibi against the sabotage. The sorcerer's wrath would not fix upon her—but, from the sound of it, whomever he *did* blame was not long for this world.

Isiem turned toward the setting sun. It blinded him, but he walked forward, shielding his eyes against its glorious glare as Uskonos's rage receded in his wake. The *itaraak* would retrieve him once he was far enough from the Chelish camp, but there was a long way to go before nightfall.

A long way to go, and a battle to plan.

Chapter Twenty-Two
Honor to the Dead

The *itaraak* do not like your plan," Kirii said.

It was late afternoon. Isiem had returned to Windspire that morning, blindfolded on the back of that unseen creature of feather and bone. Honey had been overjoyed to see him, leaping and prancing so giddily that he was afraid she might fall off the ledge, but the dog was the only one who seemed glad he was safe. Even Kirii had greeted his arrival grimly.

Isiem could hardly blame her—humans had never brought the strix any happiness, himself least of all—but he wished they would swallow their disdain and *move*. Since his return, the strix had been locked in argument about whether to accept the diabolist's proposal or pursue their own plans. Until now they had told Isiem nothing, and so he had paced around his nest-tent and stewed as he watched the hours slip by.

Velenne had wanted the strix to strike soon after Isiem killed the toads. Otherwise, she feared, Uskonos would be able to procure new ones. His supply of drugs was so critical to the sorcerer's functioning that he would almost certainly teleport back to Egorian to retrieve more, if he did not leave altogether—and while that would give the strix an even greater advantage by allowing them to attack the Chelaxians with Uskonos away, it would also prevent them from assassinating the caster.

And while that might not vitiate their secret bargain with Velenne, Isiem wasn't inclined to test her. If the diabolist hated Uskonos badly enough—or had enough to gain politically from his death—to have plotted against him since leaving Egorian, she would hardly be satisfied with driving him out of their camp. She wanted him *dead*.

Therefore, they needed to attack tonight, before the sorcerer got desperate and cast the spell that removed him from their reach. Tomorrow morning, at the latest. But it did not seem that the strix cared.

"They don't want to fight?" Isiem asked.

"They do not wish to flee," she said. "The *itaraak* are eager to fight these iron devils. They believe it will be a quick victory, as their other battles were. They see no reason to stop with the fat one or the captain of the *kotarra*. Why not kill them all?"

"Because they'll lose," Isiem said, struggling not to grind his teeth, "and if by some miracle they won, the reprisal would crush them. Not just Windspire. *All* the strix."

Kirii blinked sideways and made a long, gurgling warble that trilled up and down an octave. Impatience, Isiem thought, but he wasn't sure. "I know this," she said. "The *rokoa* knows. I have told them. Some agree. Some do not."

"But they all want to fight?"

"Yes."

"Then let them. Whether they agree with us or not." Isiem was fairly certain that the paralictor would charge into the thick of the battle, and he could kill Uskonos himself if it came to that. Velenne could keep herself safe; she always did. "We need to attack *tonight*."

"We do not attack tonight." Red Chest swept onto Isiem's ledge, raising his immense black wings at the last moment to raise a cloud of gritty dust that made Honey yelp and momentarily blinded the Nidalese wizard. Not an accident. The leader of the *itaraak* had always made his dislike clear. "We raid tonight. We kill tomorrow."

"Why?"

The strix's primary feathers bristled. "Because we are not clean," he answered, his contempt thick enough for a human to detect, "and we are not blessed. Death must wait until the morning." With that he launched himself back into the abysses of Windspire, leaving as abruptly as he had arrived. Another wash of dust billowed over them and fell.

"Well, that's one way of telling us they've reached a decision," Isiem murmured when Red Chest was gone. "Do you think I should accompany them on the raid?"

"No. You will be only in their way. The *itaraak* know how to take horses." Instead of relaxing at the news that the impasse was broken, Kirii seemed even more tense. The feathers on her wings were stiff as the hackles of a wary dog, and she kept her gaze slightly averted from Isiem, causing her eyes to glow with sideways-reflected light.

"What's troubling you?" Isiem asked. "This is what we wanted, isn't it?"

"Not what was wanted." Kirii turned away from him fully, staring at the crooked peaks, wind-carved arches, and gaping pits that her people called home. Darkness filled her eyes. "But what must be if we are to survive. Windspire fights for its life tomorrow—and I will not, *cannot*, be there." She scratched at the stone, digging

313

her small toe claws into the ledge. "The daughter of the *rokoa* must be kept safe, so that if the *itaraak* are defeated and our tribe falls to ruin, someone will remember the names of our bones."

"That is not your mother's role?"

"It should be. If she did not have me, it would be. But she believes I know enough of Windspire's lore to serve as our memory . . . and that she herself is needed in the fight. It is taboo for a *rokoa* to take lives, but she has spells that may aid the *itaraak*, and that she is permitted to do."

"Would you rather it were you?" Isiem asked quietly.

The young strix's feathers stirred in the wind. A shrug? He couldn't tell. "I have no duty against killing."

"Neither do I."

"This is so." She turned back to him, briefly. The shadows danced across her face, and for a brief, dizzying instant Isiem imagined that it was not Kirii who spoke to him, but Helis. The rocks of Windspire, black and skeletal under the moonlight, seemed an echo of shadow-sworn Nidal. "Can you kill your own clan?"

He blinked to clear his vision. This was a different woman asking for death, and for different reasons. Very different. "They aren't my clan."

"They were."

"They aren't anymore."

Kirii ducked her head in acknowledgment—the closest thing a stiff-necked strix could manage to the human gesture of a nod. "Then I hope you will do what I cannot." She dropped into the night with a violent sweep of her wings.

Left to himself, Isiem sat on the ledge with his legs dangling into darkness, just as he had perched above the gardens of the Dusk Hall so many years ago. Honey came to sit beside him, and he stroked the dog's ears contemplatively, thinking of nothing in particular. The ghosts of the past were with him, close as his own shadow, and yet they did not trouble him tonight. The strix might be conflicted, but his own path was clear. Not easy, but clear.

And so he sat and gazed at the icy desert stars and listened to the patient breathing of the dog beside him. After a while Honey lay down and slept, her head nestled against his leg.

Hours later, the *itaraak* returned. One by one they drifted into Windspire, materializing like phantoms from the black sky. If any were wounded or missing, Isiem could not tell.

The strix did not disperse to their own nest-tents, but instead gathered on the largest of the flats, only twenty yards from Isiem's own perch. A dungpatty fire burned there. It was little more than coals raked out in a pit, glowing dull and almost smokeless, but the *itaraak* ringed wide around it as though circling a bonfire.

When all were in their places, they began to sing: eerie, echoing songs that celebrated their own lives and mourned those that would be lost with the coming dawn. No instruments accompanied them; their music was the warriors' voices and the wind.

Fierce Spear stepped forward in the circle. As the others sang behind him, he plucked a small feather from his right wing and cast it into the coals. "I am *itarii* Fierce Spear, *itaraak* of Windspire. Valor is mine through my mother Fox Claw. Wisdom is mine through my father Owl Dream. I honor my blood and my ancestors tonight with my song. I honor them tomorrow with my spear."

He grasped a flint-bladed knife and cut a shallow line across his left bicep, then cut a similar line across a deer's bone, leaving a bloody gouge. Fierce Spear drew four such lines, dipping the knife into his cut each time so that each was stained with blood. "These are the lives I have taken. These are the sorrows I have made." He threw the bone into the fire. "I burn my sins. I challenge my ghosts. I go into the great storm without fear."

"Into the great storm we go without fear," the others chorused. Fierce Spear stepped back, stone-faced. The cut in his arm trickled blood, but he ignored it. The next *itaraak* came forward and began his chant.

Isiem eavesdropped for a while longer, using magic to understand their words, but after a time he dismissed the spell and listened to the song alone. Its sorrows lulled him to sleep and haunted his formless dreams.

Kirii shook him awake. The sky was gray behind her, almost as dark as her raven-feathered wings. The other strix were blurs in the chilly gloom. The aniselike fragrance of *cricscaara* stems drifted toward him: the *itaraak* were chewing the herb for bravery. It was the same plant they had used to poison Erevullo's Hellknights, although then they had used the concentrated sap. In smaller doses, if the stems were chewed and spat out rather than ingested, *cricscaara* dulled pain and increased courage.

"Go." Kirii pressed a vial of carved bone into his palm. Groggily Isiem shook it. A potion sloshed inside.

"You must fly," she said, pulling the vial's stopper for him and handing him two more. "The *itaraak* attack from the sky. To fight with them, you must do the same. Drink, and the wind will carry you."

He drank. The potion tasted like nothing. It ran down his throat, cold and quicksilver, and he felt the weight of the world lift away. Isiem gripped his tiny clay ziggurat and uttered a quick incantation, enabling himself to speak to the *itaraak*. A second spell wrapped an invisible field of force around him, offering some protection against Chelish arrows. Then he pressed his feet to the ground and leaped into the air . . . and, to his amazement, flew. Honey ran back and forth beneath him, barking, as Kirii tried to soothe the dog.

Isiem's exhilaration did not last long. The *itaraak* were already well ahead of him, and he had to hurry to catch them. Most of the warriors flew grouped in a V-shaped formation like migrating geese to draw their enemies' eyes, while smaller clusters of camouflaged scouts moved in on either side. After a brief hesitation, Isiem joined the tail end of the V.

He hadn't had time to tie his hair before leaving Windspire. The long white locks whipped at his back, lashing into his eyes when the strix veered into the wind. Isiem spat them out and tried to stay focused. He had never flown before, and although the magic required no physical skill—it was entirely an effort of will to push himself in one direction or another—he still felt clumsy in the air.

But he kept up with the *itaraak*, drinking a second potion to stay aloft when the magic of the first began to falter. Just when Isiem began to wonder whether he ought to drink the third, he caught sight of red-and-black pennons snapping in the wind, and smelled the smoke of cookfires rising on the air.

The Chelaxians were breaking camp. The *itaraak* had driven away or crippled their horses in the previous night's raid; Isiem saw vultures circling the dark lumps of their corpses outside the red walls of Tokarai Springs. The mastiffs, too, lay dead by their master's tent. Blood soaked the gravel under them and stained their short sleek coats.

But the soldiers were undeterred, and they did not seem afraid. They clad themselves in iron and steel, and they kept their eyes on the sky. Eight crimson-cloaked signifers and four Hellknights under the eye-and-vortex pennant of Citadel Enferac stood at their fore, the paralictor and maralictor prominent among them.

Squinting against the wind, Isiem scanned the soldiers below. *The battlemages are not with them.* Neither Velenne nor Uskonos and his bodyguards were in view, although both their tents had already been collapsed and packed away.

He spun two swift spells, one to bolster the web of force that shielded him from attack, the other for invisibility. Black Toes hissed at his sudden disappearance, but Isiem ignored the *itaraak*'s discomfort. He had to find out where the sorcerer had gone. Dipping lower, he broke out of the strix's formation.

A scuffed stone told him. Thirty yards from the Hellknights' camp, an apple-sized rock bounced and rattled along the ground as if it had been kicked. No one was nearby—no one Isiem could see, at least—but a second jouncing rock confirmed it. Someone was walking there invisibly, and that someone was likely to be Velenne or Uskonos or both.

Swiftly Isiem ascended back to the *itaraak*. The strix had paused behind the last remnants of cloud cover, circling as they awaited their leader's command to attack. "They're here," the shadowcaller said hoarsely, panting for breath. Red Cloud's head jerked up in surprise at being addressed by seemingly empty air, but he soon recovered his composure.

"The diabolist and the sorcerer are invisible," Isiem told him. "Thirty, forty yards west of the camp. They know we're coming."

"Can you kill them?" Red Chest asked.

"Maybe. I can't be sure. Uskonos has guards."

"Fierce Spear. Black Toes. Go with the human. Kill these wizards and their guards." Red Chest lowered his bone-crested mask. The other *itaraak* slid their masks on as well. As one, they readied their spears.

Isiem blinked, startled by the warleader's trust, but he nodded jerkily and aimed himself downward. As he plunged through the wet veil of the clouds, the two warriors following close on his heels, he heard Red Chest roar behind him.

"Warriors!" the *itaraak* shouted, pitching his voice loudly enough to reach the Hellknights below. His warriors howled and battered the hafts of their spears together as they dove, adding to the clamor. "To me!"

Wizards, Isiem thought dizzily as he dove, the air rushing past his ears, *to me.*

Chapter Twenty-Three
Tokarai Springs

His guess was on the mark. As Isiem plunged toward the ground, he saw a shimmer like a heat wave in the air, and a quick ghostly glimpse of a corpulent face turned upward toward Red Chest and his charging strix. Uskonos Greentongue was on the attack, and his invisibility was failing.

Red Chest and his strix had broken their sky cover. Shouting challenges and insults, the *itaraak* hurled a storm of spears down at the Chelish camp, but the soldiers were ready to meet them. The signifers wove spells of unnatural darkness and blinding mists to cloud the sky, while the soldiers raised their shields overhead as the strix rushed over their camp. Flint-tipped spears clanged against steel, creating an ear-shattering clamor. One soldier, a red-haired woman who seemed scarcely more than a girl in her leather and heavy chain, was skewered through the calf. She fell, dropping her shield, and two more spears finished her off. None of the others was hurt.

Isiem couldn't see the sorcerer's bodyguards or Velenne—if, indeed, they were with Uskonos— but it didn't matter. He willed himself to fall faster, hoping to catch his target before the tattooed sorcerer realized he was coming.

Fifty feet above the man, Isiem could hear his chant. He recognized the spell at once; he'd prepared it himself.

Which meant he could stop it.

Even as he continued his dive, the Nidalese wizard began reciting the incantation in garbled form, switching its verses and spitting the words out backward. He took a pinch of bat guano and sulfur from his pocket. The wind swept most of his materials away, but he kept enough between his fingers to crush the guano into the sulfur, reducing them to powder rather than the tiny lump that would ordinarily beome the fireball's heart.

The instant that he saw Uskonos release his nascent spell—a blue-edged bubble of flame darting over the broken rocks—Isiem dropped his own pinch of dust atop it, trapping the sorcerer's fireball as neatly as a fisherman netting a trout. The fiery globe sputtered out, its magics torn apart by the distorting effects of Isiem's counterspell, and Isiem felt the backlash of energy wash over him as both casters popped suddenly back into full visibility.

The tattooed sorcerer looked up, snarling at Isiem . . . and the strix accompanying Isiem hurled their skirmishing spears directly at him.

Neither struck home. Instead, each spear jerked as it thudded into apparently solid air; bright red blood sprayed the rocks underfoot, steaming in the weak morning sun. Uskonos retreated between the hovering spears, his eyes wide and face pale under the glimmering tattoos as the spears jerked about and faded from view.

The bodyguards. Although both remained invisible, the strix's disappearing spears and their own hot blood marked their positions. Fierce Spear and Black Toes touched down, trying to rush past them to get at the sorcerer, while Isiem, struggling to maintain the advantage of the air, pulled up sharply from his dive. His toes knocked heart-shaped yellow leaves from the topmost branches of a tree.

Volleys of glowing motes and crackling acid shot up into the air, streaking through their clouds of blinding fog, as the Hellknight signifers answered the strix's challenge. Others sent pillars of wind gusting upward, knocking the strix formation awry.

Paralictor Cerallius had rallied some of the Chelish soldiers along with his signifers and, while exchanging erratic shots with Red Chest and his strix, was rushing to the sorcerer's aid. The swirl of combat would soon engulf them . . . but Black Toes and Fierce Spear stayed on the ground, unwilling to give up their quarry and unable to fly away without opening themselves to blows from Uskonos's bodyguards.

Isiem tried to buy them time. When the soldiers were almost within spear's reach of the two strix on the ground, he spread his fingers outward and snapped off a quick spell.

Fire burst from his fingertips in a hissing fan, striking at the Chelaxians. The nearest pair, a man and woman each clad in chainmail and fiend-faced helms, were caught squarely by the flames. Hair and flesh burned; steel links glowed gold. Their visors flared crimson, as though the infernal visages of their helms were breathing hellfire around their faces.

The man screamed, dropping to the ground and clawing at the suddenly red-glowing oven of his helm.

The woman, intent on the strix, had been looking away from Isiem when the fan of fire struck. Flames caught her shoulder and torso, curling down her left arm and licking at her steel-rimmed shield. She grunted and staggered through the pain, continuing on her course.

The other soldiers were barely singed. Maralictor Adarai, a tall man who cut an imposing figure in heavy black-enameled plate, kept prudently back from the fore; it seemed he was aware of their plan. Isiem spiraled upward, trying not to collide with Red Chest's strix, who were diving down to attack.

Driven from the sky by the signifers' enchanted winds and blinding obstacles, the *itaraak* were taking to the ground. They split their forces, sending some to approach on foot while others skirted around the fog banks and fought past the buffeting winds to continue their aerial assault.

The Chelaxians set their shields to defend against the ground forces. The airborne strix cast spears down in a stony rain, hammering the soldiers and the signifers alike. This time, with the enemy's defenses turned away, their weapons struck true. Several soldiers collapsed under the hail of spears and did not rise again. One of the signifers fell as well. A hurled spear caught the paralictor under his right pauldron, drawing blood; another struck and vanished into one of the still-unseen mutes.

The ground party of *itaraak* landed alongside Fierce Spear and Black Toes, turning to prevent the Chelaxians from rescuing their beleaguered sorcerer. Swiftly they unstrapped the heavier thrusting spears from their backs and readied to meet the surviving soldiers and Cerallius's signifers.

Out of bravado or simple mistake, a young warrior named Blue Feather, who had just earned her mask, was first to step into the paralictor's path. The Hellknight carried a slim, silvery longsword etched with leaping flames all along its blade, and as he swung the blade at Blue Feather, those flames burst into life. White and bright as the noontide sun, they enveloped the sword and blanched Blue Feather's painted mask. She raised her spear courageously, trying to block the swing.

She never had a chance. At the same instant that he struck at her, Paralictor Cerallius released a spell with his other hand. Electricity arced across the young strix, convulsing her muscles and sparking along the bits of metal and bone in her armor. Blue Feather's hands clenched helplessly on the spear's haft. Stunned by the magic, she froze for a single fatal instant, and the paralictor's sword sliced into her throat so deeply that it nearly severed her head. Blood fountained over his snarling devil's mask, sizzling in the burning aura of his blade. The strix around him fell back, visibly shaken by the savagery of the paralictor's attack.

"Rally, my *itaraak!*" the *rokoa* called. Isiem had not seen her approach. Neither, it seemed, had anyone else. Perhaps she had been invisible. But now she showed herself openly, walking—not flying—toward the fray from the south. She leaned heavily on a gnarled staff strung with oblong beads and the small painted skulls of birds. Her ragged, graying feathers and blind white eyes gave her a look of helpless decrepitude that, in the face of so much bloody chaos, was itself frightening. For such a venerable lady to walk into such danger seemed madness, even with five *itaraak* to escort her.

But walk into it she did, and even Red Chest seemed to draw courage from her presence. "*Itarii!*" he shouted, burying his spear in a soldier's throat. The cries of the warriors, and the screams of the dying, followed Isiem as he flew steeply back up. The sun blinded him briefly during the ascent, but he heard Uskonos begin to shape a second fireball, followed by the *rokoa* countering his unfinished spell with an imperious croak and a rattle of her staff.

Isiem spun through the clouds and began a slower, more controlled glide back toward the fight. Paralictor Cerallius was surrounded by strix, but he faced them unafraid. Bellowing a war cry, he swung at them with a scything horizontal sweep, cleaving through their ranks as though the *itaraak* were so many stalks of wheat to be harvested. Fire flew from his other hand, fanning across the strix. His enemies fell broken and burning, at least two of them dead before they touched the ground. None could reach the signifers behind him.

He's too strong. None of the *itaraak* could hope to match the paralictor's vicious blend of spells and steel. Isiem pointed at the man's back, uttering a short incantation. A ray of shadow sprang from his hand, striking Cerallius between the shoulders. The magic spread over and through his armor like smoke, leaving the Hellknight wracked by an unnatural, shivering chill. He stumbled, lowering his longsword fractionally as it suddenly became heavier in his hand.

Red Chest did not miss the chance: he stabbed at the paralictor, twisting his spear as it screeched along the Hellknight's breastplate. The flint tip shattered against the metal, but enough remained to punch into a weak point between the buckles on the paralictor's left side. Cursing, Cerallius jerked away.

Isiem lost sight of the melee as he flew past and the remaining aerial strix swept by underneath him, obscuring his view, but he did not think Red Chest had dealt a mortal blow. He'd struck with his weight on the wrong foot, and the angle had looked too glancing.

And, indeed, when he circled back, the paralictor was still standing in a ring of broken foes. Slower, weaker, but fighting gamely on. Blistered, blackened blood spattered the rocks around his feet. The Chelish soldiers were fighting in disciplined pairs and trios, forcing the strix into reach of the paralictor's deadly swings, while the signifers harried them with frost and fire. The *itaraak* on the ground were losing numbers steadily.

A short distance away, the sorcerer Uskonos flickered in and out of reality, evading the jabs of the strix around him. They punched their spears into the air where he'd been a second earlier, but they seldom hit the man. His mute bodyguards were down and dead, as was Fierce Spear. Black Toes lay beside his fallen comrade, gasping bloody bubbles that grew weaker by the second.

Out of nowhere, a flurry of incandescent red motes slammed into the dying strix. Black Toes jerked spasmodically and went still. Moments later, Velenne materialized, shaking off the last of her invisibility and tucking a silver-capped wand back into her sleeve. She had taken up a position thirty feet away with her back to a high rock formation, offering some protection from the aerial strix's fly-by attacks and preventing anyone from coming at her from behind.

"Good of you to join us," Uskonos said caustically, dodging another spear.

"You seemed to be doing well enough on your own." The diabolist raised her hands, jeweled rings twinkling in the gray morning light, and gauged the progress of the oncoming strix. A few of the *itaraak* had broken away from their fruitless harrying of the sorcerer and were advancing toward her. Maralictor Adarai moved to intercept them, but she cautioned him aside with a small shake of her head.

Uskonos didn't seem to notice. "Well enough for you to waste time finishing off a bird that was already dead?"

"I like to be sure of my enemies." There was a smile in Velenne's voice; Isiem heard it clearly, even if he could not see her face. She whispered a short chant, gesturing toward the *itaraak*. They cried out in terror as she released her spell. Tripping over the rocks in their haste, the strix fled from the diabolist's phantoms. Some even hurled their spears aside in fear.

Blinded by fright, they ran straight into the maralictor's soldiers. Adarai and his men made swift work of them, chopping through feathers and flesh with grim efficiency. Isiem, no stranger to bloodshed, had to turn his eyes away.

He refocused on the paralictor. From fifty feet overhead, Isiem cast the same spell that Velenne had used to kill Black Toes. Spectral missiles, opaque as agates, erupted from his fingertips and slammed into Cerallius.

It wasn't enough. Bleeding from innumerable wounds and favoring his right leg heavily, the Hellknight nevertheless stood victorious over a field of fallen strix. Red Chest's headless body lay at his feet, surrounded by the spear-slain bodies of three Chelish soldiers. More than half the crimson-clad signifers were down, but the only *itaraak* still living were those in the air— and the *rokoa*, who was retreating with the last of her guard. As soon as she had enough room to manuever, she too sought the safety of the sky.

Isiem wanted to curse them. *Fools. Stupid, prideful fools!* If Red Chest had believed him—if the *itaraak* had focused on Uskonos and the paralictor alone, instead of stupidly trying to engage the entire Chelish force at once—they might have won. Instead they had lost their leader and half their number, and were retreating from the battle in disarray, even though victory might yet lie within their grasp.

But the strix *weren't* retreating. They wheeled sharply and came around again, brave and foolish and utterly determined. The *rokoa* rallied them again, calling on her masked warriors to defend Windspire and save their kin.

And they responded, at first haltingly but then with proud conviction. Unerringly they plunged through the signifers' shrouds of fog and shadow. This time, the strix all landed among the Hellknight arcanists, pulling out their heavy spears as they skidded to a noisy stop on the rocks. A blinding cloud of dust and grit plumed up around them, blown to greater heights by the bellows of their wings. Only the *rokoa* stayed aloft.

Uskonos hooked his thumbs together and fanned his fingers, preparing to unleash his own fan of flames upon the strix. Just as the first sparks began to gather, sparkling hazily through the obscuring dust, the *rokoa* croaked her counterspell again, and the fire died in infancy.

The sorcerer shrieked in high-pitched frustration. Veins pulsed in his neck and forehead; his flesh was abnormally ruddy, almost livid, under his lattice of tattoos. "Help me!" he cried at Velenne. "Kill them!"

She nodded, beginning a new spell. Isiem lost sight of her in the dust cloud, but he heard the infernal words roll from her tongue and felt the world shudder around him as she tore a small rift in its fabric. *A summons. She's calling devils to her side.*

Three fiends boiled up from the cloud of dust, shrieking and beating their double pairs of scabrous wings. This type Isiem recognized. *Gaav.* Their heads were yellowed, monstrous skulls fringed by broken horns, their bodies scaled and muscular. An odor of pestilence hung thick around them. There was no particular cunning in the empty sockets of their eyes, no sense in the constant chittering that hissed from their hollow tongueless mouths. They existed to serve, not to think.

As the gaav circled defensively around the diabolist, the injured paralictor made one last rush against the strix. Flicking his longsword out in low, swift arcs, Cerallius forced them back to the very edge of the dust cloud, then retreated behind the ranks of his signifers.

The strix couldn't reach him from there, but the Chelaxians were massed closely enough for Isiem to catch them all in a single spell. He regretted using his fireball to negate Uskonos's; it was the better strategy, he was sure, but the clustered signifers made a tempting target.

Still, he didn't have to pass it up entirely. Plucking a pouch of ground mica from a pocket, Isiem murmured a few short phrases and then scattered the sparkling powder in the Hellknights' direction. As the dust drifted down, his magic seized it, enhancing it to a cloud of shimmering motes that coated the red-cloaked arcanists in a curtain of blinding gold.

Now the advantage was on the strix's side, and the *itaraak* were as ruthless in exploiting it as the Chelaxians had been in crushing their fear-spelled comrades earlier. As their spears darted through the dust, punching past lowered shields and spell-woven armor, Uskonos turned his gaze back to the flying *rokoa*.

"Had enough of you," he mumbled thickly, knotting his right hand into a fist. Crackling, incandescent energy engulfed his arm from the elbow downward, forming into a spectral echo of that fist. Uskonos punched upward and the spectral fist flew off, streaking at the *rokoa* like a burning bowshot. The impact of it cracked a wing and an arm, and the elderly strix came pinwheeling out of the sky.

Flapping her good wing frantically, she managed to soften her landing rather than crashing full force against the ground, but she still hit hard enough to make Isiem wince—and, worse, fell within easy reach of the melee around the signifers.

"Finish her!" Uskonos shouted at Velenne, his entire body quivering. *"Do* something!" His hands trembled violently; sweat dripped down his cheeks and hung from the scraggly strands of his beard like a fringe of glass beads. Whether because of rage or terror or withdrawal from his toad toxins, the sorcerer seemed to be losing control of his faculties.

Isiem couldn't hear the diabolist's response. He was too busy plunging toward the fray himself.

He had to save the *rokoa*. Without her, the strix's resolve would crumble. Even with her, it might; the *itaraak* would sacrifice their offense to save her, and then the Chelaxians would crush them. All their losses would have been for naught.

But if he could protect her, the others could fight on.

The *rokoa* had fallen dangerously near the paralictor. Isiem landed and hurried toward her, afraid that she might try to crawl away on her own and thereby draw the man's attention. He crouched and reached for her cautiously, trying to stay out of the fray . . . but his caution was wasted, for a longsword beat an arm's reach every time.

Cerallius's flaming blade lashed out, unexpectedly fast. It opened a searing gash across Isiem's side and shoulder, and only the defensive spells he'd cast earlier deflected the blow enough to keep it from inflicting a mortal wound. Isiem was already bent over awkwardly, and the paralictor's attack knocked him into the ground. Dirt filled his mouth; stones scraped his chin. The strike was so sudden, and so hard, that he did not even feel any pain initially. Black flashed across his vision.

The pain soon came, however, and the confusion cleared. None too soon—Cerallius raised his sword to finish the shadowcaller. Isiem rolled to the side and wove a swift spell, vanishing from view, as the Hellknight brought the weapon arcing down.

This close, Isiem could see that the paralictor was standing by dint of sheer will. The man was gray-faced under his helm, his eyes blank and glassy with fatigue. His breastplate was scored with spear marks and soaked with blood from his wounds. Isiem's previous spell continued to sap his strength along with those *itaraak*-inflicted injuries. The Hellknight was struggling for breath, seemingly on the brink of collapse . . . and yet he still stood, and fought on.

"Face me," Paralictor Cerallius growled, scanning the battle-torn ground where Isiem hid behind his magic. The flaming aura of his sword flared and dipped, reflecting the Hellknight's desperate fury. "Fight!"

The wizard held his breath and willed himself not to twitch the smallest muscle. After an agonizing moment, Cerallius turned away, unable to ignore the battle raging behind him.

Isiem exhaled explosively. Biting back a grunt of pain, he pushed himself to his feet and scrambled toward the fallen *rokoa*.

She was dying. What bones hadn't been cracked by Uskonos's force punch had shattered during her fall.

Her pulse beat frenetically through the paper-thin skin of her wrists and neck, as though the aged strix's spirit were frantic to escape its failing shell. She let out a weak moan as Isiem, wincing silently at the fragility of the *rokoa*'s body, lifted her head.

He uncapped a potion vial with his teeth and poured the pungent-smelling liquid down the *rokoa*'s throat. Her bruised eyes opened as she swallowed, and she raised her head higher despite Isiem's efforts to keep her still.

"We have not won," she said in a threadbare rasp. "The fight goes on."

"Hush," he urged. "The *itaraak* are fighting bravely. The battle is well in hand."

It was almost true. Uskonos bled freely from several spear wounds and was swarmed by *itaraak*. Velenne, too, was surrounded, although her gaav kept her assailants at bay. The dust-blinded Hellknights were steadily losing men and ground to the strix, who whooped in glee at the prospect of victory on the horizon. Only Maralictor Adarai's knot of soldiers, fighting defensively behind the cover of their shields, had kept all their numbers.

And yet even as he spoke, a deafening boom from Uskonos's direction made them both look over in horror.

In each hand the sorcerer held a glass vial, one filled with fine white powder and the other with virulent yellow liquid. He smashed them together furiously, heedless of the glass shards that slashed his palms. Gold and green energy coruscated around him, intensifying rapidly. As the *itaraak* continued to harry him, Uskonos charged ponderously toward Velenne. "Traitor!" he roared. "Scheming wench! If you will not aid me, you'll die with my enemies."

"Oh no," Velenne said, half shocked and half mirthful. She backstepped lightly away from the enraged sorcerer, her devils shrieking and spinning around her. Her voice rose, pitched to carry over the fray. "You've gone mad."

"Help me up," the *rokoa* whispered to Isiem as the Chelish battlemages turned on each other. Her milky white eyes fixed on his face, unseeing. She clawed at the dirt, trying uselessly to rise on her own strength. "I am too broken to stand alone. Help me, please."

"My lady, you must not," Isiem protested. "Your people need you."

"Now more than ever," the *rokoa* agreed. "Help me stand."

Reluctantly, he did so. The *rokoa* gasped and teetered, clinging to his arm for support, but eventually managed to balance precariously by folding her good wing against the ground. She reached into the tangle of braided ropes and talismans that draped around her reedy neck and fished out a slim wand of frosted crystal, which she held out to the air.

It was Isiem's wand. The *itaraak* had taken it from him when they first found him among the ashes of Crackspike.

"Take it," the *rokoa* croaked, and he did. The slender crystal rod was cool to the touch; a film of condensation clouded its glistening whiteness. The magic was still there.

"We should have trusted you with it from the beginning. I pray it is not too late. Now go." The ancient strix turned away from him, toward the signifers who had seen her rise and were already advancing upon her.

"My lady —"

"*Go.*"

Duty silenced him. Bowing respectfully—even knowing she could not see the gesture, invisible as he was—Isiem withdrew. The paralictor and his surviving Hellknights closed on the solitary strix, beating back the *itaraak*'s attempts to block them, but the *rokoa* made no attempt to run.

"Ancestors defend me," she said as the Hellknights came. "Ancestors protect me. I am *rokoa* of Windspire, and I call upon you now. Avenge the *itarii*. Cleanse these interlopers from our land. They have spilled the blood of your children. They threaten the sanctity of your bones." A signifer hurled a flurry of frigid motes at her, knocking the gray-feathered strix to the ground, but the *rokoa* continued her feeble chant. "We are your bones! Your blood! Your kin! *Kirraak!*"

A whirlwind rose around her. It picked up dust and flint shards and the black feathers of the dead, whipping them higher and higher until the *rokoa* was engulfed completely. Ghostly gray figures appeared in the wind: strix, but taller and gaunter than the ones Isiem had known. Their feathers were sharp as layered dagger blades; their claws burned white at the tips. The *rokoa* moaned and collapsed in their midst, and the spectral strix struck out.

They tore the Hellknights apart. Paralictor Cerallius raised his shield to fend them off, but the spectres were undaunted. They ripped through steel as if it were fog; they cut through leather like empty air. Only flesh posed any obstacle to their claws, and that not for long.

When the storm of ghosts subsided, collapsing back into loose feathers and fragments of broken spears, the paralictor was dead on the ground. So too were the signifers who had been caught in the *rokoa*'s invocation, and the *rokoa* herself. An obsidian dagger lay near her hand: she had cut herself deeply to spur the ancestors' wrath, and either the wound or the magic itself had drained her too far.

Isiem had barely registered the deaths when a thunderous detonation knocked him off his feet. A crackling nova of blue-white frost exploded outward from Uskonos, obliterating the *itaraak* around him in a cold red mist of limbs and feathers. Several were frozen solid instantaneously; their bodies shattered like dropped icicles. Velenne staggered unsteadily away from the explosion, bleeding from a dozen shallow lacerations, her dark hair rimed with frost.

Uskonos, too, had suffered from his own spell. A glassy coat of ice cracked over his robes, and his fingers were blue-black with frostbite. He did not seem to care. "Die!" he shouted again, crushing another pair of vials between his palms and resuming his elephantine charge at the diabolist. Maralictor Adarai ran toward him, but the Hellknight's charge was in vain; he was much too far away to reach Uskonos in time.

Velenne continued to back away, lifting her hands in preparation for a retaliatory blast—but as she tried to utter the words to shape it, her expression changed from contempt to raw terror.

Somehow the sorcerer had silenced her. Isiem saw it clearly in her choked attempts to voice a spell that would not come.

She turned and ran. Uskonos lumbered after her, roaring and sloughing chunks of ice with every step. The gaav converged on him. They dropped from the air, grappling the tattooed sorcerer and beating their scabbed vultures' wings frantically to hold him back. One bit the Chelaxian's face in a macabre kiss, burying its fangs in his fleshy lips and twisting its head viciously to keep him from uttering another incantation. A second gaav sank its yellow teeth into the man's knee. Blood spurted from the nostril holes in its skull; cartilage twisted and popped between its fangs. Uskonos fell heavily.

Isiem didn't waste his chance. Leveling his crystalline wand at the devil-besieged sorcerer, he drew upon the magic trapped within the stone. Threads of frost wrapped around his hand, numbing his fingers, but he did not let go.

A torrent of elemental cold burst from the wand's tip, enveloping Uskonos and the gaav in a whirling, conical white blizzard. Something screamed in the flurry, but Isiem could not tell whether it was the sorcerer, the devils, or just the screech of metal and fiend-bone surrendering under the strain of so much cold.

When the last snowflakes fell, nothing moved. The gaav were gone. Uskonos was slumped under a mantle of magical snow, his death agonies mercifully concealed.

Through the haze of destruction, Velenne's eyes met Isiem's. She nodded imperceptibly.

Drawing a shaky breath, Isiem began what he hoped would be his last spell of the day. He pulled a bit of fleece from his sheepskin vest and rubbed it between his fingers, then concentrated on visualizing a flight of *itaraak* as vividly as he could. Their masks painted in powder and clay, the shrilling of wind through their wings, the clatter of spears rattled to threaten their foes . . . in his mind's eye he saw it all, perfect in every detail.

And when he opened his eyes, he saw it in reality, too. There was his illusory flight of reinforcements, distant but dark on the horizon. He had never woven shadows so skillfully.

"Retreat!" Velenne called to the Chelish soldiers. Many of them had survived, but of the Hellknights, only

Maralictor Adarai and one of the signifers remained standing. Isiem could not tell how many of the fallen were dead and how many were merely insensible.

The distinction hardly seemed to matter to the Chelaxians, though. The defeat of their Hellknights had visibly demoralized them, and they were all too willing to flee.

Maralictor Adarai took up her cry. "Retreat! We cannot stand against so many! Retreat in formation!"

"Let them go," Isiem called to the strix as the Chelaxian soldiers began their withdrawal. The Nidalese wizard sank to the ground, too weak and exhausted to stay standing. It was all he could do to sustain the spell, and the illusion of reinforcements, until the last of the Chelaxians had turned tail.

Then he released the weave, and closed his eyes, and let his head rest against the broken stones. He was too tired even to mourn the dead. *Let them go*, he thought. *Let them all go.*

Epilogue

This is what my mother died for?" Kirii gazed at the parchment in her hands.

Put that way, it seemed a woefully inadequate thing: a single sheet of thin-scraped calfskin marked with the imperial seal of Cheliax in red and black at its head. It flapped violently in the wind, as though the desert itself were trying to tear the thing from Kirii's hands.

But the treaty was much more than that. "It's safety," Isiem said.

"Truly?"

"If it holds."

Kirii curled the parchment tightly in a white-clawed fist. She looked away, squinting into the sand-flecked wind toward the west, where the Chelaxians were tiny specks receding into the distance. There seemed to be a haziness to her golden eyes, as if the cataracts that had blinded her mother were somehow being passed down to her. "Will it hold?"

Isiem wondered that himself. It seemed such a fragile vessel for Windspire's hopes of survival.

Fifteen paragraphs, four signatures: Paralictor Adarai on behalf of the Order of the Gate, Provisional Governor Parsellon Alterras on behalf of Cheliax's civil authority, Velenne to represent its military authority and Asmodeus's approval of their bargain . . . and Kirii's mark, alone, for the strix. It took three signatories to bind Cheliax to the treaty, but only one to bind the other side.

The *substance* of the bargain was fair, however, even if its form reflected Cheliax's habit of skewing every deal to the empire's advantage. Isiem had made sure of that.

For a hundred years and a day, the Chelaxians would be free to take the silver in the hills of Devil's Perch. But their numbers would be small, their settlements impermanent, their activities watched. Tokarai Springs was inviolate to them; the strix's hunting grounds were forbidden.

It wasn't a victory, exactly. Isiem knew that. The treaty would hold because the Chelaxians didn't *care* about Tokarai Springs. They didn't even really care about the strix, or Isiem himself, as long as their mines went undisturbed. It was the silver that interested them, and what that silver meant for their ambitions.

The rebels of Westcrown would suffer for the bargain he'd struck here. Pezzack. Sargava. No doubt there were other people in other places, beyond Isiem's ken, who would soon feel the increased might of Imperial Cheliax.

And in that fact, he thought, there might be something the strix could use. "You guided that collaborator from Crackspike to Pezzack."

Kirii turned back toward him and blinked sideways. The knotted tangle of charms and necklaces she wore, many of them taken directly from her mother's body, jangled with the movement. "Yes."

"You could guide rebels back."

"Yes." She blinked again, then flicked her tongue out between her sharp little teeth in annoyance. "That is not an answer to my question. There was much bargaining before they signed. It is different now than what we spoke of. *Will the treaty hold?*"

"As long as that seems to be in Cheliax's interests," Isiem said, taken aback by her intensity. "And as long as they have no reason to believe you've reneged on the bargain. It's the same as we discussed before the battle."

"It is not the same." The parchment in Kirii's hand trembled. With her other hand she rubbed a thumb over her right cheek, where the first of her *rokoa* tattoos had recently been inked. The flesh was still swollen under the blackened curlicues, giving the design an angry red shadow. "Now I am *rokoa*. Now the survival of our tribe is my burden. What we agreed . . . that was with my mother to guide the *itarii*. Now it is only me, and our numbers are small. Much of Windspire died at Tokarai Springs. What is left is the old, the hatchlings, and the wounded."

"Will the tribe survive?"

"Only if we can compel more of the *itarii* to join us," Kirii said bluntly. "We have not enough of our own. Even with a peace, we cannot lay eggs quickly enough to restore our numbers. If Windspire is to survive our losses, other *itarii* must leave their own tribes to join ours. This is not a thing done lightly. To give up one's kin lines, the bones of one's ancestors, the teachings of one's own *rokoa* . . . as we did not wish to give up our traditions to join Ciricskree, so others will be reluctant to join us."

"What would draw them to join you?" Isiem asked.

"Something they cannot obtain in their own tribes."

"Such as the chance to strike at humans who cannot hit back?"

Opaque membranes veiled Kirii's hawk-yellow eyes as she blinked. "Explain."

"The treaty prevents you—not only the strix of Windspire, but *all* the strix in Devil's Perch—from attacking the Chelaxians. Open aggression would break the bargain."

"This I know. We have talked of it already." Her small, slitted nostrils flared. "It will be difficult to keep the other tribes from taking up their spears. The *rokoa* of Ciricskree is a strong voice for killing the humans, and the *itaraak* of the Screeching Spire have many spears. They do not accept humans as true-people. Convincing them to change those views will be . . . difficult. Very so. My mother might have done it. But I . . ."

". . . will have another choice to offer them," Isiem finished for her. "One that allows you to harass the Chelaxians without risking the lives of your own people."

"How?"

"Use the rebels." The idea had ignited his imagination; the words spilled out almost faster than Isiem could utter them. "House Thrune has many enemies. Pezzack is rife with them. Show the rebels where and how to strike, and they'll do the fighting for you. It will be humans who sabotage the mines and rob the silver wagons. Humans who die. Not strix. And as long as you take care to cover your tracks, so that the Chelaxians do not suspect you had a hand in their misfortunes, the treaty will hold. You'll have to be careful—very careful—but it may be a useful strategy for Windspire. And for Ciricskree. Even if they don't accept humans as 'true-people,' they surely understand how to make use of an enemy's enemies."

Kirii blinked twice in rapid succession. "This is acceptable to you?"

"Whether it's acceptable to the rebels in Pezzack is the real question. I believe it will be. They understand what such an inflow of silver to the imperial treasury means for them. They'll want to stop it. They may even be willing to pay you for information, if you let the rebels believe it's their own idea and that you are but a reluctant partner in their schemes."

"How am I to make them believe this?"

"Let me do it," Isiem said. "They'll listen to a human more readily than a strix."

Slowly Kirii nodded. After considerable practice, her gesture looked almost human. "And so Windspire will become not the first tribe to surrender, but the vanguard of the battle against the humans."

"A *secret* vanguard, in a secret battle. And not against all humans. Only the servants of Imperial Cheliax. The others will be your allies—necessary allies, and ones that I hope you will find worthy of respect."

"Perhaps," the young *rokoa* said. "The chance will be theirs to earn it."

Isiem inclined his head in acceptance. It was all he could ask of them. "Will that draw the *itarii*?"

"Some. The restless and the vengeful." Kirii gazed into the distance, then ruffled her wings in approximation of a shrug. "Not a solid foundation for a tribe, but perhaps they can be made one. My mother could have forged them into strength."

"You can do the same." He smiled slightly. "You taught me to eat snakes."

"Yes." She made several quick, huffed exhalations, imitating a human laugh. "A good skill for us both. So: you go to Pezzack. Recruit some rebels. And then?"

"I can't say," Isiem told her honestly. All his life he had focused on escaping Nidal, and then on escaping Cheliax. He had never spent much time considering what he would do with his freedom once he had it. Now he faced that choice full on, and found it confounding.

What could he do? What *should* he do? His talents were narrowly focused, and they did not lend themselves easily to a peaceful life. Dealing with Pezzacki rebels, Isiem suspected, was a delay rather than an answer; he had known many rebels in Westcrown, and had never been tempted to join their cause.

In the absence of an answer, however, a delay would suffice. Pezzack suited his needs: its people were less likely to hand him back to the Umbral Court than other Chelaxians might be. And the Umbral Court knew, or would soon learn, that Isiem had defected. He had stayed in the background while the treaty was negotiated, but too many of the Chelaxians had seen him at Tokarai Springs. While none had seen him closely—except Velenne, whom he still trusted not to betray him—it would not be difficult to piece together that particular puzzle. Not many shadowcallers had vanished in Devil's Perch.

Best, then, to move and hide again . . . even if he wasn't quite sure what he would do afterward.

"I've never been to Pezzack," he said at last. "I'll know when I get there."

"But you will go?" Kirii pressed.

Isiem looked at her. Already she seemed older, weighed down by the *rokoa*'s burden. It would get no lighter, he knew. Hard choices lay ahead, and harder ones would follow.

But if anyone could guide the strix through treachery and hardship to safety, it would be the woman who had taught him to eat snakes. No doubt the old *rokoa* had known that when she left the tribe in her daughter's care. Clear-eyed, courageous, and willing to walk new ways, Kirii was the leader that Windspire needed now.

And however he could help her, he would.

"Yes," Isiem said. "I'll go."

About the Author

Liane Merciel is the author of the independent fantasy novels *The River Kings' Road* and *Heaven's Needle*, both set in her world of Ithelas, as well as the Pathfinder Tales short story "Certainty," which is available for free online at **paizo.com**. She is a practicing lawyer and lives in Philadelphia with her husband Peter, resident mutts Pongu and Crookytail, and a rotating cast of foster furballs. For more information, visit **lianemerciel.com**.

Acknowledgments

First and foremost, I'd like to thank the entire Paizo team. You guys have built an awesome sandbox with a bunch of really neat toys; it's been a joy and a privilege to play in it. I'd also like to thank James Sutter, Dave Gross, and Pierce Watters in particular, as these three amigos were instrumental in showing me how much fun Golarion could be.

I am indebted to Marlene Stringer, my agent, for her support, encouragement, and ability to ensure that I get loooong deadlines. And I am indebted to Hugh Burns for his patience and forgiveness when even those long deadlines don't prove quite long enough. I'm almost caught up!

Lastly, I'd like to thank Cliff Moore, David Montgomery, Greg Collins, and Tim Minnear, who forced me to (very minimally) learn the Pathfinder rules so I could continue whomping their PCs up and down Varisia . . . and who are awfully forgiving about a whole lotta fudging over the considerable gaps in my rules-knowledge. Thanks, guys. Someday I will learn how Stealth actually works, I promise. (Incidentally: You know who's not on this list? Ian. You know why? BeardHawk.)

And, of course, I must thank Peter, who keeps the rest of 'em honest when they lie about their feats.

Glossary

All Pathfinder Tales novels are set in the rich and vibrant world of the Pathfinder campaign setting. Below are explanations of several key terms used in this book. For more information on the world of Golarion and the strange monsters, people, and deities that make it their home, see *The Inner Sea World Guide*, or dive into the game and begin playing your own adventures with the *Pathfinder Roleplaying Game Core Rulebook* or the *Pathfinder Roleplaying Game Beginner Box*, all available at **paizo.com**.

Armiger: Hellknight in training; a squire.
Aroden: Last hero of the Azlanti and God of Humanity, who raised the Starstone from the depths of the Inner Sea and founded the city of Absalom, becoming a living god in the process. Died mysteriously a hundred years ago, causing widespread chaos, particularly in Cheliax (which viewed him as its patron deity).
Asmodean: Of or related to the worship of Asmodeus.
Asmodeus: Devil-god of tyranny, slavery, pride, and contracts; lord of Hell and current patron deity of Cheliax.

Avistan: The continent north of the Inner Sea, on which Cheliax, Varisia, Taldor, and many other nations lie.

Azlant: The first human empire, which sank beneath the waves long ago.

Belial: One of the dukes of Hell.

Black Triune: The three rulers of Pangolais; some of the most powerful members of the Umbral Court.

Blackridge: Recently established mining town in Devil's Perch, intended to be a regional capital.

Bleaching: Sickness suffered by gnomes who aren't regularly exposed to new experiences. Often fatal.

Chelaxian: Someone from Cheliax.

Cheliax: Devil-worshiping nation in southwest Avistan.

Chelish: Of or relating to the nation of Cheliax.

Ciricskree, the Screeching Spire: Largest strix settlement in Devil's Perch.

Citadel Enferac: Hellknight fortress north of Devil's Perch, home to the Order of the Gate.

Cleric: A religious spellcaster whose magical powers are granted by her god.

Crackspike: Recently established mining town in Devil's Perch.

Crosspine: Small village in the southern Uskwood.

Dawnflower: Sarenrae.

Demons: Evil denizens of the Abyss who seek only to maim, ruin, and feed.

Desna: Good-natured goddess of dreams, stars, travelers, and luck.

Devils: Fiendish occupants of Hell who seek to corrupt mortals in order to claim their souls.

Devil's Perch: Inhospitable region of mountains and desert in northwestern Cheliax. Home of the strix.

Diabolist: A spellcaster who specializes in binding devils and making infernal pacts.

Druid: A spellcaster who draws power from nature.

Dusk Hall: Academy in Pangolais where initiates are trained as shadowcallers through study of both wizardry and the dark worship of Zon-Kuthon.

Dwarves: Short, stocky humanoids who excel at physical labor, mining, and craftsmanship. Stalwart enemies of the orcs and other evil subterranean monsters.

Earthfall: Event thousands of years ago, in which a great meteorite called the Starstone fell to earth in a fiery cataclysm, sending up a dust cloud which blocked out the sun and ushered in an age of darkness.

Egorian: The capital of Cheliax.

Elves: Race of long-lived and beautiful humanoids. Identifiable by their pointed ears, lithe bodies, and pupils so large their eyes appear to be one color.

Garund: Continent south of the Inner Sea.

Gnomes: Small humanoids with strange mindsets, originally from the First World.

Golarion: The planet on which the Pathfinder campaign setting focuses.

Half-Orcs: Bred from humans and orcs, members of this race have green or gray skin, brutish appearances, and short tempers, and are mistrusted by many societies.

Hell: Plane of evil and tyrannical order ruled by devils, where many evil souls go after they die.

Hellknights: Organization of hardened law enforcers whose tactics are often seen as harsh and intimidating, and who bind devils to their will. Based in Cheliax.

House of Thrune: Often called the Thrice-Damned House of Thrune. Current ruling house of Cheliax, which took power following Aroden's death by making compacts with the devils of Hell.

Inner Sea Region: The heart of the Pathfinder campaign setting, centered around the eponymous inland sea.

Includes the continents of Avistan and Garund, as well as the seas and other nearby lands.

Iomedae: Goddess of valor, rulership, justice, and honor, who was a holy crusader in life before passing the Test of the Starstone and attaining godhood.

Isger: Vassal nation of Cheliax.

Isgeri: Someone or something from Isger.

Itaraak: Strix word meaning "warrior" or "warriors."

Itarii: Strix term for their race as a whole.

Joyful Thing: Worshiper of Zon-Kuthon who voluntarily amputates all his or her limbs as a sign of devotion.

Joymaking: Terrifying ceremony in which a worshiper of Zon-Kuthon has all his or her limbs amputated, henceforth becoming a holy invalid cared for by the church.

Keleshite: Of or related to the Empire of Kelesh, far to the east of the Inner Sea region.

Korvosa: Largest city in Varisia and outpost of former Chelish loyalists, now self governed. For more information, see the Pathfinder Campaign Setting book *Guide to Korvosa*.

Kotarra: Derisive strix term for humans.

Kuthite: Worshiper of Zon-Kuthon; of or related to the worship of Zon-Kuthon.

Landshark: Ferocious monster that burrows through solid earth and eats almost anything.

Maralictor: A mid-level Hellknight officer.

Mendev: Cold, northern crusader nation that provides the primary force defending the rest of the Inner Sea region from the demonic infestation of the Worldwound.

Midnight Guard: Nidalese spellcasters—primarily shadowcallers—loaned to the Chelish military.

Midnight Lord: Zon-Kuthon.

Nidal: Evil nation in southern Avistan, devoted to the worship of the dark god Zon-Kuthon after he saved its people from extinction in the distant past. Closely allied with devil-worshiping Cheliax.

Nidalese: Of or pertaining to Nidal; someone from Nidal.

Nightglass: A magic item useful in the summoning and binding of creatures from the Plane of Shadow.

Nightmirror: Nightglass.

Nisroch: Major port city of Nidal.

Oppara: Coastal capital of Taldor.

Orcs: A bestial, warlike race of humanoids originally hailing from deep underground, who now roam the surface in barbaric bands. Universally hated by more civilized races.

Order of the Gate: Hellknight order devoted to expanding law and order primarily through magic.

Osirian: Of or pertaining to Osirion.

Osirion: Desert kingdom ruled by pharaohs in northeastern Garund.

Paladin: A holy warrior in the service of a good and lawful god, granted special magical powers by his or her deity.

Pangolais: Capital city of Nidal, situated deep in the Uskwood.

Paralictor: A high-level Hellknight officer.

Pathfinder: A member of the Pathfinder Society.

Pathfinder Society: Organization of traveling scholars and adventurers who seek to document the world's wonders. Based out of Absalom and run by a mysterious and masked group call the Decemvirate.

Pezzack: A town of rebels and outcasts on the northwestern shore of Cheliax; extremely isolated from the rest of the nation.

Pezzacki: Of or pertaining to Pezzack; someone from Pezzack.

Plane of Shadow: A dimension of muted colors and strange creatures that acts as a twisted, shadowy reflection of the "real" world.

Queen Abrogail II: Also called "Her Infernal Majestrix." Queen of Cheliax and head of House Thrune.

Rokoa: Strix title for a tribe's spiritual leader; a wise-woman or shaman.

Sarenrae: Goddess of the sun, honesty, and redemption. Often seen as a fiery crusader and redeemer.

Scroll: Magical document in which a spell is recorded so that it can be released when read, even if the reader doesn't know how to cast that spell.

Scrysphere: Magical device that allows its creator to observe events wherever it is left; useful for spying.

Shadow Plane: Plane of Shadow.

Shadowcaller: A Nidalese spellcaster trained in both arcane and divine magic, blending studious wizardry with religious power granted directly by Zon-Kuthon.

Shadowgarm: Ravenous monster from the Plane of Shadow.

Shelyn: The goddess of beauty, art, love, and music. Long-suffering and good-hearted sister of the evil god Zon-Kuthon.

Signifer: Hellknight spellcaster, who specializes in fighting with magic rather than physical weapons.

Sorcerer: Spellcaster who draws power from a supernatural ancestor or other mysterious source, and does not need to study to cast spells.

Spellbook: Tome in which spellcasters such as wizards transcribe the arcane formulae necessary to cast spells. Without a spellbook, wizards can cast only those few spells held in their minds at any given time.

Strix: Race of winged humanoids who dwell in the mountains of Devil's Perch in northwestern Cheliax. Hostile to outsiders and regularly antagonized by Chelish miners and settlers encroaching on their territory.

Swoop: Derogatory term for strix.

Taldan: Of or from Taldor; a citizen of Taldor.

Taldane: The common trade language of Golarion's Inner Sea region.

Taldor: Nation southeast of Druma that was once an immensely powerful empire, but has lost many of its holdings in recent years due to decadence and neglect.

Thassilon: Ancient empire which crumbled long ago.

Tian: Someone or something from the Dragon Empires of the distant east.

Tokarai Springs: Small oasis vital to the Windspire clan of strix in Devil's Perch.

Umbral Court: The ruling council of Nidal.

Umbral Leaves: Holy text of Zon-Kuthon.

Uskwood: Nidal's central forest, often said to be eerie and haunted.

Varisia: A frontier region northwest of the Inner Sea.

Vicarius: Spellcasting leader of a Hellknight order.

Westcrown: Former capital of Cheliax, now overrun with shadow beasts and despair.

Windspire: Traditional Strix roosting place closest to Crackspike.

Wiscrani: Someone from Westcrown.

Wizard: Someone who casts spells through careful study and rigorous scientific methods rather than faith or innate talent.

Zon-Kuthon: The twisted god of envy, pain, darkness, and loss. Was once a good god, along with his sister Shelyn, before unknown forces turned him to evil.

For half-elven Pathfinder Varian Jeggare and his devil-blooded bodyguard Radovan, things are rarely as they seem. Yet not even the notorious crime-solving duo are prepared for what they find when a search for a missing Pathfinder takes them into the gothic and mist-shrouded mountains of Ustalav.

Beset on all sides by noble intrigue, curse-afflicted villagers, suspicious monks, and the deadly creatures of the night, Varian and Radovan must use sword and spell to track the strange rumors to their source and uncover a secret of unimaginable proportions, aided in their quest by a pack of sinister werewolves and a mysterious, mute priestess. But it'll take more than merely solving the mystery to finish this job. For shadowy figures have taken note of the pair's investigations, and the forces of darkness are set on making sure neither man gets out of Ustalav alive . . .

From fan-favorite author Dave Gross, author of *Black Wolf* and *Lord of Stormweather*, comes a new fantastical mystery set in the award-winning world of the Pathfinder Roleplaying Game.

Prince of Wolves print edition: $9.99
ISBN: 978-1-60125-287-6

Prince of Wolves ebook edition:
ISBN: 978-1-60125-331-6

PRINCE OF
WOLVES

Dave Gross

In a village of the frozen north, a child is born possessed by
a strange and alien spirit, only to be cast out by her tribe
and taken in by the mysterious winter witches of Irrisen, a
land locked in permanent magical winter. Farther south, a
young mapmaker with a penchant for forgery discovers that
his sham treasure maps have begun striking gold.

This is the story of Ellasif, a barbarian shield maiden who
will stop at nothing to recover her missing sister, and Declan,
the ne'er-do-well young spellcaster-turned-forger who wants
only to prove himself to the woman he loves. Together they'll
face monsters, magic, and the fury of Ellasif's own cold-hearted
warriors in their quest to rescue the lost child. Yet when they
finally reach the ice-walled city of Whitethrone, where trolls
hold court and wolves roam the streets in human guise, will
it be too late to save the girl from the forces of darkness?

From *New York Times* best-selling author Elaine
Cunningham comes a fantastic new adventure of swords and
sorcery, set in the award-winning world of the Pathfinder
Roleplaying Game.

Winter Witch print edition: $9.99
ISBN: 978-1-60125-286-9

Winter Witch ebook edition:
ISBN: 978-1-60125-332-3

Winter Witch

Elaine Cunningham

The race is on to free Lord Stelan from the grip of a wasting curse, and only his old mercenary companion, the Forsaken elf Elyana, has the wisdom—and the swordcraft—to uncover the identity of his tormenter and free her old friend before the illness takes its course.

When the villain turns out to be another of their former companions, Elyana sets out with a team of adventurers including Stelan's own son on a dangerous expedition across the revolution-wracked nation of Galt and the treacherous Five Kings Mountains. There, pursued by a bloodthirsty militia and beset by terrible nightmare beasts, they discover the key to Stelan's salvation in a lost valley warped by weird magical energies. Will they be able to retrieve the artifact the dying lord so desperately needs? Or will the shadowy face of betrayal rise up from within their own ranks?

From Howard Andrew Jones, managing editor of the acclaimed sword and sorcery magazine *Black Gate*, comes a classic quest of loyalty and magic set in the award-winning world of the Pathfinder Roleplaying Game.

Plague of Shadows print edition: $9.99
ISBN: 978-1-60125-291-3

Plague of Shadows ebook edition:
ISBN: 978-1-60125-333-0

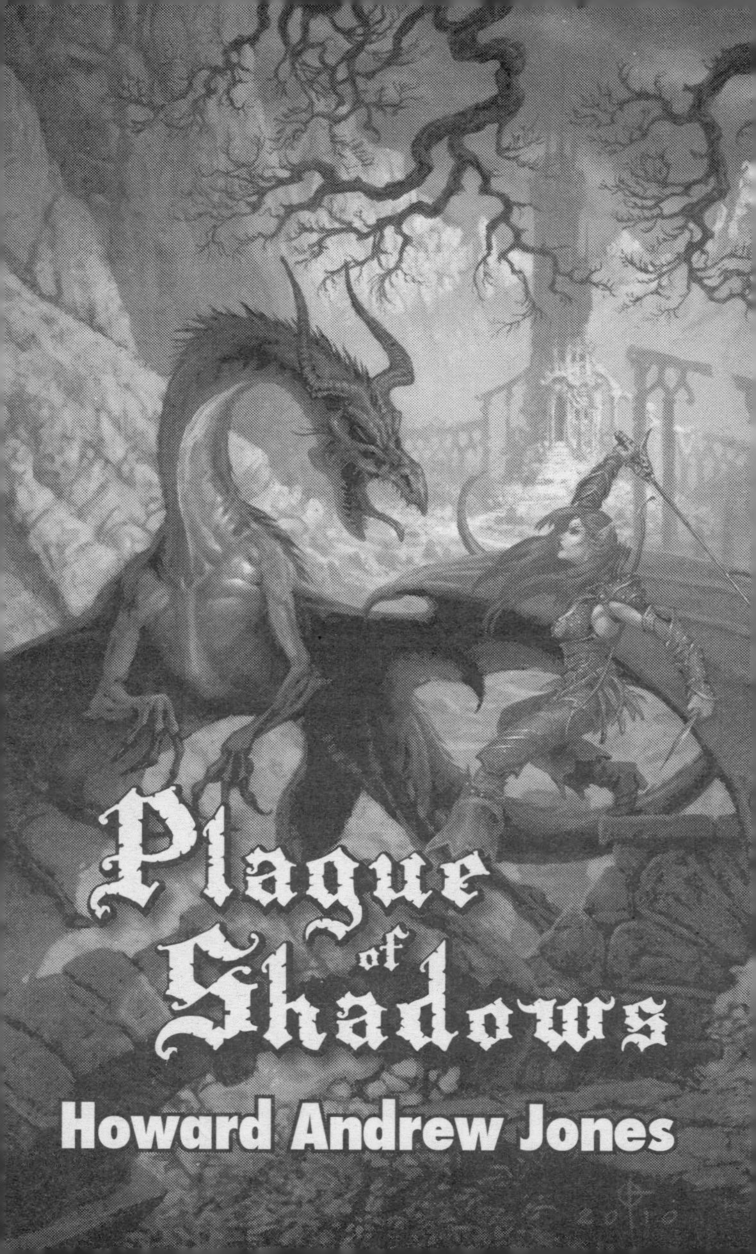
Plague of Shadows
Howard Andrew Jones

In the forbidding north, the demonic hordes of the magic-twisted hellscape known as the Worldwound encroach upon the southern kingdoms of Golarion. Their latest escalation embroils a preternaturally handsome and coolly charismatic swindler named Gad, who decides to assemble a team of thieves, cutthroats, and con men to take the fight into the demon lands and strike directly at the fiendish leader responsible for the latest raids—the demon Yath, the Shimmering Putrescence. Can Gad hold his team together long enough to pull off the ultimate con, or will trouble from within his own organization lead to an untimely end for them all?

From gaming legend and popular fantasy author Robin D. Laws comes a fantastic new adventure of swords and sorcery, set in the award-winning world of the Pathfinder Roleplaying Game.

The Worldwound Gambit print edition: $9.99
ISBN: 978-1-60125-327-9

The Worldwound Gambit ebook edition:
ISBN: 978-1-60125-334-7

the WORLDWOUND Gambit

Robin D. Laws

On a mysterious errand for the Pathfinder Society, Count Varian Jeggare and his hellspawn bodyguard Radovan journey to the distant land of Tian Xia. When disaster forces him to take shelter in a warrior monastery, "Brother" Jeggare finds himself competing with the disciples of the Dragon Temple as he unravels a royal mystery. Meanwhile, Radovan—trapped in the body of a devil and held hostage by the legendary Quivering Palm attack—must serve a twisted master by defeating the land's deadliest champions and learning the secret of slaying an immortal foe. Together with an unlikely army of beasts and spirits, the two companions must take the lead in an ancient conflict that will carry them through an exotic land all the way to the Gates of Heaven and Hell and a final confrontation with the nefarious Master of Devils.

From Dave Gross, author of *Prince of Wolves*, comes a new fantastical adventure set in the award-winning world of the Pathfinder Roleplaying Game.

Master of Devils print edition: $9.99
ISBN: 978-1-60125-357-6

Master of Devils ebook edition:
ISBN: 978-1-60125-358-3

Master of Devils

Dave Gross

A warrior haunted by his past, Salim Ghadafar serves as a problem-solver for a church he hates, bound by the goddess of death to hunt down those who would rob her of her due. Such is the case in the desert nation of Thuvia, where a powerful merchant about to achieve eternal youth via a magical elixir is mysteriously murdered and his soul kidnapped. The only clue is a ransom note, offering to trade the merchant's soul for his dose of the fabled potion.

Enter Salim, whose keen mind and contacts throughout the multiverse would make solving this mystery a cinch, if it weren't for the merchant's stubborn daughter who insists on going with him. Together, the two must unravel a web of intrigue that will lead them far from the blistering sands of Thuvia on a grand tour of the Outer Planes, where devils and angels rub shoulders with fey lords and mechanical men, and nothing is as it seems . . .

From noted game designer and author James L. Sutter comes an epic mystery of murder and immortality, set in the award-winning world of the Pathfinder Roleplaying Game.

***Death's Heretic* print edition: $9.99**
ISBN: 978-1-60125-369-9

***Death's Heretic* ebook edition:**
ISBN: 978-1-60125-370-5

Death's Heretic

JAMES L. SUTTER

To an experienced thief like Krunzle the Quick, the merchant nation of Druma is full of treasures just waiting to be liberated. Yet when the fast-talking scoundrel gets caught stealing from one of the most powerful prophets of Kalistrade, the only option is to undertake a dangerous mission to recover the merchant-lord's runaway daughter—and the magical artifact she took with her. Armed with an arsenal of decidedly unhelpful magical items and chaperoned by an intelligent snake necklace happy to choke him into submission, Krunzle must venture far from the cities of the capitalist utopia and into a series of adventures that will make him a rich man—or a corpse.

From veteran author Hugh Matthews comes a rollicking tale of captive trolls, dwarven revolutionaries, and serpentine magic, set in the award-winning world of the Pathfinder Roleplaying Game.

Song of the Serpent print edition: $9.99
ISBN: 978-1-60125-388-0

Song of the Serpent ebook edition:
ISBN: 978-1-60125-389-7

Song of the Serpent

Hugh Matthews

Once a student of alchemy with the dark scholars of the Technic League, Alaeron fled their arcane order when his conscience got the better of him, taking with him a few strange devices of unknown function. Now in hiding in a distant city, he's happy to use his skills creating minor potions and wonders—at least until the back-alley rescue of an adventurer named Jaya lands him in trouble with a powerful crime lord. In order to keep their heads, Alaeron and Jaya must travel across wide seas and steaming jungles in search of a wrecked flying city and the magical artifacts that can buy their freedom. Yet the Technic League hasn't forgotten Alaeron's betrayal, and an assassin armed with alien weaponry is hot on their trail . . .

From Hugo Award-winning author Tim Pratt comes a new adventure of exploration, revenge, strange technology, and ancient magic, set in the fantastical world of the Pathfinder Roleplaying Game.

City of the Fallen Sky print edition: $9.99
ISBN: 978-1-60125-418-4

City of the Fallen Sky ebook edition:
ISBN: 978-1-60125-419-1

CITY OF THE FALLEN SKY

TIM PRATT

PATHFINDER
TALES

Luma is a cobblestone druid, a canny fighter and spellcaster who can read the chaos of Magnimar's city streets like a scholar reads books. Together, she and her siblings in the powerful Derexhi family form one of the most infamous and effective mercenary companies in the city, solving problems for the city's wealthy elite. Yet despite being the oldest child, Luma gets little respect—perhaps due to her half-elven heritage. When a job gone wrong lands Luma in the fearsome prison called the Hells, it's only the start of Luma's problems. For a new web of bloody power politics is growing in Magnimar, and it may be that those Luma trusts most have become her deadliest enemies . . .

From visionary game designer and author Robin D. Laws comes a new urban fantasy adventure of murder, betrayal, and political intrigue set in the award-winning world of the Pathfinder Roleplaying Game.

Bloof of the City print edition: $9.99
ISBN: 978-1-60125-456-6

Blood of the City ebook edition:
ISBN: 978-1-60125-457-3

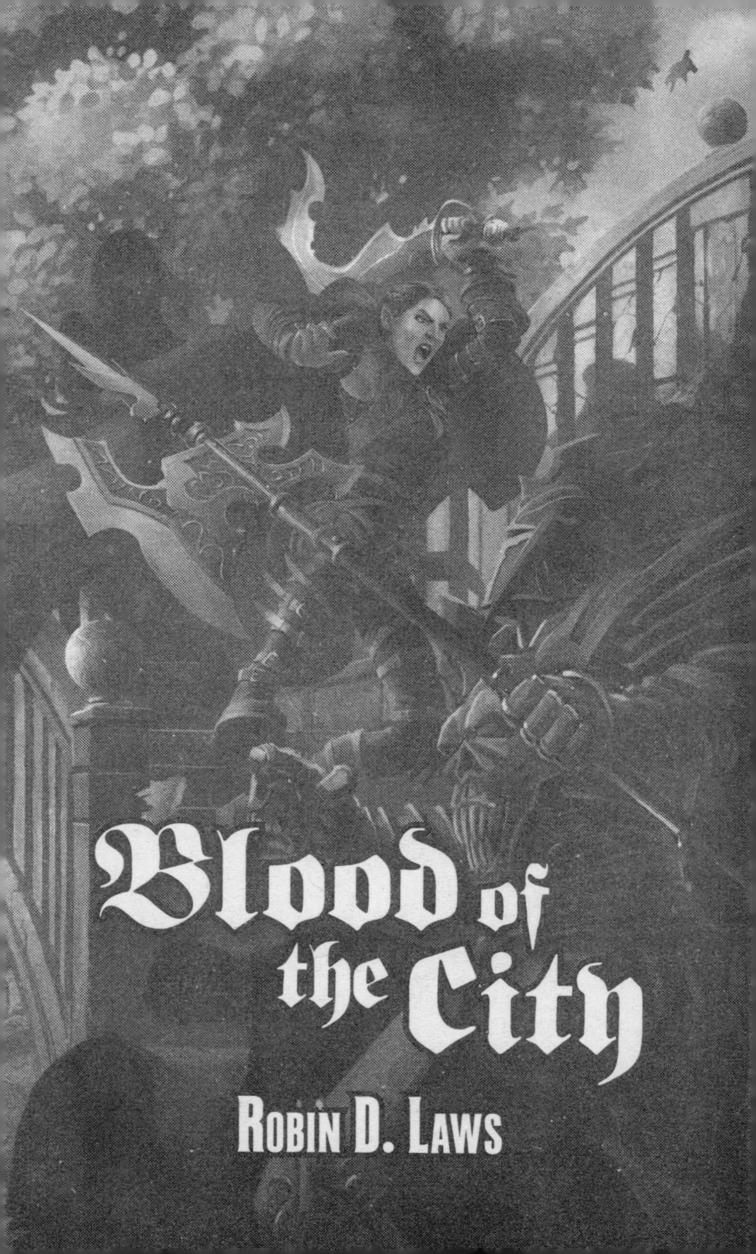
Blood of the City
Robin D. Laws

PATHFINDER
TALES

PRINCE of **WOLVES**

Dave Gross

Winter Witch

Elaine Cunningham

Plague of **Shadows**

Howard Andrew Jones

the WORLDWOUND Gambit

Robin D. Laws

Master of **Devils**

Dave Gross

Death's Heretic

James L. Sutter

Subscribe to Pathfinder Tales!

Stay on top of all the pulse-pounding, sword-swinging action of the Pathfinder Tales novels by subscribing online at **paizo.com/pathfindertales**! Each new novel will be sent to you as it releases—roughly one every two months—so you'll never have to worry about missing out. Plus, subscribers will also receive free electronic versions of the novels in both ePub and PDF format. So what are you waiting for? Fiery spells, flashing blades, and strange new monsters await you in the rest of the Pathfinder Tales novels, all set in the fantastical world of the Pathfinder campaign setting!

PATHFINDER

CAMPAIGN SETTING

THE INNER SEA WORLD GUIDE

You've delved into the Pathfinder campaign setting with Pathfinder Tales novels—now take your adventures even further! *The Inner Sea World Guide* is a full-color, 320-page hardcover guide featuring everything you need to know about the exciting world of Pathfinder: overviews of every major nation, religion, race, and adventure location around the Inner Sea, plus a giant poster map! Read it as a travelogue, or use it to flesh out your roleplaying game—it's your world now!

EXPLORE YOUR WORLD!

paizo.com

paizo
PUBLISHING

NOVELS!

Tired of carting around a bag full of books? Take your ebook reader or smart phone over to **paizo.com** to download all the Pathfinder Tales novels from authors like Dave Gross and *New York Times* best seller Elaine Cunningham in both ePub and PDF formats, thus saving valuable bookshelf space—and 30% off the cover price!

PATHFINDER'S JOURNALS!

Love the fiction in the Adventure Paths, but don't want to haul six books with you on the subway? Download compiled versions of each fully illustrated journal and read it on whatever device you choose!

FREE WEB FICTION!

Tired of paying for fiction at all? Drop by **paizo.com** every week for your next installment of free weekly web fiction as Paizo serializes new Pathfinder short stories from your favorite high-profile fantasy authors. Read 'em for free, or download 'em for cheap and read them anytime, anywhere!

ALL AVAILABLE NOW AT
PAIZO.COM!

HIDDEN WORLDS AND ANCIENT MYSTERIES

PLANET
stories